VISIONS VII

UNIVERSE

Doug C. Souza won first place in the 2016 Writers of the Future Quarterly Contest.

Jason Lairamore is a published finalist of the 2012 SQ Mag annual contest, the winner of the 2013 Planetary Stories flash fiction contest, a third-place winner of the 2015 SQ Mag annual contest, and a Writers of the Future Contest Semi-Finalist.

Margaret Karmazin's stories in The MacGuffin, Eureka Literary Magazine, Licking River Review, and Mobius were nominated for Pushcart awards. Her story, "The Manly Thing," was nominated for the 2010 Million Writers Award.

Jonathan Shipley is an active member of Science Fiction Writers of America and was a contribuitng author to the *After Death* anthology that won the 2014 Bram Stoker Award.

John M. Floyd is a three-time Derringer Award winner and an Edgar Award nominee.

Lorraine Schein's story in this volume, "Sleeping Westward," was nominated for the 2017 Canopus Award.

Books from Lillicat Publishers

Visions Anthology Series
Visions: Leaving Earth
Visions II: Moons of Saturn
Visions III: Inside the Kuiper Belt
Visions IV: Space Between Stars
Visions V: Milky Way
Visions VI: Galaxies
Visions VII: Universe (Rogue Star Press)

Northern Futures
TreeVolution
The Future Is Short: Science Fiction in a Flash
The Future Is Short, Volume 3: Science Fiction in a Flash
Dance With Me: My Journey Through Cancer
Sunshine & Shadow: Memories from a Long Life

ROGUE STAR PRESS
The Helena Orbit

DAWN LIGHT PRESS
The Night Blooming Jasmine in Your Heart

ALTERNATE UNIVERSE PRESS
Snake in the Grass

VISIONS VII

UNIVERSE

EDITED BY

CARROL FIX

ROGUE STAR PRESS
USA

VISIONS VII: Universe

Copyright © 2017 by Carol Goodwater

Rogue Star Press
an imprint of
Lillicat Publishers
9625 Mission Gorge Road, B2-159
Santee, California, 92071
USA

Cover art: agsandrew (Shutterstock)

First Print Edition: August 2017
Printed and Bound in USA

POD ISBN: 978-1-945646-32-4
EPUB ISBN: 978-1-945646-29-4
MOBI ISBN: 978-1-945646-30-0

Contents

Stepping Stones to Eternity

The *Visions Series* tells the story of how humanity must ultimately venture outward from our tiny home and explore the Universe.

Visions: Leaving Earth, the first volume, describes our first faltering steps to rise from Earth's surface and build homes in space.

Visions II: Moons of Saturn confirms humankind's success in leaving Earth and building homes in the other planetary systems circling our sun-father Sol.

Visions III: Inside the Kuiper Belt proclaims domination of all that dwells within the solar system—from our Sun to the outermost reaches of the Kuiper Belt and into the Oort Cloud.

Visions IV: Space Between Stars astounds us with the infinite possibilities of adventure and danger far from any suns or planets—in the cold, dark regions of deepest space, where dark matter and nebulas of celestial gases abide.

Visions V: Milky Way leads us to explore our own galaxy. Although vast and unreachable with current technology, the Milky Way is but a tiny point in the Universe. We must first learn about our own home galaxy before we can explore further outward to other galaxies.

Visions VI: Galaxies follows human progress into other galaxies. Humankind survives to spread across the Universe, making distant galaxies and planets into a home for a race destined to seek horizons ever more far away.

Visions VII: Universe, the final volume, opens the doors to incredible possibilities for the race called Human. We venture into realms where what seems impossible becomes fact.

Our Vision is limitless.

Introduction

There are more things in heaven and earth, Horatio,
Than are dreamt of in your philosophy.
~ William Shakespeare

This is the final anthology in the *Visions Series*, completing a seven-volume exploration of humankind's passage into space, covering adventures near our home world and farther, to planets and galaxies at the beginning of our universe.

Visions VII: Universe takes us outside our current reality and into worlds where anything is possible. If we can imagine an existence in some remote time and place, where the inconceivable exists, then it is within the speculative actualities of our talented futurists.

With no limits on what science may be like in the distant future, *Universe* stories allow us to explore exciting options and let our thoughts roam to the unexpected domains of the previously unimagined.

Relax your preconceptions and take this journey into the future, while allowing us to stretch the boundaries of what you believe is possible. We promise, you will not be disappointed.

Carrol Fix
Editor
Lillicat Publishers
July 22, 2017

Something is wrong with Marshal Colby McEvans. He can't shake the impending sense of doom, and the only person on his side is his dead wife. He knows the trans-luminal cruise circuit can be an easy mark, but even he is unprepared for the hijackers' end game.

Pseudo-Soul

Doug C. Souza

My day doesn't really get going until I hear from my dead wife.

"Fractured light thinned into wisps by superluminal speeds. Quite amazing." Susan's voice wasn't really there; I hadn't heard her pleasant timbre in three decades. Her specter-voice played in my head like a muffled holo-vid.

Outside *Destiny's Shadow's* porthole window, radiant streaks of purple and orange swirled and disappeared into one another. Gazing into the abyss, I was almost absorbed by the infinite beauty of it all.

Almost.

Exactly how long does it take to brew a freagin' cup of coffee anyway?

"Relax, enjoy the magical light show," Susan suggested.

I half-rose from my seat, about to stomp over to the corner bar, but plopped right back down.

I didn't talk back to Susan, *that* would be crazy. My fingers drummed the tabletop in a steady rhythm.

"You know I'll leave you alone if you just sit with me for a bit," Susan said.

I nodded. It was true; she did let me have the rest of the day to myself—only making the occasional one-word comment—if I sat quietly and let her talk for ten minutes uninterrupted.

The superluminal lightshow was spectacular. Ethereal colors that technically didn't exist within the visible spectrum danced in transcendent tendrils on the other side of the palladium glass. Atomic embers said to be nothing more than shadows of neutrinos and dark matter.

Susan would have given a year's pay to travel trans-luminal when she was alive.

The superluminal ship's upper deck lighting was kept low, enhancing the violet view outside. The chaotic river of color was a stark reminder that an infinite emptiness beyond normal space surrounded the cruise ship. Up here, in the small, quiet, and unpopular deck; one had time to recount the numerous ways *Destiny's Shadow* could fall into an eternal tailspin.

Some say you don't exactly die, but lingered in an emptiness of consciousness between the folds of space.

"You're in a morbid mood," Susan said, her ghostly voice a bit taunting. *"Better hope that coffee gets here soon, eh?"*

This was my first pleasure cruise as a Marshal of the Superluminal Transit. Mostly, I worked point-to-point transport jobs. The duration spent in superluminal space was much shorter on those. Pleasure cruises set out for weeks at a time, with few port stops.

A subtle bell-tone of f-sharp sounded over the ship's speakers and the house lights brightened. The purple and orange tendrils in the distance vanished, replaced by black space.

"Something wicked this way comes," Susan said. *"Goodbye, Colby."*

An unscheduled stop. Not good.

My wrist-comm showed I still had over two minutes left in my self-imposed tribute to my dead wife. I stopped the timer at 2:15 to continue later.

I paused and listened for her voice in my head. Nope—she was gone as soon as the chime sounded. She didn't appreciate not having my undivided attention. "Susan," I whispered. "We'll talk later. I'll set aside time for us. Promise."

She didn't respond.

I closed my eyes and brought the *Destiny's Shadow's* schedule to mind. My brain landed in the top point zero one percentile for spatial imaging; with a little effort, I could see the day blocked out into hours as if a holo-sheet hovered before me.

Just as I guessed; this was an unscheduled stop. I stepped away from my table and surveyed the normal space around *Destiny's Shadow.*

"Is that a broken ship?" a stocky woman with a feather-rimmed hat asked, hovering over my shoulder.

A small vessel with a section of its hull missing came into view portside. The mangled ship drifted just outside the large viewing windows.

"Ya think we'll help 'em?" she asked.

Most likely, we would offer help. But my primary duty was to insure the safety of everyone on board this ship. We shouldn't offer help—not without more information.

The barista coughed behind me, "You gonna pay for that?" He had set my Andes-dark cappuccino on the table.

"No." I turned and left, heading for the bridge.

People were in different states of festivities as I walked across the lower-decks. Few stood at the windows to examine the damaged ship.

The pleasure cruise circuit has a way of bringing out unfettered joy within her customers. Part of the lure of working this gig—easy folks in easy moods.

"No passengers," a rent-a-cop said as I approached the inner corridors. To his credit, he didn't waver as my 6-foot-4 frame towered over him. A good guy doing a good job.

I punched a few keys in my wrist-comm and flashed my holo-badge.

The rent-a-cop took too long checking it so I held my arm aloft while working the panel on the wall past his shoulder. The door hissed open and I went through.

"Should I tell them you're coming?" he asked my back.

I waved it away. An announcement played over the intercom: a standard message to quell any fears, no reason provided. I doubted half the passengers even noticed we'd dropped out of superluminal space.

Destiny's Shadow's schematics came to the front of my mind, mapping a clear path to the bridge. Sixth door on the right. No panel for a passcode on this door. I found the chip-reader and pressed my wrist-comm to it. The door opened, much smoother than the outer door.

The group stopped midsentence.

Four people: Captain Phaman Argeriche, First Mate Benedict Larson, Ship's Engineer Ramena Sahadi, and Ensign Daryl Montego at the helm.

"This is a restricted area—" First Mate Larson started.

I waved him away, crossing the cramped room in two quick strides. "Don't bother. Read it quick," I said and flashed my credentials. All around, I could sense their apprehension.

Like me, they thought this would be an easy gig.

First Mate Larson took a step back. His gaze was as inviting as an electrified razor-wire fence. The engineer and helmsman gaped. The captain gave a curt nod. His broad silhouette leaning against the wall.

"Trans-luminal Marshal Colby McEvans," I announced. They had themselves a good gander. I continued: "You have made an unscheduled stop. This violates protocol. Specifically, statute six point one nine under regulatory guidelines."

"Oh spare us the recital." First Mate Larson about-faced, returning to a sidebar with the captain.

What was with this guy?

"Amazing," Ship's Engineer Sahadi stepped forward and commented. "I've heard of you guys, but never seen one in action." Her dark eyes widened. The kid looked like she had lied about her age to land this job.

Captain Argeriche, who was unfazed by my sudden appearance, took control. "Yes, marshals only reveal themselves when they sense immediate danger to the vessel or any of her passengers. Please, Mr. McEvans, tell us what has brought you here." He was a plump man, but carried the extra girth comfortably. His face was tired, but his eyes had that sapient glow acquired by years of experience.

"It's Marshal McEvans, sir, not mister. A common misunderstanding," I corrected him. I felt like a stylus-necked jerk doing it, but it was a common mistake. Insisting on the title helps maintain reciprocity of respect.

First Mate Larson scoffed.

I continued, "I cannot allow you to assist the crippled vessel at our portside."

"How do you know we are planning to help?" First Mate Larson asked accusingly. "Monitoring our private channels?"

"There is no *other* reason to stop *Destiny's Shadow* mid-run," I aimed my meaning at the captain, hoping he'd step up to his role as leader.

The ship's engineer piped in eagerly, "We're still running preliminary scans. So far, they have come up negative for any armaments or other hostile indications."

"Nevertheless, protocol dictates that you report what you have found and then we must continue on our voyage."

"We're wasting time," First Mate Larson said. "Thanks for your input, but you don't run this ship, Captain Argeriche does."

"Nevertheless, you must rescind any offer for aid and move on."

First Mate Larson started to say more, but Captain Argeriche quieted him. "They sent a distress signal. Being the only superluminal ship within the vicinity, we have to look into it. Protocols changed as soon as we received that signal."

He was stretching protocol thin, but had a case.

First Mate Larson took the opportunity to gloat. "So forgive us if we don't just leave them high and dry. Sorry we can't just let them die, no matter how convenient it would be."

"Venturing out here was their own doing. You would not be held accountable for any result no matter how unpleasant."

"That's pretty cold," Ship's Engineer Sahadi muttered.

I threw my hands up. The first mate and engineer kept interrupting and Argeriche allowed it. A clear reminder this was a commercial crew unaccustomed to any form of order. A cargo-ship captain would've backhanded anyone who dared interrupting. A cargo-crew would also agree that we move on.

"Captain Argeriche," I tried again. "We cannot simply open our doors."

"Do you have an alternative?" he asked.

I took a moment to review possible scenarios. The helmsman busied himself by bringing up various holo-vids of the vessel while furtively glancing my way. The engineer continued brazenly looking me up and down. I imagine she'd take a skin biopsy had I allowed it.

"I have an idea," I said. "Request to board their ship and investigate. If their intentions *aren't* malicious, they'll allow it. "

His eyes wrinkled with concern. "I don't know the condition of their ship, my crew wouldn't be safe."

"Then let me go alone. I'm not your crew."

"How long will that take? " Captain Argeriche asked.

"An hour for a decent investigation—at the most."

"Ensign, where will that put us fuel wise? With the added deceleration, another start-up, and the delay."

Ensign Montego punched in the numbers. "He could take a day and we'd still leave reserves untapped."

"Very well. First Mate Larson, please join Marshal McEvans, but only up to the hatch."

First Mate Larson appeared ready to argue.

"Problem, Larson?"

"No sir," he answered crisply.

"Think of it as an outreach program. Maybe it will calm some of those prejudices you seem to have about our guest." The captain slumped into the nearest console chair. The dura-plastic cushion protested, but held.

"Sir, everything I know about Trans-luminal Marshal is based on fact."

"We're wasting time," I said and left the room.

Ship's Engineer Sahadi asked to join us and was soon at my side. She nearly ran into walls as she ogled me and tried to keep pace at the same time.

"I think someone's developed a little crush on you," Susan said.

I froze. Susan speaking to me meant, she wouldn't relent until I gave her my undivided attention.

"Can't blame her," Susan continued. *"You must remember, you're a twenty-five-year-old body of hard muscle."*

I leaned against the corridor wall and stared at my wrist-comm. 2:15 left. My finger pointed at the time, hoping Susan comprehended my meaning without me having to say it. I wondered if I should just start the time and sit quietly for the tribute.

"Don't you dare," Susan said. *"You've got a job to do."*

I blinked at the 2 minutes and 15 seconds.

"Something wrong?" First Mate Larson asked, though his tone made it clear he didn't care for my wellbeing one bit.

"No," I lied. "Just, uh, thinking." I strode forward, unperturbed. I quickened my pace to squelch any further inquiries, or doubt.

At my back, I heard Ship's Engineer Sahadi explaining to First Mate Larson how my brain works different than others.

En route, we made our way through the galley. The fewer passengers seeing us huddled together the better. These people weren't used to seeing anyone other than the service staff. The sudden appearance of the ship's crew might rouse suspicion.

The umbilical was located near the aft-port of the ship, almost the lowest section. The flexible airlock snaked away from *Destiny's Shadow*, toward the vessel.

After Sahadi handed me an earpiece, Argeriche thoroughly updated me. No medical aid required, just a simple "repair and parts" request. Sahadi plugged in commands and the umbilical locked into place with a reassuring click.

I had to shout over the hissing air as it filled the umbilical's venting shafts. "You two wait here. I'll return or send an all-clear!" I left them at the cruise ship's outer hatch.

Surprisingly, First Mate Larson didn't argue. Instead he handed me a tase-stick. "I saw you weren't carrying!"

"Not allowed." I shook my head. The shrill venting ceased. I turned and headed down the umbilical. *Destiny's Shadow*'s hatch shut behind me.

I listened for Susan. It worried me how she had spoken outside her tribute; I didn't need the distraction right now.

Nothing but the soft hiss of recycled air.

G-force lightened as I left our ship's grav-field and entered the crippled vessel's. I calculated it to be about four-fifths regular pull.

The outer hatch irised open and I stepped into darkness.

Floodlights snapped on, surrounding me. I squinted and waited for the temporary blindness to end.

Five men pointed five assault rifles at me. The high-pitched whine of electrodes charging split the silence.

One of them stuck a head out into the umbilical. "They shut their hatch! Told you they would."

"Pulse-shots?" I asked, putting my hands up.

"Two of the guns are pulse-shots, yes," the centermost man answered snarkily. "Don't be offended if we don't tell you *which* two."

Grunts of approval echoed around me. The other three guns must be classic powder projectile contraptions.

It didn't matter. I knew which two carried pulse detonators by their triangular barrels. I also knew they wouldn't risk shooting at me with the exposed umbilical at my back. No telling what those rounds would do to the pliant material.

One of the gunners reached over and shut their hatch.

"So what's the plan?" I asked. "I go back with the group of you in my wake? I'm a hostage even though you know they won't negotiate?"

"Little bit of that, little bit more, but you got the idea. We ain't too worried about the negotiating. Any marshmallow crew starts listening after a few passengers get fried."

The assault rifles wouldn't have shown on scanners. Small arms rarely do. This group of marauders could do some real damage if allowed onto *Destiny's Shadow*. Ruthlessness is technically a sound negotiating tactic. Captain Argeriche shouldn't have stopped to help.

"I won't allow you to board," I said.

More playful grunts. Creaks of machinery resonated throughout this small vessel. Much different than the gaiety that murmured across the decks of *Destiny's Shadow*.

"You should've said something more dramatic like, 'over my dead body,'" their leader sneered. They were buying time, and I didn't know why. One of the men cocked his head. He was receiving orders via an earpiece like mine.

"That one's different," Susan pointed out. *"He's doing something else."*

"Quiet," I said, shaking my head.

"Quiet?" their leader asked. "Um, no. Now, turn around. Walk forward."

"Very well," I shrugged. "I'll be dramatic, over my dead body." I darted forward and slapped a tranq-patch on his neck.

A pulse-shot ripped through my left shoulder as I tucked and rolled.

Human-shield time. I lifted their drowsy leader, keeping him between me and my assailants. They shot him up regardless.

Didn't expect that.

I threw him forward, but only half as far as I intended because my arm was losing sensation fast.

"You are gonna die," Susan said matter-of-fact.

I leg-swept two at once. Shots riddled my torso as I slapped two more tranq-patches. My lungs collapsed, feeling like a vice closing across my chest. I wrested a powder-and-bullet gun free from an attacker since the pulse-detonator rifles would be at eighth power after so many discharges. I got off a couple shots, but couldn't tell if I connected. My vision was blurring.

Pinpricks turned to numbness across my body.

I leapt and shoulder-tackled the remaining two. The haphazard move slowed them, but I wasn't able to neutralize the group. They emptied their remaining clips into me.

"This is bull! You probably took out only two of them. The rest are still alive," Susan's fading voice scolded me.

"Yeah, but they won't make it to the ship," I sputtered.

Reaching for my wrist-comm, I tried to start the timer. A boot stomped my arm to the cold floor. My world grew faint and soon the remaining time of 2:15 disappeared completely. I'd have to mourn for Susan later.

***

Voices drifted in, distant and choppy.

"Nothing. *They've* gotta undo it."

"You can't override?"

"It's their door. Call them again."

"I've been calling them."

I canceled audio and accessed video feeds to get my bearings. First things first: I retracted the umbilical and secured all hatches. Milliseconds passed that felt like minutes as I was bombarded with multiple ship functions. Finally, I had video and audio under control. I used the intercom to inform a bewildered Larson and Sahadi what I was doing.

"That you, Marshal? You sound different," Sahadi's voice was scared.

"Standard voice modulator."

"Are you still over there?" she asked.

"My body, yes. But I've been uploaded into *Destiny's Shadow's* computer. I'm moving us away from the vessel."

"You're taking command?" First Mate Larson asked.

"For the moment."

"You can take controls, huh." Ship's Engineer Sahadi pointed out.

"Yes, but only for a limited time and my access is limited to basic operations." There wasn't time to explain that the body I left behind would begin to dissolve once I uploaded to a hub successfully.

"You really botched that one, didn't you?" First Mate Larson commented.

I ignored it and prepared to awaken in my new body. An experience more painful than dying, but a necessary evil for those in my line of work.

***

The frost dissipated as torrents of warm air wracked my body. Normally, I'd have ten minutes to come to. Right now, I was trying for a record of thirty seconds. Acid burned through every muscle and my stomach hit a perpetual series of dry heaves. The jumpsuit that comes pre-worn stuck to my hairless skin as the fabric continued to dry. Smelled like bottom-of-the-basket laundry.

The fans shut off as I dropped out of my cryo-husk.

Gingerly, I set each tinting contact lens over an eye; dry eyes and uncoordinated hands are a rough combination. It took time, but eventually I got them in, only jabbing my eyes once or twice. I sat down and waited for them to auto-adjust to the light that pierced into the back of my brain.

"Ahem," a voice sounded from nowhere.

Instinctually, I placed a finger to my ear and then remembered I didn't have an earpiece on this body.

I looked upward for the intercom.

"You owe me." It was Susan.

I blinked hard. My throat felt like two sheets of sandpaper.

She continued: *"Not that I agree with your keeping a daily memorial, but if you're going to do something, do it right. Aren't those your words?"*

Sighing, I pulled up the wrist-comm and punched 2:15 into the timer. It took several tries with my jittery hands, but I got it.

"You saw what happened. I got a bit busy," I said in a wheezy croak, too quiet for any of the living to hear.

I wanted to rest there and get the remainder of her tribute over, but I had to get to the bridge. I didn't trust this crew to handle terrorists.

"Now, get off your ass and get to work," Susan ordered.

I coughed a weak laugh, stood, and slapped the panel to open the exit of my renewal-chamber room. The corridor was empty—good, I didn't want some passerby raising alarms at the sight of me.

I stumbled for the first few feet, leaning heavily on the wall. My brain felt like wet cotton. Passengers winced at me like I was a drunk maintenance worker. I didn't do anything to dissuade that notion. That and the reek of what smelled like stale body odor kept everyone away.

Two sets of hands reached down and propped me up. Engineer Sahadi's small form was easy to make out. I couldn't make the other one.

"You're bald. And very pale. You sure you're alive?" First Mate Larson mused.

My throat was too dry to reply.

Sahadi spoke on my behalf. "Hairs aren't able to survive the cryo-freeze, it's not a common—oh." She cut herself off, realizing Larson was just being a jerk.

They helped me the rest of the way to the bridge.

"You were right," Captain Argeriche greeted me.

"There was no way to know," Larson offered. "I still think it could've been handled better."

Next time, I'll let him get shot up.

I had regained most muscle control by the time we reached the bridge. Still, it was better that I sat while everyone else hovered around me.

Someone put a cup of water in my hands. Captain Argeriche informed me that all hails had gone unanswered.

"Keep an eye on them," he said. His lighthearted tone from earlier had changed. This man was a leader.

After forcing the liquid into my clammy mouth, I gave them a quick briefing of what happened. They winced when I pointed to my head and explained there was a network of wetware that enabled my consciousness to upload via the ship's communication array. Although they'd learned about it in school, seeing it firsthand seemed to bother them.

"That's not accurate," Sahadi interrupted my story. She pointed to her console.

"What?" I asked. "My story?"

"No, their ship. There's no signs of venting." She was referring to the holo-display of the crippled ship at the helmsman's station.

"Meaning?"

"Well, it could mean nothing." She stopped to think about it. "Every engine has its own method of cooling. However, most interstellar ships simply expel their excess heat. It lessens the need for extinguishers and other chemical dampeners. Nitrogen and helium are needed, of course, but not as much. Heck, cold space has been utilized since the Space Crawl Era."

"Most ships, like seventy-five percent?" I asked. This development bothered me.

"No, upper nineties." She corrected modestly, staring at their ship confused. "Also, the heat readings are steadily increasing." She punched some keys and the screen brought up an infrared view. "There. The flaps remain shut even though there's a noticeable heat buildup. For the life of me, I can't figure out why anyone would do that."

"How'd they get out here in the first place without venting their heat?" Captain Argeriche asked.

"They couldn't have. The amount of coolant required couldn't be carried on a ship that small . . ." her voice trailed off.

Sahadi jumped over to Montego's console and started jabbing at the panel. *Destiny's Shadow* lurched as we moved away from the crippled vessel.

"That girl's got spunk, I'll give her that," Susan said.

Cruise Director Rachel Trulley was going to have a hissy-fit. Space cruises are supposed to be smooth.

"Ramena!" First Mate Larson barked.

Hearing her first name didn't faze her. She merely righted the ship and pointed to the main viewscreen.

"Are we a safe distance?" Captain Argeriche asked, leaning over her shoulder.

"For what?" Larson insisted.

His question was answered as the display screen went white. The blinding light hit the *Destiny's Shadow's* windows next. The ship we had stopped to help was now flying at us in a million pieces.

I stared at the viewscreen and braced for impact.

All shields max," Captain Argerich said.

"Already on it," Sahadi answered.

"They . . . they blew up?" Montego asked.

"I could've told you that was going to happen," Susan said smugly.

Why didn't you? I wondered. *Why didn't I see it coming?*

"Dear God," First Mate Larson swallowed. A large chunk of debris flew by.

The jolting did a number on my equilibrium. My inner ear complained with vigor. "Someone want to explain?" I exhaled.

"The flaps." Sahadi watched the screen return to blackness. "I realized how close they were to blowin' and didn't want to take chances. Sorry Captain, I had to act."

"Noted," was all Argeriche said. Smaller bits continued to drift by outside the cruise ship's windows.

I figured Sahadi was apologizing for running a new course without approval. Glad to see there were some procedures among *Destiny's Shadow's* crew.

"Sabotage?" Larson asked. "Incompetence?"

"They were idiots, but not incompetent. My guess is they were scrambling those last few seconds," I suggested.

"This report's getting more and more complicated," Larson looked down at his data-tablet. "Ship concierge Trulley's demanding an explanation."

"Stop schedule?" Montego asked once he settled back into his chair.

Captain Argeriche plugged it into the nearest console, "We're fine."

"Standard restart?"

The captain considered this. "Not quite yet." He frowned, as if to say something else, and then put out a hand. "Marshal McEvans, could you accompany me to the conference room?"

I ignored the proffered help. "If it's not a problem sir, I've gotta get back on my beat." I stared down at 2:15 on my wrist-comm.

"Only for a bit. It'd be a big help." He turned to First Mate Larson. "Tell Trulley it was an abandoned vessel and that we're in no danger, help her calm things down. She's probably got a lot of damage control going on after that light show and bump."

I followed the captain into a tidy conference room. Half-walled partitions separated the room into three sections. He ran a hand over a panel and the half-wall extended to the ceiling, providing us with a private area to talk.

The captain brought up recent holo-vids of the crippled ship on the wall screen.

"Something's not adding up," I noted.

"Semi-competent crew runs a slapdash raid and then destroys themselves. You said you had neutralized the crew."

"Not certain. I hit three with tranq-patches and another got shot up by his allies. The fourth and fifth may or may not have been hit in the melee. It was unclear at the end." I thought back to that foot nailing my arm to the ground.

"That heat build-up had to have started earlier. My guess is it started as soon as the umbilical was attached."

"You think *Destiny's Shadow* was the target," I said, agreeing.

"Possibly. But even with both hatches open and facing one another, the explosion would have only caused minimal damage. Our hull is so well-fortified and reinforced, worst is a brief paralyzing, that's all. The passageway would've been destroyed, but the safety hatches shield the rest of the ship."

"Why delay the restart?"

"Just need some time to think." He pointed to the screen. "There's nothing out there. Not anymore."

"Have you considered that this could be a rendezvous? The explosion may have been designed to stop you long enough for the real threat to get here."

The captain shook his head and sighed. "You're right. I feel like a blind fool. Even as we're talking, I'm distracted by the regulations I'm going to have to look up before I call the authorities." He pulled up a different icon and relayed the order to begin the start-up.

A thought struck me about Susan's obsession with Sahadi. "Do you mind if I 'borrow' Ship's Engineer Ramena Sahadi for a bit."

"What about First Mate Larson?" he smiled wryly.

"Seems competent, but also seems pissed off about something . . . or everything."

That made him laugh. "I'll tell Sahadi. You're a good judge of talent. She's only going to work the cruise circuit a few more months before she's picked up by a bigger agency."

***

"Don't press that timer," Susan warned. *"You're not done."*

"Then what? You keep interrupting me while I'm trying to work," I muttered as I left the corridor.

"Well," she hesitated. *"I'll try not to. Deal?"*

"Deal." I moved my finger away from my wrist-comm.

I chose the promenade first, keeping along the edges and avoiding the main concourse. I'd give the ship a couple laps and hope that jostled something in my brain.

The passengers strolled around as if on a perpetual high. Some taking their yearly trek into superluminal space, others on their first and last. None seemed to notice, or care, that we hadn't reentered superluminal space. Usually, I enjoyed the contagious revelry.

"Marshal McEvans?" Sahadi's voice sounded on my wrist-comm as I lifted it to my ear.

"What is it?" I asked. I opted to have her stay aboard the bridge and work from there. Having her nearby seemed to stir Susan up, and I needed to concentrate.

"Uhm, nothing. Just wanted to check in. I've been running scans across the debris field since we'll be entering superluminal space again. Other than that, I don't really know what it is you want me to do."

"Keep sifting, I know it's busywork, but I have a feeling it's important. Really important."

"Yeah, okay. I wasn't complaining. Just asking."

"No problem. Anything else?"

"Captain Argeriche has notified the authorities and they're sending two patrollers. One to rendezvous with *Destiny's Shadow* and one to camp out where the other ship blew up."

"Thank you." I clicked off the channel.

The eerie feeling that some dangerous presence pursued *Destiny's Shadow* loomed heavily. The rational part of my brain reminded me that we were safe.

Long range scans showed nothing nearby except the approaching cavalry.

I ran a hand across my bald head, marveling at the smooth skin. Such an odd side-effect of the cryo-husk. Passengers gave me a second glance, but that was all. I probably looked like a maintenance worker playing hooky.

2:15 brightly displayed on my wrist-comm caught my eye. I made my way to the top-deck.

"I'm not gonna join ya," Susan's voice drifted in.

I sighed, readying myself for another comment about work ethic . . . or Sahadi.

"You've got other things to think about. Ships don't just blow up."

For several minutes I sat there and replayed the simple facts: Crew tries to hijack a cruise ship, crew blows self up. Case closed. Except, both the captain and I were bothered by the peculiarities. Something was nagging us. Odd questions, like: Why did they shoot up that guy I hid behind? Who closed those vents? Finally, something clicked. The guy cocking his head to listen to someone giving orders.

"Took you long enough," Susan complained.

"Sahadi," I said into my wrist-comm.

"Yes Marshal?"

"Check all transmissions aboard the other ship."

"Sir?"

"Sorry," I explained. "All logged transmissions. Your communication array keeps everything recorded right. All outgoing and incoming messages."

"Yes," she said. "Unless it was on a secure channel. Then we'll only know the size of the data-stream, but not the content within."

"Okay. Check everything that was sent during my time on the other ship. Someone was giving orders over there. Hopefully, we caught some of it."

"Got it. Give me a sec."

My quad cup showed up and I paid the barista this time. Even left a decent tip. It was government per diem anyway. The smell was enough to send my stomach to queasy-land again. This new body would take time to calibrate to my well-seasoned caffeine addiction.

"Soon," I said to the cup as I set it down. "Soon."

"Got something here."

"Really?" I said. "That was fast."

"No transmissions were picked up during your stint over there." The channel went quiet.

"What is it then?"

"Still trying to make sense of it, sir. A big chunk of data was sent shortly after . . ." her voice trailed off.

I sighed, "That's my transfer, Sahadi. After my bio-reads ended I was automatically sent into the ship's computer, remember."

"Yes, I know that, but this is something else. Regulations don't really have us checking every data-transfer so close. But I took it upon myself to bring up a catalog of all data-transfers—uploads and downloads."

"Told you she was good," Susan bragged.

Sahadi continued: "Every data-stream checked out . . . calls, vid packages to families, but there was one data-stream several minutes after yours that was very odd. Nearly identical to yours."

I shot up and I rushed out of the top-deck.

"Sahadi, clear me a path to my renewal-chamber."

"Oh, okay." My wrist-comm went quiet for a moment. "Take the back stairwell, starboard side. The doors are locked until you arrive. From there take the utility corridor. I've put out an all-call to keep it clear."

"Thanks, and have Captain Argeriche meet me there." The bridge was closer; they'd have a head-start.

"Affirmative."

An odd sensation crept through me as I raced through the cruise ship. Like I was being watched.

A security team along with Argeriche and Larson met me at the threshold of my renewal-chamber room. They followed me in.

Three cryo-husks. One empty, the chamber I had left just hours ago.

I yanked out my all-tool and scanned the remaining two. They appeared full, but U-sound specs showed one empty.

I silently cursed and pulled the cryo-husk door free. It fell easily.

***

"There's another *you* running around?" Larson asked, puzzled.

"Obviously." I spat, making the castigation clear. I was getting tired of explaining the obvious to this guy. "And he destroyed the only remaining body."

We draped a stabilizing blanket over the corpse. Notifying any regular crewmembers, such as maintenance, was out of the question. Even the onboard security detail would be subject to gossip and spreading fear. We didn't dare call in more than we already had.

Although a body I inhabited had expired before; I had never seen one up close.

"Where's he at now?" Larson demanded. "This other marshal."

Obviously not wanting to be found.

Captain Argeriche rubbed the bridge of his nose. "I'll notify ship's security, but it's gonna be fishy. They'll probably end up reporting *you*."

"Do it anyway." I pointed at the wrist-comm that was left inside the abandoned cryo-husk.

"So how do we track him down?" Larson asked. "How do we tell you apart?"

"Easy—I'm the one with the wrist-comm." I held it under his nose.

"That doesn't explain how we'll find him," Larson said indignantly, pushing my arm away.

"We won't have to track him down. There's only one reason he's here . . . to kill me."

They gazed at me like I was already dead.

"What do you mean?" Captain Argeriche asked.

"His name's Paul Collier, and he's no marshal. He *hunts* federal agents, specifically pseudo-souls. Been at it for over two decades."

"What's his beef with you?" Sahadi interjected over my wrist-comm. The voice threw me, I forgot I had left the line open so she could listen in from her station.

"This is *his* body." I leaned against one of the cryo-husks. "I am surprised that he's after me. He usually goes after bigwigs. But then again, no one's been able to figure him out. His methods are unorthodox, and he's extremely patient."

First Mate Larson turned around nervously, checking the passageway. "You said you have his body?"

"Yes." I didn't have time to detail the finer practices of pseudo-souls.

"He's one of many templates the government uses. Early in consciousness transferring, agencies sought out those most physically able and those that demonstrated high aptitude in detail recall and problem solving. Collier was—*is* both."

"Isn't it your intelligence that gets transferred?" Captain Argeriche asked.

"Yes and no. My consciousness gets transferred. My memories, my tendencies, my emotional foundation, that's all *this* brain." I pointed at my head. "It remembers everything."

I left out the part about Collier being schizophrenic.

Susan's ghost had never spoken to me until I had transferred into Paul Collier's body. Shortly after her death, I thought I had heard whispers, but it wasn't until that first upload of my consciousness that I heard her so clearly.

That was seven years after she had died.

"That's why he destroyed the spare, yours and this last body," Captain Argeriche said, gesturing at the blanket that covered the corpse.

"Yes, and his next move will be to eliminate any chance for me to upload into the ship's computer," I said.

"Wow," Sahadi said, "That's the only way he can truly kill you, huh?"

"This is precisely why pseudo-souls aren't natural," Larson said.

The comment hung in the air, like sad truths do.

Captain Argeriche and Sahadi didn't have anything to say in my defense. Neither did I.

I shook away the eerie reverie and raised my wrist-comm and asked Sahadi, "What are the chances you would've noticed the piggy-back signal if you weren't digging around?"

"Pretty close to nil," she admitted. "It wouldn't have come up until our next docking at the Ryman Port Authority. Even then, it's unlikely to have been detected."

"Exactly, so my counterpart didn't plan on being discovered just yet. That gives us a small window to work with."

"What do you suggest?" Captain Argeriche asked.

"Get a covert team set up at the array. That will be the first to go. Tell them it's a new drill or something."

"Of course," Sahadi said. "Once he kills you, he was probably just going to roam the ship pretending to be you. We wouldn't even have noticed the cryo-chamber until after our next stop."

Susan was right; this girl was insightful.

First Mate Larson pointed past me at the remaining cryo-husk. "How'd he do it? How'd he kill the spare?"

"That I don't know. It should have set off alarms."

"You said he's pretty sharp," Capatain Argeriche said. "Probably worked the schematics, since he's no stranger to uploading into cloned bodies."

"He sounds pretty pissed," Sahadi said.

Captain Argeriche turned to leave. "I've gotta get to the bridge and notify Trulley. There are several pseudo-souls on board. They have to be warned about the upload hub being threatened. It's going to be a PR mess. Larson, you get a team of men to guard the array."

"You said he downloaded from the other ship?" Larson asked as we made our way out of my renewal-chamber room.

"Uploaded, but yes."

"So he's a pseudo-soul himself."

"Technically, yes, but he doesn't see it that way. He claims only he has a right to the younger version of himself."

"Very peculiar," Captain Argeriche said as we turned the corner that led to the bridge. "What do you plan to do?"

I had to think about it. Something the captain said nagged at me. I hadn't realized Collier was a living contradiction: the original uploading into a copy of himself.

"We know where he's going," I muttered.

"Yeah, you said the communications array," Larson said.

I turned to Captain Argeriche. "Pull your men off, I don't want him deterred."

"What are you talking about?"

"We lucked out when Sahadi found that piggy-back signal."

"What's that?" Captain Argeriche asked.

"A chance to go on the offensive. A chance to stop him."

"What's the plan?" Sahadi asked.

"I'll explain on the way." I looked at the timer still beaming 2:15 on my wrist-comm.

***

"I don't like this plan," Susan's ghostly voice sounded distant.

I crouched inside the maintenance hatch, just below access to the communications array. Five meters above my head rested the only way a separated pseudo-soul could upload into the ship's computer. Shut that thing down and a person attempting to upload would have the data-stream disappear into empty space, eventually fading to nothingness. Steel plates protected the terminals and wiring that rested at the base of the array.

I glanced at the small airlock half-a-meter to my right. The only thing separating me from cold space.

"I really don't like this plan," Susan repeated.

Footsteps sounded down the bottom of the shaft. Several minutes passed before my counterpart entered, climbing the ladder. A plasma-slicer at his side. A common maintenance tool used for cutting dense metals. Deadly, if used as a weapon.

All I held was my all-tool.

"What the . . ." he said, gazing up at me.

An eerie feeling wormed through me as I looked into my own eyes. He wore a blue workman's jumpsuit. I never realized how large and intimidating I looked.

"What if this doesn't work?" Susan asked. I blinked hard, trying to quiet her.

Collier scrutinized me and then examined his surroundings. As I thought, he was planning to cut away the wiring and receiving hubs from within the ship—no reason for him to risk going space-side.

"Let's talk about this," I feigned panic as I stepped away, and backed into a crawlspace that led to the inner-airlock hatch.

"Sure, we can talk," he said, lifting a com-tab and scanning the maintenance shaft. Probably to verify that we were alone. He could still drop down a connecting shaft and disappear if he wanted, maybe rework his plan.

No, he was too eager: excited to catch his prey.

Stepping forward, Collier flicked a switch and the plasma-slicer fired up. Indigo light shone brightly at the end. I felt the energy from the lethal instrument.

I backed farther into the airlock hatch. There was a subtle jolt as *Destiny's Shadow* dropped from superluminal space to normal space. I hoped my counterpart didn't notice.

"You knew I'd hit the array. How?" he asked, stepping out of the service-shaft and following me into the airlock corridor.

"Didn't know. Had a hunch," I said. "I know about you. All the clones do, but I couldn't tell the captain—he would've tried to have me locked up. He and his crew hate pseudo-souls. Think we're an abomination to mankind."

"He has a point," Susan said.

"So what now?" I asked Collier, ignoring Susan.

He considered my question for a moment. "I'm gonna maim you," he said—now within five meters. "Then I'll hit the array to keep you from uploading your pseudo-soul."

I inched away, a bit closer to the inner-airlock. "We can talk about this. Figure something out."

"Always amazes me how scared y'all get," he said with a ruminative smirk. "You don't get it, do you?"

"'Real death'? Yeah, I get it." I said.

"No you don't!" he blurted. "You're nothing more than a program. A set of directives uploaded into a body. My body."

"And you're a killer."

At four meters away the energy from the plasma-slicer sent goose-bumps across my skin.

"Killer of what? You were never alive!" There was a brief pause as he stopped approaching. "They conned me into signing over my body for replication so they could download manufactured personalities into them. You," he eyed me disdainfully, "are nothing more than a line of code put into a *real* person."

"What're you talking about?" I asked. His unwavering confidence jarred me.

"You have no past. It's all a clever life you think you once lived." His eyes afire. "God, I love watching you fakes realize you're nothing."

I examined the back of my hand. The pores, the hairless knuckles unlike my own—they were all I knew. I remembered the first time I took a breath with the new body, how the lungs pulled in more air than I ever imagined.

"You're a soul-thief," Collier said.

It was entirely possible. My consciousness was uploaded and downloaded so many times, it was hard to remember where it really began. An emptiness stilled me.

"You don't really believe him, do you?" Susan interrupted.

I shook my head, trying to clear my thoughts. Who to believe? A ghost or a killer?

"Come on," she teased. *"Me? A planted memory? Gather your wits before he gouges you something fierce."*

I took a deep breath. Collier had closed in within three meters.

"What's a major symptom of schizophrenia?" Susan asked calmly.

I pressed the heel of my palm to my head.

"What's a major symptom of schizophrenia?" she repeated.

"Paranoia," I muttered, looking up and focusing on the man before me.

"Wait?" Collier snarled, bringing the weapon dangerously close. "Why aren't you armed? You knew I was coming this way. Why aren't you armed?"

He had figured it out. My hope had been that he'd be so eager to kill me that he wouldn't hesitate. But, now he froze and seemed to consider backing away.

I raised my arm to the inner-airlock hatch controls.

Collier squinted in confusion, probably wondering why I opened the inner-airlock—it only led to a walkway to the outer hatch: a hatch that was secured from the inside and could only be opened remotely by a crewmember.

"Sahadi, copy?" I asked.

"Yes Marshal," she answered.

Collier lunged. The plasma-slicer tore my left triceps.

I spoke quickly, "Shut off the communications array. Discontinue all interfaces from running uploads and downloads across the ship."

"Understood," she said.

"What're you doing?" he cried, sudden awareness flashed across his face. Our virtual tether to the ship had just been eliminated. The plasma-slicer impaled my stomach.

"Open the outer-hatch," I wheezed.

"Wait! Wait!" Collier said.

Collier dropped the plasma-slicer as we tumbled toward empty space. I locked my gaze on my wrist-comm, cradling it firmly. The vacuum of space grabbed us as we flew out the maintenance shaft. Struggling, I reached the timer and focused on the seconds.

I owed Susan.

2:15, 2:14, 2:13, 2:12 . . .

***

Only a small fraction of my mind panicked, probably the artificial interface trying to compute what in blazes was happening.

At 2:05 the relentless freeze engulfed me. There was no sensation of drifting in the vast emptiness. Only in my mind.

At 1:28 my vision blurred.

By 0:43 I could no longer see.

I counted off the seconds best I could. Susan laughed, *"Now? You're holding your memorial for me now?"*

"Yeah."

"You're so hard-headed."

"Some would call it dedicated."

She kissed my forehead. Then I felt her gentle lips on mine.

"I felt that," I sighed. "New level of crazy?"

"Things have changed."

The freezing turned to nothingness. Peace covered me slowly. A calmness I never expected. No sorrow, no fear. Just a surprise notion how I'd miss the job.

I thought I heard a timer beeping, but it had to be my imagination. No sound in the vacuum of space—it's a law. Besides, it had been more than two minutes. Time drifted sporadically. I could feel the artificial cortex searching for a hub.

No upload available.

My counterpart was experiencing the same thing. Space had already decompressed our bodies, but the cortex remained. A few more minutes and it'd dissolve into nothingness. The safeguard to protect the technology.

A gentle hand squeezed my shoulder, followed by encompassing complacency. Like slipping into a warm bath.

Terrible ripping!

The comforting warmth erased by cold.

***

Ship's engineer Ramena Sahadi angled her EVA-suit closer to Marshal McEvans' drifting body. She knew it would come down to seconds. The adrenaline didn't rattle her. With deft hands she manipulated the axon-sheath across the marshal's forehead.

She clicked on maneuvering jets and pulled the dead marshal back toward *Destiny's Shadow*. Paul Collier's frozen body drifted farther and farther into empty space.

Keep it short range, she reminded herself. A final order from McEvans. Can't risk picking up Collier's signal.

"No guarantees," McEvans had said earlier. "Just do what you can."

Captain hadn't agreed to the plan, said it was too risky. Captain also didn't know Marshal McEvans would pull the rank card.

Several minutes passed as Ramena amplified the axon-sheath's receivers. No glimmer on the readout. No faint fluctuation in wavelengths.

Tempted to widen the signal-field, she glanced over at Collier. Nothing more than a spec in the abyss. A wider signal-field wouldn't hurt.

Keep it short range.

She disagreed with the final order from the marshal, but she'd honor the request. Another minute was all she would allow herself before calling it quits.

She fed power into McEvan's cortex shelling, listening for any change.

"Captain." She called out and then remembered to click on her mic. "Captain, I've got something!"

Doug C. Souza won first place in the Writers of the Future Contest. His story, "The Armor Embrace" will be featured in the Writers of the Future anthology. You can read "Claim Jumpers" in Visions V: Milky Way and "Mountain Screamers" in Visions VI: Galaxies. Doug C. Souza can be found at dougcsouza.com and you can email him at dougscifi@gmail.com. He encourages readers to email him with any questions (especially those looking to give writing a serious try).

In a far future Earth, walkers cross the Dry on the path of Return, to show their adherence to the precepts taught them at the Reserve. All walk different paths, all show different talents; some can osmotically call water from even the driest of places.

Watercharmer

William Huggins

At first, she thought the buildings a mirage. Surely, they could not be the place of Return—sad, little place. She had walked the Dry so long, time ran as a droning loop of sharp sands and cerulean sky, broken only by sunsets and starscapes. Never a cloud drawn in by the mountain ranges that flanked her left and right, not in all her months of walking. At night, trying to rest in the painful sand before sleep, the heavens seemed a dark sea to her, stars glistening like the tips of wavelets.

She had known water once, in a past now half-forgotten at the Reserve, true seas of it—until Eldeen dropped her at the edge of the Dry so she could make her Crossing.

She took a sip of water from her stave, working the cap at the top—just enough to coat her tongue and swirl inside her mouth, take some of the dryness away. Out here she thought of water all the time. She needed a cleansing, a bath at the very least. Rubbing sand across her lean form every morning was not the same. But that was the point of Crossing and Return: to realize the essence of simplicity, learn to respect the meager resources of the world.

She replaced the cap and moved, shoes slipping across sands that would lash her feet if they were bare. She remembered the last place she thought a mirage, after two days of harsh wind and stinging sand: the arching, beautiful red stones of the Sandman's home. She did not think it real until she sensed the water. Her belly stirred, for she had had nothing but her pellets each day, small and long to melt in the mouth, balanced enough to keep her walking but nothing on the stomach.

In the cool shade of the curving rocks she paused to let exhaustion roll over her. Across the small center a netted hammock was strung between two stones. She wondered what it would be like not to sleep on the sands for a night. Then wondered who might live here and held the stave before her. Half again as tall as her, hard iron, dangerous, made more powerful by the charmed water within. She knew how to wield it—had used it, twice. It could break legs or skulls and she was not hesitant with it.

She breathed in: after so much time without—water, and life.

A figure moved from the shadows to her left: an old bald man, skin withered from the Dry but tall and still full of form. He wore a light red robe. He inclined his head to her, touched a hand to his breast, "Sandman am I." He looked at her a moment, smiled. "Watercharmer?"

She nodded. She had not spoken in so long, words would not come. Crossers took no vow of silence but saw so few on the walks many lost the power of speech completely, even if Returned. Some, like Eldeen, never saw another person as they moved through the Dry.

"The sun will set soon. Come, eat with me." He moved to the circle's far side and squatted, slid a rock aside and began pulling things from below it.

She stepped forward, certain for no definable reason she could trust the man. He set food on two thin wide rocks to his sides, more food than she had seen in months. She sat on her haunches before him, laying the stave close to her left hand. He moved the large rock back over his stores and handed her the plate to his right, then set the other before himself.

"The Old Ones left us very little but we still make do, yes?" She nodded to be polite. "I have no talent such as you but manage to keep this place alive."

She cleared her throat. "How?"

He grinned, and she found his calm confidence contagious. "I cheat." He nodded to the plate. "Eat. I know you are hungry."

Beyond hungry, she thought. She unwrapped the dark scarves from her head and face and saw his eyes widen. She had no idea what she looked like, in these long months of walking, not in the face—only in the body below, thin and starkly muscled. She must retain some beauty, then, which pleased her. They ate in silence. He had prepared seedcakes and meatfruits, berries of four kinds, the best of which was the green, which hit her mouth like a sparkler, and last and finest a fresh rockcrab, cured in salt. *Must be a saltspot nearby.* She savored the salt while she could, wishing she had time to borrow from it before she went on in the morning but it was no doubt too far. And she could not spare a day.

A full belly made her feel drunk. The Sandman stood and walked beyond her view, returning with two carved stones full of water. She drank deeply and the water was cool and delicious, tasting of red sand and minerals. She felt weariness hit her like the midday sun.

"Come," he said, rising, "come, rest." And he took her hand and helped her to the hammock, set her on its edge and rolled her to her side. She fell back and stretched and slept almost immediately.

She woke in the windless dark, face cold, for she never slept without her scarves. Above her face the stars. To her left the Sandman slept on a bed of red stone, curled away from her.

"Sandman," she said.

He stirred, slowly, turning to face her. A hand rubbed his eyes. "Are you well?"

She curled fingers at him.

He rose, moving as if in a dream—and perhaps he was, and her, as well. She opened her robe and he opened his and let it fall, and she took him. For he had been kind and she was lonely and full of need. He was slow and gentle and surprised her by pleasing her. They fell asleep nestled into one another's warmth, and when she woke she found he had wrapped his robe around them to fight the chill. Another little kindness. She kissed his wrinkled forehead and rose.

She took time to bathe at the spring, luxuriating in her rare nakedness, washing her face and body and hair. It felt so good to be clean. Her body drew in the water magnetically. She thought about charming the spring to increase its flow to help the garden, but the Sandman seemed to be managing the resource well. *Blessings. Simplicity.* She smiled, put a palm to the moisture, dressed, filled the stave.

The Sandman had robed himself. He smiled wistfully, laughed. "Another day would be too much to ask, yes?"

She nodded.

"Then hold. I have something for you. For the gift of your water."

She laughed, because no one had ever called it that—either a gift or water, but it seemed appropriate from him. There was temptation to stay another day, for she liked the calm of the place, and the man—but . . . no, she must be on.

His bare feet slapped against stone. He held out his hands. Across one palm lay a cloth bag, full of meatfruit and berries and salted rockcrab, no doubt—across the other lay a piece of swirled steel, like a whirligig without the means to fly. A waterflute. She had only seen one before, at the Reserve, during her apprenticeship. She looked at him in shock. "I cannot take this."

"I have another," he said. "Please. I told you—I cheat. Perhaps it will help you along your way."

"Show me the other," she said, to make sure he was not giving up something essential to keep him alive. She could not in good conscience take this gift if that were so. So, she waited until he turned and quickly moved behind the stones and returned with another just like it.

"You are honorable, Sandman," she said, shaking her head. This thing, so rare, half magic and half high technology—for no one knew with certainty how they worked—and here, in the midst of the Dry, this old man had two. "I accept your gifts." She pocketed them quickly.

"Safe passage, Watercharmer. I will not forget you or your face."

She gave him a last smile, then wrapped her head in the scarves and turned from the cool rock enclosure and did not look back.

And now here, again, something most probably not a mirage—but it did not give off the same feeling of security as the Sandman's haven: six wooden buildings, two of them nearly fallen, the others splitting and broken in various stages of disrepair. Old, but preserved in the long seasons of heat in the Dry. She had heard tales of places like this, small towns and hamlets and even great cities that existed here before the water vanished, taking civilization with it, too. *A last remnant.*

She moved forward and felt the sand change under her. She knelt, touched it with a palm. *Ah.* She felt the water call and the power of it shocked her. *Softsand.* She smiled, rose and took off her shoes, laced them together and strung them around her neck. The gentle touch of the sand felt soothing across her feet, a fine powder, like talc.

The closest building was half fallen. *So odd, to see wood.* No one used wood anymore. The Old Ones so negligent with their resources. She looked to the peaks in the distance. The forests from which they had taken this wood were all gone, long ago. And not returning anytime soon. Weeks before, she passed a massive fire burning in the mountains at her right. She walked for days with that fire in her shadow, a great smoke obscuring the sun in the day, at night glowing like a giant ember. With the right wind, she could smell the smoke. Without rain, the entire range burned. Eventually the peaks dissolved into the Dry and so did the fire.

She put a hand to the wood of the first building. It was splintered and peeling but still holding its integrity. *Hundreds of years, perhaps. A relic.* But a good strong wind, as often moved through the Dry, would blow it down eventually.

Across from the first building another stood. Beside it was a large sign, steel with fading greens and whites, and a name: Aguadulce. Though she could read, unlike so many, the word meant nothing to her. The door had fallen and she cautiously peeked inside: decay, dust, parts of the roof piled in a corner.

Four more structures, one in complete disrepair. The other two looked ready to fall at any moment, but the one furthest, on the right, looked like it might be a place to rest for the night—though the thought of sleeping in softsand pleased her, too. So rare to find such sand—only once in her walking had she come across it, and like the Sandman, it had been hard to leave.

The feel of water deep below wrapped the soles of her feet as she moved, satisfying, like the Sandman's gentle hands—and just as suddenly the feeling changed.

They came at her from the left—*three men,* she thought, though they were lean and shaggy things, wild hair and beards, thin robes. She turned to run but another man came from her right. *When attacked, be the attacker.* She charged the single man and her stave swept low and took his leg and she heard the crack of it breaking and his scream. She hit his head for good measure and as he went down she spun in the softsand and leapt at the closest pursuer, taking him across the shoulder and knocking him into the man at his side. The trailing man she took down in three hard hits across his body and neck—he lay in the sand, still. She spun back on the other two men. Weaponless, they were quick work.

She turned a circle, breathing hard, the soothing presence of water below her forgotten. She let the calm return, filling her, and turned her attention to the final building again. Perhaps best to let that alone, get out of here while she could. Where there were some, there could be more—though in the calm stillness of the early afternoon she heard no sound.

She held the stave waist-high, backing toward the open Dry again, eyes on the building.

To her left, movement—by the time she spun to catch it something struck her head. There was pain, then all went black.

She woke, drymouthed, in deep night. She turned her head and pain moved through her. She closed her eyes and gritted her teeth against it. A hand to her head came away with blood, shining on her fingers like red starlight. *They took my scarves.* She ran a hand across her hair, stiff and calcified.

She spotted a man sitting on the sand, legs before him. When he saw her eyes on him, he rose.

She shifted and her body hit something hard and cold. She rolled onto her back, ignoring the pain in her head, and realized she was caged in steel. She placed her hands on it, pushed but could not lift it. Panic hit her for a moment—she had never liked tight spaces, especially after months in the long barren openness of the Dry. She pushed again. She closed her eyes and took a breath. *Calm. Be calm.*

She could feel the water beneath her, hundreds of feet down, perhaps a thousand, and let that knowledge still her anxiety. *Options.* She put a hand to her pocket and felt it empty. The panic set in for a moment again. The cloth sack the Sandman had given her, the waterflute, her pellets—all gone. And her stave. And she trapped, pressed into the softsand like a foolish beginner—

She heard voices coming to her across the Dry, carrying in the stillness. The scent of a fire came with them, with the reek of charred meat that set her senses on edge. Shadows grew in form and she saw three men: the one who had been sitting and two others, larger men, hard to make out in the darkness but seemingly swarthy, bearded, frightening. One of them picked his teeth.

"You awake?" one asked.

She said nothing.

"Probably pretty under all that dirt." He spat. "Well, we'll deal with you in the mornin'. Damn stupid to be out here by yourself. And you kilt two of my best men. We took care of the other two." He spat again. "Get some rest if you can."

The other leaned close to the cage, waved something before her. She caught the glimmer of steel, tried not to show the longing on her face. The figure shook his head and laughed. "Flauta de agua." He laughed. "Que no se puede tener, bruja." And he tossed it a few feet away where it shone dimly against the softsands. The men spoke between themselves a moment, then two walked away while the other sat on the sand again to watch.

Options. She shifted to a more comfortable position on her side, resting her head and eyes. She wished for some water.

Water.

Though exhausted, she reached deeply with her will and called. *Blessings. Rise.* And she felt slight movement but nothing like what she needed. She took a deep breath. Her head throbbed from the effort, pain lancing her temples and jaw with each heartbeat, and she could feel the wound reopen and blood move down her face. But she drew again from herself and called, half desperate now, and a seam broke and she felt it rising—oh, water, chill, resting far below these hundreds of years, waiting, waiting—for her.

She felt the man rise and step toward her. Her head hurt so much she was loath to open her eyes but she did. He bent. "What is this thing?" he asked, with wonder in his voice, not cognizant of the water lightly pooled around his feet—water that guided him to the flute.

"A flute," she replied.

"I remember music," he said wistfully, and caressed the steel with both hands. He picked an end and blew on it. No sound emerged. He tried the other end with the same result. "It don't make no noise."

"I can play it for you if you give it to me."

He shook his head. "I don't think that's a good idea." He blew again to no effect. "'Berto won't like that."

"Does 'Berto like music?"

He shrugged. "Don't know. S'pose so."

"Give it to me," she said, and she could feel his will failing as the water pooled around his ankles. "I will make a music you will all love."

He leaned forward and opened a hatch on the cage, raised it and dropped the flute inside. She grabbed it quickly, before he had a chance to take it back, and pressed it against her belly. It was cold but quickly warmed. She rolled it against herself, almost faint with relief. The other things she could find later.

"Thought you were gonna play," he said, a slight edge to his voice.

She remembered what these men could do. What had most likely happened to the two men she killed—*little to eat out here,* she thought, with disgust. When they were done with her tomorrow that would no doubt be their plan for her, as well.

No.

She raised the thin tapered side of the steel to her mouth and blew softly and a sound emerged, low and mournful. The man sat beside her, enchanted, as the sound moved through the night. Ambient noises moved within and around it, blending with the melody, and as the water rose to his waist he noticed nothing.

Voices came through the stillness and still she played on, the sounds melding with the night. The water rose, moving into her cage now, encasing her, taking away much of the pain of the wound. The water wrapped her head and began to heal her, and just as the men came running toward her she cast out her will and the entire area collapsed.

She rolled out of the cage and let it fall into the depths she opened. She swam upward, flute in one hand, kicking, rising through the cold water until she touched softsand. She crawled until she could stand. Behind her, just a pool in the vastness of the Dry. The men nowhere to be seen.

Best not to be negligent again. She walked quickly to the tall building, cautious—but no one was there. *Could still be others out in the Dry.* In the dimness, she searched until she found her belongings, all piled in the same place, including her scarves. Walking back, she ignored what she saw stuck on steel above the diminishing fire. She stepped again into the water and washed herself, filled the stave, then stood over the pool and bowed.

Thank you. Blessings.

Slowly, as she dressed and wrapped and suited herself to walk again, the water drained away until there was only sand, as if nothing unusual had occurred.

She held the stave before her, wary. Her shoes she slung again around her neck, vowing to enjoy the pleasure of the softsands so long as they held out. And without a look back, she put out a foot, and resumed her Crossing.

William Huggins lives, writes, works, and hikes with his wife, daughter, and three rescue dogs in the southwestern USA. His short fiction has appeared in Another Realm, Expanded Horizons, Wolf Warriors, and Third Flatiron Anthologies, and he writes for Texas Books in Review. He is currently at work on a novel and a few other pieces of short and not-so-short fiction.

A miracle survivor of an eighty-five-foot fall is on a spaceship headed toward the first ever manned mission to an earth-like planet. The crew doesn't understand his presence aboard and don't want him there, but what they might find is possibly something only he can handle.

Way-Way and the Unseen

Jason Lairamore

When I was twenty, I had an accident. I slipped on a snowy slope while hiking and fell eighty-five feet off the side of a bluff. The doctors told me I should have died. That I had lived was a miracle.

I walked out of the hospital eleven days later with only a cane to show for my injuries. My great-grandmother made that walk with me. My dog, Trixie, who had died when I was six, padded alongside us.

Now, fifteen years later, I found myself in a similar miracle. As I pulled myself clear of the hypersleep chamber, I was brought back to how I had felt lying at the bottom of the cliff with blood leaking from my ears and nose. I felt cold, so cold that my very bones rattled.

"Way-Way, what are you doing up?" Jeff Balroy, the ship's mechanic, asked as I got unsteadily to my feet.

Way-Way, Wasted Weight, it was what the crew had nicknamed me just before our experimental spacecraft, Goldilocks, had launched into the heavens. I didn't take offense. I couldn't expect them to understand what it was I did, or why I was here, going on humankind's first-ever manned mission to a viable, earth-like, planet.

"I set my chamber for early release so that I could see our approach," I said as I toweled off and dressed in a set of the ship's white spandex undersuits.

Jeff nodded. "It's a sight. I don't blame you."

I walked over in the .5 artificial gravity and joined him at the viewport.

"Any problems?" I asked.

"Goldi is purring like a kitten full of porridge."

I gazed through the ship's viewport and saw all three of the gremlins on board perched on the nose of the ship. Their attention was riveted outward, toward the blue and white marble we were nearing.

"Glad to hear it," I said.

Trixie barked from behind me and I turned to give him a smile.

"He's as nervous as you are," Great-grandma said, bending down to rub a long-fingered hand down the little mutt's short-haired back.

I didn't reply out of deference to Jeff, though I had my doubts that it would help his opinion of me anyway. As it was, he noticed me looking at something he could not see.

"Always in character, aren't you Way-Way," he said.

The ship was full of scientists and army specialists. They, like Jeff, thought me a joke, a waste of very valuable resources. This was humanities first attempt to find a world that we might someday colonize and none of them could understand why I was there.

Still, Jeff was nicer than the others. I didn't want to give him a reason to despise me as the rest of the crew did.

"The world looks good," I said, changing the subject. I turned back to the viewport.

Jeff followed my gaze. "Looks even better than the vids the orbiting drone sent to Earth. You can almost feel her anticipation. It's like she's a girl waiting for her prom date."

"Yeah," I said and smiled, because he was smiling.

I looked long and hard at the growing orb and felt, not anticipation, but a swirling mass of life. This was the real reason I had woken early. I wanted to gauge what to expect when we went down there. What I saw only made my nervousness worse. The planet was full of life, and by the complexity of the auras rolling around like massive cloudbanks, a lot of it seemed intelligent.

"I was just as nervous as the girl I took to prom," I said softly, my eyes on the intricacy of twisting colors.

Jeff laughed. "Don't you worry, Way-Way. We'll be wearing our finest tux and have a nice corsage to present to her."

By that he meant the few soldiers on board had the finest armor that money could buy and the most powerful weapons the ship could carry. I shook my head.

"Yeah, I know," I said and glanced once more to the gremlins perched on the narrow point of the ship. A brownie had joined them, and one of the gnomes.

***

The others of the crew woke as the ship established a low orbit. Captain Jacobson was the first to dress and join Jeff and me by the viewport.

"How's our little miss, Mr. Balroy?" he asked Jeff. The captain had a way of ignoring me completely, even when I was standing right next to him.

"She's a rose prime for the picking, Captain—ready for the vase."

The captain slapped him on the back. "I like that, Mr. Balroy. Rose. Hang on to that when the time for naming her comes around."

"Captain, I need a private word," I said and glanced toward Jeff.

The Captain smiled amiably at me in a sidelong way, never turning to give me his full attention. "Later. I've preparations to make," he said as he walked away.

I raised my hand toward his retreating back and Jeff let loose a low laugh.

"You're a real people person, Way-Way. Anybody ever told you that?"

"Yeah," I replied, still watching the Captain's back. Trixie barked at him as he turned a corner and disappeared.

"You're going to have problems with that one," Great-grandma said from beside me.

"Yeah," I said again, shaking my head. One of the demons that had woken with the crew, a barrel-chested, red one, gave me a fierce, yellow-eyed look then followed the captain.

"It's going to be an interesting landing," I muttered.

"Interesting?" Jeff chided. "It's going to be monumental!"

I hoped not, but he was probably right. I should probably have had my talk with the Captain before we had gone into hypersleep.

"Everything is going to work out," Great-grandma said. "We are *all* here to help."

That's what I was afraid of.

***

The Captain had us gather in the mess hall about a half hour later. Even though the little area was crowded, the other crew found a way to arrange themselves so that I was standing all alone in one of the corners. I usually didn't mind them avoiding me, but now that the time was upon us to land, I found that my lack of relationship with any of them might cause me problems.

"Alright, listen up," the Captain began. "First thing, what the orbital pointed out as possible native buildings looks to be true. Our higher powered instruments confirm this. They look to be some kind of tree houses. That changes the dynamic down there, but we planned for the contingency, so you all know what to do."

"First Contact," Mary Tilton said from one of the chairs up front. She was the ship's astrobiologist.

"That's a few stages down the line, Mrs. Tilton. Be patient," the Captain said with an easy smile.

The Captain turned his gaze toward me before continuing.

"We land in a remote area and set up a zone of safety. Our military people will establish a perimeter for us."

I shook my head at him. That wasn't the protocol agreed upon by mission control before leaving Earth.

The Captain nodded. "The rest of us will stay in the ship until they give the all clear."

He stared at me, daring me to contradict him. One of the ghosts floating nearby sensed my unease and drifted out to the center of the room. The temperature dropped a dozen degrees or so. A uniformed army man sitting right next to the ghost shivered.

"Mr. Balroy, see that you look at the temperature regulators," the Captain said offhandedly.

"Yes Sir," Jeff said.

"Class dismissed," the Captain said. "Go strap in. We're heading down."

I waited in my corner as the others filed past me. Not one of them even so much as glanced in my direction. When the Captain came to the doorway he stopped and looked at me expectantly.

"I will be the first person to set food on that planet," I said. That was what had been agreed upon back on Earth. It had taken me months to convince the administrators of the need to do it that way, and now the Captain, in one little meeting, had undid all my work.

The Captain didn't respond to my statement. He looked at me steadily for a moment, smiled, and walked out the door. This time, instead of a demon following him, one of the angels did. The beautiful creature paused in her pursuit to consider me.

"I will work on him," she said in a harmonious voice before disappearing through the wall.

***

We were fully suited during atmosphere entry as a safeguard and I was thankful. I disconnected my com with a push of a button so that nobody could hear me speak.

"I didn't want to have to do it this way," I said to Great-grandma.

I could feel her grab my hand even through the thick material of my suit.

"Accidents happen," she said.

I shook my head as the bitter memory of our original Captain's death replayed in my mind. She, a stoic woman named Sherry Cotner, had been on board with what I had proved to the other administrators.

"Jealousy happens," I corrected. I had no doubt that one of the unseen left behind had killed her for spite. I had figured something like it might happen. It wasn't like I could, or even wanted, to take every spiritual force with me on the trip. As it was, the ship was stuffed to the gills.

"Don't get yourself worked up so," she said. "The others get nervous when you do, and they are already pushed to their limits. You realize how many opposing entities we have so close together."

I knew. I'd hand-picked each and every one of them.

"The crew won't understand," I said.

"You won't make any friends, that's true."

"Thanks for that, Great-grandma."

She laughed in a light, carefree way that reminded me of my easy days of childhood.

"They're a tough crew. They can handle it," she said.

"Yeah," I said. They were tough, maybe too tough. "Let's hope they don't try to kill me."

"We won't let that happen."

She was right and I knew it, but that didn't change the fact that the crew was more than likely going to witness something none of them had ever seen before, and the approaching planet paled in comparison.

***

We landed with a soft thud. The others popped their safety belts and stood. I fumbled with my belt's release and couldn't get the thing to work. A gremlin snuck in around the chair and jimmied the lock open.

"Fooled you!" it said and cackled. The thing's high-pitched laugh set my teeth on edge.

"Very funny," I said. The gremlins and the other tricksters of the group had made it their mission to sneak around and prank me in various ways. The fact that I could see them seemed to exhilarate them. I figured they enjoyed the challenge.

"Better open your coms. Troubles starting," Great-grandma said.

That hadn't taken long.

I followed the others out of the bank of seats and entered the main hold where the doors to the outside were located.

"What do you mean the doors are jammed?" I heard the Captain bellow over the com.

"Just that," Jeff answered. "The board is green, but the electronics won't fire."

I took a deep breath and began working my way through the crowd. My heart beat hard in my chest and my hands were clammy with anticipation.

There was a gremlin at work on the main door and another on the cargo bay assembly. A ghoul and a leprechaun were close at hand, helping or maybe just enjoying the group's tension. I squared my shoulders and stepped forward to where Jeff and the Captain were staring at the computer display. The angel from earlier hovered just behind the captain.

"It's no use, Clay," the angel said to me as Jeff and the Captain turned toward me. "He really doesn't like you."

I didn't need an angel to tell me that. The Captain's feelings for me were stamped on his face with the sneer he directed at me.

"I'm here to help," I said.

"You have a degree in electronic maintenance that I didn't know about?" the Captain spat.

I ignored his vehemence as best I could. "Protocol states that I am to first ensure our safety on this planet. With your leave, I will do what I came here to do."

He pointed to the door. "Go ahead. Let's see you walk through walls."

The heavily armed soldiers waiting to exit the craft laughed. I stepped away from the intense glare on the captain's face and positioned myself in front of the door.

"That won't be necessary," I said. The gremlin in the door smiled at me with its sharp-toothed grin.

"Open it up," I said to it in a low voice.

For once, the gremlin didn't try any trick. The door retracted back with a soft whir.

I caught a glimpse of a blue-green sky. There were spindly trees out from the ship, impossibly tall compared to my earthbound references. But, with the gravity here being only half of earth norm, it had been expected that the plants would be taller.

I made to take a step and got knocked aside. The door closed as I fell to the hard, metal floor. Before I could right myself in my bulky suit, the Captain was on top of me.

"No," he said. His helmeted face was against mine. I wished, and not for the first time, that I had the ability to see when a spell had been put on somebody, for I was almost certain that the Captain had received one before our departure.

All I could really see extra, when it came to the living, was their aura, and Captain Jacobson's had always been a bruised red. That, in and of itself, wasn't too rare. There were a lot of angry people in the world.

A pixie flew from above my head and poked the Captain in the eye. At the same time, I heard Trixie snarl.

The Captain jerked and smashed his helmeted head against mine.

"Captain, please," I said. Time was wasting. I needed to be outside observing the unseen.

His head and chest lifted off me then the rest of him. I rolled onto hands and knees as a woman screamed and one of the soldier's cursed.

"Observer," a voice as black as the void said in a slow, measured tone.

"What are you doing?" The Captain screeched.

I got to my feet and sighed as I turned to face the Jinn that held the Captain a couple of feet off the floor. The creature had been a late addition to our mission, and one that I was still not too sure about. But, in the end, I guessed I still agreed with my original assessment. Having a Ghoul Jinn champion was a good way to ensure any dark place would not go unexplored.

I turned to the gawking crowd and hated the thick, cloudlike auras of fear and hate that surrounded them. The army men close to me held their weapons a little too tightly for my liking.

"Hold him until I am outside," I said. It would be best to get away as fast as I could. I'd already missed too much of the action. I would explain the situation afterward, just as I had originally planned.

"Don't let him go!" The Captain yelled as he struggled against the impassive Jinn.

The crowd paused, as I knew they would. No normal person's brain would act without hesitation while witnessing somebody seemingly floating unnaturally in the air. I took advantage and slipped outside before one of the army men tried to shoot me.

***

I stepped off the ladder onto soft, flattened grass. The ship had created a small circle of smashed plant life as it had landed. Beyond the little circle, the grass stood as high as my shoulder.

As I walked toward the tall, rolling grass line, a leprechaun came strutting out like he owned the whole world.

He threw a thumb back in the direction he had come.

"The gnomes have found their best friends back there," he said in mock disgust. "Bloody, miniature troll-looking creatures with hairless skin, ye know, like an elephant, but all wrinkled up like a Shar Pei. They've already learned a lot about the vegetables and such. Above my head it was, so to speak."

That was good news.

"Why are you returned so early?" I asked.

"Nothing for me out here, not so far. Maybe I'll get lucky once we find something with a brain."

I nodded. "Once we have the rural area secure, we will reconnoiter to some of those buildings we saw from orbit. We'll hunt for a small town or something."

"Sounds good to me," he said. "Maybe I will get to have fun like the pixies up in the trees."

"Fun?'

"Oh, it's like a bunch of bees fighting miniature buzzards, only these buzzards caw like crows when they get excited."

That sounded like a fight. "Show me."

He gestured for me to follow when a great roar broke the relative silence. I flinched down instinctively. The little, green-clad fellow laughed like it was the funniest thing he'd seen.

"Might want to observe up, observer," he hooted.

I was already doing so, and what I saw up there made my blood run cold. The sky was full of dragons. I'd only been able to fit five of the great creatures within the ship, even with their ability to shrink their enormous size.

The fighting up there was titanic in proportion. Though our dragons were outnumbered a hundred to one, they were holding their own. Squinting a little, I made out the demons and the angels as well. They were giving it everything they had, and holding the enemy back, for now.

But, they were going to lose. We didn't have the numbers.

"Get down here!" I yelled up at them, though I knew that I didn't really have to raise my voice. Distance didn't really equate, like it did to humans.

Our dragons and the rest dove to the ground fast. The horde they had been fighting followed. It looked like the battle was coming to me. Well, so be it. I was here to see if we could make a go at this planet, and fighting against one hundred to one odds wasn't going to help that happen.

"Get everyone back here," I said to the leprechaun.

The leprechaun smiled up at me. His grin was the embodiment of mischievousness.

"Some fun for me at last," he said. "Don't think I've ever tangled with a dragon." Then he was gone, disappeared back into the tall grass.

I shook my head as the mass of giant, winged creatures neared. I'd never fought a dragon either.

And I didn't want to start now.

***

Our dragons landed like falling boulders around me, then turned their great heads skyward and let loose a river of fire, ice, and magic. The advancing mass of native dragons disappeared behind the wall of elemental forces, but not before I got a better look at them.

There were differences in the native dragons, but not the polar opposites we had on earth. From the little I managed to see, they had bat-like wings with bodies that reminded me of a penguin. Their heads were an ugly mash-up of vulture and owl. It was the eyes, though, that caused the shiver that ran down my spine. They were deep set, overly large, angular and ovoid, and a sickly whitish-blue.

Great-grandma laid a hand on my shoulder and I jumped. She held Trixie in her other arm, tucked close to her ribs. The little dog had its ears up and wore a look of dog-like concern.

"Maybe we should go back inside," she said.

I shook my head. We'd be no better off inside than out. I glanced at the pearl-like blood trickling from a few of the angels and the dark-purplish wounds on a couple of the demons. No, it was now or never. We had to make a stand, and that stand would be better made on the ground, where at least the others I'd brought along could enter the fray.

Ri Riu, the Japanese lucky dragon, one of the first creatures I had approached to join me on this venture, edged in closer to me. I was glad to have the mysterious creature along. We were going to need all the luck we could get.

It pointed with one sharp talon off towards the trees as the other dragons' attack began to wane in intensity. I was turning to look, when one of the pixies buzzed like an arrow right in front of my face. She had some green smears of blood on her arms, but was smiling.

"We have the trees!" she said with a smile. "At least the lower portion. The little buzzards don't seem to want to fight over anything a dozen lengths off the ground."

"Keep what you have," I said. "Don't press it right now."

Ri Riu nudged me with the back of one of its talons, nearly knocking me down. The great, white dragon pointed again.

I looked, and at first, I only saw that the attack had stilled for the moment. The hundreds of native beasts overhead simply circled, as if waiting. Then I saw what the luck dragon was pointing at.

In one of the trees, about two-thirds the way up, perched a birdlike creature. I couldn't tell much detail due to the distance, but one thing was immediately clear. It wasn't an unseen. I believed it might be one of the actual natives that called this planet home.

"Everyone," I called. "Stay here." I spied a rocky outcropping about a hundred yards away. "I'm going over there. Maybe I can talk to that fellow." I pointed to the strange creature in the tree. "Parley, or some such."

None of the unseen around me said anything, so I started walking. Great-grandma followed.

"You stay too, Grandma," I said.

She looked worried and Trixie growled, but she nodded. "Be careful," she said.

Careful. How was I to know how to be careful? It wasn't like anything like this had ever been done before.

***

The atmosphere was a strained silence with only my motions through the grass and my huffing breath breaking the charged moment. I felt like it could explode open at any time, so I hurried as fast as I could. I was breathing hard by the time I reached the summit of the little pile of rocks.

I caught my breath as I stared up at the creature in the trees. Its wings were blackish-gray and folded over its body, making it look like it wore a long trench coat. It kicked its head toward me in little jerks, just like any other bird back on Earth. It did have a beak, but it wasn't overly long and pointy. It reminded me of a narrow-headed human with a big nose. The pointy feathers on its head added to the narrowness of its features, giving it a mohawk look.

"Hello!" I called, then realized that there was no way it would be able to understand my words. As luck would have it, the creature solved my dilemma for me.

"You have come from the far sky." Its words sounded inside me head just like some of the unseen talked to me.

I nodded like a fool. "Yes," I thought back. "We are travelers."

"Yet you touch the ground. Can you not fly?"

"Ummm, some of us can, some can't."

"And that great, gray winged thing," it said. "It flies above the sky?"

I turned to look at our transport ship.

"It is a machine," I said.

I got a feeling that the creature didn't understand what the word *machine* meant.

"Your spirits fly, yet you cannot?" it asked. I could feel the suspicion in its question.

I thought back on the awful fight we'd just had up in the air above.

"I cannot, and I can keep the others from doing so," I said. We couldn't afford another battle.

"Why have you come?" it asked.

"To explore. We have no wish to fight."

It kicked its head at me a couple of times as it considered my words.

"I am Tloward, a spirit flyer. I must report to my people. Stay on the ground until my return and you will not be harmed."

"Will do."

It extended its bat-like wings and flew away. The native dragons continued to circle overhead, though they did rise a little.

***

"No fight?" the leprechaun yelled before I had made it back to the others.

"No fight," I said as I entered the little circle of unseen.

"No fun at all," the leprechaun chided.

I snorted. It wouldn't have been a fight anyway, not with the numbers so stacked against us.

"What now?" one of the angels asked.

"We explore, just like we were sent here to do," I said. "There is only one rule. No flying. Stay on the ground until we figure something else out."

"Bah!" the fire dragon spat. A waft of brimstone stench rolled over me with its outrage.

I pointed skyward, to the hundreds of circling dragons overhead.

"You fly, they attack. Got me? We had our fight, and were getting licked. It's diplomacy time."

They grumbled, but didn't object. I could only hope that they obeyed. I was dealing with spirit creatures, after all, and they weren't known for their use of logic. They were forces of nature and the embodiments of the human condition, both good and bad. Their behaviors were narrow.

"You did great," Great-grandma said.

"That's yet to be seen," I said with a weary smile. I turned back to the ship. "Besides, now's the hard part. I have to go and try to explain things to the crew. I'm more likely to be killed by them than by the dragons overhead."

She patted me on the shoulder. "You always did have a hard time finding friends."

"Yeah," I said. She didn't hear the sarcasm overlaying my word. I'd like to see her try to make friends when you attracted spirits like a magnet.

"Hey, leprechaun," I called over my shoulder.

"I have a name, sonny. Want to hear it?" the leprechaun shot back.

"Maybe later. You still looking for a fight?"

"I'll never say no to a bit of fun."

"Grab a few of the like-minded. I may need some help here pretty soon."

The little fellow giggled. Trixie barked.

***

A gremlin poked its head out of the side of the ship after I knocked.

"You've missed quite a time inside," it said, giving me an evil, pointy grin.

I'd assumed as much. The crew hadn't come all this way just to be locked away like sardines in a tin can.

"Can you keep them back while I board?" I asked.

The little black and green face bobbed up and down. "That big Jinn and a few of his ghoul kin have got things well in hand, though it took some convincing."

"And the army men?" I asked. I really didn't want to get shot the moment I stepped inside.

The little guy gave me a reproachful look, though, truth-be-told, his look was more ominous than anything else, what with his already evil, yellow-eyed face.

"First thing we did was jam up those guns of theirs. Not a machine working that they can lay a hand on."

Well, I couldn't ask for any more than that. I rubbed my sweaty palms together and tried to settle their trembling.

"Okay, open up. Here goes nothing."

The door opened and a little ladder lowered to the ground. A stench of anger and fear rolled out from the inside like an ugly, gray-orange cloud.

This wasn't going to be fun.

I squeezed the ladder rungs extra hard to prevent my trembling fingers from slipping. It wouldn't be good to fall and break my fool neck.

I stepped aboard and the door closed at my back. The gremlin working the door slipped from the wall and stood beside me. He gazed out at all the fearful and angry faces and smiled.

"Have at it, boss," he said.

I ignored him and returned the crew's stare with one of my own. The divide between us was greater than ever. I had no idea how I was going to be able to get them to believe a word of what I was about to say. They probably thought I was some sort of demon.

"Uh, I made contact with a native. We will be okay for now as long as we stay on the ground. We can't send up any drones or anything though."

My words were met with a stony silence that beat against me worse than any incrimination.

"What are you?" the Captain asked. His face was swollen like he had been pummeled. I winced at his injuries.

"I'm sorry about that," I said. "All I wanted was for them to keep order while I did what I was sent here to do. It was protocol, after all. The administrators . . ."

"Them?" a shaky voice interrupted me from somewhere in the back of the group.

I held up my hands. "Listen. What I am going to tell you is the truth. I didn't ask for it, but it is what it is." I told them of my fall, and of what happened after, of how I could see and talk to all kinds of spirits and magical creatures."

"And you brought them on board my ship!" the Captain roared.

I shook my head and the others murmured. It was true that I had hand-picked those that had come along, but I had no more *brought* them on board than I had brought the crew on board.

After a few moments, the talk subsided and a quiet expectation filled the cargo hold where we all stood. I was glad to see that a little of the sickening fear had leaked away. Knowing what was going on, even a little bit, seemed to do wonders for people's anxiety level.

I waved a hand to include the crew at large.

"I didn't bring them," I said. "We all brought them."

I held up my hands before the outrage I saw building could pour forth.

"Hold on. Let me explain."

"Yes, explain," the Captain said icily.

I sighed and dropped my arms. "How many nationalities do we have here? How many races? How many religions?"

"Most of them!" I said, probably too loud, but I wanted them to know that it was important. "We represent a big portion of all that humanity has to offer. There's Chinese, Japanese, American, Scottish, Islamist, Buddhist, Christian. So many."

"So what!" one of the army guys holding a gun shouted.

"Every one of those cultures and religions has their own folklore, their own mystical beings."

"Yeah?" Jeff Balroy asked. I looked at him. He looked more interested than scared.

"Well, don't you think that you each carry those things with you everywhere you go? You do. They surround you, always, no matter where you go. When you came to this world, you brought along all those things. And not just your specific, current cultures and religions, but your historical stuff as well. Beings and forces that you don't even know about."

"What I did was pick and choose the ones that came along. I tried to get a good group, one that might best represent the human race. Just like the administrators chose each of you."

"You can do that?" Jeff asked. I tried to pick up on any incredulity in his tone, but he seemed to actually mean the question.

I glanced to the giant Jinn and the skeletal ghouls circling the group.

"I had help." I said. I hoped they didn't dig on what that help entailed. There were a lot of intricate powers involved that helped me manipulate things the way I did.

"I'm not going to stand here and listen to this nonsense!" the Captain roared. He took one step toward me and the Jinn champion lifted him from his feet.

The others gasped. I shook my head.

"That's a Jinn that has you Captain." A few in the crowd who knew a thing or two about the Jinn gasped again.

"Go ahead and set him down," I said.

"Observer," the Jinn said and let the Captain fall. The Captain caught himself and stood erect. His swollen face had gone ashen.

"The administrators agreed to the protocol that you tried to ignore," I told him. Oh, how long it had taken me to prove to them how important it was to do it my way. But now wasn't the time to discuss that in too much detail.

"Here's the deal," I said instead. They deserved to know the whys, in any case. Hopefully, it would be enough to satisfy them, at least for now.

"The administrators knew that we were going to a planet that most likely had life. They didn't know what kind of life that might be any more than anybody else. But, if that life was anything like ours, then it would have spirits and forces just like ours. So, they wanted to make sure that we weren't blind to it. That's why I'm here. To observe those spirits and help steer us clear of any trouble that they might present."

They chewed on that for a while. Each and every one of them was a scientist to one degree or another. I knew that thinking about the spiritual and folklore folk didn't factor in very highly in their thinking. But they needed to think about it. It was a fact of humanity.

"So what now?" the Captain asked. He'd regained his composure enough that his hostility didn't outwardly show too much.

I smiled. "My initial job is done. We can explore. Just remember. We have to stay on the ground for a while. The native I spoke to is going to talk to his people. We'll see how things develop."

The Captain nodded. Nobody spoke or even moved.

Jeff Balroy was the first to do anything. He walked up to the control panel and opened the door and the cargo bay. The others continued to stand about like they'd forgotten how to move.

"Well, don't just stand there!" the Captain barked. "You all know what you're supposed to do. Get moving."

His words had the necessary effect. People started drifting to their various work stations.

None of them met my eye or even came close to me as they went about their business. Jeff surprised me when he did come to stand beside me. He slapped me on the shoulder and grinned.

"You're one hell of a strange guy, Way-Way. What is your name, anyway?"

"Clay," I said. "Clay York."

He nodded. "Well, Clay York. I'd like to have a drink with you tonight. You've got to tell me a thing or two about these beasties that are among us."

"Um, sure."

After he walked away, Great-grandma laid a hand on my shoulder.

"If I didn't know better I'd think that young man wants to be your friend."

I shook my head. "Yeah, we'll see."

Jason Lairamore is a writer of science fiction, fantasy, and horror who lives in Oklahoma with his beautiful wife and their three monstrously marvelous children. He is a published finalist of the 2012 SQ Mag annual contest, the winner of the 2013 Planetary Stories flash fiction contest, a third-place winner of the 2015 SQ Mag annual contest, and a Writers of the Future Contest Semi-Finalist. His work is both featured and forthcoming in over 65 publications to include Perihelion Science Fiction, Stupefying Stories, and Third Flatiron publications, to name a few. You can connect with Jason at https://www.facebook.com/jason.lairamore.

With the diversity that exists within our own solar system and what we are finding exists within our galaxy, what will we find beyond our galaxy? What strange things will exist as we explore our Universe? If other Universes exist what will separate them from ours and what will the similarities be?

Universe 289

W. A. Fix

Water seemed to be everywhere. It lay like glass all the way to the horizon with occasional ripples, created by the slight movements of ten large creatures that schooled in the shallows surrounding a small island. With noses just above the surface, their heads were submerged and not easily visible. Those heads, maybe a foot length in diameter, displayed large deep-set orange eyes and a mouth that was proportionally wide and fixed in an almost half-moon smile. Just above the smile was that bulbous nose that now stood like a growth on the water's surface. The ears, currently under water, were small but extremely sensitive and could distinguish the individual heartbeats from the nine others in the group. The heads were attached to very powerful shoulders by a short neck so muscular it restricted movement. Underwater the outstretched primary arms spread nearly seven foot lengths and, despite their muscularity, floated buoyant in the water. At the end of each arm was a hand with three large opposing and thick fingers. Just below the primary arms, and slightly forward on a powerful chest, were another set of arms, far less powerful, with small delicate hands each containing three refined fingers and an opposing thumb. One of the creatures stirred slightly, creating ripples that touched the noses of the others, and caused several grunts of dissatisfaction.

The offender had inhaled deeply, his massive chest almost breaking the water's surface, as he savored the sweet-smelling methane that bubbled from the decaying algae bed just below him. The methane, the warm water, the algae, and the muddy sludge all combined to provide the perfect environment for his midday nap. His mind began to drift into sleep, as hundreds of small water slugs began cleaning the oils from his body. "*Ahh yes,*" he thought, "*This is how My-God intended intelligent beings to live.*"

"Excuse me, Dr. Jarnnod." There was a momentary pause as he opened his eyes. "Sir, you have an urgent communication."

The creature very slowly raised his head above the surface. A small orb hovered four foot lengths to his right and one above the water. Disgusted, he said, "I said I did not want to be disturbed. Who is it?"

"Sir, they didn't say. They simply said to tell you that Wahdeer refused to come home."

Jarnnod sat upright, gravity pushing his naked backside deeper into the sludge and causing waves of water to wash over the noses of his companions. Within seconds the entire group was sputtering, grumbling loudly, and some even shouting obscenities. As the algae slime ran down his chest he said urgently, "I'll take the communication." A holographic panel opened, between him and the orb, displaying two of his lab assistants and the laboratory that had been his home for the last two solar years. "What happened?" he asked.

"Dr. Jarnnod, we are so, so sorry to bother you, sir. If there had been anything we could have done . . ."

"Kleen, will you stop your incessant sniveling. I simply asked what happened." Some of the slime ran from the top of his bald head, over the broad brow, and dripped on his cheek. Subconsciously, he wiped it away with his right detail hand, smearing his face with even more slime.

"You're right, sir, I'm sorry for being such an irritant. Even my mother used to say . . ."

"Kleen, just shut up! Marsick, what happened?"

Cut off in mid-sentence, Kleen bowed and turned to Marsick with a look that pleaded for her to take the lead.

"Sir, we opened the portal into Universe Number 289 three solar days ago and without incident the Wahdeer probe was sent through. Today, and at precisely the appointed time, we opened the portal again. As expected, Wahdeer was waiting. We issued the recall command and the unit failed to respond. After numerous attempts it simply sat motionless ignoring our commands. Having never lost a probe in 288 previous Universes, I . . ." She paused, lowered her eyes then continued, "Kleen decided to consult you on what to do next."

Jarnnod thought for a moment, then said, "Did you receive any telemetry?"

"No, sir. Total silence."

"Well, it sounds like we may have lost twenty-five percent of our operating budget for next year. Obviously, there was some sort of system failure. Start running diagnostics on the backup. Let's get it ready to send through. Maybe we can retrieve Wahdeer. I'll be back in the lab in the morning," he said sadly.

"Sir, please stay and finish your vacation. The backup won't be ready for at least four solar days and that's if the diagnostics are perfect. It seems a waste to miss the remaining three days of your well-earned vacation watching us do diagnostics on a probe."

Jarnnod paused again then said, "I agree. However, I want all your findings on my workstation when I return. Kleen, you are senior in my absence. Over the next three solar days, please surprise me and display the leadership qualities I'm sure you have."

"Sir, I promise to have everything in order when you return," said Kleen. "You will be amazed at the efficiency displayed by everyone on your team. Even my mother, who I have tried to please all my life, will be proud of . . ."

Jarnnod slowly turned to Marsick, "Please do all you can to help him. His mother is a dear friend, in addition to being the project's benefactor."

Marsick bowed her head slightly, "Do not worry, sir. Kleen will not fail, your entire team is prepared to support him."

Jarnnod returned the bow and said, "Thank you, Marsick, and know your efforts are recognized." He then turned back to Kleen. "You have much to complete in a short time, Kleen. You may contact me if you require my assistance. I will see you in three solar days." Then he said dismissively, "Orb, end this communication."

The holographic image vanished and was replaced by his nine bathing companions, clumped together, as if posing for a holo-image. All were in various states of displeasure, with the remnants of the lake bottom obscuring most of their dark pink flesh. Jarnnod realized for the first time that he may have pushed the limits of resort etiquette, and frantically searched his memory for the appropriate thing to do. The group glared in silence and all that could be heard was the sound of methane bubbles bursting on the surface and sludge dripping into the water—very similar sounds, but easily discernable to Jarnnod's ultra-sensitive ears.

"My dear friends," he said, even though he may have known only two of their names. He humbly bowed his head and continued, "I sincerely apologize for the interruption, but as you heard, it truly was an emergency." There were grumbles from the group that clearly indicated they did not share his opinion. He raised his eyes to the group and as a last resort said, "Please, let us continue our meditation. Orb . . ."

"Yes, Dr. Jarnnod?"

"Please transfer the group's cost of this session to my account. I simply could not rest knowing I may have ruined their mid-day repose." The grumblings rapidly changed from dissatisfaction to cheerful chatter as the group spread out and found fresh spots in the sludge. Before long, all that was visible were the bulbous noses of ten, extremely large creatures protruding from a glass-like water surface.

Marsick regarded Kleen before speaking. The furrows above his brow clearly indicating stress. "What is your direction, Kleen?"

Kleen took a deep breath, began waving his powerful primary arms above his head and held the sides of his face with his detail hands. The corners of his eyes turned down as even deeper stress flooded him. "Marsick, we only have three days! How will we be ready in three days? Let's get everyone working on this. Nobody goes home until we are done." He turned and walked to his office door. "I'll contact everyone and get them into the Lab."

Marsick quickly responded, "Well, you *are* the one in charge. However, Dr. Jarrnod didn't say we had to be finished, and what would you have everyone do? Most of the work is serial in nature and there are really only a few things for two of us to do at the same time."

Kleen seemed to relax slightly. "That is true. But I want everyone to understand the importance of preparing the backup probe."

Marsick touched his left shoulder with her right primary hand and the forearm of his left detail arm with her right detail hand. Kleen seemed to melt with the touch and all his anxiety vanished. Marsick said, "With the potential loss of Wahdeer, I'm sure they understand the urgency. What they really need is a plan that will accomplish *your* goal." She waited a few seconds then continued. "If I may suggest, why don't you divide the team into three groups of three team members and create three work shifts? You, Karrwin and I can take the first shift and get things started while the others rest. You, of course, would supervise while Karrwin and I do the diagnostics. We can pass our work on to the next shift, maybe Zrippees, Sawwed, and Deeops. They would pass their results on to the final group. Of course, Sissle, Queuen, and Moudd would pass their results to us as we come on for our second rotation. We can continue that cycle until Dr. Jarrnod returns. We won't be finished, but, we will be close and proceeding with the efficiency you promised."

Kleen's chest swelled with pride and said, "Yes. That is a fine plan, Marsick, I will adopt it as my own. Please call the team together so I can set my plan in motion."

The group was assembled, Kleen outlined *his* plan and as they prepared to breakup Marsick spoke up with her eyes slightly averted. "Sawwed and Moudd, under Kleen's plan you are free to organize your shifts as you see fit," essentially putting them in charge of their shifts. "However, I'm sure Kleen will be the first to remind you that all protocols for probe activation must be strictly followed. Also, please provide copies of all configuration scripts and test results to Dr. Jarrnod, Kleen, and, with Kleen's permission, to me." Kleen, Sawwed, and Moudd all nodded their heads in unison, leaving no doubt who actually was in charge.

During his second shift, Kleen watched the two-dimensional image of the Wahdeer probe as it waited in Universe 289. The image was real time and displayed the probe's location and current condition. This image was accomplished by the portal generator as it maintained its contact between Universe 1 and Universe 289. He did not tell Marsick what he was planning and would only say something if his suspicions proved true. Using a detail hand he increased magnification and examined the surface of the probe. He focused on the interior access hatch. He had walked through that hatch so many times, and each time used that mechanism. There should have been a red light indicating the hatch was locked. The light, however, was totally dark, indicating Wahdeer was devoid of power. Power to that latch came directly from the main supply and was the last system that would shut down during a power failure. He reduced magnification and as he pulled back he caught a slight movement of something coming into view from the opposite side of the probe. It was small and, at first, he thought it was a piece of debris from the craft. It quickly changed direction and moved toward the hatch. Kleen, in shock, realized it was a creature in a space environment suit. He instantly touched the monitor controls and began recording the scene. The little figure, maybe the size of one of Kleen's primary hands, darted over the entire surface of the hatch. Moving at incredible speed, it examined the hatch surface, reminding Kleen of a nectar bird in search of a meal. When it came to the hatch control it stopped and examined it closely. Kleen said loudly, "Orb, contact Dr. Marsick."

"Yes, Kleen. How can I help you?" responded Marsick.

"I'm watching the Wahdeer. Please join me in the portal chamber. You need to see this."

"I'm in the middle of a test. I'll be there as soon . . ."

"Come now! Cancel your test and come now! Orb, end communication," said Kleen.

Less than five increments later, Marsick entered the portal chamber, working out the final details of how exactly she would make Kleen pay for this inconvenience. Granted, he was *technically* in charge, but, he simply could not be allowed to order her around like that. She would allow Dr. Jarrnod to see Kleen's incompetence and then accept his praise for protecting Kleen and the project. Soon. Very soon she would be rewarded with her own project and be free from the weight of Kleen on her back.

Kleen looked up as she entered the chamber. "Quick, come look at this. You're not going to believe this. I'm recording it so we can show Dr. Jarrnod later."

Marsick walked to Kleen's workstation displaying her displeasure in her body language. "What could possibly be so important that you would have me cancel a critical systems test on . . . the . . . probe?" Her voice trailed off to a whisper as the scene of Wahdeer and the small figure came into view on Kleen's monitor. "What is that? And, where did it come from?"

Kleen said, "It is clearly some form of intelligent life. I have not seen a space craft of any kind. When I first saw it, it came from behind the Wahdeer. The craft must be obscured by the probe."

"What is it doing?"

Kleen was enjoying this, Marsick was asking *him* questions for a change. "I think it is trying to open the hatch. Which is not possible without power, and I can tell Wahdeer is totally without power because there is no light on the hatch locking mechanism. That also explains why we cannot communicate with it."

Marsick glanced at Kleen, surprised by his confident tone and clear understanding of the situation. "Kleen, we must inform Dr. Jarnnod immediately. You should continue to monitor what is happening and see if you can locate a craft of some kind. I'll contact Dr. Jarnnod from the lab on a secure communication. I'll return as quickly as possible with his instructions."

"Yes, of course. Please apologize for interrupting him again."

Marsick actually laughed as she returned to the lab. *Kleen is such an idiot,* she thought. *This could actually be the break I am looking for.* "Orb, contact Dr. Jarnnod, from Dr. Marsick, priority urgent."

"Dr. Jarnnod, you have an urgent communication from Dr. Marsick."

Jarnnod uncoupled from his current mating partner muttering to himself and to her, "For the love of My-God can't anyone contact me when I'm alone and unoccupied?" He reached with a primary hand and retrieved a lounging cloth, then draped it over his shoulders. His detail hands pulled the cloth closed around him, covering his nakedness as he moved to a private deck that adjoined his room. He sat on a lounge chair and said, "Orb, I will accept the communication."

"Dr. Jarnnod, again, I apologize for interrupting your vacation. However, sir, it appears an intelligent alien life form has found the Wahdeer and is attempting to open it."

Jarnnod jumped to his feet, "What? An alien life form? An intelligent life form?"

"Yes, sir, it appears so."

"How can you be sure they are intelligent?" asked Jarnnod.

"Well, sir, they *are* in space and wearing an environment suit of some kind. But to be honest, sir, we have only seen one. There must be more, but we can't see a ship or any way for the creature to have transported to the Wahdeer's location. I asked Kleen to continue monitoring the scene and to record everything. I will have the recordings and our test data ready in the morning. Given these developments, I assume you will return by then."

"I will leave the resort within one hundred increments and will come straight to the lab upon arrival. Tell me, Marsick, what made you monitor the Wahdeer?"

"Sir, as you know there has been no contact and I wanted to verify that there was power on board the Wahdeer. The hatch locking mechanism is the very last system to shut down when power is lost on the probe. There is a single light that indicates locked or unlocked on the mechanism itself. I asked Kleen to . . . excuse me sir, I forget myself . . . Kleen decided to use the portal's two-dimensional viewer to check the status of the locking mechanism or to see if the light was even operational. It was not, which of course meant there is no power on board. The loss of power, by the way, may be a fortunate development, in that the craft is locked and will remain so until they figure out how to recharge the batteries, or they cut it open."

"As usual, Marsick, your evaluation is likely correct." Jarnnod gave a small chuckle and said, "Marsick, it is just the two of us. Do not concern yourself with social protocols. Your attention to detail and ability to understand its importance has led to one of the single largest scientific discoveries in our history. Kleen, as the project leader, and I, as head of the program, will most likely receive the vast majority of credit, but I will make sure you are recognized and rewarded. In the meantime, you and I know the truth."

Marsick bowed her head slightly. "As always sir, you are very kind. I'm sure whatever the reward, it will be appropriate."

Jarnnod viewed the recording for the third time as Marsick and Kleen waited. The little creature was clearly looking for a way to open the Wahdeer. He magnified the image several times and examined the environment suit. "Look at that suit," he said to Kleen and Marsick. "It is primitive in design, but remarkably similar to our own early designs. The occupant will be approximately half the size of that suit. My-God, I wish the face shield was clear—that reflective surface is clearly designed to protect against intense solar radiation—we could learn so much if we could just see its face. Amazing, only two arms. I wonder how they can possibly get anything done." He seemed mesmerized by the scene. "Look how fast it moves. Its metabolism must operate at twenty times ours, or possibly even more."

Eventually, the little creature backed away from the probe, turned, and faced slightly to the right of the view from the portal. It accelerated quickly, and in an instant passed the portal and was out of view.

"Just look at that," marveled Jarnnod. "How does it withstand that much acceleration? How does it accelerate so quickly with so little fuel?" Jarnnod thought for a moment then said, "I wish we had more time, but if we don't retrieve the Wahdeer, they will destroy it by opening it in space." He turned to Kleen and Marsick. "If we bypass all the tests, how soon can you have the backup probe ready?"

Kleen glanced at Marsick and back to Jarnnod. "Two full work shifts, minimum."

Jarnnod saw Marsick bristle slightly, "Do you agree with that assessment, Marsick?"

She refused to even look at Kleen, "Possibly a little faster, but, I agree with Kleen's estimate."

"They will have it open long before we are ready," said Jarnnod. "What else can we do?"

"Sir, I have been thinking," volunteered Kleen. "Why are we risking another probe? Why don't we use a guidance drone to take a cable with a docking magnet over to Wahdeer. We can hook the cable to a winch and just reel it in. With all of us working, we could be ready in about a hundred solar increments. Any of the winches used to move the probes around in the lab will work. The only problem will be finding a cable long enough."

Marsick and Jarnnod exchanged surprised looks. Jarnnod said, "Marsick, find us a light cable at least two hundred foot lengths long and get it to the portal chamber. Kleen and I will prepare the winch and program the guidance probe."

Marsick returned to the portal chamber and found Kleen and Jarnnod waiting impatiently. They alternated between pacing and watching the view of the Wahdeer probe. She pushed a cart with a spool of cable not much thicker than common electrical wire. "This is all I could find. It doesn't have to be too strong, if we are careful. Anything stronger will take way too long to get here."

Jarnnod said, "It will just have to do."

They worked frantically connecting the cable to the magnet and the magnet to the guidance drone.

The guidance drones were normally used to test the probes guidance programming in the new universes. They were sent into the new universe, tested, and then simply abandoned. Unfortunately, the drones were not used in 289 because Marsick was concerned . . . because Kleen was concerned, about budget expenditures. This drone's programming was very simple, it would take the magnet to the Wahdeer and allow it to attach. That was all.

"You two go to the control room and open the Portal," directed Jarnnod. "I will stay here and make sure the cable doesn't get tangled. When the magnet is attached I'll cut the cable and attach it to the wench. When I tell you to start the wench, begin reeling it back. This all should just take a few solar increments."

Kleen grinned even more broadly and headed for the control room. Marsick turned to Jarnnod and said, "Sir, be very careful. Your personal environment generator will maintain your life support, but there is no physical protection."

"I will be fine," said Jarnnod, pointing a detail hand toward the control room. "Go. We don't have a lot of time."

She went to the control room and sat next to Kleen. Kleen said, "Portal activation in three . . . two . . . one . . ."

The holographic display of the alien space craft and the graphic animation of a small, but now expanding, magnetic field turned bright green. The craft and the magnetic field were about two hundred fifty meters apart and half a kilometer from the *Salvage Ship Peking Princess*.

"Captain, this is Collins. The magnetic field is expanding exponentially. We need to back off."

Then, from the ship's speakers, "This is the Captain. Mr. Sims, move us beyond that ship and away from the magnetic field. Let's just watch and see what happens. I'll be on the bridge in five minutes."

"All hands, brace for a five second deceleration and stop." The maneuver was completed in fifteen seconds. "All hands, carry on as you were. Sims out."

Captain Frank Mintz entered the *SS Peking Princess's* Bridge. "The Captain is on the bridge and has the Con," announced Commander Sims over the ship-wide communication system.

Mintz went to the command chair and took his place. He closed the ship-wide communication channel, then said, "Thank you Mr. Sims. What is the status of the alien ship and that magnetic field?"

"Sir there is no change in the ship's status. There is no sign of life and it appears dead in space. The magnetic field is expanding in strength. It doubles in strength every sixty seconds; however, the area of its influence remains constant within a thirty meter sphere."

"Care to speculate, Mr. Collins?"

"Sir, my best guess is an artificial wormhole or possibly some form of jump gate for that ship."

"Keep a very close eye on it Mr. Collins." Mintz turned to his executive officer. "Mr. Sims, if, at any point, it looks like that thing will go critical on us, get this ship out of here. Do not wait for my command." He opened the ship-wide channel. "All hands, this is the Captain. General Quarters... Strap in and maintain Maneuvering configuration. Off duty personnel return to your quarters and strap in. We may require emergency maneuvering without notice. Everyone just settle in. This may take a while."

In space, the magnetic field began to glow a light blue and slowly began turning opaque. A light blue sphere thirty meters across was forming just beyond the alien ship. Within ten seconds the blue began to swirl as if clouds were forming inside. Collins spoke up, "Sir the field is stabilizing at nearly five hundred times its original intensity." Suddenly the sphere cleared. It no longer appeared as a sphere, now it looked like a round hole in space that led to the interior of a ship or possibly a building. A giant grinning figure stood gazing at the alien ship. The creature moved so slowly, at first Mintz didn't realize it was even moving. He felt like he was watching a scene in an ultra- slow-motion video.

"Any idea what we are looking at Mr. Collins?"

"If that is actual size, sir, that being is at least eight meters tall. The way its moving, it must be a recording of some kind."

So slow, so agonizingly slow the four-armed being watched the ship as a device that sat on the floor next to it began moving. The device slowly rose to the creature's eye level and crept toward the perimeter of the field. As slow as this all happened the bridge crew watched with intense interest. From start to the device reaching the edge of the field took close to half an hour.

"Jesus Christ, this is going to take a week," said Mintz.

Jarnnod watched the portal as it quickly opened. He paused only a moment to look at the Wahdeer, totally motionless in space. It seemed so close he could have reached out and touched it. Without delay the guidance drone rose from the floor trailing the cable that would play out from a spool mounted next to the wench. The drone rapidly moved toward the portal and entered Universe 289. Suddenly the spool began spinning at an incredible rate. The cable was flying off the spool so fast Jarnnod quickly stepped back in fear the cable would break. He looked at the drone as it moved at incredible speed toward the Wahdeer probe. "Kleen, what is happening?" He moved quickly to the spool's breaking mechanism and as soon as the magnet attached to the probe he applied the break.

Marsick spoke first, "Sir, there seems to be a major difference in the temporal environments of the two universes. That may be why they appear to move so fast."

The spool stopped quickly but most of the cable was already floating loosely in space. Jarnnod quickly cut the cable and attached the end to the wench. "Start the wench and bring Wahdeer home."

"Sir, I really don't like this. Maybe you should move away from the portal," said Kleen.

The wench engaged and the cable began to wind onto the wench spool. Jarnnod quickly realized the loose cable was not winding properly on the wench spool and, if something wasn't done quickly, would soon foul the rewinding process. He moved to the cable and, using his primary hands, began guiding it while maintaining the proper tension.

As he guided the cable Jarnnod watched the cable slack begin to disappear. All was going well when suddenly a craft ten times the size of Wahdeer streaked to within only a few foot lengths of the probe and stopped.

Mintz watched the device touch the perimeter of the opening. The thing instantly shot toward the alien space craft. It trailed a cable or wire of some kind and within five seconds stuck to the craft. Excess cable continued to feed from the opening. It all happened so quickly, Mintz jumped from his chair. Shocked, he yelled, "Mr. Collins, what's happening here?"

"Sir, they appear to be trying to capture the space craft."

"Bullshit! That ship has been dead in space for two months. It is officially "Space Junk" and we claimed it. It's in our space and falls under our laws. Mr. Sims, get us close to that ship and secure it to our hull!"

"Aye Captain, maneuvering to within five meters of the alien craft." The Princess smoothly approached the craft and stopped. "Capturing the craft using the forward salvage arms." Two crane-like arms unfolded from the bow of the Princess, reached around the alien craft and secured it to the ship's hull.

"Very good Mr. Sims. Now back away slowly."

Sims responded immediately, "One quarter reverse maneuvering thrusters."

Mintz watched as the slack in the cable was taken up. Within seconds the cable was stretching like a rubber band and just as he expected the cable to snap, the magnet that was attached to the alien craft released. The build-up of kinetic energy in the cable shot it and the magnet back to the portal at incredible speed. He had no time to react before most of the cable and the magnet went through the portal traveling at least two hundred kilometers per hour. Before the impact Mintz could clearly see the grinning giant standing motionless, apparently unable to move. There was an explosion inside the portal and the scene disintegrated into fire and debris that was expelled into space. The portal instantly collapsed as small pieces of what was inside the portal ricocheted off the hull of the Princess.

There were seven people on the bridge of the SS Peking Princess. No one said a word for several seconds as they all stared at the now empty scene displayed on the monitor. Finally, Mintz said, "Mr. Collins, what in the hell just happened?"

Sims and Collins looked at each other, then Collins said, "Well sir, I think we just killed that thing. I'm not sure how, but the energy released was very disproportionate. Maybe we can figure out more when we get a look inside that ship. But for now, that's all I've got."

"Well, crap," said Mintz. "That certainly didn't go the way I expected. Now we have no idea where that portal led, where that ship came from or who that being was." He paused, deep in thought. "I'll report everything to the authorities on Titan, when we get back. I'll file a formal letter of apology just in case that race ever shows up again. I honestly don't know what else to do." He looked around the bridge as if looking for suggestions. When no one commented he said, "Mr. Sims, set course for Titan. Let's get home and see what we've got here."

Kleen and Marsick waited to be called before the Council of Scientific Achievement. Over the last solar year, they had replayed the destruction of the portal and lab numerous times. *Thank My-God that the recordings had survived*, thought Marsick. The recordings had allowed them to figure out what actually happened. When the magnet released, the kinetic energy in the cable pulled the magnet and cable back through the portal. When it crossed the portal, its inertia was multiplied by the temporal difference between the two universes. Marsick had done the calculation herself and the cable and magnet were traveling faster than a meteor entering the atmosphere when it reentered the portal chamber. Dr. Jarnnod was killed instantly. Kleen and she were very lucky to have survived.

An orb materialized in front of them. "Dr. Marsick, the head of the counsel will speak to you privately before the meeting."

Marsick followed the orb into a private chamber. She had expected this and was prepared to speak openly to Kleen's mother. It was time to receive her just payment for allowing Kleen to receive credit for all her work.

"Dr. Marsick," said Kleen's mother, "I will be to the point. I have read your report of the incident and find it interesting that you are willing to accept credit for everything on this project that was successful. However, when a disaster occurs you accept none of the blame. You seem to be a true survivor." She paused, watching Marsick closely, and then continued. "My dear friend Dr. Jarnnod many times mentioned what a wonderful team you and Kleen made, and recommended several times that it should continue. I agree. Therefore, we will formalize a union between you and Kleen. Kleen will become the new head of the Portal Project, with you as his deputy. And, eventually, the two of you will produce a grandson that I will spoil."

Marsick was stunned. She starred in disbelief and almost laughed as she said, "Counselor, I have no interest in Kleen as a mate. Dr. Jarnnod made several promises to me, if I would support and allow Kleen to receive credit for much of my work. Furthermore,—"

"Dr. Marsick, I have searched for any *agreements* between you and Dr. Jarnnod and found nothing. I am sure that you would have the same result if you searched."

"But, I . . . he said . . ."

"He said nothing . . . that you can prove, Dr. Marsick. You will agree to this arrangement or the counsel will revoke your credentials and you will end up as a female escort, entertaining wealthy males." The counselor stood and walked toward the exit, then paused. "Please take a few moments to consider your decision." She turned and walked out.

Marsick slowly headed for the exit. With each step, she felt a little more of Kleen's weight on her back, and knew she would carry that weight for the rest of her life.

W. A. Fix is a retired Information Technology Professional, who, with his wife and three cats, lives in the suburbs of San Diego, California. Several of his works are published throughout the Web. He is a featured author in **The Future Is Short: Science Fiction in a Flash** *(volumes 1, 2, and 3) anthologies of flash fiction and he has longer works in* **Visions: Leaving Earth, Visions II: Moons of Saturn, Vision III: Inside the Kuiper Belt, Visions V: Milky Way, Visions VI: Galaxies,** *and* **Twisted Tails IX: Wunderkind.**

Humanity has created a perfect world for itself within a computer simulation that allows everyone to be whatever they want and to be a part of whichever social group they prefer. With the technology at their disposal, the games they play span the whole universe without real risk to any of the participants . . . until, that is, they stop being games.

Burstchasers

Gustavo Bondoni

"Forget about the end of the world, people, this is the end of the universe!"

Sabrina rolled her eyes. It seemed that Brissel understood as much about astrophysics as he did about women—nothing whatsoever. He'd demonstrated his lack of knowledge regarding the second, in a feeble attempt to get her to join him in exploring the functions of their newly printed biological bodies, and was now displaying his massive ignorance of the first.

In his defense, the concept of genders was just another rule in the game they'd decided to play, but there was no real excuse for not knowing how the universe worked.

She stared out across the field of stars. Even here, at what the computers had decided was the edge of the observable universe, unnumbered galaxies spread out in every direction. From where she stood, it didn't feel like the edge of anything, just the center of something else.

As the others cheered Brissel on with much waving of glasses containing alcohol and other stimulants, she felt the urge to go for a walk. The station could be circumnavigated in five minutes, but any distance at all was better than being stuck with her moronic cohort, and the silly games they wanted to play now that they had physical bodies to play them with.

Her body worked well enough, despite the unfamiliar intoxicants she'd imbibed, and as she left the observation deck behind, she calmed down and took stock of her situation.

It didn't get any better with reflection, but at least the body the cohort's computers had printed for her seemed to work well with the memories it had selected for this incarnation. Things, she knew, could have been much worse.

The ring corridor was much darker than the brightly illuminated observation deck. From here, the stars around them could be seen. She found them much more beautiful than the violent cluster of supermassive stars the rest of them were raising their glasses to.

Sabrina wasn't expecting to encounter anyone on her walks—the cohort was intensely social—so she almost ran into a man before she noticed she wasn't alone. He was looking out at the stars.

"I'm sorry," she said.

He turned to her, a sad expression on his face. "Don't be. You have as much right to look out this section of viewport as I do."

"But no need to do so. There are thousands of others."

"Ah, but this one has the best view," the man replied. He stepped aside to let her look, and Sabrina admitted that he was probably right. A dust cloud, illuminated from within, shone like some ghostly ocean creature. It was almost as beautiful as some of the things that the combination artists created back in the Real World.

She pulled away and continued a few steps down the hall.

"It seems I've found the other dissenting vote."

Sabrina froze. When their newly-printed bodies were activated, the result of the vote had been announced. Eighteen members of the cohort had voted in favor of the activity, two had voted against. She turned back to him. "You remember?"

The man shook his head. They'd printed him as a slight, dark-haired man maybe five feet eight. "No. I can't remember. But the whole thing just seemed so wrong that I needed to go for a walk."

Sabrina nodded, surprised at how natural the corporeal gesture felt to her. She'd had the same reaction: if anyone had asked her how she'd voted, she would have guessed at 'No'. Of course, she couldn't remember much except that she was a woman who had woken up earlier that day in a new-printed body for a cohort excursion. That, and the incredible sense of wanting to be back in the Real World—the quantum computer program inhabited by every human consciousness in the universe—were all her new brain and memories were giving her. "Yeah. Me, too. So, what do we do now?"

"Well, the teams are supposed to be two to four people in size. We can be a team."

"I don't think I want to play."

"You know as well as I do that we don't have a choice. If you joined a cohort, you are subject to the will of the majority. That is the rule."

"I know that. What's frustrating is that I remember everything about life except for my life. Who am I? What kind of personality do I have in the Real World? And what, in the deepest level of hell, possessed me to join a cohort?"

The man chuckled. "Join the club. I've been wondering about that for the past hour."

"Ah, then you missed watching the cohort get drunk. You can tell they've never been exposed to alcohol before."

"They've all done Virus in the Real World, how bad can it be?"

"This is different. I had much less to drink than the rest of them and even I'm feeling it. When you do Virus, it doesn't affect your baseline. You can distinctly feel that safety line, always there for when you want to end the experience. Here, I feel that even the basic motor functions of the body are affected by the alcohol. It's not a great sensation."

"Then why are they still over there, drinking?"

"I don't know. They seem to be enjoying it, though."

The man shrugged. "I suppose it takes all kinds. I'm Tarsu, by the way."

"Sabrina."

"So, is it agreed? We're a team?"

"Yeah, I guess I'd rather be teamed with someone sober if we're going to be trying to catch a gamma ray burst. I have a feeling we'll need our wits about us."

He grinned. "Fair enough, and I guess half-drunk is better than my other alternatives, too. Any clue about how long the intoxication will last?"

"Hell if I know."

"Figures." He was in a much better mood. "Want to go back to the observation chamber? They'll probably be announcing the start of the game any time now. We probably don't want to give them a head start, drunk or not."

"All right."

They arrived just in time to claim a spacebender and leave with the other teams. True to the cohort's gregarious nature, most of the teams were composed of four members, the maximum allowed, which meant that there were two nervous-looking members of the cohort who'd been left out of the division. They were waiting for Sabrina and Tarsu to return. When they did return, the two excluded players asked whether they could build a team of four with them.

They'd asked as a formality, never expecting to be turned down. When Tarsu told them that no, the team was all full, they were shocked. Only strict cohort protocol kept them from protesting.

Their spacebender was yellow. Each team had a different color, to make sure that the competitors could keep track of one another. Sabrina held the hatch open. "After you."

Tarsu gave her a look. "I'm not certain that is how chivalry worked."

"Me neither, but still, after you."

Five minutes later, they were throttling the craft's booster engines. They needed to be a minimum of a thousand miles away from both the station and the other teams' spacebenders before the system would allow them to toggle their singularity. It was both a safety precaution and a way to ensure that the teams wouldn't simply follow each other around.

The trip gave them time to study the swollen, raging stars arrayed ahead of them.

"Looks like a good place for a game. The instruments show ten candidates, stars that could go supernova at any moment, within a twenty-light-year radius. This cluster was well-chosen," Tarsu said.

Sabrina just grunted. The person who put the game together certainly knew their stuff. They'd selected a place where a good number of stars nearing the end of their lives were clustered together. Of course, there was no guarantee that one of the stars would go supernova in the next million years, but if she knew game designers, they'd probably run a statistical analysis and the likelihood was probably that at least one of the stars nearby would explode in the next few years, decades at worst.

The task of the crews was to be there when it happened.

The screen suddenly went blank and the game control logo appeared. A simulated human voice filled the cabin.

"Now that you're on your way, it's time to reveal the final objective of the game. You believe the objective is to find the first star to go supernova, and be nearby when it does. That is only part of it, although it's a very important part.

"Humanity has been staring into the far reaches of the universe for as long as we've had orbiting telescopes. And almost since the very first days of spaceflight, we've known about gamma ray bursts.

"But all we really knew is that they were incredibly far away and that they were big.

"Since then, we've expanded to every corner of our galaxy, and to others as well. But humanity never did come into direct contact with a gamma ray burst before we retreated into the Real World, mainly because going to the very edge of the observable universe, where all gamma ray bursts had been observed, was never a priority. And, as you know, the computers that run the Real world are both shielded against radiation and backed up with redundancies without number. Maybe some of them have been taken out by gamma ray bursts. We would never have known about it.

"The objective of this game is to remove all doubt. The winners will become the first physical humans to die in a gamma ray burst, and their Real World equivalents will be awarded a million credit coins and gain a cohort social level.

"So, calculate the spin of the star you choose carefully. It would be a pity if it happened to be the right one, and exploded beneath you only for the gamma ray burst to miss you completely. Then instead of being winners . . . you'd just be dead."

The screen returned to the starchart it had shown before the announcement, and the two contestants sat in silence. Sabrina mulled the words over. They seemed familiar, as if she'd heard them before, not just once, but many times. She felt she should be able to recite them in her sleep, but when she tried, she could only remember fragments.

"All right. If we get fried by the star, we win . . . but only if we do it correctly," Tarsu said.

"Relax. It's easy. The burst is emitted perpendicular to the spin of the star, and it's wide and gets wider. Imagine a cone above and below. If we choose the right star, we just sit in space far enough away from it and the burst will kill us. No need to sit nearby and risk a miscalculation. These things are so powerful that they sterilize entire galaxies."

Tarsu held her gaze. "What a stupid game."

***

"You think that's the best candidate?"

"Definitely seems that way. An unstable monster of a star. I'd be surprised if it doesn't blow at any moment."

"So now what?"

"We use the sleep chambers and wait. That way, if it blows and we win, the sleep chamber will have backed up these memories and we'll wake up in the Real World with a full backup of this experience, and we don't have to wait for the tedious decades for a star to explode."

"And if we lose?"

"The sleep chambers are programmed to terminate the life within them once the game ends. It's pretty much the same thing, except there are no groupies waiting when you get back."

He chuckled. There was little else to do now but get into the sleep chamber and wait to see if they'd won. But for some reason, both were reluctant to do so.

They sat in silence. Until, Sabrina finally put into words the thoughts that had been nagging at her since they'd set foot in the spacebender. "How long do you think these bodies would last?"

Tarsu shrugged. "I suppose a few decades, given enough food and water. I don't have much experience with them, but I recall that they're standard human bodies, so they should last well enough."

"Well, for my part, I know about starbenders. And the one we're riding isn't limited to short hops. We might not be able to get back to human space—nearly fourteen billion light years is a big hop—but we can jump between galaxies."

"Are you suggesting that we abandon the game?"

"Only if you agree?"

"What about our real versions. This could impact our lives in the real world. It's considered treason to our cohort. They'll throw us out and we'll never get into another."

"I guess we'll have to deal with that. If my personality is anything like the one I have in this body, I'm not entirely certain that I'm cut out for cohort life anyway."

"That might be your glands, which you aren't used to, or your implanted memory talking. Your equivalent in the Real World might be horrified when it sees the feed of this conversation."

"Which is a good reason to act quickly. If we jump out of range before they can take remote control of the spacebender, we'll be free. If we wait, they'll haul us back before we can escape."

She watched his expression. They must have imprinted the capacity to read human faces into her memory, because Sabrina could tell that her companion was torn. She decided to give him a little push. "All we really have to look forward to is to go to bed and hope to be incinerated. Wouldn't you rather see the universe before you go?"

"I don't know. Would I? That's the question I have. I have no sense of what my real self would do in this situation. None."

"I assume that my personality hasn't changed."

He hesitated again, but this time Sabrina stayed quiet. There was nothing more she thought it worthwhile to say. He would accept or he would decline and she would respect his decision.

Finally, with an effort, he nodded once. "Let's do it. I think my other self, trapped inside a computer simulation, would approve of this."

"Yeah, that's what I think, too."

She flipped open the transparent box meant to keep them from spacebending by mistake and hit the big red button beneath it. She'd already programmed their first destination.

The starfield changed.

***

The first few planets were the hardest to land on. They had to learn the limits of the systems at their disposal, as well as the way atmosphere and radiation levels worked, and how to decide whether they could leave the spacebender without risk of drastically shortening the lifespans of their printed bodies.

They also learned how to refuel the boosters, an operation that mainly involved flying around in the thickest hydrogen and methane atmospheres they could locate to fill one tank, and in oxygen-rich areas for the other.

Water, they soon discovered could be split by the ship's motors and saved hours of time.

By the time they approached their tenth world, all of this was second nature. They selected a rocky planet with enough mass to give it a gravity of about one point five gees and with an oxygen atmosphere and low radiation levels for their first excursion.

As she maneuvered, Sabrina looked around. "There's a lake right at the foot of the mountains over there. I'll land on the shore so the ship can refuel while we explore."

Tarsu didn't answer. He'd quickly realized that the running of the ship was best left to her. She knew more about navigation and engineering than he did, while she was equally impressed with his knowledge of biology and medicine, which was a science that humanity had had little use for in the past millennia. He was peering down at the screen. "It's safe to go out there," he said.

She didn't question it. "All right. Let's go."

The spacebender's hatch opened to allow a warm breeze inside. It smelled of the damp earth, likely from the ground that the vehicle had torn up when it landed. Sabrina wondered how she knew that. Had she been born on a planet before they'd uploaded her? Perhaps the Sabrina alive now—both the one in the spacebender and her electronic copy in the Real World—had deep memories of planetary smells, memories that had survived the process of being turned into a complex algorithm in the last machine humanity ever built and then printed back into a human body.

She stepped out and walked around the vehicle. The subroutines she'd programmed were already in action, and pipes snaked from the bottom of the yellow craft towards the water. She knew that full tanks could keep them fueled for another landing or two.

Tarsu, on the other hand, walked towards the mountains, wonder written in every feature. He stumbled over a tiny bump in the terrain.

"Are you all right?" Sabrina asked him.

"I'm perfectly fine. But have you thought about this, really thought it through?"

"Hey, I got us down here without blowing us up, didn't I?"

"That's not what I meant. When do you think was the last time human beings walked a new planet?"

"They do it all the time. We organize games on the surface with printed bodies constantly. There must be dozens going on right now."

"Of course, but they're always on the same dozen or so worlds in human space. Think about what we're doing. From the info we have about this planet, we're likely the first people on it . . . ever. We're likely the first humans to ever arrive in this galaxy in fact."

"Well, yes. The whole point of the game the cohort put together was to get us to the edge of the observable universe, even if it turned out that it looks just like the rest of it . . . except with more exploding stars for some reason."

"Doesn't that make you feel anything? Think about it."

Sabrina did. She looked around the planet, then tried to imagine the planetary system around them, which she knew consisted of six planets, only this one rocky. Then she contemplated the entire galaxy and the unimaginable distance back to the Milky Way and the human zones, spread across a dozen galaxies nearby. All that space, empty of people.

She sat down, dizzy.

"Yeah, that's how I felt."

The spell soon passed and Sabrina was back on her feet in moments. "Well, if we came all the way, let's have a look at those hills."

The mountains were about a mile away, huge grey hills towering thousands of feet above their heads and jutting straight out of the grass in a way that contradicted everything that Sabrina imagined she knew about geology. But in an infinite universe, of course, one was bound to find unusual rock formations. And much stranger things as well.

As they approached, it became clear that the mountains weren't brand new at all. They were pitted and eroded and they could make out different shades of blue-gray coloring. The tops were different colors than the bottoms, making it look like the wind had eroded huge blocks of stone into the forms of tapering mountains.

Once in the shadow of the hills, the pitted surface came into focus as the tops disappeared from view.

"That's impossible. Those things must be thousands of miles long."

But their eyes weren't deceiving them. When they reached the base of the mountains, they could see it clearly: the mountains were made of some kind of metal plates, and the pitting showed places where windborne particles had eroded away the covering. Farther up, structural latticework could be seen, eroded like the walls.

"How can this be? Who built this? And why?" Sabrina said.

"It wasn't us, that's for certain. Even in the Colonization Era, humans have never been here. Hell, we didn't even have benders powerful enough to get us all the way out here, until *after* we all uploaded." He looked around. "And this looks like it's been here a while."

It did. The metal showed no signs of rust, and even in its severely eroded state, it hadn't bent. The only damage seemed to be that it was slowly being worn away, atom by atom. The accumulated dust of eons created a slope that ended at its base.

"Want to go inside?" Sabrina asked,

"Wait. Why aren't the openings choked with sand? They should be completely piled over and sealed."

Sabrina looked inside. And then she laughed. "Here's your answer. Stand there."

"A breeze. Coming from the inside."

"More than a breeze. Feels like a hurricane. No wonder there's no dust in there."

"And look there. I think I see lights."

Tarsu was right. Barely visible at the end of a long, straight canyon between two metal walls that went upward as far as the eye could see, there was a light. "Do you think it's the daylight at the other end?"

"I don't know. It could be. But it seems too close for that."

Sabrina had heard enough. She entered the tunnel and began to walk toward the light.

"Hey, wait for me!"

They walked about five minutes before coming to an open doorway that was fifteen feet high and eight wide. It was the source of the light, and after the relatively dark corridor, they had to shield their eyes to look into it.

This time, Tarsu didn't wait for Sabrina to preempt him. When she stopped beside the aperture, he simply kept walking with a smirk, although it only lasted a second because the wind was strong enough to distort his face.

On the other side was a chamber illuminated by the glow of thousands, hundreds of thousands, perhaps millions of translucent rectangular slabs arrayed in neat rows in a semicircular shape, radiating outward from where they stood. Outward and upward, until they curved onto the roof of the space and came back down behind them. It was breathtaking.

"What is it?"

Sabrina walked over to one of the rectangles. It was perhaps two feet tall, eight inches wide, and an inch thick. When she put her hand behind it, she could see its outline, despite the glow. With trepidation, she placed a finger on it and pulled it quickly away. Once she ascertained that she was all right, she put the finger back. "I thought it would be warm. But it isn't. It feels cool to the touch."

"Granted," Tarsu replied, touching one of the slabs, probably so he didn't feel she was doing more than him. "But what is it?"

"I have no idea. But whatever it is, the mountains are here to keep this, and I suppose thousands of places like this, going for as long as possible. Whoever built it wanted it to last, and they put a shield around it."

"But who built it? And why?"

"I don't think we'll ever know." She looked around, wonder warring with frustration as she studied the place. "But how many places like this might we be missing. How many millions, billions of intelligent races are we simply ignoring, just because we're locked in a simulation, and have been for thousands of years. Maybe the builders are out there somewhere, just waiting for someone to ask them about . . . whatever this is."

"Or maybe they're long gone, maybe these are just the ruins of another civilization, dead for eons, like all the ones we've found in human space."

"Perhaps. But we'll never know unless we look. Unless people are out here, walking into mountain ranges that turn out to be enormous bunkers with glowing things inside."

"I don't think humanity wants this. Have you ever heard of a cohort dedicated to stuff like that?"

"Maybe, if I had all my memories, I might have. But off the top of my head . . . no. Not even remotely."

"Why not?"

"Inertia. Peer pressure. People think we've finally achieved a perfect society, so anyone agitating for change gets shouted down."

"And yet, out of a cohort of twenty, two of us want this."

"Are you sure you want it? There's a digital version of you back in the Real World who might be deadly afraid of what we're discussing."

"I don't know. With my current personality, it feels right."

"It might not, if you wake up back in your original self."

"I think it would." Tarsu said it confidently, as if somehow, some sense of profound dissatisfaction with the Real World had filtered into his implanted memories.

Sabrina wondered why the memories were filtered. Maybe it was to stop people from using specific knowledge to win the games . . . or maybe it was just because the online memory banks, for each individual, had long since outstripped the capacity of a single human brain. Still, it was disconcerting to not know who one was.

Sabrina shrugged. "Well, we're not going to solve it ourselves . . . although a male and a female technically could . . ."

Tarsu blushed. While there were entire cohorts dedicated to experiencing the ancient practice of corporeal sexuality in all its possible forms, most of modern human society found the whole thing a little too biologically messy for their taste. "Even if we were so inclined, there would be serious issues of genetic diversity. We would probably be better off printing new bodies for everyone interested."

"We can't do that with the tech on the spacebender. We'd need to go back."

"And get ourselves punished for betraying the cohort? Not too much we could do after they strip all our social points away. And with a black mark like that on our record? No one would let us in anywhere."

"That might not be a problem. If we go back, before any of the other teams win, and choose a star, we'd still be in the game, and there would be no breaking of the contract. Who knows, we might even win and get all the funding we need for the project."

"What are the odds of that?"

"If Brissel and his followers are any indication of the knowledge about astrophysics held by the cadre, I'd say the odds aren't bad. I can choose a star more likely to become a burster in a minute than he could if I gave him eternity and all the galaxy to choose from."

"But what if someone's already won?"

"The likelihood of that having happened in the time we missed is just about zero. We've only been gone a few weeks. Stars last billions of years. We'll need to bend a couple of times to get back, but I'm confident we'll be fine."

They returned to their starting point and the star they'd chosen in the first place.

"I can't believe we're doing this. What if they decide to punish us anyway?"

"Why would they? Nothing in the rules against going out for some sightseeing. Only abandoning the game is strictly forbidden."

Ignoring the sudden hailing from the comm system, they went back and activated the sleep cells.

As Sabrina drifted into stasis, she wondered if any human in history had gone to bed hoping to be incinerated by a gamma ray burst.

***

"Congratulations!"

Caspel Tau Celenn woke. Memory systems slowly brought it back online as it remembered and incorporated Sabrina's memories, which now belonged within its vast memory store. It had been inactive for twelve Earth years, which meant that the star cluster they'd chosen for the game had indeed proven to be as ripe for explosions as the calculations indicated. Then it saw that its cohort social level had increased and that it was suddenly a very wealthy individual.

It wasn't particularly surprised to have won the game. It now remembered that its cohort consisted of a number of very ignorant—albeit wealthy—individuals.

Caspel immediately identified the one who'd gone by the name of Tarsu as Beni Pollux Thays, one of the oldest members of the cohort, and not an individual that Caspel would have believed to be a radical nonconformist.

Caspar commed the other individual.

"I think it's time we resign from this cohort."

"I don't believe they will want us to. We just became its most socially relevant members."

"No matter. If they want to bask in our newfound relevance, they can join the new cohort. Although I doubt the rules will appeal to them."

The waveform that had replaced laughter eons before reached Caspar through the quantum connection.

Gustavo Bondoni is an Argentine novelist and short story writer who writes primarily in English. He has recently released two science fiction novels: Siege (2016) and Outside (2017). He has nearly two hundred short stories published in fourteen countries. They are translated into seven languages. Many of the stories are collected in Tenth Orbit and Other Faraway Places (2010) and Virtuoso and Other Stories (2011). His website is at www. gustavobondoni.com.

The hammerheads were the most intelligent creatures on the planet, yet the linguists were constantly frustrated in their attempts to communicate with them. When the hammerheads sang, however, everything seemed a lot better.

When the Hammerheads Sing

John A. Frochio

Someone buzzed Captain Chantelle Cruciante while she was recording her morning log and scheduling her day's planned activities. Since everyone knew she hated to be interrupted during her scheduled times of privacy, she expected it was important. It had better be important!

"Corporal Callie Buenaventura, Captain. I was asked to inform you the hammerheads are about to sing."

She put down her recorder, pushed dark strands of black hair from her face and sighed. The endless attempts to understand the hammerheads! When will she see any progress? Anything at all.

"Thank you, Corporal. I'll get there as soon as I can."

Anticipating it would be the same old thing, she took her time shedding her leisure mistware and putting her uniform on her tired, aging body. She was still in excellent shape for her age, but lately she noticed she had been tiring more easily. Too many missions perhaps. How many? She lost count.

She called for a roboshuttle. Number 23—compact, tubular, shiny under the pale reddish sun Arcturus—arrived and hovered over Sienna's gray-green soil as the Captain boarded. She spoke her destination. It swiftly delivered her to the natives' tree-lined auditorium.

She found her linguists, Xenia Barrett and Gary Pendragon, stationed at the back with their recording equipment set up among a line of ringwood trees. As usual they were recording audio, visual, olfactory, tactile, and weather indicators.

Xenia was young and attractive with short, brown hair, petite, full of energy, and well-versed in the latest xenolingual analysis technology. Chantelle sometimes envied her energy. Gary was middle-aged, tall, well-built, with dark thinning hair, and a proponent of the tried and true xenolingual techniques.

She said, "Well?"

Xenia shrugged. "As you can see, they're still rehearsing. Should be starting soon."

Chantelle could never tell the difference between rehearsals and actual performances. The stage was simply a clearing bordered loosely by tall, dark, iron trees. The hammerheads moved around the area making random harmonies with whomever they encountered.

She said, "How many concerts must we attend before we finally understand their language?"

Gary spoke without looking up from the equipment. "The sounds are so complex and fraught with subtle nuances that it's nearly impossible to learn their language by any standard methodology. We are inventing new ways to analyze the phonemes and morphemes as we observe and listen to them."

She'd heard the same old, unintelligible song and dance from her linguists before. More of the same excuses.

Xenia smiled and said, "Not impossible, Gary, just challenging. And we relish the challenge, right? We believe some of their recent songs have been about us."

She perked up. That was a new one.

"How so?"

"We've noticed specific actions of mission teams correlate with specific musical performances. For example, recent rock and soil gathering expeditions coincided with singularly unique and comparable performances."

"Interesting." She didn't know whether this was good or bad news.

The air around them grew suddenly warm and crackled. A low soft humming gradually grew louder. Chantelle felt her defenses soften, her body relax, her tensions unwind. Soon the hammerheads let loose with a powerful burst of song, harmonizing the nine voices on stage, each a distinct sound yet perfectly blended. For several minutes, the space around them was filled with complex layers that weaved in and out of each other.

This was the part Chantelle enjoyed the most, what drew her to the performances. The experience somehow soothed her body, mind, and soul like nothing else could. And when her mind relaxed, she thought back to the beginnings of their exploration of Sienna.

***

The world called Sienna orbited Arcturus. It was a planet much like a young Earth around the Carboniferous Period. Many odd creatures, large and small, roamed the ubiquitous jungles and swamplands of Sienna. One of the oddest, descriptively named hammerheads, turned out to be the most intelligent species on the planet. Their heads, which rested atop long giraffe-like necks, were shaped much like the head of a sledgehammer, or the hammerhead sharks of Earth. They walked on two legs, but could run at great speeds when they used their long arms as an additional set of legs.

Some objected to the name because they felt it was somewhat derogatory. However, in the light of their completely alien culture, it was argued they would not understand any Earth-based historical contexts, and, therefore, would not feel they were being ridiculed in any way.

The hammerheads built small communities out of the natural outgrowth of the trees, shrubbery, and vining plants around them. Their communities grew outward from a central amphitheater, or circle of trees, like spokes on a wheel. There was a loosely governing oligarchy of seven who were also their spiritual leaders.

The mission team's language experts struggled to understand their language. They spoke in soft shushing sounds barely distinguishable from each other.

And then they discovered the singing.

***

After the alien concert, Chantelle went to see her good friend, Ship Psychologist Kierkegaard Dennison.

"Kirk, tell me I'm not losing my mind."

"You're not losing your mind."

"Tell me again and this time mean it."

Kirk was in his late middle years, somewhat bulky, yet still in good physical shape. He boasted a full head of curly black hair but needed an external eye enhancement adapter, the newer slimline model that looked like swimmers' goggles.

He took her hand gently and said, "What you want to hear is that your latent anxieties are in remission. Gone and never to return. Well, I can't promise you that. But we are managing it. That's the best I can offer."

"I can't risk a flare up now, not at this critical stage of the mission."

"You needn't worry. The external manifestations of your anxieties are so insignificant, anyone would write them off as authoritarian expressions of throwing around one's weight."

Early in the mission, Kirk had confirmed her worst fears, a positive diagnosis of a particularly volatile type of space anxieties, that were frequently a precursor to space madness. From that point on, he had been secretly treating her for the illness. She used to think she simply had anger issues, and for good reason. She grew up badly abused. She never told anyone how bad it really was.

Kirk had the authority to remove her from her post immediately if he considered her illness a danger to her crew or the mission. Since he kept her symptoms under control, he allowed her to remain in command of the mission. However, realizing the risk he was taking, he monitored her symptoms daily.

Later she returned to her cabin and wrote in her private log, "Swaying to the lull of the pensive hammerheads, I felt again that peace welling up within me that calmed my soul."

***

The linguists requested an audience with Captain Chantelle. She entered their lab. The lights were dimmed. She squinted to find them among the maze of workstations and stacks of equipment and boxes. Still wearing her protective gear, Xenia was hunched over a tablet rapidly keying. Gary studied an electronic whiteboard at the far end of the cluttered room. He glanced back and spotted her, then motioned for her to come over.

As Chantelle approached, Xenia joined them. The Captain said, "Remember. I'm not known for my patience. What's this about?"

The linguists exchanged smiles. Gary said, "Watch."

Gary clicked a remote and a video of the hammerheads singing popped up in front of them.

After a minute he said, "Now I'm going to slow this down by one tenth."

Instantly the sounds were less lyrical, more monotonic, more distinct.

Gary said, "When we significantly reduced the speed of the playback, the speech patterns were much easier to distinguish from one another. The sounds were clearer, unlike the blended shushing sounds they made with their normal speech. By analyzing this one ten-minute recording, we logged over two hundred unique speech patterns, and actual phrases, words, or word components."

"Which means . . .?"

"We are finally on our way to developing a lexicon of their language. However, without context, they're meaningless sounds. That's the next step. We need to associate sounds with meanings, objects, actions, concepts. We need to understand the purpose of the singing, what they are singing about, and why."

"Perhaps now is a good time to arrange a meeting with their leaders."

"Yes, we have something to start with now."

The Captain left, not feeling quite as confident as the linguists did. Something didn't feel right. What was bothering her? Was she simply being cautious, or was it paranoia rising up from the depths of her muted space anxieties?

***

Kirk Dennison intercepted Chantelle as she was leaving the base to find a wandering hammerhead. This was the only way they had found to request a meeting with one of their leaders. They called these hammerheads "sentinels" because of their apparent responsibility.

"Captain, could I have a few moments of your time?"

She stopped and looked into his worried eyes.

"You're feeling something?"

"Yes."

Kirk was a second stage esper, the stage below an empath, with limited capabilities to sense a person's feelings and worries, but not actual thoughts. This ability was considered beneficial for someone in his profession.

"I have some time. What are you feeling?"

"It's very odd." He stared into the wooded terrain before them, as though hypnotized. "I never had this feeling before. I believe it's been in the back of my mind since we landed here. However, it's been growing stronger. I suspect it's coming from the hammerheads."

"What kind of feeling?"

"It's vague, jumbled. Something like nervous anxiety, a growing discomfort. Which is odd considering they seem to be getting *more* comfortable with us."

"Possibly, but we still don't communicate with them beyond a rudimentary level."

She paused a moment, then said, "Come with me."

They plunged into the damp forest, thick with a varied and colorful assortment of vegetation. After a while, they came across a wandering sentinel near a large stand of fruited trees. It stopped when it saw them approach.

Chantelle said, "Tell me what you sense when I try to communicate with it."

He nodded.

She stepped forward and bowed. They didn't know if the hammerheads understood the meaning of this gesture. However, they continued to use it to show respect for their culture. With her boot, she sketched a crude picture of three hammerheads standing before two humans. Simple drawings were the preferred way to communicate their requests and intentions.

The sentinel glanced briefly at the sketch, then pointed up at the sky, then to the left towards the North Atrium. Afterwards, it turned and plodded away.

Kirk said, "I sensed nothing. A vacuum. A blank page."

"Perhaps the sentinels are a breed of lesser intelligence, raised for menial labor. It indicated a time and a meeting place. I'll need to inform the linguists."

They started back.

"Kirk?"

"Yes, Captain."

"I want you to come with us."

"As you wish, Captain."

***

Meetings with the hammerhead leaders were always strange. By the end of a meeting, nobody knew for certain whether the purpose of the meeting was addressed or not. And no one was certain how much either of the parties understood one another.

Since the hammerheads co-existed with nature so tightly, meetings were held in designated atriums formed by naturally shaped tree branches and shrubbery. Nature itself was a key member of any meeting.

During the course of a meeting, the linguists were of little help when it came to getting words or concepts understood by the hammerheads.

Today's meeting was no different.

Chantelle, Kirk, Gary, and Xenia stood in a semi-circle facing the stand of trees where three of the hammerhead leaders stood. Chantelle tried to discern which three leaders were here today. They were easily recognizable from the "commoners" since they were taller, heavier, and slower moving. However, they were not readily distinguishable from each other.

As far as they could tell, the culture had seven leaders, designated in her mind as A through G. As best as she could tell, today they were meeting with A, D, and E.

The soft shushing sound of leaves rustling in the breezes blended with the gentle hushing of Aerolian Harps. This was the customary greeting of the hammerhead leaders before a meeting.

Captain Chantelle bowed slightly. The others followed suit.

The linguists used a stack of holos, like teachers used to use "flash cards" to teach young children vocabulary. They offered a picture, spoke its name, and gestured to the hammerheads.

A tree. "Tree." A low hum followed.

Tree. Rock. Fruit. Flower. Food. The elementals: earth, air, fire, and water. And on and on.

After the meeting ended, the Captain watched as the hammerhead leaders hurried away more hastily than usual. Were they upset, anxious, angry, or pleased with the linguists' tactics? She couldn't tell.

Walking back to the base with Kirk, she asked him, "Did you feel anything from them?"

He nodded. "Yes. At the beginning, I read unwavering calmness from all three of them. As we proceeded, I noted a growing tension, mixed with confusion and concern. As it ended, I felt a strong sense of fear from all three."

"Why should they feel fear? We did nothing threatening. We've been nothing but peaceful and accommodating with them since the beginning."

"I don't think it was that kind of fear. It was more like a dread of the unknown. Perhaps it was a fear of who we might be."

"You read that?"

"Some of that was reading between the lines."

"I appreciate your input, but I need facts not feelings. I need to know what's going on. Should we be concerned about their unique reaction to this meeting?" She hesitated before adding, "They've always been friendly with us."

"But it was clearly different this time."

The Captain looked back into the forest which had swallowed up all signs of the hammerheads. She sighed and turned back to Kirk.

"It *was* different. I have to make sure we're prepared for the worst."

She contacted Corporal Callie. "Prepare for defensive maneuvers. We must be prepared for a potential attack. No, nothing specific at this point. I'll let you know when I know more."

***

Later the linguists called the Captain. Their voices were cheerful and excited on the commlink.

Gary said, "We're developing a lexicon. In the near future, we hope to begin development of an auto translator."

"I'm glad you've made a breakthrough. Let me know when they plan to sing again. I believe it's important we attend their next performance."

"Well, okay, but they don't usually have performances this close together."

"I expect it will be very soon."

***

The linguists were surprised when they received word of a new performance so soon after the previous performance. The Captain was not so surprised.

Huddled at the back of the auditorium, under a stand of umbrella trees, was a larger contingent of Earthmen than usual: Captain Chantelle, the linguists, Ship Psychologist Kirk, Corporal Callie, and two armed soldiers.

Too much precaution? Chantelle didn't think so. It was her responsibility to err on the side of caution.

The song the hammerheads sang was different. The linguists exchanged puzzled glances as they recorded their more energized performance, a musical account full of drama and passion. It was much more intense than their usual concerts.

As the performance drew to a pulse-pounding climax, the performers suddenly stopped singing and turned to face the visitors from Earth. The other hammerheads in the audience slowly turned to face them as well. Even the tree branches and vines appeared to point toward them.

A chill went up Captain Chantelle's spine. She whispered, "No sudden moves. Hold your position."

There was no point in running. It would be better if they all stayed together instead of scattered.

Minutes passed. No one moved.

Finally, the performers left the stage and the audience slowly departed. The tree branches seemed to relax, even as the Captain's tension subsided.

When all were gone, she ordered, "Back to base, everyone. Stay together."

No one spoke as they returned to base. Even the linguists, who always had something to say, were dead silent.

***

Later the Captain met in private with Kirk.

He studied her face before he spoke. She knew she must look like a wreck.

He said, "Should we talk about you or the hammerheads? I would think both."

She sighed. "All right. Go ahead."

"First of all, I'm impressed how much you've been in control throughout this unexpected turn of events. There are clear signs of stress, but this is completely normal and to be expected. You haven't succumbed to hasty decisions based on fear or panic. Your anger is in check. I've noted no external manifestations of your space anxieties. That's the good news."

He paused.

"So, the bad news?"

"None of your deep-seated anxieties are trying to come out."

"That's bad news?"

"Haven't you been listening to me during all of our sessions? Space anxieties are never completely cured. They can only be covered up, restrained, buried. Your anxieties should have shown themselves at least in some small ways."

"What does that mean? What are you saying?"

She still didn't see this as a problem.

He stood up from his chair and paced back and forth in his small office. "That's just it. I don't know what's happening. I sensed absolutely zero signs of any anxieties. What's happening to you is unprecedented in medical science."

"Maybe, you've made a breakthrough of some sort. You can write a paper about it someday."

He sat down like a heavy sack and said nothing.

"We'll figure this out later, Kirk. Now tell me about the hammerheads."

"That's also hard to describe. Of course, there were no concrete thoughts. Only vague feelings and images."

"Tell me as much as you can."

***

After received some interesting insights from her psychologist, Chantelle went to meet with the linguists. They were puzzling over their workstations when she strolled into their workshop.

Xenia said, "We were making good progress, but now we've been set back. I don't understand what happened."

"I have something for you to consider before you return to your investigations. Perhaps you wonder why I've been bringing the Ship's Psych to our meetings lately. He has limited psi abilities and has been receiving vague feelings from the hammerheads. However, I also find his psychoanalytic insights interesting.

"This is what I learned from him today. As you know, the hammerheads commune closely with nature. All of their activities are tied closely to their natural surroundings—the trees, bushes, vines, flowers. Kirk believes they have a much closer bond with nature than we realize. He believes they have a kind of psychic link, a commensal relationship with nature. This may be a vital relationship required for both to survive."

A stunned silence followed.

She continued, "Can you see it now? Think about our early encounters, how strange we thought it was they stayed so close to the vegetation.

"Now follow this carefully. When you were making your breakthrough in communications, something about us was revealed to the hammerheads which clearly disturbed them. So much so that they had to put out a special performance to let everyone know about it. You have to figure out what might have been misinterpreted by them. Once we understand what troubled them, only then can we alleviate their concerns.

"We have to address this quickly to get back in their good graces. We have no idea what they might do because of their new revelation about us."

She left them alone. Now it was up to the linguists. She hoped she had placed a good dose of urgency in their minds.

She doubled the guards at their base and tripled the number of patrols. They had to be prepared for a worse-case scenario.

She felt a growing anger and frustration toward the linguists for putting them in this perilous situation. She knew those feelings. She had to focus on the crisis at hand.

As she crossed the periphery of the base, something stirred at the corner of her eyes. The trees. Were the trees moving?

She took a few steps toward the forest's edge. She imagined a sudden and furious uprising of hammerheads pouring out of the forest and attacking the base bearing large tree branches as weapons. She didn't know of any weapons they possessed. She shook away the image.

Tree branches were gently swaying, though there was no wind. She wondered if the trees obeyed their masters, the hammerheads. On command, would they stretch out their branches like the arms of gnarled old men to do their bidding?

These were crazy thoughts. Panic welled up within her. *Don't! Hold onto your senses, girl! Your crew needs you to be calm, level-headed.*

Then she heard music filtering out from the forest. At first, she wondered if this too was her overworked imagination. It was the gentle sounds of rustling trees and softly crooning hammerheads. It blended into a music unlike anything she ever heard before.

She called out, "Corporal Callie."

"Here, Captain."

"Get your soldiers ready. Something is approaching. Tell them not to fire unless I give the order."

Behind her she heard sounds of boots and metal. Weapons clicked into ready mode, a clear and sickening sound. She didn't want to give the order.

The music grew steadily louder. Trees rustled more vigorously.

She swayed to the lull of the pensive hammerheads.

Dozens of them suddenly broke out from among the trees, appearing as though sprouting from the trees themselves. More and more poured out of the forest, quickly forming a large semi-circle facing the base.

She heard the faint voice of Gary behind her. "May we come forward?"

She glanced back and said, "Let the linguists through."

They came and stood next to her. They watched the spectacle of the hammerheads in silence for a while.

Chantelle said, "What do they want?"

Gary said, "We don't know. But maybe we can find out."

Xenia said, "Permission to go forward, Captain."

"Granted, but not too close. Wait." She turned and called Corporal Callie. "Corporal, the linguists will try to find out what the hammerheads want. Keep your soldiers alert in case something goes wrong. But stay back for now. We don't want to aggravate the situation."

"Yes, Captain." She left.

"Okay. Go ahead. But remember, don't take any risks."

Xenia and Gary exchanged glances, took deep breaths, and faced the hammerhead contingent. Or was it a mob? Or a family? Whatever its function was, Chantelle didn't know. It was up to the linguists to find out now.

Xenia stepped forward. Gary followed close behind her.

The music of the trees and the hammerheads was clear and soothing to Chantelle's mind. She felt a rapidly growing calmness. *Were they putting us into a trance?*

The linguists paused a dozen feet away from them.

Xenia began to sing.

The hammerheads stopped singing.

This caught Chantelle off guard. She didn't realize Xenia could sing so beautifully. Xenia sang a song wholly different from the hammerheads' songs, yet in a similar lulling, melodic style. The hammerheads were attentive, listening closely to every sound and syllable she uttered. Even the trees appeared to be leaning in to hear her song.

Then the trees began to sway.

Something strange is happening, thought Captain Chantelle. *Something strange and beautiful.*

She continued to be on guard, however, since this could still be a deception, a trap.

Then, to her further amazement, the hammerheads and the swishing trees joined in Xenia's song, forming a perfect harmony, at least to Chantelle's untrained ears. The performance continued another five minutes, and then abruptly stopped.

Chantelle felt a tangible tension in the air.

A soft voice, much like the hammerhead's, rose above the silence. Gary was speaking in their language, shushing sounds that were delivered slower and clearer. He wore an odd donut-shaped device on a chain around his neck that modified his voice. The natives responded, deliberately slowing their speech.

The conversation went back and forth for some time. Chantelle lost track of time.

Finally, it ended. The hammerheads rapidly dispersed, retreating back into the forest. The trees seemed to open up and absorb them among their beckoning branches, closing up afterward like an impenetrable wall.

In a minute, they were gone.

The forest and the air were still.

The Captain said, "Did they understand you? Did you get answers?"

Gary pulled his gaze away from the trees and stared for a moment at the Captain as if trying to comprehend her language. After a moment, he said, "Once I understood their concern, I had to do some fast talking. Do you remember when we showed them holos of the elementals—earth, air, fire, and water?"

She nodded.

"It was the fire. Have you ever noticed they never use fire? They tried to explain their adversity to fire. They kept saying, 'No fire to masters.' It took me a while to figure out the masters were the trees. Fire destroys the trees."

"What do you mean the trees were the masters?"

"Exactly what I said. We've been assuming all this time that the highest form of life on Sienna was the hammerheads, when, actually, it's the trees.

The trees on this world are far more intelligent than any vegetation we've ever encountered."

Xenia cleared her throat and said, "You see the hammerheads are their servants, their faithful instruments of service, used in many ways, including communication with other species. They have a unique commensal relationship."

The Captain stared at the forest surrounding them. "I'm having a hard time embracing this revelation."

Gary laughed and said, "Understandable, Captain. Like I said, once I understood their concern, I had to do some fast talking. I explained that we used fire for warmth and for cooking our food, but the logs in the holo were not tree branches, but were fire-making constructions."

The Captain's face grimaced.

"I know. It was the best I could come up with on short notice. Not a lie. We do have fake logs. I think it worked. They calmed down afterwards."

"We'll have to spread the word. No campfires."

Xenia said, "We learned something else. We learned what their singing is all about. The singing is their hospital, their church, their media. It actually heals sickness and disease, tree rot, fungus. It relieves pain, it offers comfort. It spreads joy, such as the news of new birth, new saplings. It spreads important news, like the horror of the fire makers.

"But now they will sing a new song, a redemption song. For we are now cleared of our crime and will not require exile or punishment."

"Do we know exactly what they were going to do to us?"

"No, only a vague reference to retribution."

"I suppose it's better we don't know." *No*, she thought. *It would be better if we did know what they were capable of doing to us.*

The Captain took a couple of steps forward toward the tall, majestic, and proud trees that seemed to watch over them, studying their every move. They would have to be very careful from now on.

She dismissed everyone back to base.

"Tomorrow we'll have an all hand's meeting to discuss our next steps. The tree beings seem to be a peace-loving race, but we must make sure we don't upset them again. Gary and Xenia, we'll need translators as soon as possible."

After everyone else had left, she remained for a while, alone with her thoughts.

We didn't realize how close we were to . . . what? I wish I knew.

***

Later, after wearing herself out in the exercise room and taking a hot shower, Chantelle went to see the Ship's Psych in her most comfortable wrap.

She dropped down in her usual chair and told him about their tense encounter with the hammerheads.

"Sounds like a lynch mob. I'm sorry I missed it."

She laughed.

"That was the most stress I care to handle. So much uncertainty. The one bright light was my illness didn't flare up. I didn't think about that until it was all over. Somehow I kept calm throughout the whole ordeal."

Kirk said, "The singing contributed to that, didn't it?"

"It was definitely soothing. That's true enough."

"More than that. Think back to what you told me. You said their singing cures illnesses, diseases—like tree rot."

"Yeah?" She frowned.

"I believe, dear Captain, you will no longer need my services. I believe your own particular brand of rot has been cured."

John A. Frochio. I grew up and still live among the rolling hills of Western Pennsylvania. For a living, I develop and install computer automation systems for steel mills. My wife Connie, a retired nurse, and my daughter Toni, a flight attendant, have bravely put up with my strange ways for many years. I have had stories published in the Triangulation *anthologies (PARSEC Ink, 2003 and 2014),* Interstellar Fiction, Beyond Science Fiction, Twilight Times, Aurora Wolf, Liquid Imagination, Kraxon Magazine, SciFan Magazine, *and* Time Travel Tales *(Chappy Fiction, 2016). I have also published a general fiction novel* Roots of a Priest *(with Ken Bowers, Booklocker, 2007) and a science fiction and fantasy collection* Large and Small Wonders, *(Byrne Publishing, 2012). My author's webpage is https://johnafrochio.wordpress.com/about/.*

From the railroad to the rocket and the spacewarp drive, humanity has sought to travel ever further and faster. For some new transportation technology became an opportunity for freedom, while others made it a means to expand their tyranny. But what happens when quantum teleportation completely annihilates distance?

Technoserf

Leigh Kimmel

The Gate failed half a minute before Roby's turn through. The worker immediately before him had just entered the aperture when eye-wrenching blackness gave way to dull gray plate. Half a body, neatly sliced from head to foot, peeled from it to fall at Roby's toes. There was no blood, for the failing field had perfectly cauterized the flesh.

Roby looked from the half-corpse to the dead Gate. Behind him his fellow workers whispered among themselves in speculation. There could be no mistaking their fear, never mind it was based upon all the wrong reasons. Although they possessed unmodified consciousness and sensorium, a necessity for the quantum devices with which they worked, they were individuals of limited curiosity who never looked beyond the immediate surrounds of their workplace and dormitory levels to the world upon which all of it was located. Little more than a tide-locked cosmic cinder, useful for the vast amount of energy coming from its sun, the planet could support life only because of its Gate connections to more verdant worlds which provided the necessary organics and volatiles.

Supervisors moved in, swinging the discipline wands, which delivered a painful shock but did no lasting harm. "Silence, all of you. It is not for the likes of you to question the works of the Lords Exalted."

Stupid, but the bottom tier of the Madrian Empire's managerial forms was not famous for their intellectual capacity. Having to supervise workers whose duties required a functional understanding of quantum mechanics served only to make them all the more touchy about the prerogatives of rank.

Roby opened his implanted link to access the Madrian computer net, including the levels that weren't supposed to be accessible to lowly orders. He hid a smile of amusement to know the supervisors, so alert for the first hint of subversive talk, did not even check whether their charges might be establishing far more dangerous connections on the net.

If he had hoped to gain solid information from the managerial channels, it proved sadly disappointing. They were in as much disarray as the bottom-feeder supervisors who were smacking Roby's fellow workers to a silence more fraught with restless energy than their previous chatter. Not surprising, when one considered that the highest-ranking managerial form present on this nameless planet of a nameless sun was at best middle-level, depending upon Gate-borne links to senior executive forms on distant worlds. Even the immobile forms, the megabrains who held executive rank by courtesy, filled their channels with copious speculation but little substance.

Roby had barely begun to dip into the rich stew of the megabrains' multithreaded consciousness when his workgroup's chief supervisor reached a decision. "All of you will return to your quarters until the situation is resolved."

Much as he wanted to continue exploring the net, or rather that part of it cut off here by the Gate failure's isolation of this world, it was foolhardy to maintain that level of concentration while walking, even along a path grown familiar from nearly three years' daily repetition. Roby joined the crowd of workers trooping back to their sleeping capsules.

What could have shut down not just the local Gate, but also every Gate on the planet, both internal and offworld, and all computer network links? Roby's secret explorations of the Madrian computer net had revealed the quantum mechanical underpinnings of the Gate system, similar enough to the work to which he had been assigned that he could grasp their operation with little difficulty. He'd seen the multiple levels of redundancy, the fail-safes that should have ensured that even a cascading failure could not cut off every link to the Imperial mainstream.

When the workers arrived at their sleeping capsules, the supervisor ordered them all to hook up their nutriment lines and waste hoses, just as they would during their regular sleep shifts. Roby had no intention of letting the soporific drug in the dormitory nutriment fluid feed lull him to sleep. At least it was a relatively simple trick to fiddle the commands to the mixing station so he would receive none of it. The mixing pump had minimal awareness, only enough to make the necessary decisions in processing and distributing nutriment, and did not question Roby's intervention.

His mind remained free to explore the net more deeply. The various supervisors and managers might come and go as their masters at the top levels of Madrian society deemed it necessary, so there was little opportunity to become acquainted with the flavor of their minds. By contrast, those few immobile forms who enjoyed full consciousness were permanent fixtures on the local information landscape, and he had become able to recognize each solely by that distinctive mental touch on the net. He knew their temperaments, their interests, the complexities of their relationships with one another and with similar forms on other worlds.

It was only when he heard Nereis talking that he realized he'd walked the whole way back in sick dread for her safety. Although not strictly a megabrain, Nereis enjoyed the same status because of the enormously enlarged brain by which she controlled not only her own processes, but those in ten subordinate mixing pumps, more akin to the one he had just fooled than herself.

Roby had never harbored any illusions about the unattainability of this elite mixing pump, mistress of a thousand chemical reactions. He could no more hope for a relationship with her than a peasant could hope to win the hand of a fairy princess, yet he would adore her from afar, the epitome of all the virtues he treasured: intelligence, wit, courtesy, creativity.

However, his relief only lasted until he heard what she was telling their world's senior megabrain. " . . . I can keep the Chalnar job suspended for another three hours, but after that I must get a Gate link to offload it or the reactions will run out of control."

Roby's merely human consciousness couldn't fully follow the multithreaded complexity of information Nereis transmitted, but he could catch enough to know he was looking at a disaster in the making. Even as his trained intellect recognized the several types of toxic waste that would poison their closed environment, his hindbrain flashed upon an image of Nereis lying in her support cradle with her mixing and pumping chambers torn asunder and her life bleeding out.

No, this must not be! Roby's mind raced through all he knew of the Gate system's mechanics, the symptoms flowing in, while he cursed the limits of human consciousness. How could his single thread of awareness put together all the pieces in a mere three hours?

It had to be a single point-source failure at one of the few places where redundancy could not be built in. Armed with that knowledge, he needed only to summon a schematic of the Gate and query non-redundant parts.

"It's the control coupler for the decision loop."

And immediately realized he'd not thought it within his head, but transmitted it onto the net.

But there was no time to apologize for having spoken out of turn, to try to cover for his error, before his supervisor's voice came blasting into his consciousness.

"Worker #21B-17-3519/JL5" (unlike the managerial forms, lowly workers such as Roby were not entitled to names, only identification numbers) "you are out of order."

Before he could specify Roby's punishment, Nereis cut into the link. "For identifying the cause of the breakdown?"

The supervisor remained unmoved. "Workers do not have access--"

"Is that the problem?" Nereis allowed her voice to become tinged with derision, no doubt only a faint reflection of the misery she must be in, from the backed-up Chalnar job bloating her mixing chambers. "Would you prefer that we all die to protect your precious little prerogatives over your subordinates?"

The supervisor started to bluster about long-term effects upon discipline, until Nereis' accompanying information sank through and he realized that there would be no long term to worry about if the connectivity disruption wasn't resolved. Only slightly abashed by the evidence of his short-sightedness, the supervisor responded, "Then what do you suggest we do, oh miss-high-and-noble, elite mixing pump?"

Nereis did not rise to the bait, responding, "We send him out to fix it. If he succeeds, we reward him amply for his courage and perceptivity. If he fails, at least we will not have sat around wailing woe-is-me as we wait to die." Which was a particularly ironic statement, coming as it did from an immobile form.

It remained only to prepare Roby to go onto the surface. With less than three hours remaining before Nereis had to clear the Chalnar job, there could be no question of giving him modifications. Equipment would have to do all the work of protecting him from both the searing heat of dayside and the brutal cold of nightside.

At least, someone had considered the possibility of equipment failure, since the necessary protective gear had been laid in at the mechanical airlock to the surface. However, the planners had not considered it so likely as to justify training anyone in their operation. Roby's only hope was to download schematics and experiences from the net.

Before the Madrian conquest, his homeworld had experimented with space travel and built equipment to allow people to work outside their vehicles.

But those suits of multi-layered fiber and plastic were humiliatingly crude compared to the device Roby now put on. Based upon quantum principles, similar to those with which he worked, it would temporarily superposition itself over his body, suspending the biological processes of his cells while leaving his consciousness free to direct its operations.

When he first activated the suit, he found it disorienting to be cut off from his body. But once he mastered it, he had his attention free to notice how the reflective quality of the surface interface made him look like a fairy-tale knight in shining armor, off to rescue his fair lady from duress vile and a fate worse than death.

The wait for the airlock to cycle felt like a subjective eternity, although the controls told him only minutes were passing. At last the door slid open and Roby stepped onto the surface.

His surroundings stretched around him in the stark linearity of a schematic, and he realized just how much the space armor must be filtering input, if not outright functioning as a sensorium while his own natural senses lay dormant under it. He hoped it would not interfere with his ability to work with the quantum-based Gate technology.

He reviewed the data loaded into his suit's onboard computer and compared it to what he could see all around him. It would've been easier if he had a live link to someone below who could offer on-the-fly advice, but the energy of the transmissions could have unpredictable effects upon the delicate quantum mechanisms with which he would be working. Even the light with which he would illuminate his work on darkside was not without its risks.

As familiar with the equipment as he could make himself in so little time, he set to work on the first station involved in the breakdown. However, he had no more than begun when it became obvious all the responses he was getting from it were completely within their operating parameters. Whatever had caused the Gate system to fail had nothing to do with this station.

Somewhere after the third or fourth station he was overcome with a sense that he was not alone. At first, he dismissed it with the knowledge that he was the only person on the surface. But when he crossed the terminator to darkside, the sensation became too powerful to ignore.

"Who are you?"

Even as he spoke the words, he remembered that his suit would take the nerve impulses directly from his brain and translate them into—wait, did he even *have* a transmitter in this thing?

If there were someone—or something—out there and he had no way to communicate, might that entity simply assume hostile intent and act accordingly? Especially if that entity were responsible for the breakdown and thought him a Madrian official come to investigate.

The thought of encountering a saboteur held a certain irony. Roby had no great love for the Madrians, whose policies toward their subject peoples redefined arrogance and brutality. But with no sure way to communicate—

Those thoughts ran into the sudden sharp barrier of an intrusive presence within his mind. Startled, he nearly flinched away from the station he was in the process of testing. Only by last-minute self-discipline did he avoid doing serious damage to delicate quantum entanglements vital to the equipment's functioning.

Once he had disengaged from his work in an orderly fashion, Roby opened his mind to the presence of the entity. It quickly became obvious that language would be too culturally bound a tool to serve any purpose in this encounter.

Composing his mind without putting his thoughts into words was not an easy process. Only his habit of tapping into the information feeds from the various megabrains, much of which was in non-linguistic form, enabled him to do it at all.

At first, he received no response, just the continued pressure of the entity's presence within his mind. Just as he was about to give up, that pressure underwent a shift, becoming less oppressive, more inquisitive. Yes, it was responding to his curiosity with its own, which indicated some level of intelligence.

Trying to communicate his identity proved harder. There was no use giving his name, but what images would convey his sense of self without unwanted baggage of the Madrian overlords?

He must've hit the right note, for the presence which had previously been a formless curiosity now took definite shape.

It took some effort to make sense of what he was perceiving, so alien was the sensorium that had gathered the impressions and the mind that had interpreted them into meaning. The layered images of multiple perspectives induced an overwhelming vertigo, until he realized he was witnessing quantum superpositioning at the macro scale, from the perspective of a being for whom it was an integral part of mental functioning.

Roby had been working with quantum operations on a daily basis since the Madrians had summoned him from his homeworld to serve them, but it had remained purely practical, a job to do. There had never been any reason to contemplate theoretical possibilities when the work was not of his own choosing and made him the target of endless suspicion on the part of his superiors.

The theory was simple enough—as matter was cooled to extreme temperatures, the motion of its constituent particles grew steadily less, until even the very electrons began to slow in their orbits. As atoms approached absolute zero, one would expect electron motion to stop altogether—yet in one of the peculiarities of quantum physics, they refused to reveal their positions, instead appearing to be in all their possible positions at once.

Some of the higher-level Madrian scientists had theorized about what might happen if life were to develop in such a condensate and evolve intelligence. For Roby, the thrill of gaining access to off-limits databases had far exceeded any interest in their contents, and he had never bothered to peruse any of that material further.

Encountering such a being caught him by surprise. He experienced a profound regret at having passed up the opportunity to gain information that would be of immediate use. And immediately pushed it from his mind with the knowledge that regrets would give Nereis no assistance. Already one of the three critical hours had slipped away.

The image came to his mind once again of Nereis torn asunder by the catastrophic reactions of a process that could no longer be suspended within her vast body. Although Roby had intended no attempt at communication, he was rewarded with a flash of alarm from the entity.

It took a moment to get across the idea of something that had not yet occurred, but would surely happen unless certain conditions changed. The very concept of cause and effect elicited confusion in the entity, along with visceral disgust, as if it were appalled that a thinking being should be constrained to only one set of possibilities, to a sequence of moments, rather than all eternity as seamless fabric.

Conversely, Roby found the entity's reaction disturbing until he recalled another aspect of quantum mechanics that had previously been merely a theoretical curiosity—the many-worlds solution to the wave collapse problem. But for a creature whose existence was based upon quantum rather than classical mechanics, it might well be ordinary experience.

Which made it all the harder for Roby to convey the concept that he didn't have access to an infinite range of parallel possibilities, and that the very act of choosing one could permanently foreclose others. Or that the opportunity to make a decision did not remain open indefinitely, and to delay action could lead to the chance slipping through one's fingers forever, the choice made by default.

Awareness finally dawned and the entity comprehended that Nereis had only a limited amount of time before the chemical processes she was managing would come to a catastrophic end, one fatal not only to her, but also to everyone in the area contaminated by the resulting toxic chemicals. Getting across the conditions for preventing that eventuality proved somewhat more difficult, since the entity had only a vague notion of the nature of space and the necessity of traversing it.

At last Roby gave up on the attempt to convey the theory and concentrated on getting across the fact that the equipment here on the surface was key to preventing the disaster that was about to befall Nereis, and that it was essential to get it functioning. He wasn't sure the quantum entity was responsible for the failure, and certainly didn't want to risk angering it with a direct accusation. However, he felt confident enough of the connection to hope he could gain the necessary co-operation.

He was despairing of conveying the essential concepts when he became aware of a certain loosening of the ambient tension. Could it be? He looked at his instruments, for a moment forgetting altogether the possibilities of quantum interactions with his consciousness.

Yes, the Gate system was re-connected once again with the rest of the Madrian Empire. Even as he watched, the indicators marked the passage of a massive load—the Chalnar job Nereis had needed to clear.

The relief Roby felt was a palpable thing. But even as the knowledge of Nereis' safety took a burden from his mind, another replaced it. Namely the realization that he must somehow convey to the quantum entity the peril of continued interaction with the surface equipment. But how could he communicate the necessity of departure to a being who had no concept of sequential time and only the vaguest notion of causality?

Shimmering images layered in his mind as the entity communicated its own predicament. How it had strayed from its native world and become stranded here, Roby couldn't quite interpret, since some of those images were so alien they had to come from a parallel universe, dominated by a civilization utterly unlike the Madrians. One thing was certain: the entity was not native to this world. Its original home lay on a world in the furthest reaches of its system, a snowball of frozen oxygen and nitrogen through which ran rivers of liquid helium. Exactly the place a quantum condensate would have the opportunity to evolve life.

Except Roby had not the slightest idea of how to affect the entity's return. He had no great confidence that anyone in authority would listen to him. Even Nereis' intercession would carry little weight before those with the authority to mount the sort of expedition necessary to locate the entity's homeworld. Assuming it was even possible to reach it, and it wasn't located in one of those other universes Roby had glimpsed. Things had been so much simpler when he just had to fix the Gate network before Nereis' time ran out.

A fresh image entered his mind, setting the entity's longing to return to its own kind, parallel with Roby's own feelings about having been summoned from his native world to serve the Madrians in a place of their choosing. Roby's initial reaction was a homesickness so profound it felt like a punch in the gut, followed by anger at being manipulated. Until he realized, this was the only way the entity had to communicate complex ideas, and that it was trying to express sympathy. Or maybe more, as a fresh image formed within Roby's mind. One of himself being conveyed to one of those other universes, set free to—

I will not abandon Nereis!

The entity responded with palpable bewilderment, tinged with sadness. Roby realized he'd hurt the entity's feelings with the intensity of his rejection of its offer, even if it could not comprehend the specifics stated in language.

How to explain he could not simply accept it as a gift freely given? As the price of securing Nereis' safety, he could have accepted being sundered from her forever, but he could not abandon her for his own benefit.

Roby had expected it to be a difficult concept to get across. He was surprised to discover the entity reflecting back to him that fierce loyalty with a harmonic of sympathy.

Could it too have been separated from a loved one? Alien though it might be in its most fundamental nature, it had demonstrated a capacity for affection and loyalty.

Roby amplified his assertion with an image of himself returning to the airlock from which he'd come to the surface. He'd no more than reached that point in his image-sequence than the entity pulled at it and he saw himself taken prisoner, held in absolute isolation—

Of course! His contact with the entity would've subtly altered his consciousness at a quantum level, such that any contact with unaltered minds could spread the change like a contagion. No, going back was no longer an option.

But even as Roby grieved at the thought of never again feeling the touch of Nereis' consciousness, the entity was in his mind once again. There was a push, a sort of sideways twist, and then he was no longer standing on the surface.

The disorientation of the change was so profound it took him some time to become aware that his body had been transformed completely beyond recognition. The fact that he had almost no consciousness to spare, from the chemical operations going on within his chambers, meant that it took longer to make that assessment of his altered form.

Through the lines that connected each of his ganglia to the controlling brain of the vast, elite mixing pump that loomed over his own support cradle, that tiny fragment of self-awareness was filled with the touch of a familiar mind. Although he no longer possessed sufficient independent awareness to wonder how the cryonic entity had found a universe in which he was one of Nereis' subordinate mixing pumps, neither did he have the capacity to be distressed by that loss.

Leigh Kimmel is a writer, artist and entrepreneur living in Indianapolis, Indiana, a city better known for automotive racing. She has degrees in history and in library and information science and has worked in libraries and archives. You can learn more about her latest projects at http://www.leighkimmel.com/.

The Ring

Margaret Karmazin

Erin Crowell sat in one corner of my couch with its big chenille throw pillows for the comfort of the patients. She'd been referred by a colleague whom she had approached about counseling at the hospital where she works as a part time phlebotomist. Since the two of them are slightly friendly, he didn't feel it was ethical to see her professionally. He did say he had reason to believe the woman was mentally and possibly physically abused by her husband.

"Tell me why you're here, Erin," I said.

I recognized her expression as the look of someone not sure they should have begun this.

"I felt like I wanted to share things with someone who can't tell anyone else what I tell them."

"What do you want to tell me?" I asked.

Long pause, and then she said, "I've visited another world."

"You mean physically?"

"Not exactly.

"Please explain."

She hesitated.

"Erin, I've probably heard everything. Nothing you say will shock me unless maybe you have a body in your car trunk."

She chuckled rather feebly. "Not yet," she said, and then began her story. "Have you heard of Robert Monroe?"

"The name is familiar," I said.

"He was famous for his out-of-body experiences and research into altered consciousness. He founded The Monroe Institute in Virginia and wrote several books about his experiences."

"I remember him now," I said.

"I read his books and those of others on the same topic, like Robert Bruce. Things have been hard in my life and I find subjects like that a good escape. When my husband was away—he drives a truck—I practiced Monroe's and Bruce's methods. One time, after months of trying, it happened. I got out."

"You mean—"

"Out of my body," she said. "I did it."

I made every attempt to keep my expression neutral.

"I know what you're thinking," she snapped. "This is why I had doubts about talking to someone like you. You science types are all the same! Nobody's ever seen a ghost, those that did were all on drugs or drinking, no one's ever seen a real UFO, even the cops, sea captains, and military who saw them, those were all lying or drinking too! This is pointless!" She stood up to leave.

I could have told her that my father saw his dead brother once and that on a trip out West, my whole family saw a giant glowing UFO, but therapy is not a place for revelations from the therapist. It's about the patient only. But I did soften my stance to put her at ease.

"I wouldn't categorize all psychologists, psychiatrists, or doctors, or for that matter all scientists as totally dismissing the paranormal. So, let's not assume too much about each other and proceed with good faith."

She sat back down with a look of defiance on her small, pointy-nosed, little face. Her shaggy brown hair fell over her eyes and she impatiently brushed it aside. "All right," she said. "As I said, it took many tries and I almost gave up, but one night I was feeling sort of feverish and to distract myself, tried again. It was around midnight and Shawn was on the road—he's away days at a time. I'd shut the bedroom door so the dog wasn't in the room. I was using one of Bruce's methods when I heard this really loud ringing noise and slipped right out. It was terrifying like you can't imagine, but being a stubborn person, I kept going and then lurched right through the door and into the hall."

"Were you walking?"

"Not at first. I didn't have control, sort of like you see in a weightless environment on the space station. Not quite that bad, but I couldn't make myself stand. Eventually, I figured out how but it would have looked to someone else like I was drunk."

"Where did you go?"

"Downstairs. I saw our dog Georgie. He was chewing something on the floor and I saw it was a brochure. It was one Shawn brought home about some dumbass trailer he wants to get so he can force me to ride with him all over the country. He'd be mad if it got ripped up, so I tried to get Georgie to stop it but my hand went right through him and then I did a somersault in the air. He kept on chewing."

"Did he see you?" I asked. "Did he know you were there?"

"Kind of eventually. He suddenly stopped, looked around, and wagged his tail. He loves me. I'm good to him and don't kick him like Shawn does. He couldn't figure it out though and looked around for a bit, then settled down. I couldn't rescue the brochure and knew that when Shawn saw it, he'd go after Georgie again."

"Does Shawn go after you?"

She ignored my question. "I decided to go back upstairs and immediately shot straight up, through the ceiling into the hall. My fear feeling returned and like someone in those books suggested, I desperately thought of my little toe and just like that I was back in my body. Then I woke up and felt cold and still sick, so I laid there a while shaking, before I got up the courage to get out of bed and get some aspirin."

"Could you walk all right?"

"I was careful," she said. "I held onto the walls and in the bathroom mirror my face was really white. The next day I stayed in bed late and when I finally went downstairs, there was the brochure all chewed up. Right on the floor where I'd seen Georgie go at it."

"How did you feel about this experience?"

"I was happy. To know that I had the power to do one thing right, this secret thing . . . it gave me a great feeling of power."

"One thing right?'" I repeated.

She turned her head to look out the window and did not reply.

"So," I said, "what happened next?"

"I couldn't do it whenever I wanted, only sometimes. But the shittier my life was, the more I practiced and, eventually, I was doing it almost every night while Shawn was on the road. When he was home, it was impossible, though I managed it a couple of times later on, after I got good at it. Eventually, I could leave my body after only a few minutes."

"Where did you go when you were out?" I asked instead of referring to her "shitty life" comment. "Did you stick to around the house?"

"Hell no," she said, perking up. "The fourth time out I shot up into the sky. Saw the entire neighborhood. At that point, I was still scared or let's say I never did become entirely unafraid until I went to the Ring, but that comes later. During this phase of things, I worked on how to arrive at a chosen destination, entered other people's homes, even went to the White House once."

"What was happening in the White House?" I asked. I was interested yet this was probably akin to asking a five-year-old, who said Santa flew her to the North Pole, to describe it for me.

"All sorts of things, but nothing I understood much. The President wasn't there at the time and neither was his wife. The most fun place was where they were eating breakfast. A really nice, wood paneled room in the basement. I just floated behind people. A young man and woman were discussing funding for flood victims. The man had an omelet and sausages; the woman a bagel. I didn't see anyone I recognized from TV."

"You didn't stay long? Didn't look around more?"

"I had to pee and that brought me back."

"Okay," I said. "Well, time is up for today."

On the way home, I stopped at the library and borrowed two of Robert Monroe's books. Despite having to spend more time than usual cleaning up after my mother soiled her pants and then became so agitated that I had to sedate her, I managed to skim and read much of one and part of another.

The following Friday, Erin was back on the sofa and while her expression was sullen, she immediately returned to her story.

"I've visited friends out of body and other people I know," she said.

"Uh huh," I said.

"You don't believe me? Why should you? To you the whole thing sounds ridiculous. I don't care. I did it, saw things and proved it to myself later in some cases by checking on what I saw, so it doesn't matter what you think!" Her face was red and she looked about to jump out of her seat again.

"Don't assume things about me. Please just go on."

She took a deep breath. "Okay, well, first I visited my father. Which was a mistake. This was around 10:30 at night. He lives alone in a doublewide a couple of miles from my house. My mother died four years ago, so he's alone. I guess I expected him to be propped in front of the TV slugging down his beer, but no, that wasn't what he was doing. He had some woman there, younger than him, maybe a little bit older than me. They were going at it in his bedroom and it was disgusting. Seeing your daddy naked with some woman about forty pounds overweight is a sight you can't unsee. I hightailed it out of there and back home and didn't go out of body for a good two weeks after. And you can bet I had a hard time looking my father in the eye for some time."

"Did you ever meet the woman after that? The one you saw?"

"No, but I hinted around, like 'Dad, are you seeing anyone?' and he said, 'not in particular, I play the field.' So, no, I never met her. And I don't want to."

"Did you go anywhere else?"

"Oh yeah. I saw all kinds of things. Went to visit this man at our church who kind of turns me on. Nothing could have come of it, not with Shawn around, and I'm not the cheating type, though some men deserve it if their wives do."

I was dying to say something but did not.

"Anyway, I've always liked this guy. He smiles at me and one time got me a program at this Christmas event and our hands touched. So, I out-of-bodied to his house. It was around seven in the morning."

"Shawn was out of town?"

"Of course," she said. "Anyway, I knew where the guy's place was because he rents the first floor of this house next to where my friend lives. When I arrived, he had a woman there, only I soon saw it wasn't any girlfriend. She was maybe in her fifties and wearing scrubs and then I saw she was changing something on him, like he had a hole in his side. She was flushing him out and he was crying a little. I never knew; I didn't know. He must have had cancer or something. These are the weird things you see when you do this."

"Did you talk to him after that?"

"No, not beyond saying hello. But I don't go to that church now."

"Why not?"

"After seeing the things I've seen? Well, I don't fit into that little box anymore. Anyway, I did this type of out-of-body stuff for a while—visiting people I know, or just people in random houses, and I saw them have sex, use the toilet, fight, cuddle, play with kids, smoke dope, cry, saw wood, read, sing, cook, you name it. Got boring after a while. Then I decided to go further."

"Further?"

"If you'd read Monroe's books, I wouldn't need to explain this," she said.

Perhaps it was necessary for me to be forthcoming. "I have read parts of two of them," I admitted.

"Which two?"

"*Journey's Out of the Body* and *Far Journeys*," I said.

"Hmmm," she said. "I'm surprised."

No need to say that I'd just done it recently.

"Well," she went on, "You may remember the part then where Monroe runs into a big wall and finds a hole in it? When he crossed through it into an entirely different world?"

"Mmmmm," I said.

"You didn't read the part where he found that other world? Where the streets were very wide and people drove cars run by steam engines?"

"Oh yes, where he lived that other man's life some of the time."

"Yeah, that's it. Well, I did a similar thing." She paused. "If I tell you, I'm sure you'll consider my story some form of delusion. But I assure you it isn't. As crappy as my life has been, I'm not prone to delusions to escape from it. There are other ways of handling *that*."

"That?" I prompted, but she didn't bite. My stomach did a little flip flop.

"You want to hear the rest or not?" she said.

"Of course."

"Well, then, let me just say that I found another world just like Monroe did, only not the same one by a long shot."

"Tell me," I said.

She kicked off her shoes and tucked her legs under her. She was small, maybe five-foot-two, wiry thin, and in her early thirties. She wore a slightly spotted T-shirt and yoga pants. No jewelry, little if any makeup.

She said, "I don't know how I got there. I just expressed in my mind the desire to see something very different. Didn't pass through any hole in a wall, don't remember traversing space. Just suddenly I was there and living in that world."

"Another planet?" I said.

"In a way, though not exactly. I had the understanding that it was in another dimension or universe. What I could see of it didn't look like ours—no black sky studded with stars, just a sort of red to pink, smoky background to space. The world I was in wasn't a planet but a giant, undulating ring that rotated around a small white sun. This world, everything in it, was inside the wormlike ring. Everything was contained, held inside, by some kind of membrane. Gravity was different than on our world. It seemed to occur in areas, but there was no definite up or down. Some places on the giant membrane, plants and animals clumped together and lived their lives. The intelligent species was sort of part person as we think of a person and part dragonfly. These people landed on different areas up or down or any which way and slept inside caves, or constructed homes in foliage clumps. There was an attraction like gravity in the direction of the star but this moved spatially inside the membrane since the ring was in constant movement itself, slightly twisting and turning."

I was fascinated, in spite of myself. "The whole ring thing must have been gigantic," I said. "I mean the people would never be able to go from one side to the other, would they? Our earth travels around the sun 18.5 miles per second." I got out my phone to calculate. "That's 66,960 miles per hour. You can see that a person would never be able to travel around the sun on his own. My point being that the dragonfly people inside the ring would probably never in their lifetimes be able to make it to the other side of the ring unless they lived thousands of their years."

"Well," Erin said, "This is in another universe. Or not. I don't really know. How do we know how big this *sun* and this *ring* really are? They could be smaller than my little finger. They could be microscopic."

I looked at my patient with new respect. "Indeed," I said.

"But the thing is, that a person's soul could evidently fit into one of these creatures, just like it does inside a human body. Does the soul have a size? I don't know."

Actually, did a soul even exist? I wasn't about to argue the point. What I did want to do was to get to her relationship with the apparently unsupportive or possibly abusive Shawn, which was proving difficult. My inability to do it so far was causing me to doubt my skills as a therapist.

She said, "Just as Monroe did with that man from the other world—he entered into his body and lived his life sometimes, I—"

"I did read that part," I said.

"Then you know that he was careful not to overstay and not to get the man into trouble."

"Yes."

"I did the same, as best I could. Though this was different than Monroe's experience. The host body in his case was still a man, but in my situation, while the creature was female, it wasn't human. Nevertheless, once I got inside, I understood her language, I understood what she did and did not do, and why."

"You understood her culture then?"

"Pretty much," Erin said. "Being inside her mind, it was automatic."

"What was it like?"

She shook her head in wonder. "It would take days, even months to tell you and I am not going to pay the price of therapy to explain it to you, even if insurance covers half. Shawn doesn't even know I'm coming here. Anyway, this was a life, a world, a culture! They had their ways, some like ours but most very different."

Our time was up yet again. I didn't want it to be, but another patient was coming.

That evening, I consulted my own therapist. "The subject is paranormal. I believe her and I don't believe her," I told him.

"It's a pity we scientific types have to hide our esoteric interests," he said.

"Why do we?" I asked, though I knew perfectly well why. Professional reputation, grants, avoiding ridicule.

"I do wonder what happens next," he said.

"I have a somewhat dark feeling about that," I told him.

"How is your mother?" he asked.

"What can I say, Peter? I'm fifty-one and lonely. What life I have is rushing by. She is eighty-five and apparently planning to live forever. I can't afford to put her in a home."

"I have been checking around for you, Dana. But like you say, they are out of your price range. At least you have the Ukrainian woman during the day."

"Illegal though she is," I said, before rising to go.

Three days later, I saw on the news that the body of a man was found sitting in the cab of his semi-trailer truck on a side street in St. Louis, Missouri. The man was identified as thirty-four-year-old Shawn Crowell of Montblue, PA, cause of death unknown. "An investigation will follow," said the newscaster.

Would Erin cancel her Friday appointment? Would I never hear from her again or would I get a call from her in police custody? Wait, why on earth was I assuming she did it?

But on Friday she walked in as usual, giving no indication by body language that she was anxious, frightened, or upset. On the contrary, there was a gleam of glee in her eyes. She seated herself on the couch as usual and settled in comfortably against the pillows.

"What's new?" I said, playing dumb.

She scratched her arm, and said, "Shawn's dead."

"Really?" I said.

"Yeah. They found his body in St. Louis. Sitting in his truck on some street or other. I don't know the city and don't know what he was doing when he died."

"Are you okay?" I ventured.

She smiled. "Oh. Yeah. More than okay."

"Would you care to elaborate?"

"What's between us can't leave here, right?"

I hesitated. "Doctor client privilege, yeah. There can be exceptions though. Like if you're a serial killer and about to do your next victim."

"I'm not," she said. "Though I am a regular killer."

My heart leaped.

"I killed him. With a little help from some friends."

This would be my first patient to confess such a thing. That didn't mean that no one killed anyone, just no one had confessed. "Do you mean you hired a hit man?"

She chuckled. "Not one from this reality, no."

Hmmm. "Exactly how do the police say Shawn died?"

She smiled. "They can't find any reason. There he was, nine hundred miles from where I was with witnesses. I was staying overnight with my sister and was with family hours before and after the declared time of death. Not a mark on him. Pathologist guesses heart or aneurysm but they're doing an autopsy. They won't find poison or anything criminal, unless he was taking drugs and he might have been, but that wouldn't have anything to do with me."

My heart was threatening to jump out of my chest. I kept thinking of my earlier jokey question about her having a body in the trunk.

"What do you think they'll find at the autopsy, Erin?" I asked, rather shakily.

She shrugged. "Nothing relating to murder. Who knows? He might have a tumor the size of a golf ball in his brain. He might have an artery about to blow. Doesn't matter."

I let a long silence ensue and finally said, "You wanted him dead?"

"You bet. After his last episode when he locked me in the spare bedroom and wouldn't let me out to pee for twenty-eight hours, yeah. Finally had to do it in a wooden box and got it all over my hands. No way to wash. The window was too high to climb out. I won't describe where I took a dump. And being hungry isn't fun either."

"Was that his normal behavior?"

"Oh, I could write a book, Dr. Torres. That scene was just the tip of the iceberg."

"Why didn't you just leave him?"

"He had stuff on my father, enough to put him in prison. And he threatened to do things to my sister and her kids."

"Do you want to talk about it?"

"No. No need to now. He's gone. And he had life insurance, not a new policy either, so nothing looks suspicious. We both had policies. I'm surprised he didn't knock *me* off. But that would have left him with no one to torture."

She seemed amazingly serene.

"So . . . how *did* you do it?"

"The only good thing about Shawn," she said, "was that he was away a lot so I could go out-of-body as much as I could. I visited the Ring a lot. I was careful, like Monroe, not to mess up my host body's life. The Yeelah, as they called themselves, at least in the part of the Ring I visited, were different from humans though, in that they could consciously tolerate a soul visitor. They are a very unafraid people. Also, they're aware of their spiritual part in a way that most people here are not. For instance, they know how to leave their bodies from birth. They know how to make a conscious death and, well, a few of them also know how to . . . how can I put this . . . detach the soul from another's body."

"Oh!" I said.

"This isn't something that is generally accepted there, don't get me wrong. It just happened that the mother of the body I visited was what here you'd call a shaman and she knew. Parents and their children sometimes do a kind of mind meld to share information and I was present during one of these. It was a secret, but I just happened to be in the right place at the right time."

Of course, I understood and the strange thing was that I felt no judgment towards her.

"Will you be all right?" I asked, meaning would she suffer horribly from guilt.

She knew what I was driving at. "I'll be fine," she said. "Sometimes a Yeelah has to do what a Yeelah has to do."

"Would Shawn's soul know what had happened? Can he hurt you in anyway, like in your future out of body travels?"

"Oh, he'll know. Can he hurt me? Well, I have learned other Yeelah ways to protect myself, in addition to my own *street smarts* on the astral plane, but I doubt he'd waste time trying that. He'll be too busy going over his mistakes in this recent life."

It was the last time I saw her. Online, I kept up on any news about Shawn or Erin Crowell and none, other than a normal obituary for Shawn, ever appeared, albeit one without a mentioned cause of death. No one went to prison; no lurid articles appeared in local or online St. Louis papers.

I returned Robert Monroe's books to the library and ordered my own copies from Amazon. They sit on my nightstand and I stare at them, while my demented mother calls from her room, and wonder if I dared to venture out, could I too find the Ring?

Margaret Karmazin's credits include stories published in literary and sci-fi magazines, including Rosebud, North Atlantic Review, Mobius, Confrontation, Pennsylvania Review, The Speculative Edge, and Another Realm. Her stories in The MacGuffin, Eureka Literary Magazine, Licking River Review, and Mobius were nominated for Pushcart awards. Her story, "The Manly Thing," was nominated for the 2010 Million Writers Award. She has stories included in many sci-fi anthologies. She has also published a YA novel, Replacing Fiona, a children's book, Flick-Flick & Dreamer and a collection of short stories, Risk.

Kendry McKendry, an officer in a trans-dimensional exploration agency, has a genetic talent for rifting into alternate realities. The problem is, he's never used his talent, and opening up the potential in a young rifter is a mysterious process around the agency and reputedly very unpleasant. He's about to find out.

I, Candy

Jonathan Shipley

Kendry McKendry paused at the glowing doorway, then stepped through. Electricity prickled unpleasantly against his skin and subsided. *So what am I wearing this time?* he wondered and gave himself a quick inspection. Business suit, shirt, and tie—but the bare feet seemed out of place.

He walked quickly to the opposite side of the small room—he hated small spaces—where another doorway awaited. Same prickling sensation. Looking down, he grimaced. Ballet tutu—seriously? Had to be some engineer's idea of a joke. He hurried to the next doorway, which reclothed him in leather samurai armor. The next studentfied him with jeans and a polo, and the final one gave him a priest's cassock. Then he exited the sequenced chambers and found himself in the lab wearing the same metal-embedded chameleon wetsuit he had started with.

"Any glitches?" Tina asked, coming up and checking the suit with a hand sensor. She was tech in charge of his prep tests and one of his few friends in the TransCorps complex. He was glad for a familiar face as things ramped up toward weird.

"Mostly fine, but bare feet in the first sequence," Kendry reported. "But a tutu? Was that someone's idea of a joke?"

She gave a laugh. "Probably. You know Ishi and his crew. They were told to include something unexpected to prime you for possible surprises. Letting the suit pick what's appropriate opens the door to all sort of weirdness. I would not be surprised to learn that the tutu was an actual manifestation from someone's jump scenario. A lot of strange realities out there, and the ones that seem the most normal on the surface are often weird under the skin. You have to be ready for any of them."

"I was born ready," he reminded her.

She rolled her eyes. "Right, the great rifter heritage of those genetically engineered to be perfect."

"Not true," he protested. "If I were perfect, I'd be taller and more chiseled and a little less heavy in the hips."

"You look fine, and I should know," Tina shot back. They'd been two legs of a love-triad back in academy, so she really had seen all. "And the boy-next-door look works better than tall and chiseled in the real world."

"In some worlds, maybe," he admitted. "Just saying that genetic engineering could have turned out a really superior product—"

"—befitting Crown Prince Candy. Just when you seem nice and normative, you have to turn into *that* guy. Next thing you know, you'll be completely loony like every other rifter."

"You really think I'll go neurotic the moment I start jumping realities?" he challenged. "That's an old wives' tale."

"It does happen," she shrugged. "Well, enough for today. Tomorrow you have an inquest to impress, so take some time off and relax. It's the normative thing to do," she added when he started to object.

And that settled that. Kendry swapped out the wetsuit for his regular uniform and left quickly down the glass-walled corridor before he said too much. He really wasn't worried about his inquest because of what he was. But he suspected saying that would make him sound like a crown prince among the peasants . . . again. Crown Prince Candy was the unflattering nickname he'd picked up in academy for saying things like that. He was fairly sure TransCorps had assigned him to a love-triad back then so there would be two other cadets close enough to tell him to shut up and act more normative. Great potential but socially awkward—the two great truths of being engineered in a lab.

He paused at a curve in the corridor where the glass opened into a comfortable observation lounge overlooking the Reclamation Valley where a hundred species of flora from a hundred worlds were being tested for hardiness in the unfriendly, post-Cataclysm environment. The fact that people spent as little time as possible outside the protective walls of the complex was proof of unfriendliness, though it was supposedly fine in small doses. Tina had grown up in a smaller complex to the north where tech was everything; other cadets had come in from various other complexes. Kendry himself knew nothing but the huge under-mountain sprawl of TransCorps headquarters. Here was where he'd been decanted fully grown from a pod five years ago and he'd been playing catch-up ever since.

There was always something dismal about being surrounded by normatives when he really wasn't being one, but lately he had started to dread his "great rifter heritage" as he got closer to First Jump between realities. All he had was the common gossip about what would happen when he started rifting—turning neurotic, going through a second puberty . . . when he was barely through his accelerated first one. It would have helped to have someone from the other side, an experienced rifter, talk him through it, but as a group, his kind seemed to be self-centered assholes who couldn't be bothered. Or so he'd heard. He hadn't actually met a real rifter. They seemed to be rare animals.

So here he was, about to step over the threshold and become a whole new person. So, no, impressing his evaluation inquest wasn't really a big deal. But the coming change terrified him. Maybe a better path would be *not* impressing the inquest and earning a reprieve from plunging into the unknown, except he didn't believe that. He felt ready. Maybe not happy, but ready.

As he turned down the dorm wing of the complex, another training officer fell into step beside him. "Big day tomorrow, eh—oops, that's the broody Candy expression all over your face."

"And I look forward to the end of that ridiculous nickname when I'm promoted to field-lieutenant," Kendry snorted back at Serge. It *was* a ridiculous nickname—Candy, Kendry—but no big deal. Tina used it to warn him, but

Serge, the last member of their academy love-triad, just liked to tease. If he had it to do over again, Kendry would keep the friends but skip the sex, even though sex seemed to be an important normative ritual. Frankly, he didn't get it.

"So what are they going to have you do?" Serge persisted. "Rift around the room?"

"Parlor tricks? Doubt it. I'm not opened up, so I can't do anything yet. And supposedly it doesn't work like that anyway. To rift across the room, I'd still have to rift to a different reality, then rift back with a slight locational variance—"

Serge gave a conspicuous yawn.

"Jerk," Kendry muttered.

"Freak," Serge shot back, then, "Hungry? Cafeteria's still open. And no one's there at this hour," he added before Kendry could refuse.

"OK, then." It was classic rifter claustrophobia to hate crowds and small spaces. Big, empty spaces, on the other hand, appealed enormously. Something about being attuned to the Void between realities. Normatives never understood that. Not really.

"And if you go off tomorrow and never return," Serge continued, "you know I'll come after you as soon as I get certified to jump."

"That's just clingy," Kendry pointed out. "And probably useless as well. Jumping via device is so much clumsier than rifting, you'd never find me."

Serge rolled his eyes. "Forget I said anything."

"Which I promptly will. This whole line of conversation is plain silly."

"To a freak maybe."

***

Kendry took a deep breath and entered the briefing room. He spotted the Colonel among the examiners and snapped off a salute. "Subtenant Kendry McKendry reporting, sir."

The Colonel looked up from an overly intense conversation with a grizzled older man in loose-fitting traveling grays. "At ease, McKendry," the Colonel said. "Take a seat, relax, and answer the questions in whatever way seems best to you. No pressure."

The first question was about TransCorps' organizational structure, so absolutely no pressure. As Kendry rattled off the answer, his eye wandered around the table. He recognized the chief staff psychologist among the pristinely uniformed officers, most of whom he'd had as instructors over the past year, and of course the Colonel, who was commander of the whole TransCorps complex. Then his gaze shifted to the old man beside the colonel, and he felt something akin to tension. Had to be a rifter. No one else would dare show up to a formal inquest looking like a vagabond. And he'd been arguing with the Colonel, which was unheard of. No one argued with the top of the food chain.

Kendry knew a lot was on the line professionally. If he was certified to jump, he'd have an immediate promotion to field-lieutenant, as well as freedom to go on actual missions. That was huge, but it paled against the prospect of an experienced rifter taking him through the change . . .

A question came his way from one of the instructors, and Kendry had to backtrack a second before producing the standard explanation for trans-reality parallelism. Parallel realities across an infinite number of possibilities created the opportunity to bridge other worlds by mimicking their vibrational frequencies.

"And why are there two very different methods of bridging worlds?" the instructor persisted. "And is one better than the other?"

That hit very close to home, and Kendry felt the weight of expectation from the examiners at the table. "Two methods," he began, "one technological, one biogenetic. Device-oriented jump mechanics is precise and dependable and capable of transferring cargo between worlds, but it can only follow a known path with known frequencies. Biogenetic rifting, however, allows for discovery of new worlds whose frequencies can then be fed back to the machines. Both methods are necessary to create a viable, sustainable program—"

"But if asteroids hit and TransCorps had to pick," the old rifter interrupted. "Should it save the jump matrix or the bio-pods?"

Asteroids? What? And the choice—it was an impossible choice. Kendry felt himself floundering.

The rifter gave a snort. "No pre-programmed answer this time. But if you can't think for yourself and make decisions, you're worthless. Answer the question, kid. Jump matrix or bio-pods?"

Now there was tension. Kendry recognized it wasn't just his own turmoil, but growing unease all around the table. "Jump matrix," he blurted out. "TransCorps has coordinates to over a hundred parallel realities, some of which have become important trading partners. We could survive without new discoveries, but not without our existing trade network." Then he tacked on a nervous, "Is that right?"

When the rifter sat back without answering, the Colonel cleared his throat. "There is no right answer, McKendry. It's a question that could be argued either way. The point was forcing you to make a decision under fire. Interesting that you chose tech over your own kind."

There was an unspoken world behind those words that Kendry couldn't follow. As the questions continued, it slowly dawned that this inquest was less about information and skills and more about psych evaluation. How much of a freak was the freak? And if he failed? He'd never considered that option before, but now he was morbidly curious what TransCorps did with failed rifters.

". . . and we stand adjourned with a positive consensus," the Colonel said. "Congratulations, *Lieutenant* McKendry. Stay for a private briefing."

Kendry warily resumed his seat as the others headed for the door. "Yes sir." But the Colonel also packed up and left.

That left the old rifter, the only one not packing up. Kendry felt a strange, panicky sensation in his stomach, which left him feeling lost and a little too normative. A little talk, rifter to rifter—it scared the hell out of him. Something about looking at the old rifter and knowing that was his future. Today he was starting down the path of becoming that grizzled old neurotic. "Sir?" he said politely when they were alone.

"Cut the military crap. It's just us crazies now. You come round the table and sit right in front of me where I can see your eyes at all times. Then I'll talk and you'll listen and sure, you'll have a ton of questions, but you'll keep your damn mouth shut because I don't care shit about your questions. Got that?"

Kendry nodded mutely. This was going to be bad. He came around the table and claimed a chair facing the rifter.

"Closer," the old man snapped.

Kendry pulled the chair a little closer.

"No, nose-to-nose close so I can see your eyes and everything behind them."

"I'd rather not be that close—" Kendry began.

"Shut your damn mouth and pull in. You don't get your druthers."

Kendry shut it and pulled closer. The knees were a problem—outside, inside—but he adjusted the best he could. It was heading way past uncomfortable toward downright creepy, but he knew there was no choice.

"Sex," the old rifter began. "Go ahead and jettison whatever you think you know about that, and I'll tell you how it really works."

***

Sitting head in his hands, alone in the conference room, Kendry felt something cold pressed against his hand. Raising his head, he saw Serge with an energy drink. He grabbed it and gulped it.

Serge shook his head. "Man, what happened here? You're shaking."

Kendry just shuddered. "It was bad."

"The inquest didn't approve—"

"No, they did. But then they left me alone with an old fart who explained the birds and the bees to me, rifter style—"

"I probably don't have the clearance to hear this," Serge interrupted.

Kendry nodded. "Kinda takes all the wind out of my First Jump."

"Which is when?"

"About five dozen donations to the sperm bank from now. Can't go anywhere until I contribute substantially to the breeding program."

Serge frowned. "I thought it was controlled genetic enhancement, not breeding."

"Well, we're all wrong about that. It's all breeding and rebreeding a few bloodlines with rifter potential. Lots of inbreeding, which is why rifters tend toward neurotic, and lots of fetus failures. Nothing is what I imagined, and it's going to take time to process. Don't expect much out of me for a while."

"Hold it together, jumpboy. Tina planned a surprise party tonight to celebrate your promotion."

"I can't—I hate parties," Kendry protested.

"And there's that Candy attitude again. But you're missing the point. If you hole up in your room right now, she's going to think you're already going neurotic."

"Maybe I am."

"Well, even if you are, you can pretend to be normal for one more night. For Tina's sake."

"There's not that much between us."

"Yeah, yeah. Not much between you and anybody, it seems. But pretend anyway."

Kendry nodded and finally heaved himself out of the chair. He might be an inbred, artificially engineered lab baby destined to be alone in the Void, but Serge was right. He could still pretend. And a party *had* to be more fun than his date with the sperm bank's devices.

***

Kendry was startled out of sleep by rough hands grabbing at him in the dark. The next moment he was plunged into a freezing, airless hell. Then onto a cold, pre-dawn rocky slope overlooking endless desert. He collapsed on his knees, gasping for oxygen.

Scuffed boots walked into his line of sight. He raised his head and glared at the old rifter from yesterday's inquest. "Are you . . . trying to . . . kill me?" he wheezed in short bursts.

"Trying to keep you alive. Lesson one—always gulp in some air before crossing the Void. It's got to be instinctive, like diving underwater with enough air to reach the surface again. Lesson Two—"

"I was sleeping, damn you! How can I gulp air when—"

"Shut your mouth and listen. If I have to tell you that again, I'm out of here and you can find your own way home."

That shut Kendry up. He knew he'd just been rifted from TransCorps HQ to somewhere but had no idea where, let alone how to rift back. At that moment, he really hated the old man. But needed him.

"Lesson Two—the Void is cold. Only an idiot would cross it in his skivvies."

Kendry bristled but found the strength to keep his mouth shut. He already knew that. He was only in his underwear because he'd been dragged out of bed.

"Lesson Three—always track your crossing 'cause that's your path home. Lose sight of it and you'll be years finding your way back. Lesson Four—you should have felt a quiver inside like flexing a never used muscle. Some people feel it the base of their skull, but more often it's in the gut. It's your propulsion system, but it's useless without a guidance system. That's visualizing across the Void. Jumping blind will land you in the middle of a mountain as likely as not, and you'll deserve what you get for not heeding me."

Kendry shuddered. Every rifter's nightmare—jumping into a solid mass.

"But," the old rifter continued with a sly look, "there's a moment of grace normatives don't know about. When you feel the mountain closing around you, you have a split-second to grab the Void again. Pray your jump instincts are honed enough before you need to try something like that. And always go for the greens and blues—those are the friendly worlds. The red are infernos, the blacks are frozen lumps, the yellows pretty much all desert. Hope you got all that."

Kendry saw the gloved hands coming at him and sucked in a gulp of air before he was in the freezing Void again. But this time, instead of panicking, he forced himself to watch everything. There was a moment of feeling suspended above an infinite string of enormous pulsing, colored bubbles, then plunging down toward a red one.

"Shit!" he yelled as his bare feet connected with sun-scorched rocks. This whole world was a burning hell. Instinctively, he squeezed with his gut and found himself among the colored globes again. One was bluish-yellow and familiar, so he focused on it. Half a second later, he popped out in the desert world again. He groaned and rolled to get his weight off the burned soles of his feet.

"Clumsy, but you're still alive," the old rifter nodded. "And that was all you on the return jump. I took us in, but you brought us back."

Really? Even with his burns, Kendry felt a surge of elation. He had actually rifted. So, he could go home . . . no, he hadn't been tracking on that first surprise jump. Hesitantly, he raised his hand for permission to speak.

The old man gave a snort. "You're a rifter now, Kendry McKendry—a really bad, inexperienced one, but still a rifter. You don't need to sit there mute like a naughty schoolboy."

A rifter. Kendry felt a grin spread across his face. "Then I have questions—"

"—that I don't have the patience to answer. I told you what not to do, and most of the rest you can figure out on your own. You might want to give yourself a few days before trying again. That new muscle is going to be plenty sore in the morning. And my last lesson to you is this"—he spread his arms to encompass the desert horizon—"Behold the world of TransCorps."

"But it's all wasteland," Kendry sputtered. The Cataclysm had compromised the surface, not destroyed it.

"Which nobody likes to talk about. All that reclamation they keep touting is just a drop of green in a big bucket of desert. And here's how it comes together—TransCorps is desperate to seek out new worlds because it needs new worlds to survive. And the assholes running TransCorps are the successors of the assholes that did this to the world. Never forget that. They need you more than you need them. And I'm out of here. HQ is right under your feet." He stomped his boot against the rocky slope. "Climb down the other side and follow Reclamation Valley back to the front door. And you'd be smart to walk and not try some fancy rifting you're not ready for. And better get started before the sun heats things up."

It sounded like good-bye, good riddance, but there followed an awkward silence where the rifter just stared at him. "Instead of HQ," he finally muttered, "you might just decide to head out and keep on going like some others have done. Know that it's your choice. Nobody's going to follow and bring you back. Just be sure what you want." And with a shrug, the old rifter collapsed into a thin line and vanished.

Kendry blinked, never having seen what that looked like, then replayed the last comment. It was a reference to going rogue, which was also part of rifter lore—go neurotic, go away, never return. But this had been presented as a choice, maybe even the lesser of two evils—he couldn't get a good read on the old rifter's attitude. But what stuck in Kendry's head was the rifter's "Nobody's going to follow and bring you back" juxtaposed against Serge's words from yesterday: "If you go off and never return, you know I'll come after you." It was an odd collision of worlds that he wasn't ready to deal with.

He forced himself to take stock of his immediate situation. He was on his own world—good. He had a long walk ahead—bad and very bad with burnt feet. Learning how to rift—super-good. Limping back to HQ—super-embarrassing. His mouth compressed into a tight frown. Or did he want to go somewhere else? The prospect hung before him, tantalizing. Then he shook his head with a snort. What kind of idiot went off to strange new worlds in his underwear?

With a groan, he made a start down to the valley and HQ.

***

Kendry was startled out of sleep by hands grabbing at him in the dark. "Wha—" he gasped and instinctively gulped for air.

"It's just a wake-up call, silly," Tina said from across the room, turning up the lights with one hand while holding a soup bowl in the other. Serge was the one shaking him.

Kendry pushed Serge's hands away and sat up in bed. His feet were heavily bandaged, still a little painful. "What time is it?"

Serge shook his head and shifted over to make room for Tina and the soup. "Two days later than you think," he said. "You showed up at the entrance, underdressed and not terribly coherent, and basically collapsed on the floor. You've been sleeping ever since."

"And the Colonel's been on Cloud Nine," Tina added. "Something about so few rifters coming back." She pushed the soup bowl toward Kendry. "So, First Jump?"

He took a few spoonfuls of soup before answering. Between going rogue and going up in flame on some hell world, First Jump must take its toll. But he had survived and come back. What did that say about him? "Trial by fire First Jump," he finally answered. "Not pleasant. But yours truly is now open to the Void." He gave a sudden, uncontrollable yawn. "Two days and I'm still tired. Why did no one warn me how exhausting rifting is?"

"Because we didn't know," Serge offered.

Kendry snorted. "Not you. I mean the Colonel or someone like that."

"He probably doesn't know either," Tina said. "Half the High Command doesn't even jump, let alone rift, and goodness knows no rifter talks about it. The Colonel probably thought he was doing well to get you a gentle mentor for your First Jump."

Kendry gave a short laugh. "Who said the old fart was gentle? Sadistic is more like it."

"All relative," she shrugged. "Scuttlebutt says that he's gentler than the others. Interpret that as you will."

Kendry busied himself with the soup, not liking the interpretations he was coming up with. If the Void was full of neurotic, sadistic rifters, why would anyone want to join them? Or conversely, why would anyone want to stay back and work for military types who didn't understand the first thing about him? He couldn't answer either of those questions and really wanted a third option.

He finished the soup and set the bowl aside. "I've long suspected that the academy love-triad was a blatant attempt to anchor me to a normative life."

"Right," Serge nodded. "So the Void wouldn't suck you in and weird you out. Apparently the psychs try something like that with every potential rifter who comes up the ranks."

"You knew? None of it was . . . spontaneous?"

"In the beginning, it was because our psych profiles were a good match," Tina explained. "But somewhere in the process, you became not just a potential rifter, but *our* potential rifter." She smiled. "That part was spontaneous. Apparently all previous attempts fizzled out pretty quickly."

"But we didn't even have enough to fizzle," Kendry pointed out glumly. "There was never that much between us."

That got an unexpected laugh from both of them. "Such a Candy remark," Tina grinned. "And it's all relative anyway. As rifters go, you're downright cuddly."

"But—"

"Think of the old fart," Serge added. "Compare yourself to him."

Kendry grimaced. He strongly preferred not to. But maybe that was the point—he found normatives a helluva lot better company than his own kind. And maybe TransCorps was run by stiff-collared military types who knew nothing about rifting, but maybe they'd give him wiggle room if he demanded it. No, they *would* give him wiggle room because they needed him. He could carve out his own future, a middle ground between one extreme and the other.

He looked at the empty soup bowl again and found it strangely reassuring. A reminder that life was more than just rifting. "I'll find a way," he said softly, more to himself than anyone else. "Not neurotic, not rogue, not military zombie."

"What are you saying?" Tina asked.

"Just reminding myself not to get lost or I'll have some idiot jumping all over the universe looking for me."

"True that," Serge nodded. "Unless we're talking about Crown Prince Candy who is definitely not worth looking for."

"Jerk."

"Freak."

Kendry lay back with a grin. So normative and so silly, but so comfortable. And he didn't need to let go of that just because he could rift. Exploring new worlds, yes, but forget the military types and forget the other rifters. They weren't the ones bringing him soup in bed.

Jonathan Shipley writes short stories and novels in a vast story arc ranging from Nazi occultism to vampires to futuristic space opera. He is an active member of Science Fiction Writers of America and was a contribuitng author to the After Death anthology that won the 2014 Bram Stoker Award. Over six dozen of his short fiction works have appeared in anthologies and magazines, and a full list of publications can be found at www.shipleyscifi.com.

Serge and Nancy Doucet enjoy the peace and solitude of their small holding in Fortuna's outback. When Nancy takes off for a few days to visit her mother in Homeport, Serge looks forward to time on his own. Yet, as he's about to discover, the dunes of their adopted planet harbor some surprises.

Road Trip

Lisa Timpf

"You're sure you don't want to come with me?" Nancy Doucet stood at the habi-dome's entrance, her tan-colored travel bag slung over her right shoulder. "Last chance."

"I'd love to," her husband Serge replied, leaning over to kiss her cheek. "But I have work to do here. Besides, you know I hate riding the jump-jet. Something that big just shouldn't be able to fly."

Nancy laughed, her green eyes glinting. "And, you don't like crowds. I get it." She paused, as though considering, then plunged ahead. "I left a list on the kitchen table. If you get a chance—"

The words hung suspended on the air between them. Serge managed, just barely, to avoid grimacing.

"I'll be back on Friday, okay?" Nancy checked her watch. "Got to go."

"Have a good time."

Serge watched the door close behind her and stood, as though rooted in place, until he heard the whine of the hover-car's engine recede in the distance.

The instant he could no longer hear the car, he felt a pang of regret. He *could* have gone. The crops would look after themselves for five days.

But spending that much time with his mother-in-law—he shook his head. No, he was better off here.

He walked over to the kitchen table to consult Nancy's list and groaned. These days, he felt so tired sometimes it was an effort just to tend to the test plot, let alone look after the hundred and one tasks his wife dreamed up.

Then he brightened. He had five days to get to the list. No rush.

***

After a shower, Serge felt marginally better. *Time to tackle the fields.*

Well, maybe he'd take the long way, through the dunes.

He pulled on his steel-tough, ankle-high boots and wandered to the spot that had become his favorite wildlife-viewing post. Serge couldn't help feeling a pang of disappointment when he saw the grey-brown dunes stretching away, seemingly empty of native fauna. *Patience*, Serge told himself. He settled into position beside the force-fence and gazed out over the slightly undulating land, with its moisture-conserving cactus-like plant life scattered here and there.

And then, the creatures Serge had dubbed the "dune squirrels" appeared.

Meerkat-sized, sinuous as weasels, and possessing a striped tail as bushy as a squirrel's, the creatures stood on their hind legs, their forepaws dangling in front of their cream-colored bellies. The two larger creatures sniffed the air and stared in Serge's direction. *They ought to recognize me,* Serge thought. *I've watched them, often enough.*

Having decided Serge meant them no harm, the larger of the two adult animals dropped down to all fours and squeaked at the five smaller creatures that Serge took to be their kits.

The youngsters commenced a spirited game that involved play-wrestling and chasing, cavorting among the dunes with their striped tails trailing behind them. One of the adults remained on watch, standing on its hind legs, while the other observed the kits with an indulgent expression.

Serge couldn't help laughing at the youngsters' antics.

No-one's reported these animals before, he thought. *I wonder why?*

He shrugged. Fortuna had been settled for only a dozen years. He'd venture a guess that there remained plenty yet to be learned about the desert planet.

Serge glanced at the sun and frowned.

Time somehow seemed to slip away on him when he was watching the dune squirrels.

"I'll be back," he said, rising to his feet reluctantly and brushing the sand off the seat of his pants.

As he left, seven sets of beady eyes observed his departure.

***

Nancy Doucet accepted the plas-sheet with the day's news from the jump-jet's smiling steward.

She frowned when she read the first heading. Rioting in Central City. Good thing her mother lived in Homeport, although there was no saying unrest wouldn't reach there, too.

Maybe, as Serge said, it was a good thing they lived in the outback. Of course, Serge's job as a government-employed researcher investigating crop yields required living outside the settlements.

Still, if he didn't pull up his socks, there was a chance he'd lose the contract. She'd been out to the fields a couple of days ago. What she saw made her wonder whether he was working on growing weeds or vegetables. Nancy couldn't imagine that his employers would be pleased. She sighed.

She had no clue what had gotten into Serge lately, but it was a chore getting him to do anything. He seemed to have lost his motivation. *He should have come with me, taken a break,* she thought, running her right hand through her short hair. *I could have helped him catch up, when we got back.* She shrugged. Well, he hadn't come, had he? Still, when she got home, they'd have to have a talk. She wasn't looking forward to it.

***

On Tuesday morning, Serge awoke early.

He'd been looking forward to his free time, but now the empty habi-dome felt lonely. He'd almost welcome Nancy's nagging.

Almost.

He gazed around the kitchen as he drank his first coffee of the day, and saw the list on the table. He sauntered over and picked it up, feeling a surge of weariness even though he'd only climbed out of bed a short time ago.

Serge grimaced and reached for his jacket. *I'll just stop by the dunes on the way to the test plot,* he thought.

When he reached the spot where he normally found the dune squirrels, he sat on the ground, clasping his arms around his knees as he scanned the area in front of him.

All he saw was a sun-lizard, a grey-green creature that measured, tail included, about the length of his forearm. He smiled. Not as much fun to watch as the dune squirrels, but the lizard provided entertainment in its own right, especially if you were lucky enough to observe it capturing one of the large day-moths with a whip-like action of its long, skinny tongue.

But the lizard stood stock-still, as though mesmerized.

Serge followed the direction of the lizard's gaze and grunted in surprise.

There stood the two adult dune squirrels. They'd initially escaped his notice because their coats blended perfectly with the color of the sand.

The dune squirrels seemed to be engaged in a silent duel with the lizard.

Serge rose to his feet. He shouldn't interfere, but he couldn't bear the thought of the kits being harmed. *Strange, though. I thought the lizards only ate insects.*

The smaller of the adult dune squirrels chittered, and two of the youngsters advanced on the lizard. As they approached, the lizard remained motionless. Surely, it must notice them, Serge told himself. If it did, it seemed incapable of stirring to either defend itself or retreat—though it must realize the dune squirrels had it outnumbered.

Mesmerized himself, Serge watched as the two kits dispatched the lizard, one biting behind the reptile's head and the other getting a grip on the soft skin under the neck. When the rest of the family moved in to join the feasting, he rose to his feet, feeling a sudden revulsion.

***

When he headed back to the habi-dome just before sunset, Serge felt a glow of satisfaction. He'd gotten a lot done, today! Though how he'd let the test plot get so overgrown—

His hands shook as he grabbed two Sustain bars out of the cupboard and sank down on the couch. *I can't let things get out of hand like that, again,* he told himself. *If I lose the contract, we'll have to move into the city.* Serge fought off a surge of nausea.

Best to take your mind off it, he thought, flipping on the entertainment unit to play the holotape of the hockey finals he'd ordered months ago. Since Nancy despised hockey, he'd waited for an opportunity such as this one to watch the replay.

Exhausted from the day's exertions, Serge fell asleep half-way through the first game. When he roused himself, much later, the habi-dome was pitch-dark. Even the entertainment unit had turned itself off. So, the energy-saving auto-shutoff triggered by the motion detector really worked! It'd been Nancy's idea to install it. He didn't have a head for mechanical tasks.

Serge waved his arms to trigger the motion sensor for the lights, noticing just before they came up that there was a red light blinking on the control panel. *Sat-receiver offline again. Must have been the wind.* Serge sighed.

Nobody'll phone me anyway. Though advertised to be able to auto-correct, the sat-receiver had been designed by engineers not familiar with the severity of Fortuna's capricious winds.

He hated the manual repair job—Nancy did it much better than him. *It'll wait till tomorrow,* he told himself, yawning.

***

Wednesday morning, in her mother's house in Homeport, Nancy toggled the radio on as she wandered in the kitchen.

"Do you really need to listen to that stuff?" Yvette Nadon asked as she poured a cup of coffee for her daughter. "Just like on Earth, it's seldom good, the news."

"There's something—strange going on, back home," Nancy replied defensively.

Yvette shrugged and resumed her perusal of her book.

"—and in other news, the Galactic Space Service reports that the body of Vido Aubin has been found." Nancy and Yvette exchanged glances.

"The GSS has issued a warning to all colonists and visitors on Fortuna, to be aware of a type of native animal that resembles a cross between a meerkat and a weasel, with a striped, squirrel-like tail. The creatures are reportedly dangerous. Avoid contact at all costs. If you see one of these animals, please alert the local Wildlife Containment Task Force. The GSS does report that the force fences appear effective at deterring the animals—"

"You have a force fence, right?" Yvette asked.

"Yes, of course," Nancy said, as though talking to herself. *Serge would have no reason to go outside the fence. And he shouldn't find them in the test plot—but what if they can tunnel? Or the fence gives out—*

Feeling a clutching sensation in her chest, Nancy dialed their home number. Despite her efforts at reassuring herself, she'd feel more comfortable if she could talk to Serge. *Pick up!* she mumbled into the phone. *Only static. Dammit. The sat-receiver must have gone offline.*

"Serge will be fine," Yvette said reassuringly.

If only I could be sure of that, Nancy thought. "I need to get home," she said, rising to her feet.

"But you're supposed to stay two more days," Yvette protested. "I wanted you to—"

"Mom. I need to go." Nancy ordered a ticket on the jump-jet, packed, and headed out the door, doing her best to ignore the stream of protests from her mother.

If I nag Serge half as much as she nags me, Nancy thought, gritting her teeth, *I owe him an apology.*

If he's still there when I get home. Weighed down by a sense of foreboding, Nancy tried to reassure herself. *He'll be fine,* she told herself. *He'll be fine.*

***

By the time Nancy lowered the hover-car onto the parking pad, the western horizon glowed purple-pink. She stopped to admire the sunset for a moment, feeling the weariness that weighted every muscle.

She stepped through the door of the habi-dome. "Serge?" she said anxiously.

"You're early." His voice sounded accusatory.

"You let the sat-receiver get off track," she said, not meaning to snap at him but unable to keep the irritation from her voice. "There's something I needed to tell you." She let her gaze sweep through the kitchen, noting the Sustain wrappers that hadn't made it into the compost. *The clock's still not hung back in its place,* she thought. *And I'll bet, if I checked the rest of the list, I'd find—*

Serge noticed where her glance had gone, and blushed. "The test plot. I was busy—"

"And you couldn't take the time to do one simple thing?"

"You're early. I thought I had time."

"You're leaving everything to the last minute again?"

"I have to check on something," Serge replied. She watched as he shouldered into his lightweight jacket and headed out the door.

Not the way I envisioned it at all, she thought.

She sighed and carried her travel bag to the bedroom. Maybe a sauna session would make her feel better. She grabbed a towel and headed for the back door and the sauna shed.

***

Annoyed with himself for his procrastination, and angry at Nancy for her sharp words, Serge wandered aimlessly at first. He found himself at his usual spot overlooking the dunes. No sign of the creatures. He shrugged. Perhaps that was just as well.

He followed the force fence, not yet ready to return to the habi-dome.

As he walked, Fortuna's twin moons rose higher in the sky. Their light seemed to soften the terrain, lending it a dream-like quality.

Serge felt the tension and anger ebbing away. Near gate D-4, he heard a soft churring, and stopped, scanning the area past the force fence to seek the source.

There stood another family of the dune squirrels—two adults and three kits, this time. All of them stood on their hind legs, gazing in his direction.

Serge watched the little family for several minutes. One of the youngsters pounced on a fire-moth and consumed it with great relish. *Perhaps,* he thought, *that's what they normally eat.* He shrugged. He knew so little about the creatures.

Had the dune squirrels been pets for the past inhabitants of Fortuna? They seemed charming enough to have played such a role. The moonlight made their fur look plushy. He'd love to run his fingers through one of the kits' glossy pelts, see if it felt as soft as it looked. Who knows, maybe they could be tamed. Sure, the colonists had brought dog embryos in frozen state.

But just last year the ruling council had determined that it wasn't time yet, to decant the pets. In fact, Council had decreed they were years, maybe decades, from being able to afford the luxury of pets, with their additional strain on food and other resources.

But the dune squirrels–clearly, they could look after themselves. *I wonder,* Serge thought.

When he reached gate D-4, Serge hit the manual override on the force fence. He opened the gate and gestured. The animals just stared at him.

Well. It seemed like that had some latent wariness. Perhaps Fortuna's previous inhabitants had been less than kind to them. No reason we can't be friends, he thought, easing through the gate and squatting on the ground, snapping his fingers at the nearest of the kits to draw its attention.

***

Nancy emerged from the sauna feeling refreshed. *If only I hadn't snapped at Serge. I need to get to the bottom of what's bothering him, and yelling at him won't help.* She sighed and reached for her tool belt. She'd go and fix the sat-receiver herself—she'd always been better at that than him, anyway, more patient. In a way, she could understand his reluctance to tackle it—it usually took him a good half-hour to get it right, and he'd often suffer at least one, sometimes two, bruised knuckles in the process.

As she pulled on her soft-soled ankle-high boots, she frowned at the control panel. That red light—she felt certain it hadn't been blinking when she got home. She moved closer. Manual override at Gate D-4.

Nancy stood for a moment as the implications sunk in. Then she reached for the keys to the hover-car, feeling her heart hammering in her chest.

When she arrived at Gate D-4 and glanced into the dunes beyond the gate, she felt her breath catch in her throat. Softened by the moonlight, the tableau might have been beautiful had she not known what she knew.

She saw the adult dune squirrels standing on their hind legs, bathed in the moon's soft luminance. Two—no, make that three—smaller animals, kits maybe, climbed on Serge, their claws catching in his clothing as he sat perfectly still, so as not to scare them. One of the kits took up a perch on his shoulder, its whiskers tickling his neck, while another sat on his arm, its muzzle at his left wrist.

"Serge?" she whispered. He continued to stare straight ahead, as though he hadn't heard. "Serge!" Nancy raised her voice. Still, he didn't move.

Or can't move.

With a snarl, Nancy grabbed the small hand-held laser cutter from her tool belt and fired a force-shot past the adult creatures. They jerked their heads in surprise, and Serge stirred, as though rising out of a trance.

"G'wan, get!" Nancy yelled, taking a step forward, stomping hard on the ground with her booted foot.

The nearest of the adults swivelled toward her, its beady eyes fixed on her face.

"I'm not falling for it," Nancy said, careful not to make eye contact. Despite that, she felt a pull, a draw, a compulsion, almost. "I can give you another shot of this, if you want." She gestured with the weapon.

The animal dropped to all fours and squeaked at its companions. The kits scrambled down Serge's body and dropped to the ground, following the adults into the dunes. When they were fifteen feet away, their fur seemed to blend into the sand, and the dim radiance of the moon made them impossible to distinguish.

Serge blinked, staring at Nancy, then looking at the open gate with a frown.

"How did I get out here?" he asked.

"I think I know," she said, her voice gentle. "Come on, let's get back to the house, and I'll tell you what I know."

***

In the kitchen, Serge sat with his head in his hands.

"You mean, they mesmerize their prey?" His voice conveyed his incredulity.

"That's what the Galactic Space Service says," Nancy replied. She paused. "How long have you been watching them?"

"Since two weeks before you left," Serge said, grimacing. "They became an obsession, and I didn't realize it."

"So all the time I nagged you about unfinished tasks, maybe this was the cause."

Serge nodded. "Even the test plot—I almost let the weeds get out of hand. My job—I could have lost it."

"You could have lost more than that."

"I know," Serge whispered.

"Look—no more secrets, okay?" Nancy said.

"Agreed," Serge said with a shudder. He lowered his head. "Look, this doesn't mean you want to move to the city, does it? I mean, I'm sure your mother—"

"She worked me over, yes," Nancy said. "In fact, I think that may have been her sole purpose in inviting me to visit." Nancy moved closer to the window to look out onto the moonlit vista. She turned back to face Serge. "But I love it here as much as you do. I can easily continue to do my transcript translation out here."

"Good," he said. "Because once I got back to working the test plot, I made an interesting discovery. Want to hear about it?"

"Sure," Nancy replied. "Over a glass of wine. Deal?"

"Deal."

Lisa Timpf is a retired HR and communications professional who lives in Simcoe, Ontario, Canada. She enjoys bird-watching, hiking, bicycling, and organic gardening. Timpf's writing has appeared in a variety of venues, including **New Myths, Third Flatiron, Thema,** *and the* **Dogs of War** *anthology.*

This story was nominated for the 2017 Canopus Award, given to works that "enhance the . . . excitement and knowledge of interstellar space exploration," and named after the 2nd brightest star in the sky—a major navigation point for travelers throughout history. A different kind of exploration is imagined here.

Sleeping Westward

Lorraine Schein

She was sleeping westward. Westward. Sleeping westward, she falls through the Doors of the sky. Falling, falling, a woman on fire. Or at least something like a woman, a creature whose essence was nearest to that of a woman.

Falling. The stars white and red streaks, blurring violently into each other. Everything pulsing past her, as if caught in the beat of an enormous heart. Her head was an unstoppable comet, her hair its fiery rays. There was only one destination for her to search, one place to seek among the galaxies. It lay westward.

(They had prepared her carefully, long ago, in the Women's Lab at the space scaffold that hung in Star Fractal 3. The trance state was induced—the Black Door, the first of all Doors, revealed. Aphry had raised her hand feebly in answer to their repeated question: "Do you see it ... the Black Door?" as they waited for her reply.)

Then they dressed her in a fine mesh cocoon suit and finished the surgical alteration of her hands, which gleamed silver with micro-circuitry, rudder-like in shape.

Eyes still chemically sealed shut, they had led her outside to the cold, high platform that jutted out over the endless chasm of stars cascading below, with no net beneath but deep space itself to catch her. They placed her hands in the ritualistic preparatory position, almost clasped, but still open, ready to steer.

And the Women sang the song in soft voices, standing by her side, the song becoming a ceaseless chant. "Bring us back a memory of what is to be, bring us back a memory of our true destiny."

Then with the enormity of nothingness smoldering before and around her, they surged forward and pushed her off, watching her slow weightless fall, past Andromeda, past Cassiopeia, past all constellations that ever were, and yet to be, past the past, past time itself, past the dream under all dreams, endless unto all.

The first one to sleep westward had been launched; the first hypnonaut sent to deep hyperspace, sent to discover the fate of the universe, as it hurtled toward Vega at the speed of 12-1/2 miles per second.

Am I really in a black hole now? Aphry wondered. *As they told me I would be? In a black hole, you can move through space-time. That must be what she was gliding through—hypertime's uncharted reaches. But would I even be conscious of being in a black hole if this were one?*

Except that she could not remember where she came from, could not recall any place of origin except this rushing darkness, the root of all velocity she had become.

Moving through time as well as space. Free fall, of a kind science had just discovered, with the ability to control her course by navigating using her hands.

She smiled as she heard the landing instructions come at last, the voices saying like the wind, "Left. And decrease velocity now. Use your fingers to clear the way . . . a path . . ."

The stars and planets streaked past like cosmic blood. Then they all spoke at once, "Remember the future. Remember it as you go. For you are our best hope—it is for this all your training has been. Bring us back a memory of what is to be. For the future has already happened and only you . . ."

The voices faded off. She was approaching rapidly, able to glimpse the landing platform below. The wind followed her down from the sky as she landed, slashing a cold blast through the thin hypercocoon she wore. She shivered.

The sky on this planet was a still blue, and only one moon shone in it, a quiet crescent tucked into a high corner.

She touched down onto the platform, alone as always, gliding onto an empty spot where no one waited. Farther down, she could see strangers' faces, eagerly searching for glimpses of their families, lovers, or friends. But there was never anyone looking for her, none to greet and embrace her after her long journey. Only a cold wind for her travel companion, and the violent, swift sky that was by now her natural element.

To be the ultimate traveler. They had warned her of what it would be like. But she had chosen to go anyhow, and bear the solitude of each Fall and destination, in this lucid dream that was not a dream. For there was joy in the wild freedom of it, and the knowledge that she was chosen.

Each Fall was so different. Always the Door, whatever its Color, and through it the empty platform waiting below, and the cold blue sky, so different from the black tidal waves of hyperspace. Yet they connected, one a continuum of the other.

The Doors. The Silver Door, the Green Door, the Black Door, the Red. She feared the Red Door—though it was exciting, too. The Gate of Hell, its color intensified as she grew closer, its fires of blood coming into focus, emanating loud noises and a sickening stench.

Pieces of the conflicts of centuries, bombs, conflagrations, mass incinerations, the sound of steel swords scraping against each other, agonized screams, the sounds of innumerable wars blending together as if humanity had fought only one endless war against itself since the dawn of history.

But the Red Door was not the domain of Summer. Summer lay beyond the Gold Door: enticing, glowing up at her from its depths, heat radiating up patterns of sunlight, smelling of wild clover. And the Silver Door was the true realm of Winter.

She came to the end of the platform, strode off its ramp, and onto the huge glowing Voltairine Skyway to the bar. Tall spiral buildings stood on either side of her, casting twisted shadows through this planet's perpetual mists. A solar clock gave off its long high golden whine, the huge disc boldly sweeping across the heavens' empty mass like a hand passed over a weary face.

Aphry began to walk more quickly. Then she saw a building ahead and turned left at the corner, which led her off the skyway and onto a smaller road.

The Ectoplasmic Bar was a small, dingy polyhedron that stood at the end of a tangle of sidestreets of even shabbier multiform housing. The streets here, unlike most of this planet's major skyways, were angular instead of curved, dipping down into forty-five degree and sharper angles, then rising up into steep canyons formed by hills that doubled back upon themselves, their surface changing constantly as she walked.

They formed, and re-formed themselves, offering to the pedestrian ever new pathways, arcane dimly-lit corners, and odd skewed alleys that led nowhere, creating new hypotheses of day.

A screech of children raced past her, their small figures blurred by speed, straight up a vertical pathway that looked like a huge waterfall whose torrents were made of pure liquid light—thousands of subtle, flickering colors that swirled and streamed into each other. The liquid prism rainbowed whirling cascades of all the hues in the universe, finally tumbling in rushing circular currents to pool in the street below.

The children had reached the top—she could hear the remnants of their laughter ahead as she walked through its shifting midst.

She was almost at the bar now, her head still haloed with the falls' light. Then, as she neared the bottom, the lights grew fainter, dwindled to a trickle, until all that was left was the night and the small, angular building ahead of her, hunched like an animal in the dark.

She pushed open the worn, round door.

In a corner sat Harraghy, the dream thief, his long white hands like tapering leaves, thoughtfully fingering a tall glass of glowing amber liquid, his soft, milk-colored hair drifting in vague, baroque waves across his head and shoulders. And Syjpurnia, astral anarchist extraordinaire, who leapt wildly onto a table floating overhead, as she tried to outwit the house computer in a game of odds-and-odders.

And then behind her a silence. The silence of being. Aphry turned around.

"Hello," he said softly. "Hello, my dear."

She looked at him.

"Hello, Xerxes," she said.

His head looked like the head of a child, round as a crystal ball, the features delicately molded. He was a freelance presence; his life was risky and complex. He had to be in the right places at the right times, which required endless training and calculation. And the worst part was that he never knew why he was to be there, precisely what emotional or psychological effect was being sought that only he could produce in that nanosecond of time.

She knew he was danger to her very being. Of course, the dream thieves were dangerous, too—they could throw her off course, slit her trance with their sharp moment-renders, perforate hyperspace and drain the very continuum, so that she would fall through the wrong Door at the wrong time, or worse yet, find herself in an uncharted featureless area, devoid of even an event horizon . . . panicky, unable to think back, remember . . . not hear the voices calling, calling . . .

At least there were ways to defend herself. The spinnerets of her wrist pack took care of the dream thieves, providing protection. She could just touch one of the small, finely-etched triangles tattooed on the insides of her wrists, and the negatron time-skeins would flow from the tiny punctures below the surface of her skin. Liquid purple thin streams, rapidly solidifying as they hit the essencia of hyperspace, turning into long, infinitely fine time cilia. She would gather them up in her hand, aiming for the punctured rift sensed nearby, and watch the skeins flow into it, seal the gaping vacuum, then go on her way.

But a freelance presence was worse. There was no defense against their powers—or their eyes.

Greetings over, she moved towards a back table. But before she had gone two steps, Xerxes's left hand came forward, one finger lightly touched her earlobe, then languidly moved back, entwined in her hair like a comb.

And his other hand caught hers in a strong, clenched grip and threw her to the ground.

"You shouldn't have come here," he snarled.

She kicked, lashing out, and drove her punches into him. He fell under her onslaught; they grappled on the floor amid fallen chairs and tables as customers fled. She was on top of him, hair flying, her fists and legs thrashing wildly, strong blows landing on Xerxes' vulnerable body. He fought back feebly from under her. His eyes flashed green-gold in desperation, raying her face.

And then the moment lit up, and she fell through it.

The Door was rushing toward her at great speed, as if ascending. She fell through it, gasping and tumbling, clawing to position herself, the time wind whipping hyperspace around her.

She could not make out clearly the color of the Door yawning open, but dove toward it, slowing down as she approached. The familiar voices under the blowing gusts had returned but were muted.

"Too fast," they hissed around her head. "Anchor, anchor, try the skeins—you're going to crash, too fast . . ."

The essentia started to burn around her. Her worst fear. It began to throb in black, deformed patterns, layering into bent fractals, that returned in a slow snakelike movement, only to alter and displace once more. Darkness manifest, chaos made perceptible.

She tried to activate the spinnerets, but it was no use. She could see clearly now that the Door was Green.

It loomed up, with sounds of crashing waves and seabirds. The amalgam and Portal of all Springs. Verdant, lush. From when life began to bubble up from the green fiery sea, from even before, when life and Spring were just nascent potentials in the green, flame-like waves of the giant waters that shot up and covered all Earth, a burning sea-fire of water.

The spring of Maid Marion and Robin Hood in old England. Beltane of the pagans chanting in the deep forest, Maypoles tied with bright silken ribbons tangling in the clear sunlight like lovers' limbs entwined in the grass. English springs . . . English springs the best of all.

It was night in an English forest as she fell past the two new dim moons cast next to the old: one a shadowy remnant of a long-expired parallel universe; the other a nascent moon of a ninth-dimensional universe that could only be perceived from this one.

She navigated her way past this bright spectral triplicity, using only the strokes of her hands, cleaving a safe path through the summer sky.

The voices were fading to a whisper around her.

As she approached the treetops below, she saw a tall blonde man, pale-skinned yet muscular, rolling on the grass in a clearing between the trees, copulating with the woman under him. The sunlight shone on his thick tousled hair that reached well below his shoulders. His back was bare; both wore no clothes. A white robe lay tossed on the grass to one side of them.

The woman murmured something to him in a low voice. He laughed, then rolled away onto his back. The sky he looked up into was as clear and blue as his eyes. A stream gurgled a short distance from where he lay.

He rose and walked over to it, splashing the cool water onto his face and body. Ribbon-colored wildflowers stood at his feet. Then he walked back to the woman, who was now sitting up against a tree, picked up the white robe and put it on, pulling its large white hood up over his face, and tossed the smaller gray robe under it to her.

It was High Spring, with all its timelessness, the antipathy of all Springs to past and future. Only the present, the body and sunlight existed now. History had not begun its contamination yet; ancient wisdom was still respected here.

And then the voices came and reoriented her. "When is a woman outside of history? When she is under a spell? She is always under a spell. When she is by herself, she is no more than a shadow," they echoed.

Tree tops rose suddenly beneath her, gathered silhouettes of black branches. Aphry tried to slow her descent further; but it was no use—she was going too fast. The most she could hope for was to be able to swerve enough to miss them and cushion her fall with a spinneret net.

Turning sharply, she tried to activate the skeins, pressing at her wrists frantically. Nothing happened. The trees loomed under her now, menacing in the darkness. She crashed onto the ground away from them, in a clearing, behind some tall brambly bushes that gave off a fragrant smell.

She could hardly move. At first, she thought she had broken a bone. It was some time before she could drag herself up enough to sit, in spite of the aching pain.

Then she heard the voices. Fevered chanting of deep voices, many voices nearby. Aphry peered out cautiously through a gap in the bushes before her, parting the leaves.

There was only one moon now in the night sky, lone and clear. In its light stood a group of white-robed figures gathered in a circle. Some of them started to dance, joining hands around a drummer who stood in the center, pounding out a hypnotic tempo.

The others began to gather closer around him, dancing dreamily to its sound. The moon seemed to throb to the drum's rhythm, a white heart beating in the quiet sky above, its whiteness flaring like the bonfire she glimpsed in the group's center, pulsing at each beat of the drums, then fading.

She could glimpse the edge of a pond beyond the dancers. It gleamed dark at the edge of the forest clearing.

The drumbeat quickened. Faster, hurling into sound. She watched, transfixed. The bodies swirled together, joining hands, increasing speed until they became a blur of white-robed figures, hair whipping wildly, streaking the night air.

Aphry could not see the drummer anymore; the sound seemed to be coming from the forest itself. Then the dancers started to sing raucously, keening like animals.

All movement stopped. The beat halted, after a final surge, that left the night empty and hushed.

The circle parted to show the man and the woman from the stream. They had torn off their robes. He was nuzzling her breast, head down. Following their Archdruid's lead, the others stripped also, and lay clustered together on the grass. Cups of mead had fallen on the ground.

All heads turned. A large man covered in blue tattoos also stepped into the center of the circle, pulling a small figure after him, with powerful hands.

The small figure's head was thrown back, but not, she realized, in fear or struggle. He was still in ecstasy; still rapt by the music, but allowing himself to be led. An owl hooted overhead; thin branches rustled against the moon.

He fell. The firelight caught his face—it was Xerxes. So, he had brought them here.

The Archdruid paused for a moment, then turned around and seemed to gaze at her where she hid in the bushes. She froze in fear. But he was not looking at her. He called to a man who stood nearby, and barked a command.

The blue man came forward, draining his cup of mead, and threw it on the ground. He leaned down, putting his arms under Xerxes' shoulders as the Archdruid held his feet. Together they heaved him over the heavy lower branch of a massive oak tree.

The drummer began to play again; the Archdruid faced the circle and began a new chant, echoed by the others to the new rhythm. His voice filled the circle and set the forest quivering.

Then she heard Xerxes scream, and shuddered. The Archdruid had taken a silver dagger from the folds of his robe that glinted in the firelight. She leaned forward to watch more closely. The leaves rustled and swayed slightly before her.

A hand came over her mouth, and the next thing she knew, she was being dragged, still half-kneeling, out of her hiding place, across the grassy rough ground, and thrown violently at the Archdruid's feet.

"Look what I found watching us from the bushes," said the blue man. She lay sprawled before the Archdruid now, looking up in fear at the tall figure radiating power, face half-hidden by his hood.

His voice was as hard and cold as the dagger still in his hand as he seized her head by a handful of hair and pulled her sharply up to face him, saying, "Who dares interfere with our sacred rites? We will feed the earth with your blood, too," he cried.

A woman stood by his side. "Hold her," he ordered. Strong arms pinned hers behind her back—the strength of a warrior woman.

The Archdruid raised his dagger once more, and turned his attention back to Xerxes' prone body. She was close enough to see his eyes clearly, still open though his head was thrown back. The others in the circle began chanting again.

The dagger came down, blade flashing, in a single vehement stroke piercing his neck. The woman holding Aphry loosened her grip, her breath coming faster in excitement.

"Come take the augury of the blood, read its flow," called the Archdruid to her, the knife bloody in his hand. "And bring her with you—we shall honor Tarainis and Esus again with another offering to them." He joined in the chant.

"Bring us back a memory of what is to be . . ." Her voices, miraculously back, merged with his. There was now a chance to get out of here, back on her way to some safer Door away from Xerxes.

But she would have to get past him fast, for the only way back from an opened moment was through it again. She would have to chance it—chance his eyes. Hyperspace began to ascend around her, a dark translucent mask over her whole body, blotting out her surroundings.

"Careful, careful . . . past him, but don't look up . . . don't use your hands, you'll be accelerating too fast . . . careful, don't look . . ."

She started to descend, but the scene in front of her was still visible. She tucked her head down, rolled into a fetal position, hands out but closed. Soon she would be safe. The time wind began to blow—for once, she was glad of it.

Xerxes' face loomed up before her as she fell past him—enormous, mouth agape, as his life drained from him. But his eyes were wide, changing. There was no way to avoid them now. They halted her in mid-fall.

Tugged still, her sight could focus on him. Aphry watched in fascination as Xerxes' pupils started to blur and enlarge, each dividing into three. Then they slowly spread outwards, like drops of ink fallen onto tissue paper, until both eyes were completely filled, small black universes.

Yet as life seeped from his small body, the darkness subsided, too, reversing until both pupils had dwindled back to normal. But something new disturbed her about his eyes; a final residue of the transformation they had just undergone.

Suddenly she leaned forward, transfixed by his face. In the center of each of Xerxes' irises, where a normal rounded pupil should have reappeared, there was now instead a tiny black profile of pupil size, a miniature silhouette, like two perfect cameos.

And the profile was hers.

Shocked, Aphry swerved off course, falling swiftly over the pond now below.

A Black Door, first of all Doors, shimmered in the water, a wavering darkness on the surface. As she hit it and dove in splashing, she heard the Women's voices singing.

"She approaches now . . . Rejoice! . . . Bring us back a memory of our true destiny . . . she nears . . ." There was no need to navigate now.

Arms flailing, Aphry plummeted through the Black Door.

And fell into the violent birth of the universe, the portal over whose threshold flowed the maelstrom of time, eons upon eons, torrential, and from its source knew its destination and fate.

There were no voices here to guide her. Swept up into the moment of creation, she was also swept into the roaring spiral of its destruction. How would she be able to answer the Women now? And Aphry thought, as she merged with it, before her consciousness blotted out:

Sleeping westward, I fall through the doors of the sky. The time-wind howls around me always. All I ask is for the peace of the void, free from the torrents of time that pass by me like ghosts. But I am not haunted by them, for I know now that the universe is a lonely traveler, too, falling . . .

We are all sleeping westward.

Lorraine Schein is a New York writer. Her work has appeared in Gargoyle, Strange Horizons, Nonbinary Review, Enchanted Conversation, **and the anthologies** Gigantic Worlds, Drawn to Marvel, Aphrodite Terra, **and** Mosaics: An Anthology of Independent Women. **Her poetry book,** The Futurist's Mistress, **is available from mayapplepress.com.**

In the human colonization of the stars, contact with other races brings dangers and rewards. Sometimes, in the infinite possibilities of the alien experience, they can be the same thing.

The Alien Way

Mike Adamson

Jethryll Patallo had been out of town for months, and was looking forward to her first company furlough.

The spaceport city of Sardis, on the planet Susa, third out from the G-1 sun Shamash, was a busy, dirty sprawl on the arid north equatorial region, near the conflux of three seasonal rivers and a shrinking sea. Two hundred years had gone by since colonization and many asked why the human race had been so keen to settle such a dustbowl. Its asteroids and moons had profitable minerals but the planet itself had been more challenge than reward to those hardy enough to brave the venture.

BlueSky Trucking hired the best graduates from the local academy, and Jethryll had taken to the game. She had been restless in the years of her VR instruction, the long period of early adolescence when true learning was crammed into the years between childhood and productive life; but she had realized in the months she had spent flying the air routes on the powerful suborbital freight-haulers, that real learning was not facts and figures, languages, and aptitude, it was not mending broken things or punctuality. Real learning was wisdom, and it came hard.

Home was an apartment in the Skylance Tower that rose above the dusty thoroughfares of the residential quarter, and she remembered spending too many days at her window, watching the ships come and go, and wishing she could go with them, for the burning vistas of Sardis had limited appeal. She dreamed of worlds with deep blue oceans, and would immerse herself in virtual spaces where she could swim and glide. She knew a planet named Aquarius lay across the glittering starfields of night and longed to go there. One day, she had promised herself, when she was older.

But Sardis was home and she acknowledged a pang of nostalgia when she walked out of the BlueSky compound under the brassy sky and shouldered her pack, to catch a passing railbus around the outskirts of the city toward home. But as the craft topped a rise and glided down a long incline she saw far off an area that had haunted her thoughts all the while she was gone. *The Alien Quarter.*

She had made friends with difficulty in her younger days, and her fascination with the other planets out there among the stars had drawn her to the part of town where the denizens of many lived and did business. Her mother had not liked it, had told her she spent too little time with her own kind, and worried Jethryll was somehow under an influence wholly unnatural for humans. But the fascination was too strong, and as the girl grew into a woman she had learned more from her visits to her alien friends than it seemed she ever did from her studies.

As the railbus drew close to her home station she flipped up the screen of her wristy and tapped for home, ready for the familiar face of mother and brother, looking forward to dinner, to giving the gifts she had picked up in cities far across this scorched, dusty planet. But as she waited for the call to connect, her thoughts strayed uncontrollably to a dark and exotic warren on the other side of town, and a being named Thwayan Tamble.

***

Evening came in cool as the fresh winds from the sea brought relief from the day, and the city came alive for the markets in the gentler hours.

Jethryll stood on the balcony of the family apartment and looked out across the city of her birth, seeing it anew as one ville among many. Sardis was larger but only by virtue of hugging both the sea and the landing fields, and many other centers, she knew first hand, squatted in the dust among ridges and mesas, ancient dry shorelines, and wandering dune fields. Mines gave forth the stuff of commerce and belched their waste upon the desert, as processing plants supported Susa's meager atmosphere, the carbon-based life in its deteriorating seas barely enough to support the human population's metabolic cycle.

On an early run her cargo-hauler had landed at a mining camp in the deep desert and she had witnessed the arrival of a great space freighter, coming in to collect the processed ores from the robot smelters. The scene had been awe-inspiring, machines the size of mountains moving with the delicacy of living things to couple and transfer the produce, which alone justified their existence, before the freighter had lifted away into the sky once more, buoyant as a soap bubble on its field of negated gravity.

Such things had served to expand Jethryll's world and make young eyes older, and her family sensed she had changed, evolved, as all people must. They lamented the loss of their young one, while celebrating the coming of their adult.

By mid-evening she could resist the tug no longer. She had discretely made a call and smiled to hear a voice she knew well in her ear, arranged to meet at ten, then changed into casual pants and jacket, zipped on boots, and took a pack across her shoulders. She told her mother she was going out to see the town she missed; but her mother knew perfectly well where she was going, and bit down on her disapproval only in deference to the fact the girl was home at all.

Sardis by night was a busy place trying desperately to not be a depressed slum. People smiled and called, but a sad fatalism lay behind expressions. It seemed an undercurrent in society which one did not have to be very old to sense: settling Susa had been a mistake. It was a terrestrial world in the goldilocks zone with existing life and near-earth temperatures, gravity, and atmospheric pressure and composition, and those things alone—a rare combination of circumstances—made it attractive as terraforming was not needed. Beyond those few considerations, almost everything else was wrong, and the Susian born could feel it. They belonged nowhere.

The night air brought a thrill to Jethryll's senses as she waited for a railbus, thinking back on desperate mid-teenage evenings as she had sought for meaning in life and found none among her peers. She was on her way to the only place she had ever found such meaning, knowing it made her nominally an outcast.

The shabby vehicle purred along the monorail and she caught the next service headed east, kept to herself, and almost felt consternation among other passengers when she left at stop 36, above the Alien Quarter. Human beings, despite centuries wandering the Middle Stars, colonizing dozens of worlds and encountering scores of alien civilizations, remained very xenophobic. Where humans went they created Little Earth and did not assimilate, even when assimilation was actually feasible, and Jethryll had read it was the still-breathing hand-down of ancient colonialism from the point in Earth's history when old empires had reached out to dominate for profit the newly-discovered lands of less technologically advanced peoples. Insularity, conquest, and exploitation may all have taken on genteel new images and names, but nothing had in fact changed.

Before her, however, was something which had nothing whatever to do with any of that, and she felt the stirring of her soul as she took in the organic architecture, the globes, domes, and peculiar connecting structures which made the buildings so very different from the monotonous Euclidean forms of the rest of the city. Here, designers from other worlds, other societies, had erected the styles and notions of form familiar to them, and among these labyrinthine ways flourished a closed community, a ghetto, composed of a dozen species whose business brought them to Susa.

Humans walked these streets in the cool hours too, shopping for alien wares in the bazaars and specialty shops, where a linguistic mish-mash of human and alien dialects crackled in the air, and the smell of exotic foods was alternately intoxicating and revolting. To pass the gates of Alien Town was to plunge headlong into an assault upon the senses unrivalled on this world, and as she walked into the humid, aromatic throng, Jethryll realized how much she had missed it.

She browsed through the arcade where alien goods were sold, looked at the things made for human consumption, merely human commodities such as wristies and coms, interfaces and VR pickups, only decorated with the symbology of other worlds. Then came really alien things, foodstuffs from across the stars for which some humans developed a taste; artworks which spoke to the human sub consciousness in ways hard to comprehend but no less real.

Jethryll recognized the Belchasian infinity glyph worked in a semi-rare metal as a necklace, and bought it at once, trading a few words, hard-remembered, with the milky-blue-white skinned Belchasian in the shop, an elegant race whose extended, spindly form was at a slight disadvantage in Susa's gravity. She clipped the chain at her nape at once and walked on, found a stall and browsed through scarves and shawls, human things but made from alien textiles and in alien colors. A shawl woven in a fabric which glimmered like metal and seemed to shift through part of the spectrum, deep blues and purples, shot with silver, won her over quickly and she left with it around her shoulders after managing a few words with the Maranite proprietor, one of the stockier races, clothed in yellow fur and always garrulous.

A coffee shop sold alien beverages and she indulged in Carminian mentholeum, a sort of tea, mild on the pallet but powerfully cleansing of the head, a sweet, fragrant brew which glowed faintly in the glass, like light shafting through deep water. To this she added Weltran oatcake, not oats by any stretch of the imagination but a plant which served the role of grain, and which was made into a sweet, moist biscuit, topped with a semi-solid confection in lieu of chocolate and whose flavor, despite being sweet on the human tongue, was impossible to describe.

On her way to the railbus she had stopped by a shop and picked up rich chocolate over peanuts; so simple a thing had value, for it was not just humans who found alien foods to their taste, and she remembered someone who absolutely loved them.

Beyond the retail area were winding streets, climbing among buildings of strange and organic form, and she walked a path she remembered from years ago. She had come this way many times, more often than her family had liked, and the steps flanking a strange, squat building were like coming home as she found the cavern-like entrance so characteristic of the architecture of the Brandovalii.

In many ways they were her favorite of the alien peoples here on Susa. Not as elegant as the Belchasians, not as familiar-seeming as the Maranites, but deeply thoughtful beings who inspired the strangest calm in her. She had first met Thwayan Tamble many years ago when wandering through the Alien Quarter on a hot afternoon, simply looking for diversion, and she had taken a fall resulting in a skinned knee. Tamble was a doctor for the Brandovalian delegation, and had been the nearest to assist. She had found him at first intimidating, as all his kind could be, but quickly found what seemed a humorous and benevolent being behind a very alien form.

His practice was a slow one, there were not many of his kind on Susa, and he spent much of his time playing human chess, to which he had taken keenly, and composing a lyrical poem representing his perception of the universe, something all his kind were expected to attempt as their lives grew long. He was waiting at the door to his chambers and raised a three-fingered hand in greeting when she came up the steps from the cavernous building entry.

"Greetings, young Jethryll," came his deep, breathy voice as his mouth made the sounds of human speech. He was long accustomed to the language, more so than she to his, and indeed there were elements of Brandovalian speech that the human larynx simply could not reproduce.

"Hello, old friend," the young woman said with an unabashed smile. "It's good to see you again." He stepped ponderously aside and gestured for her to enter, and she found herself in a chamber she recalled, a domed ceiling from which glowed dim lights whose frequency matched the home sun of these people. Brilliant fabrics created artistic hangings, and soft cushions scattered the floor, for the Brandovalii had never adopted furniture in the human way. A dull, vertical mirror partition reflected the chamber and Jethryll knew it was used for meditation. As she settled she saw herself, a more mature form than the child she remembered needing help in this room once. Her shoulder-length tawny hair and rough-and-ready clothes seemed to say she had found her place in the world but she knew it was all pretence, as so much of human existence was.

Tamble seemed unchanging, though probably because she simply did not know the signs of age to look for in his species. He had always reminded her of a lizard, an iguana, perhaps, though it was only the most fleeting resemblance, more in the shape of the skull than anything. His skin was dark and smooth, the morphology was tetrapod, and large, clear eyes looked out over vertical nasal slits flush with the curve of the face above a wide mouth whose lips exposed the teeth of a vegetarian. A deep cherry-red robe, worked in amazing patterns of gold thread, swathed a somewhat bulky body, a hood was up over the dome of the head, and wide sleeves with elaborately embellished cuffs accented the powerful but expressive hands.

After a respectful moment of silence, Jethryll opened her pack and brought out the candy peanuts. "I have not forgotten, my friend," she said with a smile as she presented them, and Tamble sighed with delight as he deftly opened the pack and sampled them. He let the chocolate melt on his palate and his eyes closed in a moment of rapture.

"Thank you," he breathed, and resealed the bag, laying it aside. "I sense you have much you would like to speak of." He gestured, a splaying of his three fingers. "Tell me of your travels, these long months since we last shared space."

The tales of her flight duties, of seeing the far corners of Susa, came spilling out, an edge of enthusiasm in her words, though unspoken was the fact she knew it was but a step in a journey. She would not do this forever, and also there seemed a hint of disappointment, or frustration with the unfolding of her universe. Tamble listened politely, his hands folded, and as her story continued he tapped for a moment at his wristy; soon a small bot appeared and served klyphos, a beverage Tamble remembered had been to her taste. The spicy, steaming brew came in wide, decorated cups designed for the splay of the Brandovalian hand, and which Jethryll held two-handed.

At last she had finished her account of working for the air truckers, and ran down. Tamble sipped from his cup, then made a small bow of the head. "It seems you have embarked upon life at last, young friend. But tell an old physician . . . why so wistful?"

"Wistful . . . ?" She blinked, then blushed faintly and drank to cover the moment. "It's . . . It's not what I had imagined it might be."

"What did you hope for?" came the deep, calm voice.

"I can't really put my finger on what, or why. Maybe I'm just impatient. But isn't there meant to be . . . well, more?"

"More? More than what?"

"More than . . ." She gestured at the world around them. "Stones and heat . . . and wondering where the future will take us?"

"Or if there is a future for you at all?" The reptile-like head inclined toward her a little and the eyes made a sleepy blink that was almost synchronized with the slow gape of the nostrils as his resting breath cycled. "My friend, it is not a job you seek but the certainties of life."

"Are there any?" Jethryll asked, an edge in her voice she had not intended.

"We spoke long of the philosophies of our kinds, years ago, but you were too young, perhaps, to grasp what they could mean. You wander, you seek, you fail to find, but the wisdom of your own people has long held that one cannot find without that which has not been found within."

"I didn't understand then, and I don't follow now. I wish I knew what it meant."

Tamble smiled quietly and composed his thoughts. "It is difficult to imagine that which is beyond perception. What more is there, than what comes to us through our senses? But can you hear radio waves? No. Can you see ultraviolet light? Certainly not. They exist and can easily be seen to exist because of their interaction with the tangible world. We live bathed in radiation to which our senses are not attuned." He smiled with a splay of a hand. "To which yours are not, I should say. My eyes see a slightly broader spectral range than yours. I perceive colors for which you would have no name."

"How amazing it would be to see them . . ."

"It is but one small example. My point is, we each perceive only a fraction of what we know exists, and in reality the world around us hums with a million things of which we are not directly conscious."

Jethryll paused on the verge of speaking for a long moment, then let the question come as if of its own volition. "Are there peoples who are conscious of them?"

"*Yes.*" The word was simply said. "You must understand, even though your kind have escaped their planetary birthplace and begun to move amongst a community of beings, you are still quite a young species. You have overcome many trials, but in so many ways have yet to mature. In another ten thousand years , we will see how you are faring, and *perhaps* by then you will have begun to grow up."

"Yours is an old race, isn't it?"

"'Old' is a vague term, just as vague as 'young.' We have far to go before we reach any racial senescence, but we saw your species come forth, so yes, we are an 'old' people, if you like."

"What is it you know, that we have still to learn?" The question was put in an almost innocent way. Tamble blinked his big, soft eyes, as if he saw not the woman but the girl once more.

"A question it would take an age to answer, for our frames of reference are different." He spread his hands in a very human-like gesture. "And I am a simple doctor, not a physicist or philosopher, and in truth my English may not be up to the attempt. But . . ." He leaned forward and spoke more softly. "My species has more access to these things than we generally admit to others. Are you familiar with the concept of *group consciousness*?"

"Gestalt?" she asked at once. "Many minds in communion?"

"Essentially. My species has evolved the ability to share some aspects of consciousness, and it is a state we hold dear, even sacrosanct, to use a human expression. When the dreary, plodding nature of day to day tasks draws us down, when the inevitability of mortality, however far off it may be, wears upon our sensibilities and equilibrium, we remind ourselves the tangible spaces we share are but one dimension, one aspect, of a multivalent whole." He smiled, an indulgence for her, and simplified his words. "It reminds us there is more."

"How wonderful it would be to know," she whispered, breathing the lingering aroma of the warm, spiced beverage.

"Are you sure? Is it not the seeking which defines humans? Would not certainty lead to ennui?"

"Why must it? Couldn't we grow onward in that certainty, rather than spend our lives seeking for something others found long ago? It smacks of reinventing the wheel, as they say."

"This is true from a certain perspective, but we never learn so thoroughly as when we do so through the experience of effort. At a personal level, this must be true for all beings."

"I accept that. But maybe it is this order of magnitude difference in the outlook of species which keeps them apart, when otherwise they may find better harmony."

Tamble suppressed a very human chuckle, drained his cup and set is aside. "Truly, there are times, my friend, when you speak far beyond your years." He sat forward and was at once more somber. "You truly wish to know?"

"If it is possible for a human being to do so . . .yes." The words were whispered, and her pale eyes held his over the rim of her cup. "If it will take away the void which seems to be opening inside me, yes."

"Think carefully, my friend. Have you heard of those humans who are said to *take the alien way*?"

Jethryll blinked. "I've heard it said. Parents use those words to frighten children to stay away from other races. They say sometimes children walk into the Alien Quarter and are never heard of again." She squinted with an air of skepticism. "That's not true, surely!"

"Not in so literal a way. But there is a grain of truth in all stories . . . True, it is among the young that the greatest receptivity is found, for the plasticity of the young brain more easily accepts the new neural nets needed to inscribe the experience. And when a young person has obtained this perspective it is not uncommon for them to substantially reject the world they grew up in, in favor of their expanded reality. Understandably, those they leave behind are unhappy, they call it an unhealthy influence, a cultic phenomenon. When such a gifting is made, it is only ever for the best of reasons, and we can claim the moral high ground in doing so, but it has unfortunately fed the mistrust of the human kind, unfortunate because, in essence, it should build bridges between races instead."

Jethryll breathed deeply, thinking, thoughts visibly racing behind her eyes. "Is there any risk to me?"

"There is always some element of risk when alien biotas are conjoined in any way, but I have never known any human being exposed to the Brandovalian group consciousness to be physically harmed, if that is what you mean."

"And the mind . . .?"

Now Tamble raised a finger, its prehensile tip fining down to a point to underline his words. "There is no way to unlearn what is leaned. You must make philosophic sense of it, no paradoxes are permissible or they will damage your future."

"I have looked for something more . . . I was drawn back here at the first opportunity; I was driven here by the damned *sameness* out there. It's like the world has become a two-dimensional drawing, and without depth there is nothing." Jethryll smiled tightly. "I'm no child anymore, to lose myself in the answer, if there is one to be found."

For a moment Tamble considered her words, then nodded. "Very well. And it is true your older brain is now less plastic and will yield less fully to the immersion. Never the less, it should offer a perspective, hopefully the one you seek." He smiled gently and tapped at his wristy, and soon the serving bot returned with a medical kit. Opening the plastic box with its multiple draws and trays, Tamble took out a phial of deep red liquid and made swift calculations, entering figures at the virtual keypad of the wristy, in the air above it.

"This drug has the effect in humans of increasing the suggestibility of the mind, which in this context means removing the barrier of inherent skepticism which would serve to obstruct the flow of impressions. It also primes the neural nets to capture the experience and store it. The actual trigger must come from myself. If you will trust me?"

"Implicitly," Jethryll whispered.

"Then we may begin. It will take a little while."

The bot rearranged the cushions with a rapid flutter of its manipulators, then withdrew to the doorway to await any command to assist. Tamble loaded a hypospray with a minute dose of the drug and delivered it into Jethryll's neck.

"Relax," he said soothingly. "Just relax." He assumed a cross-legged seat before her as she focused, trying to sense any operation of the drug, and he flipped back the cuffs of his robe, flexing his fingers. "Allow a few moments for the drug to do its work." Within the minute Jethryll felt especially calm and mellow, and Tamble reached to gently draw an eyelid upward and study her pupil. "You are ready. Now, spread your fingers."

She raised her hands and splayed the fingers widely, and Tamble's three digits sought out the thumb, middle and last fingers of each hand. The prehensile tips morphed, became wide and then invaginated to create cup-like structures into which her own fingers fitted, and though the inherent strangeness brought a moment's revulsion, she overcame it without difficulty. She looked into Tamble's wide, kind eyes and let herself simply receive whatever this gift may be.

A moment later she felt, or thought she felt, a sharp prick in each fingertip, and an instant's puzzlement followed as she assumed the alien's fingers contained a sharp claw of some sort, usually retracted. But she had no further time to wonder as the minute puncture allowed the transmission of some substance, whether a hormone or an enzyme, which swiftly targeted the neurons primed by the drug, and she seemed to succumb like a gliding descent into deep, warm waters.

It was not so much a loss of consciousness as a transition, in full waking state, to a new order of perception. She lost all input from her physical senses, sight, hearing, and touch fading gradually but swiftly as they were overlaid by perception coming from somewhere else. From Tamble? Were these the perceptions of his alien organs? Her human brain struggled to understand what it was sensing, and she let the confusion pass over without stressing. She knew her brain had no template by which to match a color she had never seen before, or a flavor for which she had no receptors, the information was merely blank, and she was aware of a thrill of regret that she had not done this long ago, when, just perhaps, she could have spun neural nets which were not human, though within possible human brain architecture, and thus she may indeed have perceived things where now there was only void.

Gradually she made out the fascinating image of herself seen through Tamble's eyes, and realized his vision processed information a little differently, especially the perception of color and light levels. She smiled and saw herself smile, and mentally felt his smile in response, then the image dissolved and she felt as if she were traveling in some way, or experiencing a shift in perspective. The expansion of perception was something which must be taken slowly or the brain would be unable to process the input, and Tamble kept it gentle. Slowly, one layer at a time, she felt her mind open not just to possibilities, but to realities, or at least perceptions of realities, the subjective caveat of phenomenology.

Did she see or feel those flares of energy which she somehow knew were other living beings? Were they fiery yellow or merely warm? The confusion between modes of input was disconcerting, but she focused on the warmth and let herself feel those glowing spots, first herself and her friend, then people outside, all through the quarter, then the city beyond. It was at this point she realized she perceived no distinction between species, human or alien registered the same way, as some living furnace of chemical and electromagnetic energy. In this way she let herself perceive the whole world as a seemingly infinite scatter of points which were beings, but when her perspective enlarged to take in the universe beyond, the constellation of beings expanded beyond all comprehension and became an ocean in which she was the merest drop.

The scope was overwhelming and Tamble sensed her difficulty, scaled it back and smoothed it out, to bring her gently to contact with the warm rock of a planetary surface. Not this planet, she realized, as she saw the ruddy glimmers of an alien terrain stretching far away under a night sky. But *what* a sky . . . The stars were blazing but only because the sun was behind the larger of two moons, across whose dark faces were scattered the lights of cities, while before her sat what seemed to be Tamble, or another Brandovalian. The being sat in what she took to be a meditative posture, naked to the stars, but the morphology she perceived only dimly. Indeed, the alien's outline seemed to be constructed of translucent blue glass, probably another artifact of her brain's inability to correctly process the perception of unfamiliar senses.

All these things she took in at once, a wash of data in her visual cortex, but now there was something else; not just the celestial majesty of the eclipse but a sense of depth. Though she saw only one being, she perceived a multitude. Not here but *everywhere*. Was this the gestalt? The sense that this one was many, or that all partook of some common channel of being . . . And more, there was *sound*, a sound not heard with the ears but felt in the chest and inside the head.

She seemed to tune into the sound, becoming aware of it, and the first thing which struck her was that it was familiar; she had heard it before at some unguessed-at time, in some unknown place or context. It was not a song, but a conflux of voices, an infinity of voices, all raised in wordless harmony, and she felt an overwhelming urge to contribute her own meager voice to it, to swell the choir whose sum was a vibration filling her being to overflowing. A million billion voices all spoke at once, but with the same message, a unity which was not a choice, not an ideology, but a natural reality. An impression both huge and simple; for a moment she felt herself a spectator at an event not meant for human eyes; but this was Tamble's gift, a perception from beyond the human experience, and she was humbled and very, very grateful.

As long as it lasted, which may have been only moments but seemed an eternity, she resonated with that booming, soaring note, feeling in it a celebration of a universal life force, transcending the mortal state and redefining it, and she felt herself settle on the warm rock, to look up at the mesmeric sky, the luminous starfields backing the eclipse, as the further moon's lighted crescent swelled gradually to overcome the darkness. She knew the sun would appear from totality soon, and the night was pent with this expectation. The chorus swelled with a feeling of deep joy in appreciation for this spectacle, and reached a crescendo which filled every part of her body and mind as the sun burst above the horizon of the larger moon and the sky flushed toward a strange blue-green at once, the rocks tending purple to her eyes. The alien became ever more transparent as light levels rose, and as the chorus began to fade the serene being moved; it turned and looked right into her very soul.

Darkness, warmth, silence . . . The loss of sensory input at first seemed unfair as her conscious mind craved more, then she felt a relief, a certain gratitude, as she sensed herself readjusting, carrying the memories but no longer the direct line to their source. Gradually she felt hearing and touch return, sensed she sat on soft cushions and breathed shakily, feeling for the world she had been born into as, little by little, she came back from the place she had been gifted to visit.

"Gently," came Tamble's voice in her living ears. "Take your time. Do not open your eyes yet. Breathe . . ." She drew in slow, deep breaths, did her best to find balance between knowing where she was and remembering where she had been, and at last, when she trusted her own equilibrium, she opened her eyes very slowly. "How do you feel?" was the doctor's question.

"Okay . . . I'm okay." Jethryll glanced at her fingertips but could see no mark. If there had been some exchange, it had been very subtle. "Thank you," she whispered. "Thank you so much . . . I understand how special a gift that was." She tried to smile but was still too haunted.

"Do you understand what you saw?"

"I felt life everywhere, life living a common thread of existence all across the stars. Whereabouts they were seemed to not even be a factor worth considering. And all species resonated a very similar way."

"Interesting that you choose that word."

"The harmony . . ." The girl shivered involuntarily. "I *knew* that sound, but I have no clue from where."

"We all know it," Tamble said softly. "We are born knowing it, for it is the wordless chant of universal life. Occasionally, a few amongst your kind experience it, in meditation, in dream; for my kind, it is a level of being we can consciously reach out to, couple, and temporarily become one with."

Jethryll stretched and her smile was cathartic. "I understand how much it means to be able to do that. How it fills the void . . . Not a matter of faith, but tangible perception of realms." She shook her head faintly. "For humans, faith has been the only access to them." She looked at her hands and for a long moment was nearly overcome with emotion. Tamble let her be, and when she opened her eyes once more the bot hovered close by with a drink extended to her. She took it and thanked both with a smile and nod.

"Are you sure you are well?" the doctor asked once more.

She nodded, her smile now the long-lasting satisfaction of having seen through a doorway which had never opened before—an epiphany in every sense, and she was thankful to have come upon it so early in life. *Now* the world had meaning and the business of life could unfold relative to that perception.

Sipping the drink, she mused on her new condition for a while. "If *that* is the vista that opens to kids, and they can immerse themselves even more deeply than I could, then I can easily see how they become totally absorbed by it. Even for me, to go back to my job, to go home, seems banal. I will, because I know I must have a place I belong, but I'm taking perspective with me. No wonder youngsters dive into the sensation and don't want to come back."

"They become interpreters and advocates between the human and nonhuman worlds," Tamble said with a nod, adjusting the cuffs of his robe. "Humans are—what is the word? Xenophobic . . . and the contact period has been difficult. Old hates have blossomed and those born of other worlds have often been made the object of them. For we older beings, it has been a difficult time, so when, occasionally, a human comes to understand us better than others of his or her kind, we see the opportunity for a channel of understanding to come into being."

"Many feel those special few are being brainwashed in some way," Jethryll murmured, "and each time, they trust aliens even less. When a kid seems to go into a trance and walks into "alien town" there's many would drag them back by force." She shrugged with a sad shake of her tawny head. "But there is another perspective, spoken of less often, but it's just as real. Those kids are also *revered* by some as blessed. Some feel they are gifted with a perception of the universe ordinary mortals may only dream of." Her smile was warmth, but a pale echo of the things she had perceived. "I can confirm that. Oh, how I can confirm that."

"I am glad if I have been able to offer you something of what you seek, my friend." Tamble raised his cup in a silent toast which she returned. "It is the task of a doctor to serve those around him, but not often do we have the opportunity to help when the soul lies ill at ease."

His precise, ponderous words faded away and they shared the silence of the chamber as the balmy night wore on, and the girl found her mind going back again and again to the eclipse. She found she could now barely recall the actual sound of the great harmony, but its power, its import, its all-embracing gravitas, these things would never leave her.

When she stepped out into the cooling air of the closing markets, she looked up at the wan stars of the midnight hours and for a moment imagined she could feel the harmony of life threading all the galaxy, all the universe, together. She could not, and perhaps never would without the direct assistance of one for whom it was a natural perception.

But she had found what she needed on this furlough, and was content. As she set out for home she reflected with some satisfaction that though she was not in the same league as the young advocates who formed a buffer between the species in these edgy, suspicious times, she, Jethryll Patallo, ne'er-do-well daughter of a world which should never have been settled, had indeed, in her own small sense, *taken the alien way.*

Mike Adamson holds a PhD in archaeology from Flinders University of South Australia. After early aspirations in art and writing, Mike returned to study and secured degrees in both marine biology and archaeology. Mike currently lectures in anthropology, is a passionate photographer, a master-level hobbyist and journalist for international magazines.

Could our universe be a small part of a giant multiverse that contains alternate versions of Earth? Could those alt-Earth denizens travel between universes? Amelie, the sole survivor of a Cold-War disaster that destroyed her small town, fears the answer to that question is 'yes', because she's being stalked by a clever, almost otherworldly enemy.

Last Girl Standing

Mary Madigan

When I first saw the Professor, I thought he was a dingbatter, the kind of tourist who would come to our little Outer Banks Island, lean out the car window and shout, "Hey kid, what time does the 4 o'clock ferry leave?" But he wasn't that way at all.

I met him when I was working behind the counter at Momma's video store. My real job was to get on my bike and deliver videos, but Momma wanted to go out to lunch, so she said "Amelie, you're on the register," and I was stuck inside.

Luckily my best friend Jen showed up. Momma was gone and when the cat's away, the mice will play. We got a pile of returned videos from the Adult Section and tried to find the funniest titles. Jen very delicately put her long, black hair behind her ear and presented *C. Assablanca*. I found *Tom Dare, Crack Detective*. We were already giggling ourselves silly when the Professor came up to the counter with *Paper Moon*. That sent us into hysterics. No one can laugh harder than thirteen-year-old girls.

He brushed the sleeve of his jacket and said, "Young ladies!"

I stopped laughing. The man had the whole professor look down, from the tweed jacket with elbow patches to the shock of white Einstein hair. His dark face was framed by a grey goatee and topped off with little gold-rimmed glasses. Why would such a respectable dude be renting porn?

Then I remembered—*Paper Moon* was a legit title from the Drama section, a heartfelt tale of father-daughter team of con artists during the Depression. It might have even won an Oscar. I got my breath back, wiped tears from my eyes and said, "Sorry, sir. Did you want to rent that?"

"Perhaps. But first, a question. I can see that, from the artwork on this cover, Earth once had a moon. Yet you have rings around the planet now. Why?"

He reminded me of that actor who always played the President. Or God. The kind of guy who knew everything. But he must have been really out of it if he didn't know what happened to the moon.

"Oh boy," Jen whispered, rolling her eyes as she stepped back. He was my problem, not hers.

"It blew up back in '83." I said. "The Russians wanted to show us how tough they were, so they used the moon as a nuclear testing ground."

He was shocked. "They literally nuked the moon?"

"Pretty stupid, right?"

"Very!"

"But the little pieces of moon gathered up together, and gravity turned them into rings. They're kinda pretty."

"Ah, so that's why it's 2020 and you don't have Satellite TV. The satellites would be crushed by the debris. No GPS, no eyes in the sky."

"Uh, I guess."

"That explains why this Earth is still stuck in the Eighties."

I pulled up a drooping anklet and fluffed my permed brown hair. "What do you mean?"

"Hmm, If the Cold War never ended, the political instability that followed might never occur," he said, as I rang him up. "No terrorism, no nationalism. Maybe this version of earth will be safe."

I had no idea what he was talking about so I laughed. Normal tourists were annoying but I liked the kooky ones. They kept it interesting.

Fast-forward five years. Now I was eighteen years old, crouched in the shadows of Vern's hunting blind, Dad's M16 in my hands. I was on the watch for Rabid Infected, the diseased yet fast-moving cannibals who roamed the ruins of my home town. I wasn't laughing any more.

Two years ago, the pandemic hit. It was a virus that combined the speed of the Spanish Flu of 1918 with all the fun of rabies. Most journalists and doctors didn't even live long enough to give it a clever name. They named the bug after the day it happened, 6/8.

We called it 'Mommucked', a Down-Easter word for totally messed up.

Most of the people who got 6/8 died fast, but others turned into raging, rabid monsters who ran fast and had a talent for eating faces. The RIs were the absolute worst.

The virus and the RI's tore through our small town like a hurricane. Some of us hung on for a while, but when Jen and my art teacher, Miz Daisy died a week ago, the Mommuck had officially wiped out every human on Avalon Island but me. I was as far from safe as a girl could be.

But that's not why I was thinking about the Professor.

Five years ago, minus one day, he brought *Paper Moon* back to the store. As luck would have it, I was working the counter again.

"Are you a teacher?" I asked him.

"Clever girl."

"What do you teach, science? Physics?"

"Cinema."

"Awesome!"

"I specialize in time travel. Because time is like a movie, a combination of stills that, when they're played at a certain speed, appear to move. Our minds create the illusion of film just as they create time."

"Uh, what?"

"I know, you don't understand. Because you don't have editing capabilities," he said. "You're a three dimensional being. Only beings from the fifth dimension can edit time, like a director editing a filmstrip. When, say, George Lucas made those changes to his Star Wars films, he was behaving like a fifth dimensional being, creating another version of his world."

"Ugh! Lucas destroyed a masterpiece! Those crappy edits were an atrocity!"

"Ah, you do understand. There are similar, misbegotten edits of Earth out there. There's an Earth where the dinosaurs escaped extinction, where Rome never fell, another where all of mankind died in the nuclear apocalypse of 1962. They're different sequels generated by the same basic story. The characters are different, some of the places change, but they're similar, like movies packed right next to their own sequel. *Aliens* next to *Aliens 2*. Or the many different versions of Star Trek. One generated the other, but the characters inside the story don't comprehend the higher dimensions, the other versions that exist outside of their container. They can't see the alternate universe that's sitting right next to them. They can only see it if they enter the fifth dimension"

"I know a movie you'd like. It's about an astronaut who turns into a fifth-dimensional being."

"Could you show me?"

He followed me down the aisles, saying "I was hoping this earth might not be doomed to suffer the fates of the other alternate Earths in the multiverse. Perhaps the Cephalopods saved you."

"Cephalopods? You mean Octopi?"

"Octopuses. Using Octopi as a plural for Octopus is misbegotten Latin. But yes, the Octopus is a creature that can consciously change its own genetic code. Which means its awareness is present at the molecular level. If the Octopus is aware at that very small level, perhaps it's also conscious at the quantum level. If humans could do the same thing we could cure so many ills."

"How?"

"We would become fifth dimensional beings. We wouldn't need a spaceship to travel great distances, we could take advantage of quantum superposition. We could change our genetic makeup. Cure disease. Travel to other parts of the multiverse. We could be at two places at the same time. Sort of."

"Umm . . . are you talking about an alien octopus like Cthulhu?"

"Yes, the monster from the H.P. Lovecraft books! Are there movies made from his work?"

"Yeah! There's a great one, *The Color Out of Space*. It's in German, though. There's another one with the guy from *Stranger in a Strange Land*."

"*Stranger in a Strange Land*?" He laughed. It was a weird laugh, more of a bark than ha-ha. "Yes, I'd like that one."

As I wrote down the due date, he said. "Let me give you a tip. For the future. Respect the octopus."

"Oh, I do. Especially the way Momma makes them, roasted in olive oil with lemon juice. My favorite!"

"No, you should not eat them! Swim with them. Listen to their song."

"O-kay" I said as he walked out the door. Very kooky.

He never returned the video.

Now that memory hung in the air, floating like the camo above my head. Looking back, it was pretty obvious that he wasn't talking about movies. But what the hell *was* he talking about?

I thought about it as I stared at my bashed and broken octopus traps, scattered on the sand below. Something or someone had been smashing them during the day when I was asleep, so I was guarding them. The rifle had been pressed to my face for so long, my cheek was damp and red.

I guessed that the traps had been bashed by a RIs, but why would they go for empty traps? I could only think of one former person who would do that.

The weird Professor who had a thing about Octopuses.

When the traps got smashed, I'd gone back to what was left of the video store and dug up the old receipts. The Professor's name was Dr. John Parker, and he was from Washington, D.C. Our Island is about 300 miles from D.C., but he still could have walked it. RI's will walk for hundreds of miles until they drop dead of exhaustion. Sometimes I'd find them, face down in the sand, groaning and still moving their feet. One clean shot through the temple put them out of their misery.

A light glinted over the horizon. At sunset, the rings rose over the shallows like a white knife slicing blue jello. Time to take the hunt outside. I got Momma's makeup out of my backpack, smeared blue eyeshadow over my face in a wave pattern and put Dad's hat on. Then I slung the M16 over my shoulder, put the pistol on my belt and my knife in its sheath. Sunglasses on. I flexed my muscles and put on Dad's camo jacket. Totally rocking the Hamilton in *Terminator 2* look.

I got on my bike and rode.

Some said the pandemic came from global warming, the temperature changes that came when we lost the moon and the axis went off-kilter. They said it released old viruses into the environment.

Some blamed bioweapons made by companies like GenAPure. Others said it came from space, brought down to earth on dusty debris from the crushed moon.

Dad was in the capital on 6/8. As a Military Policeman, he was right in the thick of it. The viruses hit so hard and fast, everyone thought it was a bioweapon launched by the enemy. So, the Cold Warriors did what they did best, took a bad situation and made it a million times worse. We launched our missiles against the enemy because we thought they'd already launched something against us. They did the same.

When the shit started flying, Dad had a choice—protect the politicians who were destroying what was left of the planet or go home and protect his family. Like most of his men, he chose family.

He fought like hell to get back to us, then fell dead as he crossed the doorway. Momma and I were too busy mourning him to try to make a run for it. Besides, Momma had gotten cancer in that past year, and with her leg, she couldn't get very far. Lots of people tried to leave Avalon Island on 6/8 but the one bridge out was dive-bombed by tons of rabid and dying birds. Planes fell from the sky. One hit a ferry. There were twisted wings everywhere.

The bridge burned and fell into the water. What the water didn't get, the sharks took. What the sharks didn't get turned into RIs.

Momma went the bad way, sick to her stomach at first, then dizzy, feverish, and hungry. Raging hungry. I didn't know how sick she was. I was sixteen years old, I thought everything was drama. It was perfectly natural for her to be very pissed off. I locked her in her room but stood outside, talking to her, waiting for it to blow over. That's what she did for me when I had a hissy fit.

When she slammed herself against the door over and over I realized this was more than anger. I ran to get the doctor but he was gone. I got back just before she died. In a last moment of sanity, she said to me, "I couldn't outrun it, but you can. Ride, baby. Ride like the wind."

And that's what I did. I loved my bike. Cars were faster, but they ran out of gas. Anyone who tried to outrun an RI wound up dead. On my bike, I could ride and shoot with no windshield, nothing in my way.

Sand and gravel crunched under my wheels. I steered into the water, wide tires hissing as they carved a path through the shallow waves. I dodged the uprooted trees, house parts, and dead horses that had washed up in the shallows. Before the warming this was a road, Highway 13. Now it was sand and crumbled asphalt.

The billboards alongside the highway were all tore up, but they were still standing. "Come to Dirty Dicks—we've got lots of crabs!" That one always made me laugh. And "Avalon Island Video Mart. You order, we deliver." That one always made me cry. Momma's place. She loved movies so much, she named me after one. She said I looked like the girl in it. "Such big brown eyes," she said.

But I was nothing like that girl, personality-wise. She was cute and nice. I was as far from nice as a girl could be. When Momma, died I got Dad's guns and declared war against anything that wished me harm. They've been by my side ever since. Like family.

Off the road were the ruins of a glassy building, covered with graffiti. GenAPure. "Genome editing for healthy happy babies." "Better living through Science."

"Science is the devil" and "burn in hell" was sprayed over it. That's what happened when Miz Daisy got her hands on a can of paint.

But even before 6/8, everyone hated GenAPure, even Daddy. He said it was a modern form of Eugenics. Breeding people like dogs. He was probably mad because the GenAPure advisor told Momma to abort me. The advisor thought I'd be deformed because I was a genetic jumble—Nigerian, Asian, Native American, Irish, Italian. He said all of Avalon Island was a genetic mess—too many mutts. I'm surprised Daddy didn't punch him. But my big, scary deformity turned out to be a rosy birthmark on my belly. And freckles, lots of them.

I rode past the graveyard. There were no headstones, those washed away years ago. Now there were just the skeletons of trees, bony branches hung with lattices of wood, moss, and ribbon. Jen and I made those lattices. Memorials to the dear departed.

Yes, I missed all the people who passed, but it was dangerous to let yourself feel too much. Slows you down. On my bike, M16 slung over my shoulder, nothing could touch me.

Ride, baby. Ride like the wind

The last orange light shone on my trap marker, bobbing in the water. I was coming up to a blue hole made by one of the meteorites that had been pelting the planet since we'd lost the moon. It was shallow, it only went down a hundred feet. This was the hard part. I had to slow down in the open shallow water. If any RI were hiding in the pines I'd be toast. They were stupid but they were fast.

I skidded to a stop near the edge of the hole, got off the bike and pulled on the rusty chain. It was already covered with oysters. They grew like weeds all over the ocean now, the calmer tides were perfect for them. I put a bunch in the bucket, but they weren't what I came out here for. I wanted octopus.

Out of the corner of my eye I saw something swimming towards me, got a hand on the Glock. But it wasn't an RI, it was just a corpse, floating aimlessly, like a bloated starfish. The thing was so far gone it would have fallen apart if it weren't for the expensive coat wrapped around it. Probably from one of the D.C. copters that crashed. Could be the President for all I knew.

I pushed it away with my foot. A bunch of crabs skittered out of its eyeholes and danced across its white bony cheeks. My stomach did a backflip. That's why I didn't eat crabs any more.

I pulled the seaweed-greased chain and brought up my octopus trap, made from a traffic cone, weighted with a detachable door on the bottom. The entry hole was small, three inches wide. They love a challenge. Heavy locked clasps kept 'em in there for a while.

I twisted the lock open, licking my salty lips with anticipation. Must be a big one inside.

But it was empty. "Damn!" I squinted in the ringlight, desperate to figure out what happened. Octopuses were damned smart—they could thread themselves through a hole not much wider than their eyeball. They could change the color of their skin to blend into anything. But the lock had been cut, snipped with something much harder than tentacles. It couldn't have been an RI; their brains were too boiled to do this. This trap was opened by someone, not something.

I was suddenly aware of the darkness surrounding me. Wind hissed through the pines. A shadow wavered behind them, moving but not with the wind. With a shaking hand, I got my rifle cocked and ready. It might be the Professor, or another kind of RI, a new and improved version smart enough to figure out my traps.

Or another last one standing.

"I'll have you know . . ." I shouted, trying to make my voice sound low and male. "You're stealing from a USDA approved Marine!" I fired a volley of shots in the air. They echoed against the trees and rang in my ears.

The shots scared the crap out of me, but whatever was out there didn't flinch, just kept pretending that it was invisible when I was staring right at it. It was either very stupid or very brave.

"You hear me?" I shouted.

Silence. My stomach did another backflip, so hard I felt like throwing up. With one hand on the M16, I dumped the oysters into my basket, jumped on my bike and rode back to camp.

Dinner was oysters, peach brandy and seaweed salad with tamari soy. No gluten—that stuff'll kill you. I finished with Miz Daisy's shrooms, sat back and remembered. Only with a full stomach and a lot of drugs could I think about the past without sinking into despair.

Most of the men on Avalon Island were fishermen, Coast Guard, and Military Police. Since they were out on the ocean or in D.C., most died in the first few days after 6/8. Miz Daisy, my former art teacher became the mayor of our all-woman town. No one voted for her, but no one else wanted the job.

Miz Daisy lived up to her name. There were daisies threaded through her braided white hair. She favored Daisy-print muumus. Friends of hers said she was an anarcho-syndicalist hippie. Enemies said she was a witch. The funny thing was, she didn't mind being called a witch, even though she was one of those church ladies who talked about Jesus like he was sitting right next to her. But she was from New Orleans. Nothing's simple down there.

We made camp in the old elementary school, the only property on the island that was fenced in. Kept the RIs out. But the Mommuck virus was still in the air. Some got sick even if they weren't bit by an RI.

Miz Daisy said that if we were going to survive emotionally as well as physically, we'd have to learn to deal with death. So she made up a funeral service, based on church tradition, zombie shows, and some good old NOLA Voodoo.

Dying of Mommuck had three stages. If someone got bit, the blood vessels branching off from the wound would turn black-blue. Then there'd be a fever, an all-over shaking thing. Then they'd start talking to people who weren't there. If someone didn't get bit and started doing that, it wasn't a sure sign. Everyone had gone a little crazy lately.

Throwing up was sign #2. Passing out was #3.

Sign #4 was, they bit you in the ass. Everyone wanted to avoid #4.

So, after the victim passed out, that was your chance to make it right. Tie them to a surfboard. Get the peach brandy out and mix in a cup with few ground-up oxycodone, enough to knock them out again, but in a happy way.

Then, draw a spiral on the ground and shake an empty gourd. Send them on their way by cutting off their head with one quick swoop of the machete. Because beheading is the only way to be sure they won't rise again. Then get everyone together, douse the dead with brandy, and set off the Fireworks. When the healing flames scrubbed everything clean, Jesus would step down from his heavenly rings and take their spirits to heaven. Only then would they be saved.

That worked for everyone except the last two to go, Miz Daisy and Jen. I didn't like this memory but couldn't chase it away. I was coming back from the hunt with a couple of rabbits in my basket and an octopus so big it made my handlebars wobble. Jen usually waited for me to bring her the game before she'd butcher them, but this time she was walking towards me, shadowy in the dusky light. Not walking. Running.

I waved. She didn't wave back. My hand was on the Glock, because my instincts knew what my brain didn't want to believe. Jen hadn't eaten anything last night. Said she was dieting. And she slept in, something she never did before.

But by the time I'd justified pulling the trigger she was already shrieking in my face. I could smell bubblegum and vomit as her nails came clawing at my eyes. I put up a defensive arm, rolled off my bike and fell in the sand, fumbling for my knife.

Miz Daisy came running and pulled Jen off me. I twisted around and plunged the knife into my best friend's chest. My eyes blurred with hot tears as she fell. Miz Daisy was crying too, cradling her bloody arm in the folds of her muumuu. Jen trembled as the last bit of energy left her body. Her mouth was wet with Miz Daisy's blood.

I started to mix up the Oxy and Brandy, but Miz Daisy didn't want to go that way. We knew she had two days, so she decided to sleep on it. But the next morning, before I got up, she had left the camp and walked off the ocean side. I found her heavy footprints in the sand, wavering as they disappeared into the shallow waves.

She left a note. "I didn't want you to see me this way. Love, Miz Daisy."

Daisy once said, "Funerals aren't for the dead. They're for the living, for the memory." So, I had a funeral anyway and did the fireworks thing. The remnants of Miz Daisy and Jen's memorials were still scattered around the camp.

Enough remembering. Time to sleep. I drank some more peach brandy.

As my eyelids got heavy, Daisy herself stepped over the red charcoal, her pink feet wispy in the flames. I wasn't all that surprised. This wasn't the first ghost I'd seen on shrooms and brandy and it wouldn't be the last. She sat next to me, so real I could almost smell the patchouli. She had an aura around her that was yellow and white.

"Sorry I missed my funeral," she said. "I thought it would be easier for us both if I just left."

I nodded. "How is it on the other side?"

"Ah, *comme ci, comme ça.* It's peaceful. I've found my answers. But the harps, they ain't playin' *zydeco. Tant pis.*"

"You found answers? To what?"

"What do you want to know?"

"Who's been messing with my traps?"

Like she was reading my mind she said "Not the Professor. I rented a room once to him and his family. Good man."

"So, who's doing it?"

She stirred the fire. "Why you so obsessed with those traps?"

"I want octopus for dinner."

"I think it's because you like a mystery. It distracts you."

"That's not why." I pulled my knife out and started whittling.

She shrugged "Vern had a Dalmatian dog. Remember that?"

"Yeah," I said as I sliced a bit of bark.

"I've seen him. In the ringlight, with a pack that hides under the boardwalk."

"I thought the dogs died off."

"Nope. They're the ones coming after your traps." She threw a log in the fire. Sparks flew. "Any more questions?"

I pretended to agree, knowing full well dogs couldn't cut through a lock. But it would be silly to give my imaginary ghost friend grief. She had enough to deal with.

"Sometimes I don't think I want to stay in this world."

"Oh, don't say that, darlin'. Jesus is always with you, waiting to welcome you through the pearly gates. No reason to rush things."

"I'm not talking about death, I'm talking about other worlds. Other earths. The Professor talked about that."

"Oh, no, I feel small enough in *this* world. Don't tell me there are more of them."

"There might be."

She laughed, her belly rippling under her flowered muumuu. "You'll never find a world with peach brandy like mine."

I smiled, put my knife down, closed my eyes, and rested on her imaginary shoulders.

In the middle of the night my stomach was aching, so bad it woke me up. I tried not to vomit but couldn't stop it. All those oysters. And the brandy didn't help.

Miz Daisy's ghost was still there, but her aura had turned dark blue, shadowy as the pines. She said. "You were raised on oysters. That's not what's making you sick."

"It's a sign I need variety . . . in my diet," I gasped as I wiped my face.

"Like—crabs?"

That set me to hurling again.

The next afternoon I managed to drag myself out of bed, but only after considering it and reconsidering it for a couple of hours. My body never felt so heavy, and the weather made it worse. No wind. Slick calm.

I got on my bike and rode, hoping it would make me feel better, but it didn't. I only started to feel good when I spotted a sprung trap. I felt much better when I pulled it up, unhooked it, and found the octopus inside.

"Well, hey there. Couldn't handle a titanium lock, could you?"

It looked at me with big round eyes and changed color, turned itself reddish brown, the same color as me. It even gave itself freckles. I laughed. That got it mad. It flapped at the walls of the trap with its tentacles.

"Sorry buddy. Sometimes you win, sometimes you lose."

My hand shook as I lowered the trap into my basket. Something dripped from my chin. I was drooling. Literally drooling. Dribbling right onto my camo. Ick. I should have had breakfast. Too hungry.

Then, with the snap of a gunshot the trap flew out of my hand. I forgot the drool and the shaking as the trap and octopus plunged into the blue hole. I dove in after them, water bubbling in my ears, caught them, and came up fast as a whip. I grabbed my rifle, lowered my voice to marine level and roared "Now you're really pissing me off!"

I fired a shot. The trees shook. Whoever took the shot was beating a hasty retreat.

Okay, you son of a bitch, let's see who's faster. I hooked the trap over my handlebars, got on my bike and chased the shooter through the pines. Couldn't be an RI, they couldn't shoot for shit. That shot was precise.

It couldn't be the Professor, he was too old to run this fast. Sweat poured from my skin as I slapped the branches out of my way, crashed through a tangle of vines and came into a clearing. There was a tent staked out in the middle, so neat it looked like it had been ironed. A man stepped out from behind it, young and tall. His dark face was framed by black Einstein hair. He had a .22 rifle in hand. "Stay right where you are," he said in a shaky voice.

I thought back to my conversation with the ghostly Miz Daisy. Weird that a drunken delusion told me something I didn't already know. The Professor had a family. This guy—crisp white shirt, gold rimmed glasses—had to be the professor's son. I took aim and kept walking closer, with him in my sights.

"I said stop!" he shouted.

"No," I said, still walking.

"This is a standoff. So stand off! Umm . . . away, I mean."

"We can't have a standoff if your gun's not loaded."

"It is!"

"If you had bullets, you wouldn't have run," I said. But I forgot to lower my voice.

He squinted through his glasses "You're no Marine. You're just a girl!"

I pulled the bolt back loudly "Say that again, buster . . ."

"Okay, okay." He slowly put his gun down, got his hands up.

My arm was starting to shake. I took deep breaths to get calm. "You're the Professor's son, aren't you?"

"You knew my Dad?"

"He rented a video from my store. Never brought it back."

He smiled and started putting his hands down. "That was Dad, neither here nor there."

He said 'was'. The Professor was dead. Tears flooded my eyes. I don't know why it hit me that hard, I barely knew the man. I swallowed the tears down and said, "Why'd you waste your last bullet trying to save an octopus?"

"He can save lives. Like yours."

"I'm not sick!"

"Your blood vessels have gone black. You're very sick."

I looked down. My shaking hand was covered with scratches, bright red, infected. I dropped the rifle and yanked up my sleeves. A bite! Clear as day.

Dizzy with fear, I remembered. Jen did that when she jumped at me. It was my blood on her mouth, my blood on Miz Daisy. I tried to remember more but just thinking about it made me sick.

"The first symptom isn't the veins." He took a step forward. "It's denial." His white teeth and shirt rippled like a mirage on a hot day. He was getting so close I could smell him. So—tasty. So nice to sink my teeth into him.

Oh, shit. Did I just think that?

"Get away from me! I'm—Mommucked." But he was getting closer.

I didn't have my rifle but all that mattered to me was the grass, because I was falling into it.

When I woke up, Professor Jr. was standing over me, a tall silhouette in the orange light. I was sloshing from side to side. Why was the grass sloshing?

"You're one of the few survivors, the best of the best," he said.

"I know," I said.

When he jumped, I realized he wasn't talking to me. He was talking to the octopus.

I tried to sit up, to catch my breath, but found that I was strapped down into one of those rescue boards the lifeguards used. And I was in the water. "Goddamn!" I struggled to get free, sloshing back and forth.

He crouched down beside me, holding the octopus. He'd taken it out of the trap and was cradling it gently in his hand. "Sorry, but I had to bring him back home. And I couldn't leave you alone."

He was scared, I could smell it. My newly boiled brain had only one objective. Hunt. I figured if I whispered something, he'd come closer. Close enough to taste. "I feel better," I whispered.

He was too smart for that. He stayed back. "The symptoms will return. I should know, I've been bitten two times already."

My brain was starting to boil. It was getting hard to make words. "You . . . thurvived?"

He rolled up his right sleeve and showed me the scars, bite marks crudely stitched, ripples of veins that had blackened and healed many times over. He pulled a syringe filled with a blue liquid from his shirt pocket. "This is the cure." He lowered the octopus to my level. Its tentacles wavered in the calm water. "This is made from his blood. The octopus can deliberately and consciously reprogram its own RNA to fight disease. This serum can give you the same ability."

So many words, spinning in my head like those winding tentacles. I turned to the octopus. I swear, it winked at me. I tried to take a bite. It smacked me on the nose.

Professor Jr. held the needle up to the light. It sparkled like hope.

But then something dark rose behind him, wide and muumuued. Miz Daisy, raising something up high. A big old log. I blinked. Was this real?

The sun was not shining through her. I tried to say "Don't," but no sound came out. Then she did it. Bashed him on the head.

He splashed down beside me. The syringe and the octopus floated past my head, out into the big blue ocean.

"Jesus will take two to heaven tonight," Miz Daisy said as I drifted into darkness.

I opened my eyes. The world was bleary.

"You wanted to eat him alive. Not that I blame you, he is pretty tasty," Miz Daisy said as she sharpened the machete, pulled it backwards over the strop. The sound it made, tzzt, tzzt, made my brain ache. "When you're a teenager, there's not much difference between lust and hunger."

She'd tied me onto the surfboard and laid me down flat. Professor Jr. was strapped onto the rescue board, propped up next to the window. His head lolled to the side, but it was still attached. Guess I'd be the first to go.

"The two of you are so cute together. A Zombie Romeo and Juliet." She smiled and took a sip of beer. "I'll play the Friar, to send you into the hereafter."

The thing about being Mommucked was, I couldn't talk but I could still think. Like remembering that Miz Daisy couldn't tie a knot for shit. Always forgot that last loop. My fingers searched for that loose bit.

Found it!

"I knew you were a goner," Miz Daisy said. "But I couldn't deal, you know? I didn't want to have to kill you, so I pretended to die and watched you from afar. Hoped you would just—disappear. But then you met this fellow." She reached out for his arm turned his wrist, streaked with the veins and scars, towards me. "Poison hath been his timeless end."

I shook my head, tried to tell her he wasn't Mommucked, that he'd been cured, but all that came from my mouth was a snarl.

She patted her buxom chest. "Bless your little heart darlin'! I'm going to miss you."

Professor Jr. groaned and opened his eyes. He had words, lots of them. "Where's my octopus. And where's the syringe? What did you do with my formula! "

"Your octopus is in that bucket there. Anything else is lost, lost at sea," she said.

"I worked for a year on that formula! It's the only thing that can cure her."

"I got the cure right here," she said, checking her reflection in the shiny blade.

My stomach growled. Eat.

"You idiot!" he screamed at Miz Daisy.

She grabbed the machete and pressed it against his throat. "Respect the one who wields the blade, for she is Godly!"

He gave her a look that was mean as her machete. "Respect is earned."

She turned away and sat back down. "You best make your peace with God."

He sighed. "Let me make this as simple as I can. My father had many degrees, but his first doctorate was in Biology. He told me he could travel between worlds because of the research he'd done on Coleoids, umm . . . octopuses, animals that can deliberately and consciously reprogram their own code. This gives them the power to change their appearance, increase their intelligence, even to travel between universes. People can unintentionally change their genetic makeup, but they can't make deliberate changes. This serum gives you the ability to do that. It gives you a mind like an octopus. It's not just a cure for 6/8, it's a cure for everything!"

I loosened the last knot.

"Pull the other one," Miz Daisy said.

"The other what?"

"Leg. What a crazy, tall tale you tell." She picked up the bucket. The octopus sloshed inside. "You're gonna be so tasty," she said to it.

"That octopus is very rare! He's the last of his breed, found only in these shallows. He's a super-intelligent creature who could save your life!"

"He's gumbo!"

I got up slowly, about to chomp down on both of them, but was stopped by a loud slurp. The Octopus had thrown its tentacles around the edges of the bucket and was loudly sloshing itself out of it. Even in my mommucked state, I was impressed.

Then it leaped to the floor, catlike, stood up on all eights and held out a tentacled arm. Wrapped within the tentacle was the syringe. It held that arm way above its head, then let it drop to the floor, like a rock star dropping the mic after a great performance.

"You may be right," Miz Daisy said to Jr. She put the machete down and loosened the straps that held him in the carrier.

But all I cared about that moment was Eat. I leaped towards Daisy, teeth bared. She screamed, dropped to the floor and rolled. Hey! I taught her that move.

The octopus picked up the syringe and tossed it to Jr., who caught it and gripped it like a knife. He held his hands out, defensively.

I growled and crouched, prepared to leap right for his neck. Warm blood, sweet as pie.

"This might pinch a little!" he shouted as I leapt. There was a hard punch in the center of my chest. I screamed as the needle pierced my heart, then fell flat on the floor, writhing in pain. The sky above me swirled, blue as blood. It picked me up and coursed through me, quivering and bending like a video with a major glitch.

Then the pain faded and I was in it, the sky and the stars. I was floating past dogs with gossamer wings. People small as bugs. Volcanoes of red clouds bursting into a yellow sky. I floated past an earth filled with humans ignoring their beautiful white moon, staring at card-sized computers. A cloud of burning metal dust surrounded me, then faded into tightly wound spools, like beads in an endlessly long necklace. DNA. My code. I'd found it. I swirled around the strands, swam in the endless whirlpool, threading and rethreading the beads with eight hands. Somehow, I knew what needed to be changed.

Then I was back. On the floor. The needle was still in my chest.

Miz Daisy's face rose above me, full of concern. "You ok?"

For the first time in a week, I didn't feel like eating or puking. "Yeah. I think. How long was I out?"

"A few seconds."

"Wow. It felt like days." Then I blushed. "Umm . . . sorry about trying to eat you."

She laughed. "No worries, little darlin'"

Professor Jr. gingerly pulled the needle from my chest, sat down next to me and took my hand. "You just saw the world through octopus eyes. Pretty trippy, huh?"

I tried to describe the way it felt, floating through the small, the huge, everything outside and within me. I was dead and alive, timeless in time. But all I could say was "Can I go back?"

He smiled. "You never left."

Mary Madigan loves to read scientific journals to imagine where new discoveries could take us. She takes those daydreams and spins stories that usually involve space cowgirls, ace pilots and mad scientists – or mad cowgirls, space pilots and ace scientists. Then she goes downstairs to make dinner. Mary's short fiction has appeared in many anthologies, including Lillicat's **Visions III, IV,** *and* **VI.** *More info about her stories and projects is at* **marypmadigan.com.**

Sometimes, victory comes with a price on the grandest scale.

Universal Hero

Darrel Duckworth

Among the dimensional essences and pan-dimensional beings of the multiverse, there is one universe respected and honored above all for her courage. A quiet universe, unremarkable except for her subtle complexities, intricate beauties, and seemingly-tragic flaws . . . yet, she alone was able to stem the darkness that devoured universes, the Enemy that threatened all of the multiverse.

This is the story of her courage.

***

Since the Beginning beyond the Beginnings, there had been existence and co-existence for the universes. Each was complete in itself, in its purpose and form, and had no need of anything from the others except discourse. Even those newest-formed were formed with all they needed. It was the Way and no universe felt desire for more or for 'different.'

And so, none anticipated the coming of the Enemy.

Although forces such as Mutation and Evolution were known to all—even to those that did not employ those forces inside themselves—such forces were not possible in the static non-Causality of the multiverse structure in which the universes existed.

But then, the impossible happened.

A universe mutated.

It was a dreary universe in the perception of most others. It avoided any forces that provided variety, such as Chaos, as much as it avoided discourse with other universes, preferring to focus its perception internally on maintaining precise orderliness among the endless, black-on-black, multi-phasic, string structures it contained.

Still, the other universes withheld comment, for orderliness was the Way for many universes, although none to the extreme of this one, and it was the Way to accept infinite diversity among their own. For each universe was meant to be what it was.

But then, without cause, this dreary universe was suddenly different than it was meant to be.

And it did the impossible.

The dark universe reached out beyond itself and engulfed a pocket dimension.

Pocket dimensions were so tiny that the universes rarely noticed them. They were so simple in their self-realization that they had little to discourse with complete universes and mostly kept to themselves.

Yet they were not so small or unrealized that the other members of the multiverse could not feel the shrill discord as one winked out of existence.

Such events were not unknown. Smaller existences such as pocket dimensions sometimes destabilized by an error in judgement, not being as realized as a full universe. But usually there were traces to be found among the strata of the multiverse. This time, there were none.

It was simply gone.

Then another.

And another.

More.

Smaller existences just disappeared, leaving no trace.

***

The members of the multiverse were puzzled. For so many existences to destabilize within a region of the multiverse implied external cause, which was impossible in the non-Causality of the multiverse structure.

And why had the destabilizations left no traces?

Then, one universe witnessed the hideous act.

If it were possible for a universe to feel horror, that universe would have felt it as it watched the inconceivable happen.

The dreary, dark dimension that seldom discoursed with any other universe suddenly turned its perception on a barely-sentient, fledgling dimension . . . and engulfed it!

Instead of manipulating the strata of the multiverse between them to form a discourse wave in the usual manner, the dark universe exuded some strange, black, extra-universal force across the ephemeral strata of the multiverse—impossible though that was—and touched the fledgling dimension. The tiny victim screamed in shrill discord as the dark force wrapped around it. Then the force withdrew back to the dark universe and nothing was left in its wake.

Almost imperceptibly, the dark universe grew.

A universe had just fed on one of its own kind.

***

Discourse raged among the universes in a way not known since their self-realizations in the Beginning before the Beginnings.

It was inconceivable to them all that this could happen.

But the shared experience from the witnessing universe was undeniable. Universes were not capable of deception.

But then, universes were also not capable of devouring or absorbing anything, much less each other. Not even minor versions of their kind. They simply had no functions with which to perform the act.

Yet, it had happened.

The multiverse was filled with discourse concerning options to take.

Until now, no universe had ever needed to consider choices outside its internal self. They had always co-existed in the Way and there was no variation in the Way. Even the appearance of new beings, or their dissolution, did not require choice. Such things simply were part of the Way in the multiverse

Further, they had no concept of crime . . . or punishment. No crime could be committed in the multiverse because they had no means of affecting each other except discourse. For the same reason, there could be no punishment. Even internally within itself, a universe did not deal in crime or punishment; events simply occurred as they should for the parameters of that universe.

And, they had no concept of conflict . . . not among themselves. There was no need for conflict among beings that were complete and weapons were not possible for beings that had no function outside of themselves.

Yet now, the impossible was obviously possible.

Then they discovered that feeding was not the only impossibility the dark universe was capable of.

***

They watched, stunned, as the dark force exuded from the dark universe once more . . . this time, reaching out and touching a small universe vibrationally adjacent to the dark universe.

This time, the dark force did not engulf . . . it speared the small universe.

As they watched, another impossibility occurred . . . and the members of the multiverse learned to feel something akin to the emotion force called Fear.

They watched as darkness spread within the small universe . . . outward from the spear of dark force impaling it. They watched as the bright and whimsical Chaos inside the small universe transformed into dark regularity: black-on-black string structures . . .just like those in the dark universe that had speared it.

The effect spread like a dark infection through the chaotic brightness while the small universe shrilled in discord.

Those universes that did not contain the concept of infection learned it from those that did and the newly-learned emotion of Fear grew.

They watched as the process completed and the small universe fell silent.

It was now a small but exact copy of the dark universe.

The other universes realized that the dark universe hadn't just fed off the pocket dimensions. Inside himself, he had used the tortured existences that he had engulfed to learn how to reshape others to his own form.

It was insanity in a realm that had always been sane . . . violence in a realm where violence had never been possible.

The universes of the multiverse had an Enemy.

***

While they debated and discussed, the Enemy infected another, small universe. And another.

When a mature universe vibrationally close to the Enemy's resonant discontinuity tried to discourse with Him, the dark universe thrust out again, infected it, and reshaped it—a universe larger than Himself—into a larger copy of Himself.

Perceiving this, the others knew that no universe was safe.

The Enemy could enslave them all to His way, devouring their infinite diversities and reshaping them into His likeness. And, He was clearly determined to do so.

In desperation, some rallied together and attempted to force Him back to the Way by directing their strongest discourses at Him.

It was like a man shouting at a gun to stop the bullets from coming out.

He infected and converted them.

The other universes realized that they would not survive such direct confrontations. But a few—those abundant in Thought—had noticed that the lost group *had* actually hindered His progress in one direction of resonance when their attempts at forceful discourse had created discord in the strata of the multiverse structure.

They proposed a concept never seen in the multiverse itself: a defence.

And so, all the universes joined in a common effort, surrounding the resonant discontinuities of the Enemy and His enslaved universes with discord.

It proved to be a weak defence.

The Enemy probed incessantly, pursuing His madness obsessively.

Finally, His dark force snaked through a weak point and speared another universe.

The others watched the transformation begin even as they shifted their pattern to include the newly-infected universe.

It was a battle of attrition . . . and they would lose.

But they knew no other way.

***

Then a quiet, firm voice spoke through the clamour.

"Let me face Him."

The other universes regarded she who spoke and thought that this must be another form of insanity.

She was a fair-sized universe, but not large by their reckoning, smaller even than the Enemy. While elegant in her subtle complexities and rich in some ways, she was tragically- crippled by one of her dominant parameters and sadly-flawed in her internal choices.

The Enemy had already taken a larger, more stable universe than she and others that, frankly, showed more wisdom in their self-management. How did she intend to stop Him?

They implored her to return to helping them hold the barrier.

"The barrier will not hold Him. We have seen that already. We can wait for Him to break through again and again, growing stronger each time while we grow fewer and weaker. Or we can attack Him directly now. I choose now, before He grows too strong."

"Attack Him with what?" The others asked, still struggling to understand the concepts of defence and attack. "Already we have done all that is new. There is nothing else."

An emanation emerged from her that some universes recognized in beings they contained internally: mirth.

"It has been my experience, while dealing with the beings in my charge, that there is never an end to inventiveness."

It was beyond comprehension! She was actually quoting the wisdom of the internal beings which had developed under her flawed choices?

She shrugged off their criticisms.

"Think as you like, but accept my choice. I would rather fight now than wait for the Enemy to take me."

Discourse was made and consensus reached. It was enough of a departure from the Way that they had to contain the Enemy and the darkened universes. They would not deny choice to one of their own.

They shifted the resonance of their discord in synch with her discontinuity.

Then, to their astonishment, she altered her interaction with her resonant discontinuity in a way none of them had perceived before.

She shifted her existence *into* the infected zone.

As her existence approached the Enemy's resonant discontinuity, she did not open discourse, as had the larger universe. Instead, she continued on, waiting for Him to act as she knew He would.

The Dark Enemy was a being of strict order—and it was ironic that only such a being could bring Chaos to the multiverse itself—so, she felt sure that He would begin as He had before.

Indeed, the dark force exuded out, straight towards her through the extra-dimensional strata that comprised so much of the multiverse.

She altered her quantum-dinubial potential gradient. Not all universes incorporated quantum concepts and so, not all could do what she did. But even those that did include variations of quantum di, tri, or higher nubiation were stunned to perceive what she did. They had never considered varying themselves as she did and so, watched in astonishment at the way she moved.

She "sidestepped" and let the spear of force pass her.

This was something she had learned while watching many of the fragile beings in her care. So many of them could withstand only trivial damage and so, had developed many methods of not being in the spot when "damage" arrived.

By contrast, universes never needed to dodge.

But then, few universes ever thought to learn from the beings within them.

The Enemy tried again.

She ducked 'below' and shifted her resonance even closer to His discontinuity. She had to interact quickly she knew. He had mutated and was therefore, unpredictable. He might also have the ability to learn and adapt, a function that universes also never *needed* to do. Until now.

"Dodging" a third attempt, she finally "closed the distance" enough to do the impossible herself.

To the amazement of the other universes, she exuded a small part of herself to reach out to Him.

Unlike other universes, she had never contentedly viewed herself as complete. She saw that as a limit to her purpose. Perhaps that was because she had Begun with such an abundance of the conceptual forces of Thought and Emotion.

What the other universes called poor choices on her part, she called experimenting. And experimenting required observing, learning, and adapting.

She had observed the Enemy attacking the other universes, learned from it and experimented with her own existence. She had learned how He did it and adapted herself to do it. She was not as powerful as He nor able to reach as far, but she could and did touch Him.

In that contact, she shared with Him all the positives that she contained, from emotion forces such as Compassion and Love, to conceptual parameters like Creativity, to meta-forces such as Awareness.

In dismay, she perceived the results.

Creativity shattered upon the sharp, unyielding corners of His black, string structures.

Love and Compassion were sucked into the infinite cold and darkness within Him, gone as if they had never existed.

Awareness withered in the vacuum of His absolute self-focus.

All the positives she shared with Him met similar, futile fates.

He had defended against her efforts with just His nature.

In return, her brief contact with Him had damaged her, leaving the part that had touched Him colder than the spaces between her galaxies. Dead. Inactive. It was as if He had drained the very energy of Existence itself from that part of her.

***

She quickly shifted her resonance and "backed off." From a state adjacent to His discontinuity, she tried something else the multiverse had never seen before. Using a variation of the method by which universes discoursed, she affected the strata of the multiverse between them, but opened tunnels instead of forming discourse waves.

Through these conduits, she hurled bolts of Thought.

Most universes contained some manner and measure of the conceptual force of Thought.

But for her, Thought was a fundamental force, a partner in creation within her, greater even than the parameters of Time or Space. She did not *contain* a measure of Thought; it was a primary part of her as a universe.

She threw that part of herself at the Enemy, hoping to alter His Realization again, as the mutation must have done . . . if not back to His old state then perhaps to another state of sanity that did not involve the destruction of others.

The bolts struck His existence and sank into His being. She watched His existence ripple in confusion . . . watched the black, string structures within Him shift, grating and tearing against each other and then being torn apart as they shifted out of their intricate balance with His multi-phasic Time.

She watched His existence shimmer and writhe under the assault of Thought.

Then suddenly, His existence snapped back into form. The sharp edges of the string-structures realigned with each other and back into chronal-vibrational synch with His multi-phasic Time.

Her bolts of Thought no longer penetrated His being.

He had reinforced His rigid parameters, making them capable of withstanding the changes that outside Thought could bring.

And too late, she discovered that He too could also move.

***

He closed with her, making full discontinuity contact.

Again, she felt the cold deadness leeching her but now it assaulted her entire existence.

In desperation, before He could spear her with His black force, she lashed out with her third attack.

Through the painful contact that He inflicted upon her, she inflicted upon Him the plodding trench of linear Time.

Most universes were not encumbered with such an affliction and wondered how she endured such a devastating disability. But now, they watched as she turned her tragic burden into a potent weapon.

Unprepared, His multi-phasic, crystalline-like, string structures—formed within the elegant complexity of multi-phasic Time—could not adjust to the crushing strictures of linearity and rent themselves apart as the onslaught pushed through Him.

And this effect was only the physical manifestation of larger corruptions.

All His internal forces and parameters were in harmony with multi-phasic Time. As the march of linear Time pushed through His being, it disrupted intricate balances and created a chronal-discontinuity along both sides of its intrusion.

Onto that horror and into that chrono-discontinuity, she threw Entropy, an impossibility in multi-phasic Time. He had no defence.

**

Beyond the defensive wall of discord, the other universes perceived His "bellow" as her attack tore through Him, penetrating deeper.

Perhaps she would do it, they hoped.

But that hope was tainted with the new feeling the Enemy had inspired within them.

For now, there were two universes that could inflict harm on their own kind.

**

Weakening under the onslaught of His energy-leeching contact, she fought to keep fighting. She called deep upon herself to continue to press her attack. It was a contest of Will now, she realized. Would He succumb before He drained so much of her that she could not continue? Or would she fall?

It would not be her, she decided.

She would draw upon her every force, every parameter . . . her last quantum of probability rather than succumb and let herself become like Him.

She felt galaxies dying within her as His damage drained her.

She fought on.

**

But it was not enough.

He had learned to learn.

He lanced spears out to His enslaved universes once more, penetrating into all of them at once . . . but this time, He drew on them. They were duplications of Himself, their parameters now the same as His. From them, He drew elements of their parameters into Himself, uncaring of what the result for them might be. He could and would make more.

He replenished His essence with theirs, re-establishing His parameters with theirs, using those to push back her chronal-entropic intrusion and repair the damage as He regained control.

He had many to draw upon. She was but one.

Soon she would be one in His many.

**

She perceived His spears, His feeding, His restoral . . . and the press of her attack being forced back.

She felt herself losing again.

Then He struck.

**

With their discontinuities directly adjacent now, no amount of alteration allowed her to "dodge" His spear.

It tore into her and sank deep.

She screamed as she felt it tear through her never-before-breached being. Then she felt the infection begin . . . and the coldness that had been pressing *against* her, was now also inside her. The infection began to spread, changing her as He forced His parameters upon her.

He had begun the hideous process of enslaving her.

She had often sampled the emotion force of Fear, to better understand the beings in her charge. But now, she was not sampling; it surged through her being. It filled her.

She fought against the panic as she fought against the infection spreading inside her, weeping as she perceived the beauties within her being crushed and reshaped into cold, black, crystalline strings. Stars, nebulae and galaxies turned black and dead, the tiny beings within them now just inert parts of a growing lattice. His contact continued to drain her from the outside while His spear and its infection weakened her from within.

Then He drove another spear into her. And another.

She screamed and felt the infection and drain spreading from multiple wounds now. She struggled futilely to disengage but He held her pinned with His spears.

She felt His "satisfaction" . . . his belief that He had defeated her.

But she was not done.

She had seen that His spears could carry change in both directions when He had begun pulling parameters and energies from His enslaved universes.

So, she tried again to insert her parameters and forces into Him—directly this time through His own spears.

But He still drew upon the other universes and immediately blocked her efforts.

She thrust Chaos into Him, but it had even less effect on His multi-phasic nature than linear Time had.

The infection inside her was spreading more rapidly. Soon, it would reach a point that she would not be able to stop or repair it.

She hurled every parameter and force she had into Him in a frantic effort to stop Him. Most had no effect. A few managed to slow the change a tiny amount, nothing more.

Then desperation drove a new idea into her being: something she had never considered a weapon before.

She drew upon a part of herself that she had carefully nurtured and held apart from the rest . . . kept apart to watch how they would develop. A tiny species that was different from any other she had created, different from any that she had ever heard any universe even mention.

To the cognitive-complexes of many other universes, it was a sign of her oddness that she chose to create and then endured the presence of such errant creatures within herself.

However, it was also a sign of her strengths that she had been able to contain such beings.

For each of the creatures was a potential—if malformed—pocket universe in itself. She had imbued so many of the elements of creation in each one: Matter, Energy, Life Essence, Thought, Quantum-dinubiant interaction . . . and more.

Why she had imbued them with so much had always puzzled the other universes. It gave these internal beings too much unpredictable latitude to change themselves and to interact with and affect their host universe at fundamental levels. They were unstable and possessed the threat of inflicting instability.

But they were a delight to her, among her favourites. Within them, she perceived so much potential.

And so, she did not want to do this. But if she did not, their potential would be destroyed anyway.

So, she accelerated their development several points along their potential, then released them from their physical forms and thrust them into the Enemy, back through His own spears.

She caught Him completely unprepared.

He perceived her new attack and set His defences to repel them as He had her other parameters and forces.

But these were not parameters or forces. They sailed past His defences and entered into His structure . . .

. . . where they took hold.

He paused in His attack against her, genuinely puzzled by these complex, unidentifiable things inside Him.

Then He began to feel their effects and forgot His attack against her entirely.

He reeled back from her, withdrawing His spears to stop the inflow.

Too late.

He was now the infected universe . . . infested.

He railed against the infecting creatures, throwing all the forces within Himself at the tiny beings: to destroy them, to contain them, to enforce His type of order on them. He even tried to infect and convert them as He had with the pocket dimensions He had engulfed.

But these beings had been created and developed in a universe of linear Time and physical constraints.

With no more physical form to constrain them, they displayed the third of their special talents with astonishing speed: they adapted to everything that He threw at them, mutating themselves into ever more diverse and resistant constructs.

He also quickly discovered the first of their special talents: procreation.

In biological form, in linear Time, they had multiplied exponentially.

In the multi-phasic Time inside Him, and freed from singular form, they were no longer limited by mere exponential growth.

For every billion He managed to destroy, trillions more were procreated by every means available to their adapting mutations. Further, each generation that emerged scattered itself among the multiple directions of His multi-phasic Time, cross-breeding and creating generations that were more mutated and resistant to Him than their progenitors. Some even managed to navigate the Time channels to arrive at the original insertion and cross-breed with the original progenitors, passing along the adaptations gained by many generations to the initiating group's first offspring.

And, the tiny, potential universes did the one other thing that came so naturally to them: violence.

Their mother, when she had accelerated their potential and released them from physical form, had also told them why she had to sacrifice them.

And that none of them would be coming home to her.

Whatever mutated form they held, there were some things too integral to their essences to forget.

They adapted. They multiplied. They tore the Enemy apart from the inside.

They interacted with Him at fundamental levels causing the sort of instabilities the other universes had predicted from them.

He fought to the bitter end, His spears still draining the duplicate, dark universes.

She watched the duplicate universes wither and die, one after the other, drained of their very Existence.

Then she watched the tiny beings that had delighted her so much . . . claw and rend an entire universe asunder.

***

In the end, she lay alone and crippled on the multiverse's first and only battlefield, surrounded by the horror of drained, dead universes . . . watching the shreds of the defeated Enemy disperse into the strata of the multiverse.

From beyond the defensive wall, the other universes slowly silenced their resonant discord and looked upon the wounded and dead universes.

There was no discourse.

***

Aftermath.

She was less now than she had been. Smaller with fewer subtle complexities. Large parts of her intricate beauties were destroyed by the Enemy's attacks and energy leeching. Yet she clung to what remained of her tragic flaws . . . even her questionable, internal choices.

She kept to herself, hardly discoursing with other universes anymore. She devoted herself to her efforts to rebuild what was within her, though the others could perceive that some of what she tried to do would never be possible.

She still mourned for the beings she had sacrificed, themselves destroyed as the dark universe died.

The other universes mostly left her alone, partly out of respect for her wishes, partly out of fear of her abilities.

And partly because to look upon her was to know their own vulnerability.

Universes should not have scars.

Among the dimensional essences and pan-dimensional beings of the multiverse, there is one respected and honored above all for her courage. A quiet universe, unremarkable except in her ability to be more than she was supposed to be.

This is the story of her courage.

After a career in high tech Darrel Duckworth returned to his first love, writing. He now spends more time on other worlds, occasionally returning to Earth to refill his coffee mug. His stories can be found in magazines such as LORE, Bards and Sages, and Plasma Frequency and in anthologies such as Coven and Wild Things.

Ebla was a dead planet, and Junior Survey Engineer Martin Rider's assignment nothing more than a formality. Until he heard the signal.

Signal

Neil Davies

It was on the third day of his solo tour at the base of Mount Pleajalta that Junior Survey Engineer Martin Rider first heard the anomalous signal. It interrupted the background static of his scanner.

Ebla, in the Esperas System, was a dead planet. It would never have been marked for terraforming otherwise. Away from Base, in the shadow of the highest mountain on the planet, there should have only been silence. Leaving the scanner open was just standard practice. He had never expected to actually hear anything on it.

Dimming the interior lights of his Rover, he peered out through the panoramic window. He did not expect to see anything unusual, but, nevertheless, pearls of sweat shone on his forehead in the filtered light of Ebla's parent star, Espe. He was tense as he swiveled his seat 360 degrees, his imagination conjuring visions of alien creatures lunging at the Rover, the five-inch thick plasteel window cracking, the deadly atmosphere of Ebla slithering inside, hissing with the sibilance of a venomous snake.

Stop it!

Had he not been on *down time* and not wearing his Monitor, every detail of his behavior would have been relayed to Base and, ultimately, his boss. At the very least, he would have been demoted, possibly fired. Psychological stability was minimum requirement for solo assignments.

There's nothing there. Ebla is a confirmed lifeless world.

He brought the lights up once more, glancing nervously towards the scanner. Nothing but the familiar low, white noise emanated from the device. The signal he thought he heard had most likely just been interference, possibly from a passing satellite, or a magnetic flare from Espe.

Shouldn't jump to conclusions.

He was firing up the Rover, *down time* almost over, when the same signal stuttered through the scanner once more.

It seemed stronger and, he thought, demonstrated patterns consistent with speech, although the language, if it was a language, was unintelligible. He struggled to remember his lessons from training. Every survey engineer received instruction in language patterns, speech constructs, and how to recognize them. Was that what he was hearing? Someone trying to speak to him in a foreign language?

He flicked the communicator to *on*.

"Base, this is Rider out at Mount Pleajalta. Come in please."

"Rider this is Base." The voice was clear and boomed in the confines of the Rover command pod.

"Are there any other assignments out this way?" said Rider, clasping his hands together, conscious of how clammy with sweat they felt. "Any reports of landings in the area?"

"There's nothing out there but you," said the disembodied voice. "Why? You see something?"

"No," said Rider, his mouth feeling dry. "Not seen. Heard."

***

Rider waited, nervously, as Base accessed the signal from the Rover Central Backup. They played and replayed it, over and over. They left communication open, and he could hear several voices offering opinions that ranged from interference, through an uncharted satellite, to proof of alien life somehow hidden from all surveys of the planet.

While the disembodied voices discussed and argued, Rider periodically flicked the Rover lights off, peered through the window for a few seconds, and then turned them back on again. He could not tell whether his anxiety was greater with the lights on, reducing outside visibility, or the lights off. Numerous detectors around the Rover would warn him if anything actually approached close enough to be a danger, but somehow knowing that could not stop the fear of what he might see with his naked eye.

"Rider, this is Base."

Rider jumped at the sudden, louder voice from the communicator. He closed his eyes for a second, composing himself. It would not do to sound nervous.

"Rider here," he said, relieved at the steadiness of his voice.

"We can't reach a consensus here. It does, however, seem of interest."

Of interest meant they either thought there could be money in it, or they feared it might bring a halt to operations. Rider knew, with a sinking in his stomach, that either option would mean they needed to know more. And he was the man on the spot.

"We've calculated the probable direction of the signal," continued the voice. "The heading has been programmed into your NavCom."

"You want me to try and find the source?" said Rider, trying not to allow his fear to seep into his tone.

"Yes," said Base. "We need to know whether it's worth sending a full team."

Rider knew he had no choice. But even as the Rover fired up and began to trundle, ponderously, along the programmed route, he could not stop wishing he could turn it round and drive as far away as possible.

***

The auto-driver steered the Rover through the foothills, winding a meandering but safe path around the edge of Mount Pleajalta. The Caterpillar tracks squelched through mud acidic enough to dissolve human flesh to the bone in seconds. On the horizon, storm clouds dulled the natural gold of the sky. Distant lightning ripped through the gloom. The first surveys had measured winds up to seven hundred miles per hour in Ebla's frequent storms. And if the wind did not kill you, the acid rain was only slightly less destructive than the combination of rainwater and ground dust that splattered the reinforced cab of the Rover.

"My mother wanted me to go into finance," said Rider, a watchful eye on the approaching storm. "But no, I wanted to travel, to be at the forefront of human expansion. I wanted *adventure*." He shook his head. "What a dick!"

"Who you talking to, Rider? You picked up an alien hitchhiker or something?"

There was laughter on the other end of the communicator. Rider blushed. He had forgotten the damn thing was still open.

"Just thinking out loud, Base," he said. "Got a storm moving in."

"We see it Rider. Just let the Rover follow the programmed route."

Rider closed his eyes, embarrassed. At least mentioning the storm had directed things back to business. But no doubt he'd hear more about talking to himself when he got back to Base. The senior engineers were not ones to miss the chance to humiliate one of their juniors.

The signal interrupted the static of the scanner, louder again, less fractured. "Base?"

"We hear it, Rider. Just keep going."

Just keep going, thought Rider. *So easy for them to say.*

The Rover's powerful headlights sparkled as rain began to drive through them. Drops speckled the window. Rider imagined he could hear them *hiss* as they hit. He had seen the pockmarked glass on some of the older Rovers, and was pleased he had been issued one that had seen less service. The built-in repellent was still able to disperse the acid before it could inflict damage.

Another signal, even louder, more complete. Just as indecipherable.

"That's given us a better fix," said Base, making Rider jump in his command chair.

"Great," he said, glad the communicator was voice-only. "How far?"

"It's close," said Base. "But it's too far for you. Abort the mission."

Rider was stunned, confused.

Abort? Why?

"But you said the source of the signal was close," he said. "What's happened? It can't be the storm. All Rovers are built to withstand even the worst of Ebla's storms."

"It's not the storm," said Base. "Rider, the signal is close, but it's up."

"Up?" Rider peered out of the window at the reasonably level path in the Rover's headlights. Then he turned and stared at the jagged rock of the mountain. "You mean somewhere up on Mount Pleajalta?"

"I'm afraid so," said Base. "And there's no way the Rover is going to be able to make it up there."

The Rover slowed to a gentle stop as Rider continued to stare at the mountain. The strengthening wind buffeted the vehicle. It was only the edge of the storm and the wind had not yet reached Earth hurricane level, but he could feel it, rocking the cab.

"But the signal could be important," he said, surprised when Base responded. He had not been speaking to them.

"Yes, Rider, it could be important. It could also be nothing. It doesn't matter. There's nothing you can do."

"But what if it stops? We've never heard it before. It could disappear again."

"We have co-ordinates," said Base. "We'll get a fully equipped team out there as soon as we can spare the men. It's not your problem, Rider."

"So, what am I meant to do?"

"Find something to shelter the Rover from the worst of the storm and sit it out. Then get back to your original assignment. Forget the signal. It's not your concern anymore."

Forget the signal?

As if on cue, the signal called out from the scanner. The strongest yet. The steadiest. Rider imagined he could make out speech patterns more than ever before.

"Can you hear that?"

"Of course," said Base, sounding irritable. "I've already told you to forget about it."

"But what if it's a cry for help?" said Rider.

"You're talking nonsense," said Base. "And it's no longer your concern, as I said. Leave this to the experts, Rider. You get back to what you're trained to do."

"Yes," said Rider. "I'm sorry. As soon as the storm's passed, I'll get back to my work."

"And if you hear the signal again, ignore it," said Base. "We're recording it all and we'll take care of it."

But if it is a cry for help, you might be too late, thought Rider. But he did not say it to Base. There would be no point.

He could not ignore it, either.

With sudden clarity, he knew what he had to do. He also knew he had never been more scared in his life.

***

He could hear Base calling for him over the communicator back in the command pod as he entered the airlock. He had not told them of his plans. He knew they would veto them. But this was important. He could feel it in his gut. That signal meant something, and he intended to find out what.

Anxiously checking that all life support systems were running, he snapped the helmet onto his suit and activated the outer door. He winced as a buckshot spray of acid rain pattered and fizzed on his visor. A heavy, violent gust of wind pushed him to the back of the airlock.

Leaning into the storm, each step a struggle, he exited the Rover.

The rocks at the base of the mountain were treacherous, slick with rain, jagged with acid erosion. He placed each step with caution. Even the thick protection of the suit would not help if he should fall onto those sharp points and razor-edges. The storm was growing, the wind strengthening, the rain near horizontal. His nerve almost failed him. A quick return to the Rover seemed the sensible thing to do. But then he thought of the signal and what it might mean. And he thought of the process of terraforming, and how it would erase all uniqueness from Ebla, its climate, its geography, its history. Moulding it into a replica of Earth. If the signal was anything other than natural interference, he needed to find out.

Base had said the source of the signal was near, and up. It seemed reasonable to assume that, if he kept the Rover below him as he climbed, he would be heading in the right direction. That was his plan. He was prepared to accept demotion, even dismissal, because of his actions, but, instinctively, he knew he was doing the morally correct thing.

The lower slopes were reasonably gentle, and he scrambled up them on all fours with little problem. Very soon, however, the mountain became serious, the cliff face angling upwards to near vertical. With only a moment's hesitation to catch his breath, Rider began to climb.

He had done some climbing as a teenager, back on his home world of Hutsoon. Nothing too serious, and always with full safety and climbing gear. And he had never been alone. Now he climbed with nothing, except his protective suit. No ropes, no harness, no spring-loaded cams. The boots of his suit slipped on the wet rock. The fingers of his gloves were thick and made feeling for the next handhold difficult. But he kept climbing, forcing the toe of his boot into one crack, jamming his fingers into another higher up. He pulled and pushed, making slow but steady progress up the rock face, while the winds slammed him, and the acid rain began to scar the visor of a helmet not designed for long periods in such conditions.

Although he had disconnected the communication feed from Base inside his helmet, he had kept open the feed from the scanner. The signal would repeat periodically, the gap between broadcasts shortening as he climbed higher.

Closer.

The signal was not only more frequent, but stronger with each broadcast. And some of the patterns were unmistakable.

Definitely speech, he thought. *There is life on Ebla. The terraforming project will need to be cancelled.*

He almost stumbled at the thought, his boot slipping, his gloved fingers barely hanging on as he scrambled for a better foothold. The cancellation of a multi-billion-dollar contract would not sit well with the Company. He was not sure he wanted to be the one to bring them the news. But if he was right about the signal, then surely the preservation of an alien species was more important than profit?

He felt a push in his back, crushing him against the rock. It took him a moment to realize it was a particularly powerful gust of wind. The storm was getting worse, and his muscles screamed agony through him with each push of a leg or pull of an arm. He hoped he reached the source soon, or he would never reach it at all.

Acid rain dripped from his gloves and helmet, sizzling against the rocks, leaving fresh scars among the old. A latticework of scarring seen on surfaces all over Ebla. The rain must have been falling for thousands of years. Were the originators of the signal impervious to the acid? Had they evolved to withstand the frequent storms, or did they hide from them, only venturing out in dryer weather, or in protective suits?

Questions lingered in his mind, however much he told himself they could not be answered until he reached the source. His only previous experience of alien species had been through documentaries during his training back on Hutsoon. This would be his first face-to-face, in-the-flesh meeting. He felt excited, but sick. It took effort to concentrate on the physical act of climbing. Otherwise he could fall, or be blown from the mountainside by the increasingly ferocious gusts of wind. He *had* to concentrate on the climbing. Everything else would have to wait.

Patience.

By now, he imagined the disembodied voice of Base would be screaming for him in the emptiness of the command pod. They would guess what he was doing, but they could not stop him. The team being put together to investigate the signal would be too late. He could *feel* that he was near. If he could just find the strength to climb a little further.

When a circular patch of the mountain face dissolved before him, his first thought was of massive acid erosion from the rain. It was highly improbable, he realized, but perhaps no more than the tunnel revealed behind the dissolved rock. Smooth walled, perfectly circular, leading into the interior of the mountain, much further than the available light could show him.

A sudden burst of the signal screamed in his ears. Almost immediately, it repeated. And again. It had not done that before, and Rider was certain it was connected with the opening of the tunnel.

Frightened, but determined, he climbed inside the mountain and crawled, hesitantly, forward.

A darkening of the tunnel made him look back. The patch of dissolved mountain was re-growing, spikes of rock reaching out from the edges, expanding, joining with others. There was something natural in the way it spread, organic, as though the mountain were a living creature, repairing itself.

Could that be real?

He did not move, listening for breathing or the thump of a heartbeat. Half expecting the tunnel to pulse with life. When there was nothing, he let go a deep sigh of relief.

Complete darkness closed in, cloying in its impenetrable thickness. The hole had been closed. The weak light from outside could no longer reach him. He turned on his helmet-lamp, but it illuminated little, quickly smothered by the blackness ahead of him.

The threat of panic was growing in his chest, his stomach. He could feel the tightness, the rising sickness, the trembling. It could not be allowed to take control. To surrender to panic would do nothing but ensure his death, whether it be through his oxygen running out, or the catastrophic failure of his suit as he scrambled and tore at the closed tunnel entrance. He must remain calm. With eyes closed, he struggled to suppress the growing fear, trying reason over despair.

He had never been claustrophobic; therefore the enclosed space should hold no fear. Even as a child he had not been afraid of the dark, so the lack of light should hold no terror. It was logical to be nervous of the unknown, but his desire to learn the source and the secret of the signal was the sole reason for his being there. And the *unknown* could only become *known* if he could override the fear and embrace the knowledge.

His panic dampened, and with the little light the helmet lamp afforded, he crawled further into the interior of Mount Pleajalta.

***

He had been crawling for almost thirty minutes, his knees and back aching. A nagging doubt picked at his brain. Had he been wrong about the signal? Was this tunnel a natural feature in the mountain that would lead to nothing but a dead-end? But there had been nothing natural about the dissolving entrance in the side of the mountain. That was no natural phenomenon, but an alien mechanism, alien technology. He *had* to be right. He had gambled so much on being right.

He paused. Considered, for a moment, turning back. But he did not know if the doorway would open for him. And if it did, he had no idea how severe the storm had become outside. He could leave to be whirled to his death by vicious winds, his body lost in the foothills, the suit gradually succumbing to the acid rain until it fizzed and sizzled on his bare skin.

Stop it!

At times, he believed his imagination to be a curse, not a gift. It would lead him down dark roads he had no wish to travel. It would confuse and depress him. He needed to be positive, to deal with the *now*. He must go on. Otherwise there had been no point in him entering the tunnel in the first place. No point in him trying to find the source of the signal.

He crawled on, the helmet lamp illuminating unnaturally smooth walls curving all around him. Although he thought of it as a tunnel, in some ways it had more in common with a tube or pipe. Was it an entrance to somewhere for the alien inhabitants of Ebla? And if so, did it indicate that they were serpent-like in form?

Falling into his imagination again, he did not, at first, notice the tunnel widening, the curving sides moving beyond the limit of the helmet lamp, the roof, so close above his head, sweeping upwards. He was still on his hands and knees when a brilliant light flared, revealing an enormous chamber hewn out of the rock.

He blinked, momentarily blinded. As his sight returned he stood, knees cracking, back complaining at the change in posture. He could find no source for the light. It seemed to emanate from the walls, the ceiling, even the floor he stood on. Yet it gave off no heat. As his eyes adjusted further, he began to make out detail. The sinuous pattern engraved in the floor reminded him of a meandering river. In the walls, stretching away either side of him, were what looked like rows of portholes, each one not much bigger than his fist. He counted over three hundred rows, before they became difficult to see, up near the roof. It was impossible to estimate the number running around the walls, but he could easily imagine that there were thousands of the small, round objects.

He made to move towards them, to examine them more closely, but felt a sudden, strong impulse to stay on the sinuous floor pattern. He tried again, but could not make himself step to the side. Cautiously, he tried a step forward. No problem. Another step forward. No strange impulse. A step to the side. A demand from his brain to stay where he was. It was obvious that something wanted him to remain on the pattern, a pattern that he now saw as a pathway. It could override his wishes with relative ease. That sort of power was frightening. He gave up resistance and followed the path.

As he walked, the walls ahead of him faded into clearer view, and he realized the light around him was not light at all, but a luminescent fog, obscuring the far end of the chamber. He wondered what else the fog might conceal, but there seemed nothing but the monotonous regularity of rows of portholes. Until the vague shadow across the pathway solidified.

It was another wall, but one devoid of any portholes, and the pathway ended at its base. As his eyes adjusted, Rider saw that it was not the flat, featureless wall he had first thought. At intervals, there were indentations. Circular, octagonal, rectangular, and more. A variety of shapes and sizes, some at floor level, others at differing heights. Their depths differed too, some so deep he could not see the back, others shallow, barely indented at all.

Select and enter.

The instruction entered his head as naturally as if he had thought of it himself. For a moment, he puzzled over its meaning, before following a gentle impulse to walk the length of the wall. He barely noticed that, for the first time since entering the chamber, he could step off the patterned pathway.

He had not walked far when he came upon a tall, rectangular indentation, several inches taller and wider than himself. It was deep, but not so deep that he could not see the back of it, partly sheathed in dark shadow. He stepped inside as though it was the only natural thing to do.

Understanding poured into him, a sudden rush of data and knowledge that left him dizzy but deliriously happy.

This wall is an Educator, the indentations shaped for the known life forms of the galaxy. It's here to explain the chamber. It's why I couldn't step off the pathway. I wasn't ready. I wasn't Educated.

He did not question the knowledge, simply accepted it as truth. His way into the chamber, he now knew, was a maintenance pathway, not designed for humanoid life forms. That it had activated on his approach indicated the system was failing. It was, perhaps, not surprising. The chamber had been created centuries ago, and technology, however advanced, deteriorated over time and exposure to the severe weather of Ebla.

The portholes are windows into chambers, and each chamber contains the consciousness of a Reader or Storyteller.

He began to see the true purpose of the chamber, the reason for the immense time and effort put into its creation. It saddened him, stripping away the joy he had first felt at his discovery. The dominant species of this world knew it as *Nbg'azrea*, which Rider found he could roughly translate as *The Ground on Which We Stand*. They had evolved into a highly sophisticated, technologically advanced race. But they had been dying.

Nbg'azrea was changing at a rate and ferocity they couldn't counter, thought Rider, the story clear in his mind. *The climate deteriorated. The rain became more acidic with each storm. The atmosphere turned increasingly toxic. They found no reason for the change, and they had no solution. Nbg'azrea is a living planet, and like any living thing, it can evolve. And so, they began construction of this chamber, deep within a mountain they felt sure would withstand erosion for many centuries.*

This is a repository, a library. Between them, the Readers hold the history, the science, the philosophy of this long extinct race. The Storytellers have the myths and legends. It's a treasure house of knowledge. An alien species, talking to us across the centuries. It's invaluable.

He finally understood the source of the signal that had brought him here. The seals on the portholes were deteriorating. Some of the chambers were leaking their knowledge, their stories, through the rock of the mountain and into the atmosphere. The chamber needed not only preserving, but also repairing. The terraforming could not be allowed to proceed. It would destroy the chamber. It would silence the voices of a long extinct alien race. It would wipe them from history.

Genocide!

***

It was over an hour since Rider had activated his communicator and given the news to Base. They had told him they needed to give the information to the SEO orbiting Ebla in the main survey ship. They would get back to him.

He had used the time to learn about the Entrance and Exit controls of the chamber, only to find they were broken. Even the maintenance hatch, which had given him access, was now sealed and would not open.

With not much over two hours of oxygen left in his suit, he hoped Base would get back to him soon. By now, the team sent out to investigate the signal would surely have reached his abandoned Rover and begun their ascent of the mountain. They would have to blast their way through the rock to get into the chamber. He hoped he could direct them to the maintenance tunnel, tell them to blast there. It would cause the least damage to the precious contents.

His communicator crackled to life, the signal weakened by the thickness of rock surrounding the chamber.

"Base to Rider. Come in, Rider."

"Rider here," he said, his stomach knotted with a fear he could not quite identify.

"I have the reply from our SEO here," said Base.

Rider thought the voice sounded hesitant. The fear in his belly tightened.

He waited for Base to continue, wondering at the silence, the faint background of static the only indication the communicator was working.

"Base?" he said, adding worry to the fear he already felt. "Are you still there? Is everything okay?"

"Still here," said Base, the voice flat, sounding tired.

"So, what did the SEO say?"

He thought he heard a sigh on the other end.

"I'll quote direct from the message," said Base. *"Erase all mention of anomalous signal from record. Terraforming will go ahead on schedule. List engineer as missing."*

Rider could not speak, the words seeming to become clear only gradually, his mind struggling to comprehend. He now understood the fear in his belly, as it twisted tighter than ever. He felt sick.

"I'm sorry, Rider," said Base, and the voice sounded genuine. "There's nothing I can do."

"What about the investigative team?" said Rider in sudden hope. "They must be outside by now. They could blast through . . ."

"Already turned back," said Base. "On orders from the SEO."

As the truth of his situation filtered through his disbelief, Rider sank to the floor of the chamber, staring at the Educator wall, the thousands of portholes showing through the luminescent fog.

No rescue.

"But there's a whole civilization here," he said, more to himself than Base. "The records of an entire alien race."

"The terraforming machines will achieve orbit in seven days," said Base. "I'm sorry."

Sorry, thought Rider. *But no one is sorry enough to challenge the SEO, the Company. The voice of another race is here, never to be heard. Silenced for profit.*

He switched the communicator off, not wanting to hear any more pity, any more empty words of compassion driven by guilt.

With sudden determination, he pushed himself to his feet. He had been abandoned, left to die along with the knowledge and stories in the chamber. But that did not mean he had to lie on the ground and wait for his oxygen to run out. He understood how to access the chambers in the walls. He had two hours. A man could learn a lot in two hours.

Before the end came, there would, at least, be one human who cared enough to understand something of the people who had once lived on Ebla, on *Nbg'azrea*. It was the rest of humanity he felt sorry for, not himself. They would be forever ignorant of the secrets, the wisdom he would learn. And all in the name of profit.

He pitied them.

Neil Davies was born in 1959 and has found everything else to be an uphill struggle. He currently lives in the North West of England with his wife, two grown-up children, and a cat. He divides his spare time between writing horror and science fiction, painting, and music. For more information please visit http:// www.nwdavies.co.uk.

Horrors of the future breeding monsters of the past.

The Plumed Serpent

Elana Gomel

Tanya dozed off, lulled by the smooth motion of her body through the sunlit grass. She could not sleep at night because that was the time when her host hunted, while she, a rider in its busy flesh, strained to catch a glimpse of the sky. She hoped to see a gliding shadow eclipse the gibbous moon. Perhaps, if she was lucky, the shadow would see her as well and dive down, affording her a full view of its gargantuan majesty. So far, she had not been lucky.

Tanya was a cimolodon—a small mammal, smooth-furred and quick-eyed. She looked like a rat but the rat family had not evolved yet in this era of brittle rocks, shaken by giants' tread, and shallow seas, roiled by flying dragons. Unlike rodents, Tanya was particular in her diet. She ate stick-like insects that reminded her of flaxseed crackers.

The cimolodon stopped and sniffed the briny air, overwhelmed by the tang of sea-salt and the fishy stench of an enormous dung-pile. Tanya was sure that her human senses could have distinguished many more odors; after all, wasn't there a beautiful star-shaped plant covering the dunes? Despite common preconceptions, the human senses were better that those of most other mammals, especially primitive ones. But while implanted in an animal brain, she could only use her host's resources. She was a parasite, and a helpless one at that, for she could not influence the actions of the cimolodon, nor guide it in the direction she wanted to go. The demobbed technician who had hooked her into the net, his melted face a testimony to the depleted resources of army hospitals, told her that she could not mess with the host's body. There were filters installed in the implantation device to prevent this. She was reluctant to ask him whether they could be overridden; his hostility to her was palpable, coming off him in waves of sullen anger. She was going on a vacation into the past; he had to wait for the catastrophic future.

A shadow mantled the dunes and Tanya tensed, hoping the cimolodon would look up. Its eyesight was its best sensory channel, color-sensitive and stereoscopic, which was one reason it had been chosen to host the biologist's mind. The other reason was money. The price of implantation rose with the size of the host. Tanya's underfunded university lab could not afford any of the theropod giants who ruled the Cretaceous world.

The cimolodon's snout whipped around. She glimpsed a bristling wall of peacock-bright feathers. The theropod paused on top of the dune, its fuchsia-bearded face turned inland. It was as big as a gantry crane; probably a

Giganotosaurus. It was a predator but the tiny cimolodon would not qualify even for an *amuse bouche* in the giant's meal. In any case, she was not affected by any damage to the host and if truth be told, was curious about the sensation of being eaten. If her host died, Tanya's mind would be automatically ejected back into her own body, cradled in the silvery tempo-net in the future where the walls of the academy protected her from the military chaos outside. She still had enough grant money left for reinsertion.

The snout started digging in the sand under the tough roots of sea-grass and Tanya mentally groaned. The last thing she wanted was more memory-shots of Cretaceous worms!

She let herself drift while the cimolodon went about its routine. As always, an image rose before her, both grotesque and sublime; both sharply delineated and tantalizingly vague. A crouched shadow towering into the clouds, the folded wings scrabbling at the ground with clawed hands, the beaked head nodding between their peaks. An impossible creature wing-walking through the desert of her knowledge.

Quetzalcoatlus northropi was the largest flying animal of all time. Or was it even flying? It had the wingspan of 18 meters, or more than 50 feet. It must have used its wings for something. But nobody could understand how a creature weighing more than 400 pounds and taller than a giraffe could launch itself into the air. And what for? What did it eat? Was it a predator or a scavenger? Did it actually attack theropods? How could such a creature have evolved?

These were the questions Tanya had come to answer. The fact that very few people cared for the knowledge she sought only strengthened her resolve. On some level, she knew her scientific curiosity was simply another way of not facing the reality of civilization's terminal illness. The world was trying to vomit itself up, sickened by the unrelenting drip of low-grade bloodshed. Everybody sought distraction and forgetfulness. But digital simulations were getting ever more threadbare as computer resources were swallowed up by the military's insatiable demand. Drugs were scarce and prohibitively expensive. Wartime austerity had made a comeback; and science was one of the few venues of escape left open. Some sought solace in sex; some in suicide; for Tanya, it was the *Quetzalcoatlus.*

But if the Cretaceous sky-god was around, he refused to show himself. Preliminary probes had established that this landscape of marshlands, salt-flats, and a shallow inland sea overgrown with horse-tails the size of baobabs was the most likely place for Quetzalcoatlus roosts. But so far, she had only seen a couple of medium-sized pteranodons.

The ground vibrated and the cimolodon's ears pricked up. Its muzzle swiveled. Tanya instinctively tried to flex her absent muscles.

A predator was coming. Even though all theropods looked big to her host, Tanya had gotten pretty good at estimating their sizes. This one was around 8 meters long, skipping spastically on its bony legs and clacking its keratinous beak. Its fingers, clawed and skeletal, emerged from the scarlet ruffles of feathers that decorated its arms. Similar feathers adorned its flat head. The rest of its skin was bare and corpse-pale. Tanya recognized a Gallimimus: a minor omnivore, big enough to draw the attention of flesh-eating giants but small enough to notice a tiny mammal. She mentally urged the cimolodon to flee but the stupid creature just froze, its whiskers twitching nervously.

The Gallimimus zeroed in on the prey, its feathery head-crest standing erect. Even as it ran toward the petrified cimolodon, Tanya had a moment of sheer wonder at the baroque strangeness of the creature. That was one of the unsolved mysteries of evolution that the mind-implantation technique had only brought into sharper focus but never solved. Why were these animals so weird? Predators the size of a building clothed in the plumage so luxurious and bright that Victorian milliners would have given an arm and a leg for their feathers; plant-eaters that flattened rain forests as they walked; creatures that looked like a voodoo doll made of chicken bones and corpses' hands. Compared to them, mammals were as drab as Sunday school.

The cimolodon trembled, pressing its tiny body into the sand. Tanya's amused distance from the body she inhabited, evaporated. A rational part of her mind kept telling her there was nothing to be afraid of, but the rest of it was suddenly flooded with overwhelming terror. A mute scream tore through her absent throat as she strained to move the creature's recalcitrant muscles, as the Gallimimus' head dipped toward her, a warty tongue emerging from the yawning gulf of the beak.

She felt something give at the junction of body and mind . . . and the cimolodon twitched, its hind legs backpedaling in the soft sand as its forepaws scrabbled to propel the body forward. Tanya tasted the burnt residue of its adrenaline. But the tiny animal's reflexes were scrambled by her sudden presence in its brain. The two of them jostled for control as Tanya was blindly rummaging through unfamiliar fight-or-flight sensations. She had no idea what she was doing or how she was doing it. But, somehow, she reached into the quivering flesh and felt it give under the pressure of her panic. But then the host's simple mind gave a pushback and she was a helpless passenger once again.

The cimolodon tried to run but the inner struggle had cost it precious moments. The Gallimimus tossed its head back like a chicken preparing to swallow a worm. But instead of darting forward, the head continued its backward arc, exposing the tender throat. Something grabbed feathery crest and twisted the scrawny neck. Pale flesh parted with a wet sound, blood drenching the quivering cimolodon. The shadow that had fallen out of the sky settled on the corpse, burying it under its wings. Clawed fingers the size of a human arm tore into the Gallimimus' underbelly.

The cimolodon, forgotten, scrambled away. But in its last fearful glance at its rescuer's meal, Tanya caught an image of the long jaws lined with broken teeth. Broken teeth that squiggled and moved.

As the cimolodon recovered in its lair, its heartbeat slowly returning to normal, Tanya tried to process what she had seen. Had she finally achieved her goal? Had it been a Quetzalcoatlus? It was certainly big enough—bigger than she had expected, with the wingspan of at least 20 meters. And it had flown in, swooped down from the cloudless sky. But what was in its mouth?

The creature she had seen had a flat triangular head and scissor-like jaws. This fit with what was known from the fossil record. But the jaw bones pried from the Maastrichtian Javelina Formation in Texas had been toothless. The creature, on the other hand, seemed to have a dentition unlike any known to paleontology. Its jaws had looked as if they were fringed with ivory sculptures, with bony eidolons, reaching down to dig into the prey's flesh with their own hungry ferocity. It was as if the creature—she was *almost* willing to call it a Quetzalcoatlus—had an army of tiny human skeletons in its mouth.

She reviewed her memory-shots over and over again but they were disappointingly vague. The technology allowed storage and retrieval of any images seen by the host's eyes but it could not show any more detail than what had been captured in the moment.

And had she actually controlled the cimolodon's body in those few moments of terror? If so, wasn't it a great victory? Now she could actively seek out her target, have better shots, perhaps reapply for an additional grant.

But there had been something profoundly disturbing about it. She tried to figure out whether the distress had been hers or the cimolodon's and could not. Still, she had her own body to go back to. Suddenly she was glad she did.

Her body and her science—it was all she had left. Her father had been killed in Lithuania, her mother had died of starvation in New Mexico when the supply lines had been disrupted by the rebels. Casualties of a forgotten cause. By now the war had dispensed with such niceties as reasons and goals.

Quetzalcoatlus was named after the Mesoamerican god Quetzalcoatl whose symbol was a feathered snake. The cult of Quetzalcoatl had involved human sacrifices, prisoners of war, flayed alive on stone altars. But what relevance did this have to a giant flying reptile?

She decided that tomorrow she would try to control the cimolodon, directing it toward the still-unexplored stretch of the shore. Most theories about the Quetzalcoatlus argued it was a short-distance glider; some claimed it was a four-limbed land scavenger, more like a hyena than a bird. Well, she could now put this to rest: the animal definitely flew! But surely it could not have flown far, so there must be a nesting site somewhere close by!

The cimolodon curled up to rest and Tanya let herself drift into sleep. In her dream, she saw a plumed serpent lapping up the blood of bound men and then picking up their bodies and setting them in its gaping maw.

Night; and the cimolodon was hunting. Tanya rode in its head, restless and uneasy. The animal poked its nose into the sand where its whiskers sensed hibernating insects. But now most of the whiskers seemed to have fallen out. Was it sick? When she had tried to force herself into its motor centers, she had the queasy sense of pushing against something soft and rotten, and withdrew immediately.

The night was moist and clear and peppered with stars. From the direction of the sea came a melodious honking like that of a truck-sized goose. A splash; and a supple neck tipped with a miniature head rose high into the air and snatched a skin-winged flier.

An avalanche of sand slid off the nearest dune and the cimolodon scrambled to get away. The ground shook with the galloping tread of some giant ungulate.

And here it was, towering into the sparkling dimness. It ran on all fours, its lumpy neck straining to support the pointed head. But its forelimbs were wings. Folded back from the clawed hands, the spotted membranes shone with refracted moonlight, rising above its sloping hindquarters in sharp triangles. Its back and hind limbs were bare, covered with the inflamed vulture-like skin. But the chest sported a bristling bib of black and red plumage, each feather longer than the cimolodon. Pieces of rotten meat were stuck between them.

The Quetzalcoatlus opened its maw and a deafening moan issued from its gullet. The moan was syncopated, riffed and repeated by a chorus of tiny voices, as skeletal figures writhed in its jaws. Its eyes focused on the tiny mammal. Eyes as multiple as those of an insect, for where an ordinary theropod had a single eye set into each side of its head, the Quetzalcoatlus had many. Its sloping cheeks were adorned with clusters of human-looking eyes, grey, blue, and black, shedding watery tears down the gaunt jaws.

This was a biological absurdity! Perplexed and horrified in equal measure, Tanya pushed herself into the cimolodon's motor centers, gaining control over its body. But now she did not know what to do. Should she stay and observe through the process of being eaten by this impossible aberration? Should she flee? Fear overcame curiosity and she propelled the cimolodon toward the moon climbing above the dunes.

But then the creature froze in sudden darkness. A lumbering behemoth, bigger than a Cessna plane, swooped down on parchment wings. The cimolodon gave a desperate shriek as it was picked up and torn apart—and Tanya blinked out.

She was floating in a formless void. She tried to orient herself but had no body to give her directions.

This was not right. When her host died, she should have been ejected back into her own flesh. She was ready for the aches and discomfort of re-insertion. But she did not know what to make of this slippery feeling of weightlessness.

Something appeared in the void and glided closer. It was a man, naked and flayed. His bunching muscles ran with blood.

Tanya stared at the hallucination and the man stared back at her. His teeth were pink. The lips had been torn away.

Words formed in her mind and writhed in the void like digital worms. And then something blinked and she heard her own voice, strangely distorted as if by a poor recording.

"Where is the lab?"

"Gone," the man said. He had a pleasant Australian accent.

"And my body?"

"Gone as well. War."

"But the war has been—"

"Yes, dragging on so long that we thought it was like the weather. Terrible but always there. Until one day it wasn't."

"Who won?"

The man shrugged and Tanya realized what a stupid question it was.

"So, I'm dead," she said.

"No. You are going back."

"To Cretaceous? But the cimolodon is dead."

"Eaten," the man corrected. "And now you'll become part of the eater. As nature intended."

"But . . ." Tanya started objecting and then stopped. The writhing figures in the Quetzalcoatlus' jaw, the clusters of eyes . . . It was a predator, consuming other animals' bodies. But what happened when these bodies contained human minds?

"How many people have been implanted in past animals?" she asked.

"Millions."

Of course, what an idiot she had been, thinking that the technique was only used for scientific research! In a world on the brink of destruction, wearied by war and sucked dry by overpopulation, people would pay through the nose to get a temporary respite! They would go for a vacation in Cretaceous, confident that if their host were to die they'd be inserted back into their own bodies. But if these bodies were vaporized by a nuclear explosion . . .

"So, we are all trapped there . . ." she said slowly. The flayed man shook his head.

"Not trapped. Escaped. Some of us."

The war gods. Leaders, bankers, and generals. Slavering giants adorned with royal plumage, squatting atop the ecological pyramid! It was very expensive but so what? People who wanted to be gods had the means to pay for their divinity.

"*Quetzalcoatlus northropi*," she said. "Are you . . .?"

The man shook his head again.

"I was just a lowly Troodon. But now I am part of my master. As you will be."

Tanya felt a stirring in the nothingness that embraced her, as if a current was building up, gently bearing her away. The flayed man watched her impassively.

"Wait!" she cried. "The Quetzalcoatlus . . . it was deformed! Bizarre! Fossils never showed . . ."

The man may have smiled—she was not sure because the torn mouth could not really move—but even as the current became a torrent, she realized she knew the answer. A human mind controlling an animal body: of course, it would create somatic changes, profound deformations. Even her brief mastery of the cimolodon had changed it. But what extensive modifications would result from a self-deified mind in a theropod's alien flesh! And as this mind consumed others, modifications would become deformities. Fossils did not show multiple eyes or other soft-tissue grotesqueries. But they did show impossible sizes, peculiar crests and spurs, flamboyant feathers, grasping hands. And they did show that a creature too big to fly ruled the skies.

The torrent of nothingness roared with a sound like soft thunder. Tanya had one last thought. The plumed serpent would rule for a long time, but not forever. A stronger god was coming, the god of fire and cosmic wrath: the meteor named Chicxulub.

Elana Gomel is the author of five non-fiction books, published by Routledge, Macmillan and other academic presses, and of numerous articles on subjects ranging from science fiction and fantasy to posthumanism and Victorian literature. Her stories appeared in New Horizons, Aoife's Kiss, Bewildering Stories, Timeless Tales, The Singularity, Dark Fire, Fantasist *and other magazines; and in several anthologies, including the* Apex Book of World Science Fiction. *Her fantasy novel* A Tale of Three Cities *was published by Dark Quest Books in 2013. She can be found on Facebook and on Twitter as @ElanaGomel.*

What if you were that lucky child who could have the Earth all to yourself, at the bottom of your pocket? Would you play with it? Would you lend it to your brother? If so, what would the two of you discover?

My Own Private Earth

Lawrence Dagstine

The Earth rolls around at the bottom of my pocket. It is my favorite planet. One I take with me everywhere. The funny part is, it's the worst looking one of the lot. It doesn't come anywhere near the pockmarked craters with active volcanoes or the gas giants with massive hydrogen storms. The one I love is made of blue oceans and green continents, and like a marble in this great big universe, the glaze has chipped off here and there.

I love that planet. It's nice to have the Earth tucked away in my pocket, with the mountains and valleys and rainforests and everything else that once existed. The best part is I just stare into the planet's core and I can make these wonderful landscapes appear again, breathing new life. I can concentrate real hard and see what the people were like, or I can focus on starting a new civilization from scratch.

A finger prods me. "Well? Can't you make up your mind, Del?"

My brother Flan is waiting, sitting on the metal walk in front of the nutrient center. Between his legs is a pyramid of six globes: three on top of the other three, two moons belonging to the planet Jupiter.

He goes into his little case and dumps a few more out, and says, "I'll see you two carbon worlds, and raise you one."

Naturally I can't make up my mind, and I definitely don't want to part with my Earth. I've shot ten times already and missed everything, like an asteroid coming within close trajectory but barely skimming the firmament. Only my thumb and forefinger is piloting it. Flan's vest compartments bulge with the planets he won at recess. There are also a few others he purchased from the vending machines outside Duffy's, but these are from entirely different solar systems. Now he has way more than me and we merely play to kill time. Now we wait for the food bell. Before I know it, I'm down to my last one. My beloved Earth.

"You think I'm going to sit here on my can until the next cycle?"

"Don't be so impatient. You're making me nervous."

"Just go!"

The Earth trembles in my palm. I shoot—and miss! Well, that's that. Miracles don't happen. We have to go in and eat now.

***

I wake up. The circle of the flashlight blinds me. It's pitch-dark. "Quick, get dressed," a voice says. "Don't make a sound."

What's going on? The others are asleep in the tent. In the darkness, I pull on my shirt. Damn it, I've got it on inside out. I sense my brother close to me, scraping his soles on the floor.

"Who are all these other people?" I ask.

"Well," says the voice, "I ought to tell you that most of these people are Jews."

This can't be a Gestapo raid; there would be cries, everyone would be up. The man holding the flashlight goes by the name Stevynski. I recognize him.

"Come on. I'll meet you in the office."

Outside the night is cool. There are millions of stars; I wonder if anybody is looking back at me. The tent is already wet with dew. One other tent is alive with noise. A large one. It is jammed with people, children, suitcases. The noise from that one tent is infernal. Its occupants are to be transported someplace. They each hold numbers. Everyone else in the camp is asleep.

Near me stands a single couple in their late fifties, and they welcome my presence. The man is bald, wearing his Sunday best. The woman's short and frail, and must have just had a permanent wave. He's wearing a brown suit with matching loafers. She's wearing a blue and gray polka dot dress. From time to time they exchange glances, and I'm afraid. As young as I am, I understand that those two older folks are looking at each other like people who have lived together all their lives. Deep down they know they are about to be separated. Each will go the rest of their ways alone, especially if it is the *only* way.

The office is open. Stevynski lights a small lantern and I see that he's carrying two knapsacks. One for me, one for my brother. "You're leaving right now. I've put everything you'll need in these bags: clean shirts, underwear, stockings, canteens, and a bite to eat. I'm also going to give you some money. You'll cut across the pumpkin fields. Then you take a train for France. From there you'll go to a village south of Paris. A woman waits for you there. Her name is Martha. The village is called—"

My brother interrupts him. "What's going on?"

Stevynski lowers his eyes. "Your father was arrested in an SS roundup yesterday."

Everything is starting to spin. The Gestapo is stronger than I imagined; they managed to get my father.

"That's not all. Your father was carrying his identity papers, made out in his own name. It won't be long before the Germans link you with him and they'll be looking for you."

After hearing that, my brother puts his knapsack on. "What about my mother?"

"They warned her in time. I can't tell you where she is, but you can be sure that your relatives had a hiding place picked out. But go now. And don't write! They might be watching the mail."

We start out. Everything has happened so fast that it still hasn't registered with me. I only know my father is in Nazi hands. What a triumph for the Gestapo if they get us in their clutches. But what about Stevynski? Anyone caught helping a Jew must share his fate. No, we'd better not get caught.

The earth is hard and dry, but as we brush past weeds and vine leaves the dew wets our short pants and our shirt sleeves. The camp already lies far behind us. The night is so light that the crest of the hills casts its shadow on the terraced farmland. The train station is a long way inland, and we must remain undetected. It makes me sad to leave my home. I'll come back to it when I'm bigger, and when there's peace.

***

The storefronts along the space walk are spectacular, most, if not all, wavering crazily. They sell items from galaxies and cultures long extinct. Shop owners are well rehearsed in the histories of the objects they supply. They have to, for these are not your ordinary merchants. What they choose to specialize in and carry are more than just keepsakes. To the right customer they are collectibles. I look to the left, because Flan is walking to the right of me. That way he doesn't see his younger brother crying.

"Quit your blubbering," he says.

"I'm not blubbering, damn you!"

"When you look away like that, I can tell you're blubbering."

"I am not!"

"Bah, you're a sore loser. It's not my fault I save my credits and can keep buying and keep playing. You should have known when to stop. Besides, it's just a planet."

"You know how much it meant to me."

"Then you shouldn't have played. You could have talked me out of the game, but you didn't. You decided to go through with it. The best part is you're getting all misty-eyed over a world that wasn't even that fantastic. Trust me, there'll be others. Better ones. You'll see."

"It's not the same." A wipe of my jumper sleeve and my tear ducts are dry. We're going to get a scolding; we should have been back at the living units an hour ago.

"Here, tell you what. Take my Callisto." He goes into his case. "I already have two just like it."

"I don't want your Callisto," I argue. "And I don't want your Ganymede either!"

"I'm nice enough to give you free satellites, and you shun me?"

"Those moons are insignificant. The planet you won off me has something of value. It has a *chance*. It has hope embedded within it."

I talk our game over some more on the main boulevard. The mall shops here have never looked prettier. The signs are enormous and jut outwards. There are advertisements for anything and everything just about everywhere. The orange and yellow and purple glow speaks volumes. Visitors from all over the cosmos come here to buy or barter the recorded accounts of empires long forgotten. History is a big business in the Cat's Eye. Sometimes, if you're lucky, you can pull it from a vending machine. The right one, at least. Duffy's has the best machines. Other times you can download it directly into your memory from these cute little kiosks. That's why all the cool kids come here.

But now it is hard to imagine new tourists. The atmosphere is always full of laser fire and colliding freighters. Interplanetary war and space politics. I am a kid like any other. Now, all of a sudden, they stick a jumper on me and turn me into a human. What is a human, anyway? Supposedly I look like one. Supposedly that's who my ancestors were. I feel anger welling up inside me. I suddenly want to learn more about these humans and how we ended up related. But I can't. And I probably never will. Flan won my Earth. Fair and square.

We leave the space walk and go home.

The courtyard to our facility gleams so you can see it from a distance. "That you, boys?" The processing of liquids and proteins accompanies my mother's voice. "Go wash up before you sit down to eat. Is your brother with you?"

I soap my hands with some kind of foam that slips through my fingers without producing any suds. "No, but he's coming. He stopped really quick at a science shop to pick up some more planets."

My father tousles my hair. "If that boy didn't have enough already."

"He took my last one from me. Now I have none."

"Well, maybe if you'd save your allowance more often, you'd be able to stock up like he does."

Flan comes in, gulps down his meal, and gets out of his seat at the same time as I do.

My mother is peeved. "Now where are you headed?"

Flan launches into a complicated explanation. The shopkeeper has sold out all her planets, but can get some more in exchange for fixing her display cases. For that, we have to persuade the owner to trade our services for a *special* order.

Father raises his head over the top of his reader. "Not late. Understand?"

"Yes, Father."

Outside, Flan says, "Is this *Earth* really that important to you?"

I'm quiet at first, then, "Yes. It has personal meaning."

"Then come with me." We start heading back to the space walk. "You're lucky you're my brother."

***

The path to freedom goes uphill. We've got to stay away from farmhouses so the watchdogs won't bark, and that takes us out of our way. Finally, my brother stops. We can see a road ahead of us. "We're going to cross," he whispers.

There's no one coming, so we dash across the road. After we scramble up a bank, the sea appears at our feet, broad, gray, shimmering. Now we've got to traverse the beach and get back on the trail. Then we'll work our way through miles of vegetable gardens to the train station. As dawn comes, we see boarded-up villas, and finally reach the center of town. A few people pass us on bicycles. Shopkeepers are beginning to raise their shutters. But the windowpanes provide grim reminders of the night before and the night before that.

Stevynski has told us stories. All children love stories, but these particular ones are something special. My brother and I are the heroes in them. I am weaned on stories of Stevynski's adventures, and we are to follow in his footsteps. At first, I am told not to be scared. I am told to just listen. I envision rifle butts smashing doors, breaking windows, and families being pulled apart. There is the wild flight of peasants, houses, and shops in flames. There is a whirlwind of saber blades, the breath of charging horses, the glint of spurs, and, towering over a tragic scene, the flying Swastika.

As the massacres intensify, the streets become peopled with refugees who leave dark, rainy townships with dark, ornate architecture. There is an infernal series of tortuous passes and glacial steppes. There are stormy nights, revelry, laughter, tears, and death. The day the good guys cross the last border and find a beautiful sunlit plain, with birdsong, wheat fields, apricot trees, and whitewashed cities with red rooftops, is where the story comes to a close. Then all the refugees set down their bundles and the fear has left their eyes, for they have arrived in Unoccupied France. Stevynski says these people have never been surprised by the love of the French for their own land. But he knows of no one who has ever loved that country as much as they do.

There's the station. It's already crowded.

I run up to the window. "Two one-way tickets for Paris," I say.

The clerk consults books and timetables. "One hundred and fourteen francs, twenty centimes."

My brother scoops up the change while I ask, "Where do we have to change trains?" This is all so very new to us.

"It's complicated. Go to track D and take the express to Marseille. There you change for Lyon. If there's no delay, you'll only have to wait two or three hours. At Lyon, take the motor train. Or you can go another way; via Saint-Germain-des-Fosses or the Bourges track. But, whichever way, you're bound to get there. Only I can't say *when* because..." Spreading his arms to represent an airplane, he imitates the sound of exploding bombs. "Understand?"

We nod, fascinated. "Thanks, monsieur."

We're lucky to have stumbled upon that informative ticket agent; I launch into an improvisation: "It's complicated. Go to track A, B, C, then X, Y, and Z." My brother is hysterical. "We change in Marseille. No, I mean Saint-Germain. Actually, the Bourges track. But whichever way you go you're bound to get blown up!"

My brother perks up. "Even I could do a better job."

Finally, we board the train. At Marseille, contrary to what the ticket agent told us, there is a connecting train for Lyon almost immediately. Paris will be our final destination. But once we go through Avignon, an unexpected enemy confronts us.

The cold.

The trains are unheated, and we are going farther and farther away from the warmth of our home. We seek refuge in the toilet and put on all our clothing. But our arms and knees are still bare. In Lyon, where the station platform is swept by a damp, chill wind, we hold a contest to see whose teeth can chatter the loudest. When the train leaves, the situation becomes serious. It is only October. Never has there been a winter so early as this one. The other passengers are already wearing overcoats and thick clothing, while we are still dressed for summer.

Blue and trembling with cold, we get off the train into one big, icy draft. People tramp up and down the sidewalks, trying to keep warm. Despite a triple layer of stockings, my toes feel as hard as marble. My stiff brother manages to say, "We've got to do something before we catch pneumonia."

The well-known axiom, "Run a little—that'll warm you up," is one of the biggest absurdities that adults can utter to children. After my experience that day I can safely state that, when you're really cold, running tires you out but doesn't warm you up at all. After half an hour of frantic galloping and hand-rubbing, I find myself puffing like a walrus but shivering even harder than before.

"Listen, we've got to buy jackets."

I look at my brother. "You have ration stamps for clothing?"

"No, but we've got to try."

We see a tiny shop. It has faded lettering: CLOTHING FOR ALL AGES.

He nudges my forearm. "Let's go."

When the door swings shut behind us, I experience one of the greatest sensations of my life. The shop is *heated*. The warmth enters each of my pores at once, then on to my bones. Without so much as a glance at the good lady behind the counter, we rudely glue ourselves against her potbellied stove.

The proprietress asks us, "What would you like, children?"

My brother tears himself away from the heat. "We'd like coats or heavy sweaters. We don't have any ration stamps, but maybe if we paid a little extra..."

She shakes her head. "I'm sorry. We haven't seen a coat or sweater in so long that we don't know what they are," she admits. "The only thing I can show you is this." She reaches under the counter for a pair of mufflers. It's better than nothing.

We stay by the stove until it is dark outside. It is too late for Paris, and it is far too late to take the bus from Lyon to the village where this Martha lives. We must find housing for the night.

I'm explaining my fears to my brother when the woman looks at us with compassion. "You won't find any hostels in Lyon," she says. "They've been requisitioned for the Germans and their militia. But I *can* offer you my son's room. The bed will be a little narrow for the two of you, but at least the room is warm."

We practically jump for joy. That evening she cooks for us, and we delight in hot chocolate after our meal. I fall asleep instantly, buried under a comforter stuffed with goose feathers. There is some kind of an alert during the night, but the sirens don't even wake me up.

When we leave in the morning, the proprietress kisses us and won't let us pay. It's not that cold now, and we have our new mufflers. She tells me that we want to take the first bus of the day, and that we'll cross the Alps. We want to end up in the mountains, she assures us. But the ride will be costly. Outside, my brother waits for me. He's lost that wan look from the day before. The sleep has washed away the fatigue of the trip.

The two of us walk the streets. There is a crowd in front of the baker's shop: young men with resistance armbands and small pistols stuck in their belts. Some of them wear berets and smoke long and thin cigarettes. They don't look like real members of the underground. No. These guys have blossomed out on the very morning that the krauts have packed up to go farther north, which probably explains the sirens the night before.

The bus station isn't far now. Behind the counter the man doesn't even look up as my brother asks for two tickets. So here we are again, with two tickets in our pockets. We don't have much money left, but it doesn't matter. *Free* France isn't far off.

We soon board. The asthmatic vehicle holds two-dozen people and chugs its way across a countryside, which seems terribly grim compared with the one we have left. There aren't any leaves on the trees, and it is beginning to drizzle.

***

The methane showers begin to subside, and Flan tugs on my jumper. He assures me it is safe to click off my protection bubble. "Let's go already!"

"Are you sure this woman's shop will be open?" I ask.

"Trust me. She stays open later than Duffy's."

"And you say she's human?"

"Yup. Pink like you and me, bro."

"What's so different about *her* merchandise?"

"Ah, man. More questions? You're kidding me, right?"

"No, tell me."

Flan laughs. "Boy, are you in for a treat. Rumor has it this woman comes from that planet you love so much."

"Impossible," I say. "Earth doesn't exist anymore. That's why it's so rare. It's a cinder in space."

"Hmm, maybe that's the reason you miss it."

"Not really. Just that the people who lived there were interesting."

Flan crosses his arms. "I thought you said it was embedded with hope."

"It is. Well, when I *want* it to be."

"Yeah? Well, the word in the shopping center is that this woman is some kind of time gypsy," Flan explains. "She can construct worlds out of putty— duplicate planets!—puppeteer and imitate ancient races, and become a living, breathing part of them. She can even physically cross time streams!"

"She sounds like your run-of-the-mill historian. The Cat's Eye is littered with them."

Flan shakes his head, annoyed. "She's not just an historian."

"Impossible," I argue. "Matter transference and temporal shifting is a mythological process. Nothing comes out of wormholes. As an advanced species, we've proved as much."

"All right. See for yourself, Mr. Incredulity. She's just around that corner."

"I don't need some history lesson," I say. "Nor do I need another collector planet from some chip-operated kiosk. Flan, I'm tired. I'm sorry I acted like a baby. Just give me your Callisto and we can call it a day."

"No!" he insists. "Not until you meet this woman."

***

We stop just outside the village. On the road, a car passes us with German officers. I act scared for a few seconds, but they pay no attention to our rattletrap bus. The sky is clear, the country flat. The houses are huddled around the steeple of the church. The wind meets no obstacle and roars right into our lungs.

My brother hitches up his knapsack. "Let's get moving!"

Upon further inspection, it appears more a hamlet than a village: one or two narrow streets, a school for all ages, a butcher-bakery shop, a shoemaker-dressmaker, a grocery-hardware, a tobacconist's store-bar, and one or two rundown cafes.

The main street goes uphill a bit. Our wooden heels resound on the uneven cobblestones. We come to a fountain under a portico. There isn't a soul on the streets. An occasional dog sniffs around our legs. The town smells of cow manure and woodsmoke. Two grocery stores face one another; both are closed.

"Damn," my brother growls, "it appears dead."

The silence makes an impression on me, too. After the din of the train, the long cold journey, the plight of our arrival, we feel as if someone has stuffed cotton balls into our ears.

Over our heads the church clock strikes. "That's right," my brother says. "It's noon and everybody's eating."

That's a word he should never have mentioned, for the sandwiches have been gone a long time. The morning coffee seems way in the past, and the country air is sharpening my appetite.

We wander aimlessly around, and find another square. Across from a building that must be the town hall stands a café-restaurant. I look at my brother pleadingly, "Maybe we could get something to eat."

My brother hesitates. "All right," he says. "We don't want to collapse from hunger."

The streets may be empty, not so the café. Much to our surprise, almost a hundred people are jammed around the tables. A half-dozen waitresses run through the aisles, carrying plates, pitchers of water, silverware. An enormous terra-cotta stove heats the place. An antique coffee machine decorates the front counter.

"What do you want, boys?" One of the waitresses, red-faced and disheveled, tries to catch a curl that's falling over her face.

Bewildered, my brother replies, "We'd like food."

She pushes us to a bare wooden table. "We've got bacon and stuffed eggplant. For dessert, there's cheese and fruit. That's all we have. I can give you tomatoes with salt to start."

"No. That'll be fine." I look at the other diners. They aren't countryfolk; they're probably from Lyon or Avignon. There are children, too.

My brother lowers his head. "We're going to bump into everybody from the camp in this place. Just you watch."

"They're like us," I note. "Jews waiting to cross the border or get back to Paris. But what are they waiting for? Maybe it's harder than we think." Our waitress comes back with our eggplant. I ask, "You're always this crowded?"

She raises her arms. "Believe me, when the Fritzes put that line a kilometer from here, they helped a lot of people in this ramshackle town get rich." I follow her gaze and see the *patronne* delicately drying a coffee cup behind the bar. She is wearing lots of flashy jewelry and her hair dyed a carrot red. For a woman, she is large and there is a distinguishable air about her. "With what *she* makes here, she could spend her whole life at the beauty parlor."

"Who is she?" my brother asks.

"Her name is Martha. She pays the bills."

My brother and I look at each other.

The waitress takes away our empty dishes. Nothing goes down faster than eggplant when you're hungry. When she returns, I ask, "What about Paris? Is it easy to get back to?"

She shrugs. "You'd have to talk to Martha about that,"—and with that, we realize that the large woman is involved in the resistance effort—"but mostly they get across without trouble...only you've got to wait till after midnight because it's too dangerous during the day. Excuse me."

She comes back with various cheeses, sets them before us, and goes off again. The second helping of eggplant is stringy and the stuffing nonexistent. The cheeses, too, are flat and dry. The apples are withered, but our waitress makes the mistake of leaving them near our table; they all end up in my knapsack.

Behind us a thickset man motions to us. Seeing that we are petrified, he smiles and pulls his chair toward us. His frightened eyes, his nervous hands, everything about him says that he is trying to get to Paris or some *other* part of Unoccupied France.

"Are you Jewish?" he asks us.

I shift my apple-filled knapsack to my other hand. "No. I mean, um, well—"

The man's jaw tightens. "I am. I've got my wife and my teenage son hiding in the woods. I'm trying to get across."

"What happened to you?"

He slaps his trouser leg in a hopeless gesture. "Yesterday I was about forty kilometers from here. I found a man. He charged thirty thousand francs for the three of us and took us out. Ten thousand a head. We walked for a long time, and then he told us to wait while he went to see if the coast was clear. When I insisted on going with him, he punched me and ran away. We spent the whole night in the woods. We've been walking since daybreak. That is until a farmer came along and told us about Martha. Are you here to see Martha?"

"Why, yes, we are," I say.

Little by little the café empties out. We pay our bill, which looks outrageously high. The man puts on his hat and says before he leaves, "You kids better hurry. Martha is an important woman. She won't be around forever. She comes and goes."

My brother pushes me forward. "Go ahead."

I slowly make my way through the exiting crowd toward the bar. There the woman waits, her eyes rounder than planets. "What can I do for you, son?" she says.

"Stevynski sent me," I say. "He said we should see you."

***

"My brother said I should talk to you." I point behind me. "That's him."

"Oh, yes, I know you. You buy here often. Flan, right?"

"Hey, Martha!" My brother smiles.

A brief pause, then: "Hmm, Earth. Let me see what I have in stock."

The shopkeeper goes in back.

I remember first entering and being greeted by those familiar colors. They are like the ones you see advertised on the kiosk screens or vending machine labels. Every childhood has its own particular color, sometimes black and white, even *gray*. Mine has them all—the whole range from red to blue to green to yellow, with splotches of orange, purple, and pink in-between—one of the benefits of growing up in the Cat's Eye, I suppose.

I can see those jars on the shelves, still recognize some of the moons and clusters, show ordinary customers what galaxies and solar systems they come from. I can even point them out on any one of the space charts that line the store's walls. If you hold any one of them in your hand real close to your ear, you can still hear the voices of the peoples who lived there. You can hear the past saying things. You can't communicate back, but at least you can listen. You can learn a lot from the past.

When Martha returns she places a small orb in my hand. "I'm sorry," she says. "This is the closest thing we've got."

It looks like the Earth. It feels like the Earth. Blue oceans, green continents, tall mountains. But it is not the Earth.

"No thanks," I say, and I hand the sphere back.

"I'm sorry I couldn't better help you. The planet you speak of is very rare."

"That's all right. Really." I leave the shop feeling more depressed than before.

"Del, wait!" Flan comes running after me. He is having a change of heart.

A brother is someone who gives you back your last planet after he's won it from you. Flan digs me with his elbow. "Here, idiot." He hands me the Earth. "Don't ever say I never did anything for you."

I get back my miniature world. It's still blue and green with small chips and cracks, just like I left it. Tomorrow I'll win a *pile* of planets from him. He'd better not go around thinking he's the boss just because he's older.

I mean it.

Lawrence Dagstine is a native New Yorker, video game enthusiast, toy collector, and speculative fiction writer of 20+ years. He has placed more than 400+ stories in online and print periodicals during that two-decade span, especially the small presses. He is author to numerous novellas and three short story collections. Death of the Common Writer, Fresh Blood, and From the Depths (TBA, w. Illustrator Bob Veon). His work is available on Amazon and B&N.com. www.lawrencedagstine.com

When a young woman wakes up in a world far from Earth, she finds herself at the mercy of a strange and terrifying creature.

Travelers

John M. Floyd

Jenny Beemon woke up scared.

She was lying on her back on the floor of a room she'd never seen before—a long, bare room with an arched ceiling and what looked like metal walls. The floor was as cold and hard as marble.

She lay still, waiting for her heart to slow down. Was this a dream? Only a moment ago, she'd been hiking in the sun in the Chugach mountains east of Anchorage, in the middle of nowhere. To be here now, in a place like this . . . It *had* to be a dream.

With that thought to comfort her, Jenny swallowed, rose to a sitting position, turned her head to look around—and felt her heart freeze in her chest.

Something was in the room with her.

It was crouched in the back corner, still as a stone, and it was looking at her. At first, she thought it was a man, but as her eyes focused she saw the thing's long hair and gray skin and oversized head. Only its eyes and mouth resembled a human's; it had no nose or ears. A simple brown robe covered its body, and hands as big as dinner plates lay folded in its lap. The feet beneath the hem of the robe had eight toes each. As Jenny watched, stunned, the creature opened its mouth and grunted.

Jenny could only stare. Her mind was spinning, her pulse pounding in her ears. Whatever this was, it was no dream; she, of course, knew that by now. She was somehow actually *here*, in a shiny, windowless room that looked like the inside of a mailbox, staring at a monster.

And it seemed to be waiting for her to say something. When she didn't, it raised a huge hand and pointed a finger at the wall to Jenny's left. She heard a CLICK, then a humming noise. Apparently satisfied, the robed creature lowered its hand, looked at her again, and spoke—but this time, though its lips moved, the sound came from a speaker somewhere inside the wall.

An electronic voice said, in perfect unaccented English, "Understand now?"

Jenny Beemon was beyond surprise. After what she had seen over the past few minutes, the use of some kind of real-time remote translating device held little wonder. Trying to hang on to what was left of her sanity, she drew a deep breath and asked, in a small voice, "Where am I?"

A silence fell, and though Jenny heard nothing, she sensed that the voice-recognition device had already translated and transmitted her question to the thing crouched in the corner. It studied her a moment before responding.

"The Gatehouse of the Opala Legion," the creature answered, through the wall speaker. "In Kingdom of Zontar."

Jenny felt her stomach turn over. She didn't know what answer she had expected, but it wasn't that one. "Zontar?" she murmured.

"The name of our planet." The creature examined its pointed fingernails (claws, Jenny corrected herself; they're *claws*), then raised its head and looked at her. "By what name are you known?"

Jenny felt her eyes fill with tears. *Don't scream,* she told herself. If she started screaming she didn't think she'd be able to stop, and she somehow knew that her only chance was to stay calm and strong and alert. Roughly she wiped the back of her hand across her eyes and sat up straight.

"Jennifer Beemon," she said. Her voice was less steady than she had hoped. "And who are you?"

The creature inclined his shaggy head and looked at her. "I am the Gatekeeper."

Of course, she thought. Who else would you find in a gatehouse? But then, even in the midst of her despair, Jenny saw the irony of that statement. The room around them was no more than thirty feet by fifteen, with smooth, unmarked walls, and no doors or windows. "What gate do you keep?" she asked.

The question seemed to surprise him. "The one you came through."

As he spoke those words, he moved his gaze to a point over Jenny's right shoulder. She turned, and saw only a fourth blank wall. But something was odd. When she squinted her eyes, there seemed to be tiny lights flickering just behind its surface.

She turned again to face the creature from Zontar. "I don't understand."

He gave her a long, measuring look, then rose to his feet. As he did so, Jenny realized he hadn't been crouching at all. He had been sitting on a low, rigid shelf that now slid noiselessly into a slot in the wall behind him. She also saw that he was much larger than she had thought. His back was hunched, his heavy shoulders slumped and apelike. His robe, bound at the waist by a knotted cord, made him look like a deformed monk who had gone a little too long without a haircut.

She tensed, every nerve in her body on red alert, as he shuffled toward her.

In another part of her mind she said, *Watch over me, Mom. Help me get out of this.*

***

Jennifer Beemon was no stranger to tough situations. Her deadbeat father had moved the family to Anchorage when she was seven years old, and had soon decided that the downtown bars held far more appeal than either his job or his wife and daughter. He was dead within two years, not from liquor but from a midnight knife fight in one of his haunts. Left with no husband and no insurance and no marketable skills, his wife Katherine had toiled at minimum wage at a cleaning service for the next ten years to support herself and her only child, and just after Jenny's high-school graduation Katherine Beemon had died also, like an exhausted climber who, upon reaching the summit, realizes the ascent has sapped the last reserves of strength.

But to Jenny her mother was, in a way, still with her. Jenny had not been idle during her high school years—she had worked many jobs, one as an after-school runner for a local bank, and following Katherine's death Jenny hired on as a teller trainee while taking college finance courses at night. For six years she handled First National's customers' transactions and studied nonstop for five days out of each week. Come Friday afternoons, though, Jenny was off to the mountains, and spent every weekend hiking the backcountry. She loved the woods and the wildlife and—most of all—the solitude. She still did. Her only company was the warm and loving memory of Katherine, and every night, whether in her own bed or inside a sleeping bag underneath the stars, Jenny spoke with her mother, talked about daily problems, asked for guidance. So far it had worked.

Jenny was twenty-five now, with a business degree from UAA and a position at a top consulting firm. Mr. Right had yet to make an appearance in her life—a fact that didn't bother her nearly as much as it seemed to bother her friends—and, all things considered, life for Jenny Beemon was satisfying. All she really required for her well-being was her weekly trek into the wilderness. It was her haven, her therapy, her getaway from the pressures of the world.

That, and those regular conversations with her mother.

And never had she needed support more than now . . .

***

Silently, her heart in her throat, Jenny watched the creature approach. She searched her mind for some way to defend herself, but found nothing. When whatever happened had happened, back there on the wooded ridge deep in the mountains, she had left her backpack—and her hunting knife—under a towering black spruce where she'd planned to make camp, and was tromping around off the trail, looking for firewood. Talk about poor decisions.

The thing from Zontar stopped six feet away, just on the other side of a straight blue line painted on the floor. The line, which Jenny noticed now for the first time, ran all the way from the left wall to the right, and divided the room in half. Without breaking eye contact, the robed figure pointed a finger downward, a motion that produced another CLICK, and a whirring sound. Jenny watched as a shiny cylindrical stool appeared, rising from a hidden circle in the floor. When it locked into place the Zontarian sat down facing her, his toes only inches from the blue line that bisected the room.

"Wall behind you," he began, "is not wall. It is mouth of tunnel that separates your world from mine." He paused for a beat. "When you, on your planet, entered this tunnel—"

"A . . . portal, you mean?"

"I suppose. Some call it a wormhole. A rip in the fabric of reality. When you entered it you were swept into a tube, an invisible river through space and time, at a rate far greater than speed of light. River that empties—and deposits its travelers—at this spot, in this room."

She swallowed. "That's impossible."

"I am afraid not. Unlikely, yes. Amazing, even. Not impossible."

"But . . . why?"

"Why does it exist? No one knows. Our scholars believe it is because the two planets are so similar. Some think they were created as one, then split apart while tiny and spun away into separate galaxies. Apart . . . yet still connected."

"Do you believe that?"

"They do not care what I believe."

Jenny studied the wall a moment. Except for the dim, pulsing points of light, it just looked like a wall. And solid as steel.

"A tunnel," she repeated.

"As good a word as any."

"How did I fall in?"

"You walked in, probably. There are six entrances—Gates, we call them—on your end. One is in tropical rainforest, one in open sea, one in Alaskan coastal mountains, and two somewhere on continent of Asia—did I pronounce that correctly? No idea where sixth is. All are remote, all are transparent, and all lead to this point, where you are now."

"But . . . how do you know all this? Have you been to Earth?"

"I have not had the pleasure."

"Your people, then. Your scientists—"

"We are not space travelers," he said. "What we know we have learned from others."

She felt cold sweat on her neck. "So I'm not the first?"

"How do you think we know your languages?"

"Where are they?" she asked, raising her chin in defiance. "The others. Where are they now?"

He waved a hand in dismissal. "They have been processed."

Jenny blinked. Processed? For an instant, she pictured groups of visitors being welcomed and tutored in the customs of this strange new world—but only for an instant. The more realistic part of her brain told her the word had a very different meaning.

Even as these thoughts registered, as the chills began their crawl down her spine, she knew she had to *do* something. And not only to save herself. If she died here, others might soon follow. No matter how remote these Gates were, she had apparently managed to stumble into one—and even though she'd been way off the beaten trails, there was always a chance her backpack would be spotted one day. If that happened, whoever discovered it might look around for her, and step through the same portal she had.

She remembered where she'd been. If she could get back, she could sound a warning.

If she could get back.

She squeezed her eyes shut. *I won't give up, Mom. Not without a fight, I won't.*

With a great effort, she rose to her knees, then to her feet.

"Let me out of here," she said. She tried to stand rigid, to look the creature in the eye—but something was wrong. She felt a physical weakness that went far beyond stress and terror. She was exhausted. She staggered, then sank once more to her knees.

"You are hungry," the Zontarian said. He turned and pointed. After the now-familiar hum, a waist-high shelf emerged from the rear wall. On the shelf was a bowl of greenish wafers. The creature stood, retrieved one of the wafers—it looked like green chocolate—and handed it to her. As he did so, Jenny realized this was the closest she had yet been to the Zontarian. He smelled odd but not unpleasant, animal-like but not dirty. She was reminded of the odor of her sheepdog just after he'd been scrubbed clean in the washtub on her back porch.

"Take this," he said. "You are near collapse."

"I just . . . I don't understand," Jenny said again. She was young and fit and healthy, and had eaten a full breakfast only a short while ago.

"Time passes faster here," the creature explained, as he sat down again on the stool. "Though you have only been here few minutes, many hours have passed in your world, and in your body." He nodded toward the wafer in her hand. "Eat that—but only tiny bite."

She did. It was tough and dry, but as soon as she swallowed she felt a warm rush of energy. Fascinated, she lowered herself once more to a sitting position. Her skin was tingling. She looked around her in awe, taking in colors and sounds and smells she hadn't even noticed before. She could see every thread in her shorts and sweater, every speck of dirt on her hiking boots.

"I'm high as a kite," she whispered.

"That piece of wafer," the Zontarian said, "is equivalent of much food and water—and other stimulants as well. It alone would keep you alive and strong for many days, on your Earth."

That made her look up at him. Now that her head was clear and her senses focused, she came to a sudden conclusion. She had known it all along, but now it seemed truly inevitable.

"I won't see Earth again," she said. "Will I?"

"No," the creature replied.

***

Jenny swallowed again, the sound loud in the empty room. *Be brave*, she told herself. *I'm not dead yet, and if I'm not dead I'm alive, and if I'm alive there's still hope. Right?*

But she had to get one thing straight.

"What happened to the others?" she asked. "What does 'processed' mean?"

The Zontarian regarded her for a long time before answering. "We get one or two Earth dwellers here each week or so," he said finally. "That is one every few years, your time. The System alerts us—alerts *me*, on this shift—when someone is coming. That is my signal to switch on the processor." He nodded toward the floor on which Jenny was sitting. "Forward half of room," he said, "is porous network of lasers, aimed upward from floor to ceiling. Thousands of them. When switched on, result is impressive. Humans unlucky enough to arrive here are incinerated. Their remains filter through flooring as input to extraction system."

She gaped at him. "So, as soon as they arrive—you kill them?"

"We process them."

"But that's . . . barbaric."

"It is practical. Human body, when broken down into basic compounds, provides water and nutrients our people can use." He paused and added, "We did not ask you to come here."

"Then let me leave." She felt tears in her eyes again.

He blew out what sounded like a sigh. "Outside, you would be doomed. I told you, time is different here. You would age and die quickly."

"Then let me go back." Wiping her eyes, she glanced behind her, at the strange, flickering wall. "I'll step back through, and go back to Earth—"

"You cannot," he said.

She studied his face. "You mean you won't let me?"

"Correct. You are forbidden to leave this room. But there is another reason." The creature rose and lumbered again to the back wall, where he picked up the bowl and dumped its dozen or so wafers onto the top of the shelf.

Then he shambled back to his stool and sat. The empty bowl looked tiny in his Chewbacca-sized hand.

"When someone is inside tunnel," he explained, "Gate on this end becomes kind of membrane, soft and thin. At all other times, like now"—he raised his arm in a surprisingly quick motion and threw the metal bowl; it hit the wall hard, bounced off, and clattered to the floor—"it is rock-solid."

Jenny stared at the bowl, which lay upside down with a dent in the rim.

"Besides," he said, "it only goes one way. From Earth to here."

She looked at him then, and saw something odd in his eyes. He turned also, and their gazes met.

And suddenly the miles and the years fell away, and she was looking not at a monster but at her mother, telling six-year-old Jenny not to wander far from the house or the boogeyman might get her, telling her this even though her mother knew perfectly well there was no such thing as the boogeyman. Katherine Beemon's expression, a look of both wisdom and deception, had been exactly the same.

"But not always," Jenny said.

"What?"

"It's not always one-way, is it," she said, holding her breath. "I can see it in your face."

He seemed ill at ease. "Our scholars have said it goes one direction only. Why should I think differently?"

"I don't know." *But you do, don't you.* She hesitated, then forged ahead. "Maybe you've heard something—seen something—to disprove it."

The Zontarian let his gaze stray once again to the wall behind her. "Nothing has been disproven. But, yes, something strange did happen. Once." He stood, moved past her to pick up the bowl, then returned to his seat. "It is of no consequence."

But she kept staring at him, and finally he spoke again.

"Some time ago," he said, studying the dented bowl, "I brought my young son here with me, to this room. He was playing there in corner, bouncing his ball on floor, when alarm sounded, signaling that tunnel was in use. I then did two things. First, I grabbed son and held him out of harm's way. Second, following usual procedure, I prepared to turn on processor. But before I could switch on lasers, and before arrival of whoever was coming, my son pulled free and threw his ball at wall—Gate—which was pulsing and flashing colored lights."

The Zontarian paused as if remembering. "That time, what was thrown did not bounce off. The ball went straight through, and disappeared into wall. And something else happened as well. Great wind, great howling suction, began to come from tunnel. I have never seen its like, before or since. Lasted short while, then was quiet."

The creature raised his eyes and stared at the Gate, apparently deep in thought. "The ball," he said, "did not return."

For a moment neither of them said anything. Finally, Jenny asked, "What about the traveler?"

"He never arrived."

Jenny thought that over. "Do you think he . . . went back?"

The man from Zontar shook his head. "I do not know." Then, as if to himself, he added, "There are many things I do not know." He bent down and set the bowl on the floor.

Jenny, who had also been studying the wall, said, "Is that why you haven't killed me yet?"

"What?"

"That's it, isn't it? There's something you want from me. Something I know but you don't. That's why I'm still alive."

The creature frowned, then stood and moved to the left wall, the one containing the speaker. "You are still alive," he said, "because I made mistake." He waved a hand and a horizontal panel emerged from the wall, a foot-square shelf containing a red toggle-switch. "When alarm sounded—alarm signaling your approach—I was gone to washroom. There is alarm in there also, but it malfunctioned. I knew nothing of your arrival until I returned here, to find you lying unconscious on floor." He glanced at the control panel. "This switch, when pushed to right"—he raised his hand to indicate this—"activates processor." He asked, "Would you like to see?"

Jenny stiffened, wondering if her time had come, but he nodded toward the back of the room. "Go there," he told her.

She stepped over the blue line on the floor and moved past him to the back wall. She stood uncertainly beside the shelf of spilled food-wafers, waiting.

"Watch," he said, and threw the switch.

Jenny flinched as the whole forward half of the room was bathed in sizzling white light. Shielding her eyes, she peeked through her fingers at the firestorm of vertical rays that had erupted from the floor where she had stood a moment earlier. The glow held steady for half a minute or more, then winked out when the creature pushed the toggle back to the left.

Jenny Beemon lowered her hands from her eyes and gulped. The floor looked exactly as it had before. "Is it still hot?"

"Not at all. Cools instantly." He turned again to face her, but left the switch-panel in place behind him. This fact was not lost on Jenny, who was watching his every move.

"That would have been your fate," he said, "had I been here to do my job. But I still have not answered your question: Why are you still alive *now*? Why did I not process you while you lay there on floor, unconscious?" He leaned against the wall beside the switch and folded his huge arms. "I will tell you, Jennifer Beemon. You are right: you know something I want to know." He paused. "My knowledge of you and your homeland consists of what our System has learned from your people. And that knowledge was not—*could* not have been—gathered through interviews. It was gathered through technology. Retrieval of memory banks found inside minds of the travelers selected for that purpose."

Holding her breath, she asked, "And am I one of those?"

"No. Those were chosen by our scholars, and procedures were set up to transfer needed information. All that is past. You are exception. Accident. In fact, you are second such accident to happen on my watch."

Jenny said nothing, waiting.

"Some time ago, another traveler arrived unprocessed. His survival was also result of equipment failure. We lost power to lasers just before he came through Gate. Problem was repaired, but not quickly, and during that time I had chance to speak with him, as I now speak with you. He was from place called France, and knew two languages—one was same one you speak. He had been on holiday, he called it, to mountains of China, after visiting King Kong."

Hong Kong, Jenny said to herself.

The Zontarian paused then. "He told me strange things," he continued.

"Things unknown in our world. Memory dumps, you see, give us facts. No insight into what you call emotions, or feelings."

"What do you mean?" she asked. "Are you saying you people have no feelings?"

"Of what use are feelings? From what my France traveler told me, they seem a burden. He spoke of your planet's fondness for charity and good deeds and 'helping fellow man.' We on Zontar know nothing of, and care nothing for, these things. Here there are no emotions to interfere with logic and efficiency."

She leaned back and hugged her elbows. "Then why are you so interested?"

The creature was quiet awhile, then said, "He told me one thing I have not forgotten. He said something like: 'Love is finest of all gifts.' I find that confusing."

"Why?" Jenny said. "You told me you once protected your son so he wouldn't be hurt by the lasers—"

"I protected no one. I restrained him because he is needed to work in the gas fields."

Jenny gaped at him. For an instant, her grim situation was forgotten. "My God. Have you no *heart*?"

He frowned and put a huge palm against his chest. "Organ which pumps blood?"

"What I mean is, have you no love? No compassion?"

The creature from Zontar stared at her. "Why should I?"

Here it is, Jenny said to herself. *Here's the reason I've been spared. I've been kept alive so this pathetic monster, this hairy oversized Yoda, can satisfy a point of curiosity, and if I give him an acceptable answer he'll be finished with me. He'll push me over the blue line, throw the switch, and fry me like a bug on a griddle.*

But she found she wanted to tell him. For one thing, she was going to die anyway, but more importantly, she wanted to tell him because she knew the answer.

"Your traveler was right," she said. "It *is* a gift." As she spoke she stood up straighter, and despite her sweat-soaked hair and dirty clothes and unlaced boots she felt proud. "To be loved is a great thing, a great feeling. And it goes both ways. To *show* you care for someone, if only to perform a simple act of kindness, can . . . well, it can warm you, inside." She paused, thinking about her beloved mother, and urging him with her eyes to believe her. "If you ever did something good for someone, and did it just because you *wanted* to and didn't really *have* to . . . then you'd know what I mean."

She blinked suddenly, and realized her face was flushed. There was no way to tell whether what she had said had made an impression, but she knew she'd said all she had to say, and she figured the thing from Zontar knew it too. She just stood there alone at the end of the room and waited for whatever Fate would bring.

But what it brought was an alarm—a piercing monotone that made both of them flinch. Following the Zontarian's gaze, she turned to the front wall—and felt her mouth fall open.

The Gate was going wild. It was blinking and shuddering and flashing a thousand colors. It looked . . . alive.

"What is it?" she shouted, above the blaring alarm.

He glanced at her, then turned again to watch the Gate.

"Someone is coming," he said.

***

She stood speechless, watching the streaks of breathtaking color that scissored across the once-solid wall at the front of the room.

Finally, the sound got the better of her. She clapped her palms over her ears and called to the Zontarian, "Shut it off!"

He gave her a blank look, then pointed somewhere. The alarm stopped.

She lowered her hands, her ears still ringing. "Before he gets here," she said, "are you going to . . .?" Her eyes strayed to the red toggle-switch.

"Turn it on? Yes. That is my job. But there is no hurry." He cocked his head, watching. "Transfer takes three minutes, our time."

Jenny looked again at the Gate. It was moving in and out now, as if breathing. "Where is—whoever it is—coming from?" she murmured.

"Which Earth Gate, you mean? Who knows? There are several. One is even somewhere in ocean."

"So you said." It occurred to Jenny, as she stood watching the colors, that she had probably just heard the answer to the mystery of the Bermuda Triangle. "How much time's left?" she asked.

"Here. I will make it easier." The creature studied the arched ceiling, then pointed to a spot near its center. A second speaker came to life, reciting in English: "NINETY-FOUR . . .

NINETY-THREE . . . NINETY-TWO . . . NINETY-ONE . . ."

"When it reaches zero," he said, "our traveler will arrive."

The countdown continued. Jenny listened, as if in a dream. She felt paralyzed.

"SEVENTY-SIX . . . SEVENTY-FIVE . . . SEVENTY-FOUR . . ."

At sixty seconds, the Zontarian shuffled to the control panel, raised his hand, and pushed the red switch to the right. Once more the forward half of the room was engulfed in white fire. Involuntarily Jenny stepped backward. With a part of her mind she felt the shelf of overturned green-chocolate wafers digging into her back as she stared, horrified but fascinated, at the buzzing, hissing display fifteen feet away. And just beyond the lasers' blinding needlework, she could see the colors dancing inside the wall.

Unscheduled flight from Earth, she said to herself, *arriving now at Gate number one . . .*

She wondered if she were going mad.

"THIRTY-SEVEN," the speaker announced. "THIRTY-SIX . . ."

Jenny glanced around the room, her mind racing. In thirty seconds, she would see a person die a horrible death—a death she herself would face shortly afterward. She knew she had to do something, to at least *try* something.

Mom? she thought. *WHAT SHOULD I DO?*

Then she froze. She stared wide-eyed at a spot on the left wall, just behind and above the Gatekeeper's head. "Oh no," she whispered.

The creature noticed, and spun around to follow her gaze. "What—"

As soon as he turned, Jenny plowed into his back with all her strength, running full speed with her left shoulder lowered like a linebacker. Though she was not a large woman, surprise was on her side: the Zontarian's head slammed into the wall and he slumped to the floor. Before he could recover she grabbed the red switch and jerked it to the left. The lasers winked out.

"TWENTY-FOUR . . . TWENTY-THREE . . . TWENTY-TWO . . ."

She shot a glance at the Gatekeeper. He was still down but trying to rise.

The deadly half of the floor was safe now, the colored lights beyond beckoning to her like a crooked finger.

The ball went straight through, he had said . . .

"NINETEEN . . . EIGHTEEN . . . SEVENTEEN . . ."

It was now or never.

She crossed the blue line and sprinted toward the wall.

***

It was her bootlaces that betrayed her. Her left foot stepped on her loose right lace, and she sprawled flat on the cold floor five feet short of the Gate.

There were fourteen seconds left.

Scrambling to her hands and knees, panting and sweating, she threw a quick look over her shoulder—

And her heart sank.

The creature was up and standing, and watching her. There was a hint of pain in his eyes, but nothing else. And his hand was poised on the red switch.

She stayed on all fours, afraid even to move a muscle, and stared at him.

"TEN," the speaker said. "NINE . . . EIGHT . . ."

Then, all of a sudden, she saw his face change. Stunned, she watched him take his huge hand from the switch and let it drop to his side. For an instant their gazes locked, and deep in his eyes she thought she saw a glimmer of emotion.

"Go," he said.

She didn't have to be told twice. She heard the speaker announce that there were three seconds left as she bunched her legs beneath her, clenched her teeth, squeezed her eyes shut, and dove headfirst through the Gate.

***

Light. An instant of brilliant light, so intense she could see it through her closed eyelids. Then darkness. She felt herself floating. When she opened her eyes again, dim colors lingered in the distance. Lingered, then faded. A terrible, roaring wind seemed very near, but she felt peaceful and protected. Was she in some kind of bubble? The gelatinous material of the wall? She didn't know. One thing she did know, however: she was moving. And not slowly, either. She was moving the way you move when the captain asks the chief engineer for more power and your head slams backward against the seat rest and your cheeks pull back into a scary grin and the stars turn into lines.

Her last waking thought was a memory of having done this before.

***

She woke up flat on her back again—but not in an empty room, and not on a cold floor. This time her resting place was warm and lumpy, and she felt a breeze on her skin and heat on her face.

She stretched and opened her eyes and looked up at the sun.

Slowly Jenny rose to a sitting position. Her first thought as she looked around was that she was home. Somehow it had worked. *I'm home, Mom. I made it.* Hot tears stung her eyes.

Her second thought was that, if this was indeed Earth, she was a long way from her starting point. From the looks of the place, this particular tunnel had not ended up in Alaska.

Jenny Beemon was sitting alone on a wide stretch of white beach, twenty feet from the water's edge. Foamy waves lapped at the sand. An ocean? If so, which one?

She wiped her eyes and pushed such thoughts from her mind. She had another matter to attend to, first.

Being careful not to shift too much from one side to the other, Jenny fished a keyring from her pocket. Four keys were on the ring—keys to a car and its trunk and an apartment and an office, relics from a different existence. She unclipped the first key, drew a deep breath, and threw the key straight ahead, into the ocean. She watched it splash, then unsnapped the second. This one she threw to her left. It landed in a puff of sand thirty feet away. The next key was thrown behind her, toward a horizon of barren yellow hills, and her eyes followed it until it plopped into a clump of brush.

But the fourth key showed her what she needed to know. It was thrown to her right, and before it had sailed six feet it vanished into thin air. She looked wide-eyed at the point where it had disappeared, and though she could see nothing but a continuation of the long, empty beach, she knew she was staring through one of the entry points into the tunnel.

Okay, she thought. Now I know where *not* to walk.

Still seated, she looked down at her feet, and the sight of the loose bootlaces brought back visions of the Gatehouse and its keeper. Of all the incredible things that had happened to her since being swept off the mountain ridge near Anchorage, the thing she would remember most was the look in the Zontarian's eyes as he took his hand from the red switch.

With a heavy sigh, she laced her hiking boots and wondered about whoever had been inside the tunnel at the moment she had plunged through the wall and disrupted everything. Had he returned to Earth also, to exit at one of the other Gates? She hoped so. As for the tunnel itself, and her passage through it, she found she had no memory of that at all.

Jenny struggled to her feet, dusted sand from her clothes, and looked down the beach to her left—to the south, according to her pocket compass. A line of hazy blue mountains rose in the distance. It was, she decided, as good a direction as any.

She had one final task. Before leaving, she fashioned a rough landmark from rocks and driftwood so she could find the place again. Though she hadn't worked out any details yet, she was fairly certain she was the only person alive who knew the location of one of these things (no, not one but two, counting the one she had walked into), and since people were dying here something would have to be done. Maybe get the marines to come blow it up, she thought. If the government refused to believe her, she'd invite a few doubting bureaucrats to step inside and test it out.

She finished her marker. It was time to go. With her gaze fixed on the distant mountains, with the comforting feel of her mother's presence in her mind, she trudged down to the firmer sand at the water's edge and headed south. She had no idea how long it would take her to reach civilization, but she was confident of at least one thing: food and water would not be a problem.

In the baggy pockets of her shorts, along with her compass and penknife and now-empty keyring, were thirteen tough, dry wafers that rattled like wooden coins with every step.

They looked like green chocolate.

John M. Floyd's work has appeared in more than 250 different publications, including **The Strand Magazine, Alfred Hitchcock's Mystery Magazine, Ellery Queen's Mystery Magazine, The Saturday Evening Post,** *and* **The Best American Mystery Stories.** *A former Air Force captain and IBM systems engineer, John is also a three-time Derringer Award winner and an Edgar Award nominee. His sixth book,* **Dreamland,** *was released in 2016.*

When a physicist disappears in a lab accident and is presumed dead, and his daughter arrives to the lab to collect his personal effects, she discovers he is not only alive, but trapped in a "pocket universe" with only two chances to return. Can she and her father's lab assistant recreate his experiment before the two universes drift apart forever?

Universal Connection

S.M. Kraftchak

Hannah felt strangely empty of emotion at her father's memorial service. Without seeing his body, it was like he was buried in one of his projects a galaxy away, and she'd receive a congratulatory note and a box of chocolate from one of his assistants for some accomplishment she'd completed two months earlier. Since there was no other family to speak, she dutifully went through the motions of receiving condolences from his co-workers, the occasional dignitary, and delivered her father's eulogy like he'd been attentive and affectionate. The deception seemed awkward and bothered her.

The day after services, she shuttled to the satellite research facility where all dangerous experiments were conducted. It seemed like any other day as she entered the Astrophysics pod where her father and his assistant worked.

"Hannah! Such a pleasant surprise. What are you doing here so soon? There's no rush. I'm so sorry for your loss." Her father's latest lab partner, Dr. Edward Sheen, rushed with outstretched arms to embrace her.

"Hey, Eddie. Thanks," she said accepting his affection with a pat on his back. "I came to collect my father's personal stuff, if there is any."

"Other than the picture that was on his desk, I don't know if there is any. If there was, it would have been on his desk in the lab." Eddie pointed toward a closed door that had a red warning sign, HAZARDOUS AREA—DO NOT ENTER, on it. "The company sealed his lab until I could complete an investigation, but I guess I can let you in." He started toward the door and paused half-way. "It's a real mess."

"I'm used to the clutter of experiments."

Shrugging, Eddie punched in the code to unseal the external spherical lab, one of four, that surrounded the Astrophysics office pod. He stepped aside as the door slid into the wall. "But not quite like this."

Hannah scowled at Eddie and halted in the doorway. "Holy Mother . . ." With her mouth agape, she gazed around the wreckage in the spherical lab. Where a-half-dozen experiments shared a curved table top flush against the walls, there were piles of shattered glass and twisted metal. The stacks of ancient books that perched atop the corners of his desk like precarious castle spires looked as if someone had swept them against the wall. Her father's smart-board, usually filled with long equations and bits of details he needed to remember, hissed with static; and his white board was a scorched, melted puddle of plastic. Everything was covered with a fine green dust, except for a single pair of shoe-prints in the middle of the room. "What happened?"

Eddie peered over Hannah's shoulder, shook his head once, and walked back to his own orderly desk. "We're not sure yet. He always pushed the limits with unstable elements, and often peered over the cutting edge into some great abyss, but this time he obviously went too . . ." He glanced at Hannah's back. "I'm sorry. Maybe it's too soon. Let me send you—"

"Did he have notes?" Hannah continued surveying her father's lab.

"As a matter of fact, I'd badgered him enough that he finally relented. He dropped this on my desk, just before he . . . the incident, he made me promise not to open it, and keep it safe. After Salister stole his earliest prototype, ten years ago and he spent five years getting the rights back, he was paranoid someone else was going to steal his work." Eddie pulled a neatly organized, four-inch thick file of papers from his drawer and dropped it on his desk. "He went old school to prevent cyber thievery. I haven't had the courage to start sorting it, yet, but the corporation wants answers . . . and you deserve to know what happened to your father."

Hanna turned away from the destroyed lab. "Want some help?"

"Oh, I couldn't ask you to do that so soon after . . . You must still be heartbroken."

"Eddie, you obviously didn't know my father, so let me tell you about him. While he was important to me and I loved him, and looked up to him, we never had the opportunity to be close. My mother, an opportunity seeker who thought she was hitching her wagon to the rising star in Physics, the great Dr. Aaron Dubois, soon left him and his four-year-old daughter when she realized life was endless hours of waiting for her husband to come home, punctuated by the monotony of Mary had a Little Morphet and endless playdates."

"I didn't know . . ."

Hannah shook her head. "He did his best to be a good father and divide his time between his research and domestic obligations for almost a year. However, he lost track of time working on one of his projects and completely forgot about, me, his five-year-old daughter, for six days until his new research assistant asked about the picture of me on his desk. I was fine, of course, having been self-sufficient with modern technology, but the Corporation was horrified that they might be liable for child abandonment or neglect. They demanded he give them custody of me. It was presented as an altruistic gesture to allow the great Dr. Dubois to continue his, oh so important, research uninterrupted by day to day concerns, and that Spatial Advancements for People would 'bear the burden of raising and educating the next great physicist.' A crock of self-aggrandizement if you ask me. Father sheepishly agreed and then returned, unfettered, to his research, while I was shuffled off to the corporate space station along with dozens of other researchers' day to day concerns who were being cared for where they wouldn't disturb their parents' work. Those were the best and worst days of my life. I wanted for nothing, but friends. Most of the corporate children were more interested in the latest superhero saving the Universe, not in a geeker girl who wanted to understand it."

"Did you ever see you father again?"

Hannah nodded. "Over the next ten years I excelled in Science and sweet-talked my way back to this research facility. I spent many hours shadowing various researchers, including one or two special assignments at my father's elbow. I quickly accumulated multiple Junior Achievement Awards in Astronomy and Physics and became the poster child for the SAP's child rearing program. At sixteen I left the corporate station and this research satellite to attend University in our quadrant."

"They must have been thrilled to have Dr. Dubois's acclaimed daughter."

Shaking her head, Hannah continued. "I changed my last name to avoid the adulation and expectations, but I sat secretly proud when he spoke at my commencement and introduced me as Valedictorian and his daughter. Despite our separate paths, I know he loved me and I cherish the connection we have . . . had through Physics. It seems only fitting to help figure out what project has permanently absorbed his attention."

Eddie raised his eyebrows and nodded. As he unwrapped the bound packet of papers, the intercom sounded.

"Dr. Sheen?"

"What is it, Lila?"

"The Corporate JG representatives request your presence in the main conference room."

Eddie let a heavy sigh. "Tell them I'll be down in twenty minutes."

"Yes, doctor. I've already dispatched a shuttle."

"I'm sorry, Hannah, I managed to put them off until after your father's memorial service, but—"

"No, it's fine, go. I understand. If you're okay with it, I'll get started laying out his papers. I have a pretty good idea of how he might have organized them. We were of like minds on the Arlon project."

"Are you sure you want to? I mean, if it . . ." Eddie stopped as Hannah raised her eyebrows at him. "Okay, then. It's just the preliminary hearing so I'm sure I can keep them away from here by telling them the lab is still under decontamination protocol. I should be back in an hour, two at most. There are some snacks in the cupboard next to the food dispenser. You know how—"

"My father hated synthesized food and had what he called real food shipped half-way across the galaxies at triple the cost of the energy to synthesize it."

"That was your father," Eddie laughed and then headed toward the entrance. He turned just as the door opened. "I've already digitally catalogued the condition of the lab, so if you need to go in there for some reason, you can."

"Thanks," Hannah said without looking up from the third paper in the stack.

Hannah tipped her head backward and then slowly forward to her chest as she rubbed the stiffness in her neck. With both hands still pulling the tension from her muscles, she scanned the ten-foot long table where she'd carefully laid out nearly all the papers from Father's file. She'd arranged them along the time-line he'd established for his experiment, turning the occasional paper sideways to indicate a gap in time. She noted that while his theories and supporting evidence was sound, the way he got to them was often vague and very unscientific. She glanced at the clock above the door and realized that Eddie had been gone for over four hours. She hadn't realized how time had slipped away. When her stomach suddenly gurgled, she glanced at the remaining papers on the corner of the table to gauge whether she could wait to eat or whether she'd be better to grab a quick snack.

A click from the destroyed lab behind her, like someone snapping, spun Hannah around. "Eddie?" She waited a long minute. "This isn't funny. I'm too tired for games. I promise you're not interrupting. I want to share what I've found, so far."

When Eddie didn't emerge, she turned back to the table of papers and stifled a small gasp. A three-inch by five-inch envelope, with her name written in her father's hand, lay on top of the last stack of unsorted papers. She was certain it hadn't been there. Her eyes widened when she realized it was covered with a fine green dust and the paper below it was not. She stepped back and looked around the lab. "Hello?" she called, cataloguing each empty desk in the silent lab to be sure Eddie hadn't returned and left her undisturbed to finish her task of sorting.

When the room remained silent, she stepped forward and lifted some green dust from the envelope on her fingertip and rubbed it with her thumb. Even though she barely used any pressure, her fingertips warmed significantly and then cooled when the dust disappeared. She swiped more dust from the envelope and rubbed it gently between her fingers again, but had to separate her fingers suddenly as the warmth strengthened to a burn. Looking at her hand and then over her shoulder at her father's lab, she considered how the dust covered both the envelope and the lab, and where it came from. Hannah suddenly went to the threshold of her father's lab, knelt on one knee, and performed the same test on a small amount of dust from the lab. When she got the same result, she touched her finger to the dust again and simply pressed her fingers together. Nothing. The dust remained on her fingers.

Her eyes wandered the lab again. Nothing had changed, but from her new viewpoint, there appeared to be a four-centimeter black orb suspended in mid-air above the foot prints. She slowly rose, tipping her head from side-to-side to keep it in sight. It didn't move. Perplexed by the minute discovery, she suddenly returned to the table of papers and carefully picked up the envelope. Walking slowly, she took it to a nearby lab station, and shook the dust into a petri dish. When she was sure all the dust had been removed, she opened the envelope.

Scanning the sentimental words on the front of a birthday card, Hannah pursed her lips. It was happening again. She looked back at the table to see if there was a box of chocolates, shook her head and opened the card. She chuckled when her eyes skipped the rest of the syrupy words and read the scribbled, "Love, Dad", that was supposed to replicate her father's hand. She looked back at the envelope, double checking that the writing on the front was her father's and then closed the card. As she turned it to stuff it back in the envelope, she noticed the back of the card was filled with his scribble. 'Hannah— U.s only align 3Xs before shift too far. You must re-trigger bridge. Use scalar as invariant, vector to track vacuum fluctuations—expansion/ contraction. Used DE distill XENON1T2 to trigger bridge to pocket U., expand WIMPs reaction with TGseaweed. Estimate alignment times: 47 hrs post IC, and 61 hrs post IC. After that, it's all yours. Either way, I'm proud of you. I love you. Dad.'

Hannah stared wide-eyed and open-mouthed at her father's note and looked up with the same expression when the door to the office pod opened.

"Hannah, I'm so sorry it took so long. They kept running me in circles—" Eddie halted and stared at her. "What's the matter? You look like you've seen a ghost."

"I don't think my father is dead," she whispered.

"What?" Eddie rushed to stabilize Hannah who was swaying precariously.

"Here, sit. I knew it was too soon for you to be going through . . ."

Hannah allowed Eddie to guide her onto a nearby stool.

"Now, what did you say?" Eddie stared at Hannah as she stared into her father's lab.

"He's not dead. My father is still alive, in a Pocket Universe."

"Oh Hannah, Sweetheart, you're overwrought. I shouldn't have left you—"

"No! Stop, Eddie. I'm fine." She held up the card. "He sent me a note. I found it on the stack of papers. He's still alive."

Eddie glanced at the card and shook his head. "Hannah, I got that for him two weeks ago and signed it for him. He must have laid it down and then accidentally collected it up with the rest of his papers."

"No! You don't understand. It wasn't there, and then it was. And only it was covered in the same green dust—seaweed of all things—that combusts when you apply pressure . . . he's alive, but he needs me to rescue him."

Eddie's face puckered with concern as he barely shook his head and spoke. "Hannah, I understand it's difficult to believe he's really gone. But—"

"Read! He wrote a note, instructions, and managed to trigger a big enough event to get this back here so I'd know what happened." Hannah held the card out to Eddie, who took it, and shook his head when he opened it. "No, the back!" Hannah turned it over in his hand and tapped the paper. "He is alive. He wrote this and sent it back when our Universe aligned with the Pocket Universe he discovered. He's alive and has only two more opportunities to get back."

Eddie took a full minute to read the note. "I don't understand."

Hannah rushed to the table covered in her father's research, scanned the table, and grabbed a sheet of paper, rattling it in the air. "He's discovered the existence of parallel universes, a Pocket Universe, to be specific. He used a scalar field to map our Universe and then used the electromagnetic energy from dark matter to trigger an event that brought together our Universe and a Pocket Universe. From there he produced a vector field map of the expansion and contraction to predict when the two would share the same point on the Scalar and Vector fields and created a bridge using WIMPs, amplified with powdered thermogenic seaweed."

"You got all that from this?" Eddie's eyebrows rose in disbelief as he shook the card in the air.

"It's perfectly clear to me."

"It's a perfectly wonderful story to ease your broken heart."

Hannah shook her head. "No, it's all here." She waved her arm over the table and then snatched the card from Eddie. "And here. See, I'll explain it," she said stepping closer to point to each line of the note. "Due to the expansion and contraction of dark matter, and the fact that it expands more than it contracts, we must assume at different rates in each Universe or we'd be permanently connected, the Pocket Universe and our Universe will only ever match parallel points in each Universe three times."

"It says all that in one short line?"

"Well it's supported by the next line and," Hannah scanned the table and pointed to several piles of paper, "and that research study, and that ancillary study."

"Okaaay. It's far-fetched, but I follow the theory. What's this XENON1T2?"

"Back in the early 21st century an international research group built the first dark matter detector, called XENON1T. It used Xenon to detect WIMP dark matter. It was quite ingenious, but now primitive by our standards. My father perfected and improved upon the design by creating a dark matter distillery—of sorts—and called it XENON1T2. It gave him the ability to power many of his experiments without having to request energy from the Consortium, which of course requires justification, and opened him up to the possibility of having his most sensitive research stolen again."

"I didn't know he was using dark matter!" Eddie said.

"Not many people do. Old Doc Carrigan knew before he died, and I believe Dr. Sara Gillett, the head of SAP's resources division keeps it as a very closely guarded secret. Anyway, according to . . . " Hannah pointed to another large stack of papers, "that study, he was able to use the dark energy to trigger a physical connection or bridge between our Universe and a pocket universe he'd discovered. Somehow, don't ask me where this harebrained idea came from, he used powdered seaweed, which is plentiful across almost any galaxy of choice that hosts an ocean and prolific botanical specimens, to amplify the reaction."

"So, the green powder covering his lab is the residue of him blowing up his lab with dark energy and seaweed?" Eddie asked looking toward the lab.

Hannah nodded. "I'm not quite sure how he augmented it to have thermogenic qualities—that's the study on the far top corner."

"So, if he blew up his lab, how is he not dead? Sorry to be so indelicate."

"I believe he was either blown into the pocket universe or had planned to cross the bridge and stepped over before the explosion. The second is more likely, because of the foot prints in his lab."

"But if everything else in his lab was blown away from the point of convergence, then how was he not thrown?"

Hannah waved him over to the lab's doorway, bent very low, and pointed. "He has a micro-XENON1T2 suspended directly above where he was standing. The blast would have gone over his head and not affected him."

"Not to destroy your overly optimistic hopes, some would say delusions, but you still haven't proved to me he's not dead."

Hannah drew a deep breath, chewed on her lower lip for a minute and then raised her birthday card. "We just passed the second alignment."

"Okay, I'm skeptical, but am willing to believe. Now, if this pocket universe is habitable, how long do we have to rescue him?"

"He tells us. His initial calculations of the vector field versus the scalar field show that after Initial Contact, the two Universes are close enough to bridge at 47 hours and 61 hours."

"But that's only twice."

Hannah shook her head. "Initial Contact is the first of three bridges. After that, the independent expansion and contraction of the two Universes will no longer line up."

"And that means your father . . ."

"And I will be a universe apart, forever."

"Well, let's see if we can stop that from happening. Tell me what we need to do."

Hannah sighed and looked at her father's lab. "I need to finish sorting Father's papers and review the procedure. After that, I'll determine the exact time of the past two events to calculate the third. The micro-XENON1T2 needs to be reset to coincide with the time, and I've got to figure how this damn seaweed plays into the equation." She gently pinched a bit of green dust from the petri dish and let it fall.

"Will the Hazmat vacuum work on the dust without setting it off?" Eddie pinched the dust in the petri dish and let it fall.

"It should, but be sure to empty it every five to ten minutes to avoid heat build-up."

"Okay, let's get started."

Nearly an hour later, Hannah finished sorting her father's research and was studying papers from several piles to get a sense of the overall procedure when the door chime sounded, just as the vacuum shut off. She looked at the door and then over her shoulder.

Eddie appeared in the entrance of the lab.

"Are you expecting someone?" Hannah asked holding the papers in mid-air.

"No, but that doesn't mean that Corporate doesn't invite themselves."

"You never did tell me the outcome of your meeting."

"I . . . got sidetracked when I saw . . ."

"Is there something I should know?" Hannah's forehead creased as the corners of her mouth pulled down.

"They weren't too happy and wanted full disclosure of all projects he was working on."

"Okay, that makes sense. He does work for them."

"Yes, but . . . your father wasn't necessarily a good Corporate employee. He worked on projects that interested him most, a few he thought had important implication for humankind, and then the ones he was assigned."

"Was this one assigned?"

Eddie skewed his mouth to the side and shook his head.

"What did you tell them happened?" Hannah glanced at the door when the chime sounded again.

"I kept telling them it was too early in the investigation to determine what had happened."

"Then why is someone here?"

"They may not have believed me since your father has had other accidents where we have been less than forthcoming with information."

"Did you tell them I was here?"

"I might have mentioned it and . . ."

"And . . .?"

"They weren't too happy to have an outsider in their lab after such a public incident. I assured them you were here on personal business."

"And so I am. Get rid of them. We don't have time to argue with some half-wit PR monkey if we're going to be ready for the next event."

Eddie gave a huge sigh and nodded before placing the hazmat vacuum in its isolation chamber. He resealed Dubois's lab and arrived at the door as the chime sounded a third time. He pressed the intercom button. "Who is it?"

"This is Dr. Sara Gillett, Chief Energy Officer. Let me in Eddie."

"I'm not sure I should do that, Doctor. I'm in the middle of an investigation."

"Oh, cut the crap and let me in. Is Hannah in there?"

Eddie looked to Hannah for permission with raised eyebrows and a shrug. "Does my father like her?"

Eddie gave a long whistle. "Now that's a loaded question, but I think it might be better coming from one of them. I think it's safe to let her in though."

"Plenty of time for family drama, after I rescue my father. Let her in if you want, but no one is stopping me."

Nodding, Eddie entered a code and the door slid into the wall.

"What took so long?" Dr. Gillett said, looked him up and down and then added, "Can't be that much contamination if you're not in an environmental suit."

"Nice to see you too, Dr. Gillett. Yes, it's safe to come in. We just didn't want the PR monkeys nosing around and messing with things before we got them figured out."

"We?" she said stepping in to the office and then stopped, folded her hands in front of her, and put on a saccharine smile. "Ah, this must be the famous Dr. Hannah Chapman, or is it Dubois now?"

"Dr. Hannah Chapman-Dubois, to please my father."

"Did he know?"

"Yes, he does." Hannah re-ordered the papers in her hand and stacked them together neatly before lowering them in front of her.

"Umm, then it must have been your doppelganger that spoke at your father's memorial service. You know he was lost in a tragic accident a little over two days ago, right?"

"Lost is not quite the word I would use. Stepped out for a while, traveling, perhaps lost in the sense we aren't exactly sure where he currently exists, but I believe he's still very much alive."

"Ah, the sweet sentiment of a loyal daughter."

Eddie cleared his throat and stepped forward, almost in between the two women. "Sara, you can drop the superiority act. I believe Hannah. We think Aaron is still alive in another universe."

Sara's smile melted and her eyes filled with tears. "Really? But that's impossible. You said everything in his lab was destroyed."

"He wasn't in his lab when the explosion happened," Hannah said.

"How can you be so sure?"

Hannah turned to Eddie and hmphed with annoyance. "We don't really have time for this." She then turned back to Sara. "If you trust me, then find a way to make yourself useful; if you don't, then leave. Either way I have a two-day long experiment to recreate in less than eighteen hours if I have any chance of seeing my father again."

"Are you talking about Aaron's bridging universes?"

"You know about his experiment?" Eddie and Hannah said simultaneously.

"Well, a little. He came to me over a year ago needing an extraordinary amount of energy. I couldn't give it to him. Well, I could, but justifying it wasn't possible, so I suggested an alternative."

"Dark energy," Hannah said.

"No, I told him dark energy was too expensive, at least the collection of it is. The technology is still too unreliable. I suggested a thermogenic seaweed from a little-known outlying planetoid over in the Lorentz galaxy. It provides an amazing amount of energy."

"How did you know about that?" Eddie asked.

"She is the Energy Resource Officer for the largest research corporation in our universe," Hanna said.

Sara nodded with a wide smile. "You'd be surprised what I know."

"But did you know that when you mix dark energy and your thermogenic seaweed, you get a very unstable energy output?" Hannah waved the papers in her hand.

"He didn't!"

"He did, and now we get to figure out how to make the reaction stable enough to create the third and last event to bridge our universe and the pocket universe my father discovered, or we'll never see him again. Per his documentation," Hannah dropped the stack on top of another stack of papers, "we can't recreate the energy needed without blowing ourselves up. He must have made an adjustment without documenting it."

"Big surprise," Eddie said.

Sara covered her mouth with her hand and shook her head. "It's not possible. The collector needed for the dark energy is much too large and there are only two others in use, and they are still in the experimental stage."

"Well, it seems he was good at keeping a lot of secrets. Eddie, open the lab," Hannah said and waived Sara to follow. Once the door opened, Hannah stepped just inside. Sara stepped up next to her.

"Holy Mother . . . He really did it," Sara said gazing around the lab.

Hannah pointed to the air in the middle of the lab. "It's hard to see, but there's a micro-XENON1T2 suspended just there. Although Eddie's cleaned most of it up, the whole room was covered in a green dust, except where my father's shoe prints were directly below the collector."

Sarah took a step forward to inspect the dark matter collector, but Hannah grabbed her arm.

"Please don't. I'm not sure of anything right now."

"He's actually microtized a dark energy collector and he didn't tell me? That son of a . . . he sweet talked me into getting him the plans for a theoretical prototype over two years ago. He promised he'd keep me apprised of his progress." Sara said still bending to be able to see the tiny orb Hannah had pointed out.

"Can the seaweed be reused?" Eddie asked. "We don't have any more in inventory.

Sara shook her head. "Re-used? There isn't usually any residue. That's the beauty of it."

"Even if it's retained its thermogenic property?" Hannah asked.

"It did?"

Hannah left the lab and retrieved the Petri dish of green powder that had covered the letter from her father. "When I rubbed it between my fingers, it burned," she said presenting the dish to Sara who gently tapped her finger into the dust and rubbed her fingers together and shook her head. "It shouldn't have that much thermogenesis left in it. In applications where we've used this, there was no residue. Is this from the initial event?"

"No." Hannah said. "It's from a card my father sent back during the second event and Eddie just finished vacuuming the lab of all the residue from the initial event."

"Hmmm." Sara stood gazing at the green powder for nearly a full minute.

"No offense, but we are on a deadline here," Hannah said.

"Is this the rest of his documentation?" Sara pointed to the table blanketed in papers.

"Yes, as much as he ever documented. There are a couple of gaps, but those are easily filled in. My biggest concern is balancing the energy. My father's calculations are woefully incomplete."

"How about I calculate from what we know of the previous two events—"

"Which isn't much," Hannah said.

"There's more there than you think. Based on the energy left in the seaweed, and any estimations of required energy in Aaron's documentation, I can make a pretty good educated guess."

"Close enough to bet Aaron's life on it?" Eddie asked.

"Close enough to bet all our lives on it, because if I'm wrong, we won't be as lucky he was." Sara looked at Eddie and Hannah with an apologetic shrug.

Hannah pressed her lips together. "I'm sure we'll all do our best."

For the next eight hours, the three scientists worked silently on their tasks. Eddie carefully finished cleaning and preparing the lab. Sara took over Eddie's desk and poured over stacks of papers that Hannah had given her. Connecting and comparing twenty pages of long hand computations that included energy equations, containing both constants and variables of electro-magnetic, radiational interference from the nearest stars, often had Sara growling with frustration and a nearby waste bin full of crumpled up paper. After one especially loud outburst that left her pacing with her hands locked onto her head, Hannah stood and stretched next to the table of papers.

"You don't have to do it long hand, you know. We have enough time that you could go get a computer to do the calculations for you."

"I've known your father for some time now and often questioned his chronic need to do everything by hand."

"And I'm sure you got the standard lecture; 'A computer has a fraction of the capacity of the brain to extrapolate numbers and circumstances out beyond a set of established parameters. Computers only do what you tell them to do; I'm looking for answers that only a sharp mind can perceive and question what next or what more.' Each lecture ended the same way whether I was five years old or twenty-five. He'd smile, tap me on the nose and say, "And that is why you're going to go sharpen these pencils and pull a fresh ream of paper. Nothing like the smell of wood and graphite to shift the brain into high gear."

Sara tossed her head back and laughed. "And I thought he was only being condescending to me."

"It was never meant that way. It was intended to help people understand what a wonderful gift the mind is." There were a few minutes of silence as Sara sharpened several pencils and then Hannah asked, "How well do you know my father?"

"How well can anyone know a man who is so driven by his work that he'd forget to take care of life's most basic necessities, unless he's reminded?"

It was Hannah's turn to laugh. "So not much has changed in twenty years."

"I did find that asking him for detailed explanations of his latest project and their energy requirements pulled him away from his lab for several hours. I managed to gently persuade him to go back to my quarters once or twice for a decent meal and glass or two of wine, but he never mastered small talk and our conversations would invariably wander into the latest project that confounded him. Not that the conversation was unpleasant . . ." Sara leaned back in Eddie's chair

"Just not what you were hoping for," Hannah said with a bittersweet smile. "That's why my mother left and why I was taken away from him, although they didn't call it that at the time. I know my father loved us. My mother never understood his passion for his work. It took a while, but I eventually understood his passion by having the same one."

"You know there was one late night," Sara looked across the office as if she were watching someone, "here in the lab, when I was trying to keep him company and he became so totally flummoxed by some minute detail that he threw his arms up in the air. He paced the office for five minutes, with his arms tightly folded to his chest and then stalked into his lab and shoved his white board aside. There he opened a small compartment in the wall and stood staring into it. I was afraid to disturb him, so I stayed out here for over thirty minutes, until I heard what sounded like a cry from the lab. I quietly approached and peered over his shoulder . . ." Sara suddenly stood and turned away.

"What? What was he doing?" Hannah asked.

Sara shook her head as she sniffed and wiped her face and then wiped her hands on her legs.

"What?" Hannah insisted.

"If your father makes it back . . . he's a very private man . . . perhaps when he makes it back, he can tell you," Sara sat down and began pouring over her papers again without looking at Hannah.

"Well, that's a right nice way to crack a rotten egg and then pretend it doesn't stink," Hannah said and then turned to Eddie. "Do you know what she's talking about?"

"No idea," he said as he shook his head.

Hannah turned back to Sara again. "But what if he doesn't make it back. With all this," she spread her arms to include the table of papers, "his chances of returning to our universe are pretty slim. My brain hurts, my eyes are blurring, and I can barely think for trying to convince myself he won't have to live out his life alone, in some other universe, or worse."

Throwing her hands in the air, Hannah stalked to the corner of the offices, tucked her arms tight to her chest and paced. As she was about to turn away from her father's lab for the ninth time, she stopped and stared into the dimly lit sphere. It was silent without the hissing smart board, and seemed empty without the melted whiteboard. In the place the whiteboard had been was the outline of a twelve-inch square compartment door. She rushed to the door, examined it for no more than ten seconds and pressed the buttons on the top two corners. The door opened out, creating a small shelf. Inside was like a time capsule. She reverently picked up a picture she had drawn for her father, when she was three, of the two of them in long white lab coats pointing at the stars. A small bundle of letters, wrapped in a pink ribbon were tucked in next to an old fashioned holo-frame. With a trembling hand, she reached in and pressed the on-button. Instantly she recognized a picture of their first quarters where her parents had been married planet side. It had been a long time, but she remembered her mother's face. Pictures of her smiling and caressing her swollen belly, faded to a picture of her mother and father cheek to cheek with their newborn daughter. When she turned three, her father had gotten his first assignment off planet and there was a picture of the three of them stepping from a starliner onto the Corporate housing satellite. After that, there were no more pictures of her mother, only several dozen pictures of a time and place she barely remembered, after her father had surrendered her to corporate rearing. The same picture, and the only one ever publicly displayed on his desk, of her and her father at her University graduation, pointing to the stars—like in her hand drawn picture—was the last one. She watched the loop of pictures two more times and then turned the frame off, replaced the hand drawn picture, and closed the compartment. She allowed her hand to linger and then left the lab.

"Let's get some rest. Working our brains until they are numb won't reach a productive solution. We'll meet back here in four hours. That will give us four hours to complete our preparations."

"But, I'm not finished . . ." Sara looked up with bloodshot eyes.

"Yes, you are. We'll have enough time to finish everything, if our brains are fresh. Please go."

Sara and Eddie tried protesting as Hannah herded them out of the office, to no avail.

"But where will you go?" asked Eddie with Sara waiting expectantly by his shoulder for the same answer.

"There's a cot behind Father's desk that I used to sleep on after Mother left and before the corporation took charge of my life. I'll get the rest I need there."

When Sara and Eddie returned to the office pod, Hannah was already busy assembling the stacks of paper into one single stack.

"I thought you were going to get some rest?" Sara asked.

"I did. I got the best four hours of sleep I've gotten in years and everything I'd been pouring over for the past day, suddenly became clear," she said stacking the last of the papers together and leaving a single sheet on the table. "Here's all we need to do."

Eddie came over and picked up the sheet and read through it. "It's that simple?" He handed the sheet to Sara who read it.

Hannah nodded as she tucked the stack of papers back into the file envelope it had been in and laid it on the table.

"It really is," Sara said.

Laying her birthday card on top of the stack of papers, Hannah smiled. "Yes, it is."

Within three hours they had set the proper parameters, checked and double-checked the exact amount of thermogenic seaweed, confirmed the micro-XENON1T2 was properly accumulating dark energy and was ready for the electro-static connection of the two universes to trigger the third event. They looked around to see if there was anything they'd missed.

"Are you sure—" Sara began.

"Yes. It's too late to change anything," Hannah said.

"So, what do we do now?" Eddie asked.

Hannah walked out of the lab, motioned the other two out, and pointed to the key pad, indicating for Eddie to close the door. "Wait for my Father to knock. But in the meantime, tell me about your childhood, since mine was anything but normal."

Whether voyaging the universe, or journeying in a fantasy world of my own making, I'm passionate about discovering engaging characters and relentlessly tracing their heartfelt stories so I can relate them to you. I love sunrise on the beach, sunset in the mountains and portraying Elizabeth Tudor. I have one dog who thinks she's a footrest, another who catches a Frisbee, and a cat who rents me my desk for open-window-time. I have three awesome daughters and a husband who is my best friend, my harshest critic, and my most fervent supporter. Please visit my website for more of my stories. smkraftchak.com

On the fringe of the galaxy, an old enemy's attack on a Coalition survey ship ends centuries of cold war passivity, thrusting both civilizations to the brink of interstellar war.

First Strike

Robert J. Mendenhall

The alien war vessel lurked in geosynchronous orbit on the opposite side of the planet, hidden from the survey ship's telemetry by the planet itself. Obsidian in color, it blended seamlessly with the jet black of space, its articulating tentacles and bulbous mass occluding the stars behind it. The dreadnought stalked the survey ship, listening to its transmissions. Silently waiting for the opportune moment to strike.

***

The dim light above Captain Alec Landon's head flickered in rhythm with the subtle vibration of the *Horizon's* idling engines. Normally, it went unnoticed, but Landon had sequestered himself in the survey ship's cramped captain's pod for the past several hours, and he was now hyper-sensitive to it. The bulkheads of his make-shift office closed in on him. The stale, filtered air irritated his throat. And that damn flickering grated on his nerves.

The Quartermaster's report further frustrated him. This assignment nearly depleted the survey ship's finite supply inventory and they were dangerously low on the basics: food, sealants, coolants, and medicine. They would exhaust critical supplies long before they made it back to a Coalition Sector Base.

The intercom buzzed and a small LED above his membrane screen blinked. He thumbed the open key.

"Landon," he said.

"Dr. McKay's survey team is aboard, Captain."

"Outstanding, Exec. Prepare to break orbit. I'll be there in a moment."

"Aye, sir."

Landon toggled the intercom. He was eager to get clear of the Tau Sigma system. The Crellat Demilitarized Zone was entirely too close and Fleet Command had not provided them a single escort. Not one. Granted, there hadn't been direct contact with the Crellats for decades, but he was tense from looking over his shoulder, nonetheless. And he yearned to pick up where he and Peyton McKay had left off. He signed the Quartermaster's report and saved the file.

They would have to divert to Rantoul Station. The port facilities there were rudimentary, but they were the best this remote sector of Coalition space had to offer. And, the crew could use some well-deserved liberty.

Landon logged off and secured the stylus to the desktop. He performed his daily systems check of the pod's on-board computer system, ensuring each module was active and recording. Once finished, he rolled his chair back on the rubberized deck, clipping the narrow bunk behind it. He stood, zipped his khaki flight suit to regulation level, and knuckled the pressure plate next to the hatch. The inner door popped inward on well-oiled pivots. He pulled it fully open and stepped into the narrow space between it and the outer door. Another pressure plate, a sequence of colored lights, and the outer door popped outward. He stepped into the open bay of *Horizon's* Primary Operations Center, feeling the coolness of fresh air on his face as he moved from the confinement of the tiny pod to the spacious bay of the *Horizon's* nerve center.

The POC resembled the mission control center of a ground-based launch facility: tiered rows of systems consoles descending to an assemblage of screens and monitor membranes flanking a deck-to-overhead main monitor. The overhead lighting glowed softly, indirectly, and unobtrusively. Most of the illumination in the Center came from the consoles, their membranes and readouts tinting faces with swatches of color. Electronic chatter and muted conversation harmonized into a familiar melody of efficiency. Filtration fans whispered with recycled air, but unlike the stagnant air in the pod's independent system, the air in the POC, and the entire vessel, was kept fresh by the natural oxygen/carbon dioxide exchange of potted foliage. The subtle scent of spearmint lingered.

Landon slid into his seat at the command console on a raised platform at the back of the POC.

"Status?" he asked his executive officer seated to his right.

Lieutenant Commander Eric Ballantine, a tall, dark-skinned man, lean and in his early forties, didn't look up from his own checks. "All systems are green. All personnel accounted for. Ready to break orbit on your order, sir."

"And not a bit too soon." He tapped a key on the command console, linking him to the communications console, several rows to his front and right.

"Comm," he said. "Send to Coalition Fleet Command. The *Horizon* has completed its assignment on TS-5 and due to supply shortages, is en route to Rantoul Station for resupply . . ." he paused a short second and added, "and liberty."

A quiet murmur of approval rippled through the center. Landon stifled a smile.

"Aye, sir," Lieutenant Ann Shelby at the communications console replied. "Coding."

Behind him, Landon heard the main hatch open and turned as Dr. Peyton McKay, the *Horizon's* civilian Science Director, strode into the POC. She stepped onto the platform and slipped into the empty seat on Landon's left. They shared a brief moment of eye contact. The barest hint of a smile passed between them.

He turned back to his console and focused on the business of the ship, but the after-image of her, trim and lithe in her flight suit, remained at the periphery of his thoughts. She was his age, mid-fifties and, like him, healthy and possessed of intellect and drive. She tied her maple hair neatly behind her back. Her eyes were dollops of sweet cocoa and he thirsted for them. They could be a good match, he and Peyton. A good match.

Landon toggled All Ship on his console. "Attention all hands. This is the captain. De-orbit in thirty seconds. Transition to Gray Space in de-orbit plus two minutes. Landon out." He cut the ship-wide connection and activated the

POC link. All stations in the Center were now tied into the command console.

"Tactical view on the Main," he said in a low tone. His voice issued clearly from speakers at each console.

"Aye, sir," the young officer at the systems console said. The video feed on the main screen wiped off and a broad schematic of the Local Spur arm of the Milky Way Galaxy wiped on. The image zoomed in until it displayed the graphic representation of the Tau Sigma star system on the leading edge of the spur.

The overhead lighting sparked out for a split second, brightened, then softened to normal illumination.

Landon looked up. "What the hell?"

"What was that?" Ballantine asked, checking his own readouts. "Chief?"

"Checking, Exec," the Chief Engineer said. He and several other engineers ran a series of rapid diagnostics and system checks through their consoles. After consulting with each other, the Chief Engineer reported back to Ballantine.

"We're not finding a problem. All systems are nominal. Do you want me to send up a tech crew?"

Ballantine looked at Landon. "Sir?"

Landon considered. It was a minor glitch, and one that seemed to have corrected itself. Shit, the lights in his pod flickered all the time. Still, he felt . . . uneasy. "Keep running diagnostics, Chief. But, as long as all systems are green, let's get underway. We can dispatch techs once we're in Gray Space."

"Aye, sir," Chief said.

"Pilot," Landon continued. "Engage de-orbital thrusters."

"De-orbital thrusters, aye," she replied.

There was a perceptible shift in the survey ship's attitude as it slid cleanly out of orbit, angling up and away from the system's ecliptic plane.

Ballantine confirmed and digitally approved the calculations from the Standard Space Navigator. "Transition to Gray Space in thirty seconds," he announced.

Landon repeated the announcement ship-wide, adding, "Secure all stations. Stand-by for disorientation."

"We're clear of Tau Sigma V, sir," Pilot said. "Ready to engage Aiken Drive."

"Aiken Drive at one hundred percent," Chief said.

Ballantine keyed into All Ship. "All decks, all stations. Situation Condition Zeta. Repeat. SITCON Zeta." The overhead lighting shifted from soft white to emerald green.

"Engage the Aiken," Landon said.

In the POC and at active stations over the entire ship, crew members tensed for the rush of sensations and confusion that occurred when the fabric of standard space was breached. Those crew members not on duty sequestered themselves in their cabins, most preferring to lie in their bunks during the transition from normality to the folds of space between space. Gray Space.

But . . .

Nothing.

No whine of the dimension-rendering Aiken Drive. No rush of vertigo. No pressure on the eardrums and eyeballs. No nausea.

Absolutely nothing.

Landon leaned forward. "Pilot," he said evenly. "Status?"

Landon could see the pilot in the lead console confirming her readouts and meters. Likewise, all the engineering officers frantically checked their instruments.

"Sir, my systems indicate the Aiken has engaged," Pilot said.

"Confirmed," Chief said.

Ballantine looked over at Landon. "First time I didn't nearly puke," Ballantine said.

Landon stood. Despite what the instruments told them, his body knew better. "All stop," Landon said.

"All stop," Pilot repeated.

But again, there was nothing to indicate that had occurred.

"Captain," Pilot said. "My board shows we're still in Gray Space."

"Not a chance," Ballantine said.

"Gray Nav," Landon said. "Can you confirm?"

The Gray Space Navigator sharing the console with the Standard Space Navigator glanced over his shoulder. "My board shows we're in Gray. On course for the reentry point."

Landon rested the tips of his fingers on the command console, feeling its vibration.

"No, we're still in black space," Landon said. "Exterior views on the Main."

The schematic wiped off and live feeds from the hull cameras blinked on in six individual tiles. Each tile displayed a dedicated viewpoint: bow, stern, port, starboard, keel, and topside.

"What the hell," Ballantine muttered.

They were, indeed, still in standard black space. And they were still in the Tau Sigma system. The watery crescent of TS-5 sparkled in the stern view.

Landon cleared the command platform and stepped down to the tier of engineering consoles. All the POC engineers pounded keypad membranes and fast-talked into headsets. Landon leaned over the chief engineer's shoulder. "Talk to me, Chief."

"We have a data-mal, Captain. I've found a viral program inserted into the POC main frame. When it went active, it overwrote the logics for helm and navigation, and severed the Aiken Drive interface."

"A data-mal? Why wasn't it discovered when we went through pre-flight?" Landon asked.

Chief turned toward the captain. "It was dormant at that point, and buried under other code. My guess? When the lights sputtered is when it was activated."

Landon silently swore. "Activated by whom? And how?"

"We're running a key-logger now, sir. We should have—" An engineer at the far console signaled Chief. Landon and Chief made for the station.

"What have you got?" Chief asked. The engineer pointed toward his monitor membrane and scrolled the data.

"Wait," Landon said. "Scroll up a bit. Go back three time-frames. There." He and Chief exchanged a glance. Landon straightened. Both turned toward the Comm console.

Lieutenant Shelby sat rigid in her seat, eyes forward and unblinking.

Landon eased his way to the Comm.

"Lieutenant," Landon intoned. "Did you send my message to Fleet Command?"

Shelby's voice was even, and toneless. "I did, sir."

"The key-logger says otherwise. Can you explain that?"

"I can't, sir," she said.

"But you did send it?"

"Aye, sir."

"According to the key-logger, two signals were sent from your console in the last few minutes. Neither of them were my message. One was a micro-pulse sent toward TS-5 through the main array. The second was an internal ping."

Landon paused. Shelby said nothing.

"The time-stamp coincides with the fluctuation in the overhead lights, so I think it is safe to surmise your internal ping activated the data-mal."

The muscles in her neck tightened. Not by much, no more than a slight twitch, really. But Landon saw it. He gave a curt nod to Ballantine. The exec slipped a wire set over his ear and spoke low into the mic end.

"Two questions, Lieutenant. First, who did you send that pulse to, and second . . . why?"

Shelby slowly rose and faced Landon. She was a tall woman, nearly Landon's height. Her short, copper hair fell across her forehead in a neat line and circled her face like a metal scarf. The muscles in her oval face tensed, her almond eyes narrowed.

"We don't belong out here," she hissed.

"I beg your pardon?"

"This isn't our space. We're intruding. No. We're invading this world and others like it for our own expansion."

"Lieutenant, TS-5 is 97% ocean. There are no intelligent species, human or otherwise on it. Our presence here is strictly scientific. Research. Knowledge. Period. Aside from the instrument module we deposited on the ocean floor and the relay-sats in orbit, we are leaving this world as we found it."

"Don't you mean the weapons cache you deposited on the ocean floor?" She cocked her head and flashed a defiant smile. "Yes, we know what you're really doing here."

"We?" Landon asked.

Shelby said nothing.

Peyton stepped down from the command platform. "You belong to Sons of Sol. Don't you."

"Sons of Sol?" Landon asked.

Peyton nodded. "They're an isolationist group. I encountered them once before, but they weren't violent. Just xenophobic."

"Not xenophobic," Shelby said. "We simply feel we should stay within the confines of our own solar system and not encroach on others."

Landon turned back to Shelby. "Lieutenant, the Orion Coalition is made up of dozens of other societies in the Local Spur. We haven't invaded a single one. We join together in the spirit of cooperation and for the advancement and betterment of everyone."

"Do you hear yourself? You sound like a spinner. For every society you say has willingly joined the Coalition, there is another that you've subjugated."

"Where are you getting your information?"

Again, Shelby turned silent.

"What I want to know," Ballantine said, "is how did you get into the Fleet with these kinds of beliefs? I find it hard to imagine Socio-Screening overlooked this."

"I thought like you once," Shelby said. "Until I met someone who showed me the light."

"The light?" Peyton asked. "What light?"

Shelby smirked.

Landon stepped closer to Shelby. "Exec, run 'The Sons of Sol' through Central Data."

Ballantine tapped several membranes. "Got it."

"On the Main," Landon said.

The exterior tiles wiped off and a full screen image of a dark male filled the viewer. Long hair, thick brows, tight beard, sinewy arms laced with wiry hair. He wore a steel-colored tunic that simulated chain-mail, burgundy pants that might have been genuine leather and ebony boots shined to brightness. On the flanking display membranes, rows of text and graphics scrolled.

"Son of a bitch," Landon said.

Shelby smiled. "Son of Sol," she said.

"So, you recognize this man," Landon said. "Do you know who he is? Do you know where he is?"

"Lieutenant Shelby, is that the man who influenced you?" Peyton asked.

Shelby's smile broadened. "Since you already have his bio-data, then you know this is Jax. And yes, he is the one that gave me the gift of the light. He is our leader. We follow his guidance."

"His name, Lieutenant, is Xeron Antelean," Landon said. "And he's a Crellat."

Shelby faced the captain. Her smug grin twitched slightly. "Ridiculous."

"Oh, I'm sure Antelean wouldn't have mentioned that little fact to you. Fleet Intel identified him years ago as a Crellat operative, but he went off the sensor-grid about eighteen months ago. He's on every watch list there is."

Shelby paled, her smile waned. "No. That's not true. He doesn't even look like a Crellat."

"Minor surgery and skin grafting. We have his DNA signature. Or the Crellat equivalent."

"Alec," Peyton said. "Up until now, the Sons of Sol have been pretty benign. Peaceful protests and annoying demonstrations. Things like that. Hijacking a Coalition Naval Vessel is not their norm. What's changed? What's different?"

Landon nodded in Shelby's direction. "She is. Antelean found someone in the Fleet he could influence. She was perfect. Young. Pliable. Idealistic. And assigned to a survey ship, a much easier mark than a heavy cruiser." He turned back to Shelby. "Where and when did you meet him, Lieutenant?"

Shelby looked as if she hadn't heard him.

The main hatch opened and two, armed security officers marched into the POC. Ballantine jabbed his thumb toward Shelby.

"Where and when," Landon repeated. He held up a hand to the security officers. They stopped short.

When she looked up, her eyes glistened. Her defiant face now sagged.

"I . . . I met him about . . . about eighteen months ago . . ." her voice trailed away.

"Go on," Landon said.

"We met at a bar. Hit it off. Fell in love."

"Love," Ballantine muttered. "Shit, he used you."

"I . . . I thought . . ."

Landon got her back on track. "Focus, Lieutenant."

"He told me the Coalition was a fraud. He said it enslaved worlds. Stole natural resources. He showed me vids and docs. They looked authentic. At first, I didn't believe him. But, gradually . . . I began to see things differently. He never asked me for anything, Captain. Never wanted me to do anything. Until

. . ."

"Until . . ." Landon repeated.

"He met me at Rantoul on our last port call. He was very concerned. Agitated, even. Said our true mission was to drop a weapons cache for a future raid. He . . . convinced me to help expose it. He gave me a data-mal. Said it would simply disable the Aiken Drive so we couldn't get away. He said he was going to go public with the drop and all I had to do was signal him when the data-mal was active."

"Signal him here? In the Tau Sigma system? How was he supposed to get here?"

"I don't . . . I didn't . . ."

"I'm confused, Alec," Peyton said. "What would Antelean want with the *Horizon*? As you said, It's a survey ship, not a combat vessel."

Landon, Ballantine, and Chief responded in unison. "The Aiken Drive."

Shelby opened her mouth, but could not speak. Peyton shrugged her shoulders.

"The Crellats have a rudimentary faster-than-light drive," Langdon explained. "It operates in standard space and allows them to travel outside their own galactic arm, but at a cost of time and energy. The Aiken Drive is a dimensional drive that breaches the boundaries between our normal space dimension and what we call Gray Space. The Aiken allows us to circumvent the FTL barrier."

Peyton nodded. "I know how the drive works."

Landon continued. "It's the one advantage we have over them, technologically. If they ever develop dimensional travel of their own, they could be at Sol's doorstep in practically no time. Literally."

"Or if they should steal the tech and reverse-engineer it," Ballantine added, "same outcome."

Shelby stepped forward. "Are you saying I just handed the Aiken Drive over to the Crellats?"

"Shit," Ballantine said.

Landon motioned to the security officers. "Take her into custody." They moved forward. "Battle stations," he ordered.

Ballantine toggled All Ship. "All stations. All decks. SITCON Delta. Battle Stations. Battle Stations."

A rapid, low-pitched claxon sounded throughout the entire vessel. The steady emerald green light of SITCON Zeta shifted to crimson. The main hatch and all maintenance crawlways into the POC locked. The hatches to the captain's pod remained open.

Landon dropped into his seat on the command platform. Peyton McKay followed suit.

"Energize the deflection net," Landon ordered. "Weapons hot. Chief, do we have mobility?"

"Negative. Systems still register we are in Gray Space."

"Can you disable the data-mal?"

"I would need to know the exact main frame address of the data-mal to introduce the mal-wipe without damaging critical programs."

Landon turned toward Shelby.

"Lieutenant Shelby, I need to know where in the main frame you inserted the data-mal."

She remained silent.

"Look, you were duped. You can mitigate your circumstances by cooperating."

"Mitigate?" she looked dubious. "According to you, I just committed treason. What could mitigate that?"

"Then let me be blunt." Landon said. "We don't know if the D-Net is up. We don't know if the weapons systems will respond. We don't know if our telemetry is trustworthy. If we don't get our systems back under our control, we won't stand a chance when the Crellats attack."

"Attack?" Shelby whispered.

"What. You still thought Antelean was just going to shoot a few vids?"

The *Horizon* lurched.

"Telemetry," Landon called out.

"Nothing on exterior telemetry, Captain." The telemetry officer ran her stylus up and down her membrane screens.

Ballantine toggled All Ship. "All decks, all stations, damage rep—"

The *Horizon* bucked upwards as if punched. The overheads blinked. The ship righted itself.

"Telemetry, full spectrum sweep," Landon ordered

"Already doing that, sir. I'm showing nothing."

"Forward view on the Main," Landon said. The image of Xeron Antelean wiped from the main viewer as the bow tile zoomed to full screen. A tiny green LED in the upper corner indicated the exterior camera was operational, but the remainder of the tile was totally black.

"Where . . . where are the stars?" Peyton asked.

"Stern view on the Main," Landon said.

The image switched to a view to the ship's aft section. There were plenty of stars, and the crescent disk of TS-5 was bright in the upper corner of the image.

"Telemetry?" Landon persisted.

"Sir, I'm showing nothing out there."

"Look," someone said. All eyes shot up to the main monitor, still focused on the aft angle. The image of TS-5 was occluded by a moving edge of blackness that seemed to wipe the planet and the stars away. In an instant, the view to the aft was as void as the view forward.

Landon angled around his console, took the two steps from the platform to the deck in one stride and was leaning over the telemetry officer's shoulder before she had a chance to respond.

"I'm not registering the black mass, sir, but I'm picking up . . . I don't recognize them."

Landon stiffened. "I do. Forward view on the Main."

The image shifted. The stars appeared again as the trailing edge of the moving blackness receded. And some of those stars appeared to be moving. Fast.

"Those are Crellat fighters," Landon said. He leapt up to the command platform

The *Horizon* pitched. The lights shimmered. The ship lurched again. And again. The hull reverberated like a metal drum as the fighter-craft tore into the survey ship with their lethal fire. The acrid stench of burning insulation rose from consoles and chalky smoke billowed from vents.

"Where's the D-Net?" Ballantine shouted over the din.

"My board shows the net is up," Chief said, one hand gripping the console for support, the other tapping membranes.

"It's not," Ballantine countered.

"All weapons systems, fire at will," Landon said as he pulled Peyton to her feet.

"Sir," Tactical responded, "Weapons are . . ."

"Spit it out, Tac," Landon said. He pivoted around Peyton and bounded to the tactical console. "Readout shows weapons are online, but nothing is firing. Projectile. Plasma. Pulse. Nothing is firing."

And then, as quickly as it had begun, the onslaught stopped. The grav-gens stabilized. Instinctively, everyone looked up.

"Telemetry?" Landon barked.

"I've got nothing, sir."

Through eyes watering from smoke, Landon surveyed the confusion-ridden POC. The operations officer was unconscious. The telemetry officer was pulling herself to her feet. His exec was already back at his station.

"Damage report. Quickly, Exec, before the Boarders lock on," Landon said.

"If we can trust these readings, the D-net is out," Ballantine reported, scanning his read-outs, "We've lost communications. The port thruster array has been completely destroyed. Aiken Drive is down. A hull breech on Deck Five. Casualty numbers are still coming in."

"Weapons status?" Landon prompted.

"Weapons systems are not responding, Captain." There was a hint of resignation in Ballantine's voice. "And the lateral cannons have all been destroyed. They knew exactly where to hit us. We're helpless."

Landon turned to an ashen-faced Peyton McKay. Their eyes met and locked in regret. Images of her, of them together, intruded on his orderly, partitioned mind. He tried to marshal them aside, but they remained at the edge of his thoughts. A tangible presence that saturated him with longing, remorse, and an absolute sense of finality.

The ship shuddered under a series of dull impacts. Not like the barrage of weapons fire, these were contacts between the hull and things solid. A subtle vibration ran through the structure of the hull.

Landon scanned the overhead as if he could see through it. "Those would be Crellat Boarder Craft."

To the right of the main monitor, plasma sparks spit out of the bulkhead and into the center with a molten crackle and noxious fumes. The plasma cut a smoldering arch in the metal.

"We're being boarded," Landon said, his utter disbelief muting his voice into a coarse whisper.

"Oh my God," Shelby said.

"SITCON Gamma," Landon said on All Ship. "We are being boarded by Crellat military. Small arms authorized. I say again. Small arms are authorized." He cut the link and darted around the console to the arms locker on the aft bulkhead. Ballantine had it open and was already issuing side arms.

Another plasma torch had started cutting into the bulkhead to the left of the Main. The screen went out as its circuits were severed.

"Now hear this," Landon raised his voice so everyone in the POC could hear him. "Lock down your stations. You, you, and you. Cover the starboard breach. You three, cover the port breach. You and you cover the aft hatch. We don't know how many breaches there are over the rest of the ship, but if they get into the POC, they sure as hell won't be getting out of it."

The POC officers took up ready positions behind consoles not on fire.

Landon tuned to Ballantine. "Eric," he said in a low voice. "Initiate the Omega Protocol."

Ballantine gave a deliberate nod and turned back to his console. He pulled a crimson key from a chain around his neck, thumped open a covered port, and inserted the key. An audible tone caught Peyton's attention. Ballantine keyed in a long sequence of strokes from memory.

"Omega Protocol, Alec?" Peyton McKay asked. "I don't like the sound of that."

Landon handed her his pistol. "I want you to take this and secure yourself in the captain's pod."

"What? No, Alec, I won't. I'll help you fight."

"You're a civilian on a military vessel. My duty is to protect you."

"I'm not the only civilian on *Horizon*, Alec. What about the others?"

Landon's face withered. "I can't help them. I can only help you. Listen to me. I use the pod as an office, but it's an escape pod. The only one on board. It has an independent environmental system and power supply and a single burst Aiken engine. But more important, it's the *Horizon's* black box. All data, all telemetry, the POC recorder. Everything is backed up to the pod."

She glared at him.

"Peyton, listen to me. I can't let the Crellats obtain the Aiken Drive. I have to scuttle the ship. I have no choice."

She paled, her eyes grew moist. "I'm staying."

He straightened. "I need you to live. I need you to get the data to Fleet Operations. They need to know about Shelby and Antelean and the Crellats. They need to know what happened here."

"Then launch the pod without me."

"The data can only provide . . . data. You can provide the human perspective. You can answer questions. Give the data context."

"Alec. I'm not going."

A rush of pride and gratitude made him warm. He savored the feeling. Then shoved it aside.

"I'm sorry, Peyton," Landon whispered. He glanced over her shoulder and gave a curt nod. Ballantine bear-hugged McKay off the deck

"No!" Peyton shouted.

Ballantine maneuvered her to the pod hatch.

"Alec, don't do this!" She squirmed and dug her fingers into Ballantine's arms. He twisted her through the inner hatch.

"I'm sorry, Dr. McKay." He released her and backed out of the pod. She lunged. Ballantine pulled the inner hatch closed. The muffled sounds of her pounding cut off when he pushed the outer hatch closed. He turned to Landon. "Pod secured, Captain."

"Thank you, Eric." Landon took his seat and keyed the video intercom to the pod. The monitor membrane in front of him displayed a static view of the pod's interior just as Peyton sat down at his desk.

"Damn you." Tears drained from her eyes, wetting her cheeks. "I hate you for this."

"No, you don't. I know you don't. Strap yourself in. I'm launching you in thirty seconds. The pod's navigation logic is perpetually locked onto the nearest Coalition Sector Base. Once clear of the *Horizon*, the pod will align itself, then fire its Aiken Engine. It will be fast and rough. Much rougher than you've ever experienced. Once you drop out of Gray Space, the pod will emit a distress signal. Hopefully you'll have enough provisions until you're picked up."

"Alec . . ."

"I have to get back to work. Peyton . . . I . . ." he couldn't voice the words he wanted to say to her.

She nodded. "I know," she whispered, and wiped her cheeks with her fingers. "I won't let you down."

He held eye contact another second, then cut the feed. He thumbed open a cover plate and keyed in a security code. A small plunger rose from the console. He jabbed it with the heel of his hand.

A clang and a whoosh and the pod shot downward through the breadth of the ship. It burst free at the keel as if fired from a cannon.

Landon wasted no time tracking the pod's progress. He pulled his crimson key from beneath his flight suit, rolled to Ballantine's position and completed the Omega sequence. The overhead lights began alternating in color from red to blue. The sequence was repeated throughout the ship. There was no verbal announcement of the impending self-destruct. There was no need.

Ballantine handed Landon another hand-gun and they both perched themselves on the console, taking deadly aim at the smoldering bulkhead.

The first breach was nearly complete. The second would be only a moment later.

"Safeties off," Landon called. "Open fire on my mark."

They all took careful aim on their designated targets.

The molten cutout of the first breach crashed to the deck. Plasma bolts spewed through smoke ahead of the boarders.

"Fire," Landon shouted.

The *Horizon* crew opened up on the first breach, crossing the boarders' barrage of plasma with their ribbons of laser fire.

The initial squad of Crellat boarders set foot on the deck, one after the other, fanning out as they cleared the breach point. The first ones were cut down by laser fire and trampled by the boarders behind them.

The second breach exploded inward.

Smoke and weapons fire and the chaos of the moment obscured the intruders, making it impossible to identify them. They were shooting at shadows in the smoke, but the crew had the high ground and the boarders were falling faster than they were boarding. If they could push them back into the boarding craft—

A third breach began sparking above them.

A fourth to port.

A fifth to starboard.

The overhead lights sequenced faster. Red . . . Blue . . . Red . . . Blue . . .

Pilot took a plasma bolt square in the chest, killing her instantly. Telemetry went down writhing. A bolt blasted Chief into the bulkhead and he slid to the deck, mouthing a silent scream.

Red. Blue. Red. Blue. Red. Blue.

Shelby lunged forward. "Wait! Jax and I—" Her words cut off as a plasma bolt incinerated her.

The third breach blasted open and boarders rained down though the smoldering hole.

Landon's hand-gun grew warm in his hand. He had grown used to Ballantine being at his side, had been bolstered by the whine of Ballantine's laser fire counterpointing his own as if in musical duet. The sudden absence of that accompaniment was like a hammer blow to his chest. He turned his head to see his First Officer sag to his knees, a smoking hole in his sternum.

Throughout the carnage, Landon had remained fixated on the enemy. Had set aside his feelings for Peyton McKay. Contained his outrage at Shelby's betrayal. Steeled himself against the Crellat onslaught and suppressed his anguish as his crew was killed or mutilated, one at a time. But, when Eric Ballantine went down, his resolve faltered. The crushing weight of despair bore down on him, squeezing breath from his lungs and moisture from his eyes. Futility penetrated his iron defenses, just as these intruders, these Crellat bastards, penetrated his ship.

RED-BLUE-RED-BLUE-RED-BLUE

The fourth breach opened.

The fifth . . .

They poured in like sand.

Landon took a bolt to his left side. He cried out as his hip incinerated and the flesh and muscle around it seared.

He pitched forward, struck his head on the console, and fell to the bloody deck.

VIOLET

***

Dr. Peyton McKay awoke reluctantly. The persistent tones of the medical scanners incited a throbbing in her temples. Her throat burned and her stomach churned, but she was alive.

She opened her eyes and eased her head to the side.

"Easy, Dr. McKay," a white-robed tech said.

"I'm okay," she said. She hardly recognized the raspy voice as her own. Three weeks of breathing dry, stench-ridden air had taken a toll on her esophagus.

"You still need to take it easy. Another day or so and your vitals will be closer to normal."

Even though she had rationed them, her provisions had run out after two weeks. She spent another week without food, the last few days without water. When they found her, she was emaciated and severely dehydrated.

"There's someone here to see you, if you're up for it," the tech said.

Peyton's heart jumped. Could it be Alec? Could he have survived?

"Y-yes . . ." she replied.

A tall man, broad-shouldered, wearing a crisp, pine-green flight suit eased his way to her bedside. He wore his dark hair regulation-short and the sporadic gray throughout gave it the appearance of cedar bark. Etches at the corners of his eyes and mouth highlighted a confident face that projected his authority, yet garnered her trust. When she met his eyes, she saw in them a depth of sadness his erect posture and commanding presence could not conceal.

"Hello, Dr. McKay. I'm Captain Warren Gale." His voice was as deep as she expected, but tempered with compassion.

"Hello, Captain," she said.

"I want you to know how sorry I am for what you've been through."

She gave a weak nod of her head. "Th-thank you. Where am I?"

"You're aboard the heavy cruiser *Legacy*. We received your automated distress call and found your pod."

She managed another slight nod. "And the *Horizon*?"

His rich voice lowered to a whisper. "I'm sorry. There were no survivors."

She closed her eyes. She wanted to cry, but her body would not produce the tears.

"There's no doubt?" she asked.

"None, I'm afraid. We're in the Tau Sigma system now and we're examining the debris field. It's clear from the wreckage, that Captain Landon employed the Omega Protocol. Between the data logs in your pod and the remains of the Crellat ship, we have enough evidence to bring to the Coalition Security Council. They'll file an official protest with the Crellat Ligation."

"An official protest?" she rasped. "That's all? An official protest?"

"A formality, Doctor. The Fleet is mobilizing."

"Are we . . . are we going to war?"

"The Crellats have been violating the DMZ for decades. We've attributed half-a-dozen raids on automated stations to them. And we know they have spies in the Coalition. But, this is their boldest action. They have to be pushed back to their own space, so yes, Dr. McKay. I think war is inevitable."

She closed her eyes and sank into her pillow.

"When you're rested and up for it," he said, "I'll need to debrief you. We have the *Horizon's* logs, but I want to get your personal perspective. I'll need you to put the data into context for us."

His words were nearly identical to Alec's and now the tears did come.

"I'll leave, now, Doctor. And again, I'm sorry for your ordeal."

She barely heard him speak and didn't hear him leave.

Waves of sights and sounds and scents engulfed her. Vivid and precise memories. Of Rantoul Station. Of the bungalow. Of long walks and longer talks. Sadly, they had never committed to one another, never gave voice to their emotions, but she thought they could have been good together and she thought he had felt that way as well.

Eventually, exhaustion and grief diffused her recollections into misty tendrils and ushered her toward the periphery of sleep. But as she drifted off, Warren Gale's terrible prophecy lingered in her mind. War is inevitable, he had said.

She was a scientist, not a soldier. She loathed the prospect of war. But she understood it and why men like Warren Gale and Alec Landon served to prevent it while preparing to wage it.

Her final thoughts before succumbing to sleep were of Landon and the last words she said to him. She whispered them aloud like a vow.

"I won't let you down, Alec. I won't let you down."

Robert J. Mendenhall is a retired police officer, retired Air National Guardsman, and former Broadcast Journalist for the American Forces Network, Europe. A member of Science Fiction and Fantasy Writers of America and Mystery Writers of America, he writes in multiple genres including science fiction, crime and suspense, horror, and pulp adventure. Visit his website at www.robertjmendenhall.com or follow him on Twitter @ RobtJMendenhall. He lives in southwest Michigan with his wife and fellow writer, Claire. And many animals.

A prehistoric man mistakes time travelers for gods and discovers that no matter what they are, his existence to them is trivial.

Simpler Times

Nick Manzolillo

Null watched the purple lightning stab into the valley, wondering what could make the gods so disturbed. Roasting from an intense heat, a segment of the forest began to smolder while the greenery blackened. Drumbeats of thunder started as a rhythm and descended into chaos. The high-pitched sharpening of stone screeched through the air. The space around the jungle vegetation before Null began to ripple, like an unborn babe prodding against the walls of its mother's belly. Something was coming.

He white-knuckled his club, sweat from the mid-day heat running slick along his forehead, stinging his eyes. His mate Miri's father, the last living elder among their clan, had often spoken of gods presenting themselves to men, offering blessings or demanding certain tasks be performed. If this is a god, Null thought, then why was his skin twitching as if one of the thug lizards were creeping nearby, waiting to sink its curved teeth into the back of his neck?

A whine from the late summer storm melded with the death call from a gabber bird caught in a thug lizard's jaws and a headache shot through Null's skull. His club became heavier than his newborn boy and the ground began to shake, threatening to bring him to his knees. Ripples of purple light speckled with circles of color richer in blue than the sky began to dance around Null. The air began to grow hot, scorching worse than the stones around a pit of fire. Too late, Null realized that whatever was coming through could care less if he stood in its way. He turned, his thoughts fleeing from the gods and the nature of the divine. Something was coming and with its searing heat and terrible sounds, would it stop out of mercy for his clan? Would it be humbled by the cries of the young and the squeals of his mate?

The skin along Null's backside burned and flaked away before the force of the *arrival* lifted him through the air. For a single moment, the world became a rockslide of violence colliding with the ear-popping clap of thunder. In a broken heap, as the vegetation burned with purple flame around him, Null marveled at how quickly the gods could command the world to go silent.

***

He couldn't sleep, could only taste the black pool of dreams before the pain along his back, scattered along his limbs, brought him back to his peril.

The heat around him began to die down even as his wounds began to flare and fill his seared mind with the sensation that he was still on fire. It was more intense than a lightning bolt from the gods, faster than the fires that erupt in the thin forests during the pre-winter dead season. Something had arrived, Null knew, as he turned his blood and blister-oozed body over to gaze at the gleaming deity before him.

Carved from the smoothest, silver rock, the thing reminded him of an egg. An egg colored in strange paints—blue, purple, and green—that began to shift and move along the walls of the dome. The front of the egg slid away and humanoid-like things stepped out, single file, covered in thin silver armor and see through headpieces, also egg-like.

"Of all the screw ups . . ." One of the figures, a male, said. His voice sounded as if he were speaking into his fist. Null could hardly moan as he continued to watch the people, three of them, putting their backs together as they inspected the scorched forest around them. Gods, Null thought, and tried to lift his hand to beckon to them.

"Look at the damage we've done, we could've started a fire that spread for miles. Aren't you supposed to be smart?" There was the main male, a smaller man, and then a female. Null couldn't quite figure how he could tell it was a woman, given the thick clothing she wore. The slender arms, the absence of bulk across the chest. Null's clan wore little more than a sash and, in the cold season, deerskin and thug lizard leggings. He had heard of tribes to the east layering themselves in richer furs and skins but nothing like the rock these gods wore. They truly were beyond the scope of reality.

"The landing is never exact. We can only guess where there's likely to be little vegetation," the little male said.

"Little vegetation?" The female snorted, gesturing to the jungle before stomping out a small tuft of purple flame.

The male who first spoke began inspecting a curved tool. They all had that same tool, the female tapping hers against her leg. Cautious, ready to use it. Curved with strange spikes attached, not unlike a thug lizard's hide. The little man had several different tools in varying shapes and sizes, slung over his back. Null could sense, like his own club and the spears back with the clan, that the tools they so readily carried were weapons.

"Spectacular miscalculations aside, are there locals nearby?" The male, the chief, as Null began to think of him, asked.

"You mean animals or what passes for man?" The little god knelt, picked through a singed weed. "The whole region's full of them. I wouldn't expect them to be like the Neanderthals you've read about. There were many variations of early man, and most of them killed each other off. Further yet, even archeological history has a funny way of filling your head with lies."

"I wasn't expecting to find anybody living in a cave," the female said, cocking her head at the distant cry of a blood hawk.

"No, no, the natives are more like wolves. Hunting, breeding, wandering together. Not quite nomads, not quite setting up villages." Null couldn't entirely understand some of the words the gods were using. It was a funny thing, listening to them. At first, he heard an unfamiliar squabbling that then rearranged itself in his head and became words. It was as if someone were shouting from far off in the forest and Null had a companion to lean close to him and whisper what was said. Words like "nomad" and "Neanderthal" put strange images in his head, of dark, hairy things similar to the half-men the elders would tell stories of in hushed tones when Null was a boy.

"Let's hurry," the female said, resulting in a bark of laughter from the chief male.

"I don't see the rush, given our predicament?" The chief male said and, curse Null if he was wrong, but he began to believe that these were not gods. Not the ones he'd been told about, at least.

First off, they were not animals. While it was true the gods could take any form they wished, this seemed wrong. Null had heard of the gods appearing as beautiful, heart wrenching specimen, as well as the ugliest of hags and wretches. The thin rock, see-through things around these being's faces obscured their features, and so they were neither ugly nor beautiful. Little as he knew of the gods, Null found it hard to believe that they wouldn't pursue one extreme or the other. Perhaps they were spirits or a kind of demon, sent by the gods.

Null watched as his arm begin to rise, slowly, like a Jaguar stalking its prey. He couldn't feel his arm, nor the left side of his body. The burning encasing him was deeper than the flesh. His very blood was wounded, he thought. The clan's shaman was a meager replacement for his mate's father, who died last winter. The fool could hardly alleviate the rashes children or naïve hunters sometimes got from brushing against a cluster of blister leaves.

"There's a man . . ." The little emissary with the tools noticed Null, before the chief male sprang into action. The curved tool in his hand straightened, made a strange echoing sound as its tip began to glow blue.

"He's spotted us, damn it, and the translators are on," the chief male said and Null wasn't sure how, but he knew the man was going to kill him.

"He's wounded," the little emissary said.

"From us?" The female asked as the chief hulked over Null, the weapon leveled toward his face. What kind of knife or club was that? Of rock, curved with an arch for the chief to stick his fingers through. Up close, the armor these emissaries wore was even more beautiful than Null initially perceived.

"He's dying." The chief cocked his head, lowered the weapon. "And unless they've invented napalm, it's our doing. What's the call cap?" he said to the female.

"Exactly how intelligent are these people supposed to be?" the female asked the little man.

Null attempted to speak, coughing for his effort. He then persisted, through a throat that was increasingly beginning to dry up. "Are you gods?"

The chief snorted in response to the female, "Does that answer your question?"

"It's still a person. The translators are working excellently, by the way, Danny." The female approached Null, her weapon tucked into the sash across her hip. "We are friends," she said, not answering his question. The chief turned away, raising his weapon toward the tree line.

"Get the med kit ready, Danny. He's no ape. He can help us."

"Not that an ape wouldn't be better than you now, hey?" The chief addressed the little man, who seemed to have two similar names. Why would someone have two names?

The taunting blackness began to fade in and out and Null found himself beginning to care less for these divine beings. The sky was beautiful, the clouds soft and rolling through their kingdom.

"As soon as he gets a whiff of this, we're really going to be gods," the one called Dan/Danny said, rubbing some type of tool like a stick covered in wet leaves across Null's arms, his back. The burning sensation began to increase as Dan/Danny removed the shorter tool from his back. Fire emerged from one end of it, only it wasn't quite fire, but a glow, like the peripheral edge of flame. He lowered it to Null's wounds and the numbness, scattered with stinging, became a spread of warmth. Then the numbness shifted in, becoming permanent.

"What are you called?" The female asked Null as his vision swam.

When he awoke a moment later, he must have managed to mention it.

"Null, can you understand me? You're going to be okay." Dan/Danny leaned over Null, patting an arm that was formerly burned black and flaky. Null winced, expecting pain or, at the very least sensitivity, but there was nothing. He was healed, but he could no longer feel, not with his right arm.

The female held up what Null could only think of as a drawing, except instead of a slab of stone the rectangle was see-through, like their helmets. Within the rectangle was a symbol, as clear as if it were really in front of Null. Something pulled from the world around him and made two-dimensional. Did these beings possess that power? To make whatever they wish flat and flimsy, on their little tool?

"Have you seen this before?" The female asked, moving the image closer to Null as he shrunk away, wary, feeling like a newborn in the care of these things. Null, who once survived being washed into the great river during the stormy season. Null, who had once beaten in the skulls of a pair of starved rogues who were exiled from some distant tribe and had attempted to force themselves on a female member of his clan. Sitting, wounded before these beings who could set the earth aflame and heal their damage just as quickly, Null imagined he truly understood, for the first time, the concept of being a mortal.

The idea, the image upon that device, Null *had* seen it before. It was a crystal, the likes of which cluttered the caves in the valley to the south, near the river where Null was once swept away. "I have," Null said, as the realization dawned on him. Elders and prophets have occasionally claimed that the gods desire more than love. Depending on the season, they wish for the clan to toss into the fire the heart and lungs of the animals they slay, especially if the hunting has been particularly bountiful. It has also been said that the gods desire more than flesh. Beads and totems of clay, speckled with gems. And crystals.

As the clan had grown smaller and the world ever harsher since Null had been a boy, such admiration for the gods was a rare display. Now, Null thought, the gods were angry. They had sent these emissaries to not only show him their power to destroy and heal, but to make him give the gods the worship they deserved. Humbled, Null knew he was lucky that the gods were the forgiving sort. Despite the fear brimming in his breast, he became calmed that the worst of the god's wrath was now over with his blackened flesh turned whole once more.

"Oh boy, count our lucky stars, can you bring us to them?" Dan/Danny asked and the female smiled through her clear helmet. Up close, she was unlike any female Null had ever seen. The tone of her skin, the slope of her nose, and the curve of her eyebrows. He had heard stories of distant clans with strange features, some of which only grew to be as tall as children, while others were giants, stupid and fearsome. These people had a grace to the way they moved, even in those suits of armor. How they stood looking at the world around them, prepared for violence with their weapons, but lacking the tenseness that Null learned as a boy, prowling through the unknown depths of the jungle.

"Can you?" The female repeated. Null's eyes were wide, his mind plunging into a chasm. "These are very important to us."

"Yes," Null said, feeling a fluttering within his stomach as the female smiled and Dan/Danny whooped with joy.

"You know, plan for one thing and fail and then you find the unexpected and, oh, Null you, this is wonderful! We might be out of here by nightfall!" Fear tinged Dan/Danny's excitement and Null squinted, uncertain. What would emissaries of the gods have to fear but the gods themselves? Perhaps they too were tasked with a trial similar to Null's.

"Captain, be careful," the chief male said to the female, and a paradox began to form in Null's mind. The word "captain" was essentially chief or leader, and the chief male said this to the female? The mother deities of the earth and forest were one thing, but a female leader? More uncertainty began to unfurl through Null's veins, clashing with the adrenaline spiked throughout his blood. He began to feel dizzy, yet excited at the same time. It was as if he were with an entirely new clan, made of a people that were almost a different species entirely. "Think through everything you tell him," the male, who perhaps wasn't a leader, said.

"Don't go jumping at the butterfly theory now. What's at stake here matters more," Dan/Danny waved off the other male, wanting to hold on to his excitement.

The other male tapped his helmet with the tip of his weapon. "The bacteria in our tongue could potentially end mankind before we get a chance to invent the wheel."

"Unlikely," Dan/Danny snapped back.

"Unlikely is not a certainty. We are not certain. For all your calculations, we can't even accurately say what year it is, what species he is, what those birds are. We know the birth crystal and how important it is. I am not your bodyguard. I am here to make sure we don't ruin everything that ever will be from this moment forward through the millennia and . . ."

"Cole," the female said, placing a hand on the man's weapon. "I need you to calm down. Are you experiencing any STDS? Do you need to be restrained?"

The man called Cole shrugged, lowered his weapon. Dan/Danny giggled and said, "I love that term. Better than what it originally stood for. Look at that, isn't everything funnier now? Cole, we're okay, yeah?"

"Yeah," Cole said, staring at the vessel they arrived in. "We have gone further than any expedition in history. Literally, almost. Paradoxes are microscopic."

"Understood." The female turned to Null, who was feeling as though he were listening to apes bellow to one another. Only every other phrase the beings said made sense to him. Their tones, from aggression to amusement, were clear.

"How far to these?" She held up her screen, tapped the image. She spoke to him soothingly, as if he were a child, or one of the dogs at camp, and not a father of two.

The question confused Null, who then interpreted it as the same thing as asking, "will we be there before nightfall?"

"Before the sun sets," Null translated and the female nodded in agreement, once more flashing that smile of hers. Cole, who seemed too concerned with the particulars and specifics, grumbled something.

It took Null a few moments to find his club. When he told the emissaries what he was looking for Dan/Danny laughed hysterically while even the female chuckled. Cole seemed to snort out spite, and Null began to wonder if these emissaries and their strange weapons were ridiculing him and his tool. He was confident the laboriously carved hunk of wood hadn't been vaporized by the flames and he was right, when he found it beneath a clump of ashes that were formerly leaves. Along one side the club was scorched black, but it was otherwise unharmed and capable of cracking as many more skulls as Null needed it to.

Cole painstakingly stayed by his side as Null led the way through the thick underbrush. He kept flexing his arm, his back. The numbness was unsettling, but not exactly uncomfortable. The female and Dan/Danny formed a single line behind them and mostly, the party was silent.

Null found himself wary of asking all the questions he used to ponder while lying beside his mate, basking in a fire's warmth, and looking at the canopy of stars above. The power to confirm your beliefs seemed risky. There's no way to un-know something, Null thought. As it is, the entire clan would have to work harder to please the gods now, which meant less time to hunt and enjoy themselves. Answers to the big questions are laced with both wonders and nightmares.

Dan/Danny was the only one chattering away, commenting on the vegetation, the birds, and the small creatures that hopped away from them. "There's so much more life . . ." he said, and Null didn't like what that implied. He also began to grow concerned because the emissaries were following him. Wouldn't a trial from the gods mean he had to do it alone? What were the emissaries gaining from following him, if they didn't have similar trials to overcome? They needed him to reveal the location of the crystals. They were not all knowing.

A thug lizard leapt from one tree to another overhead and Dan/Danny reacted like an infant, screaming while the female and Cole raised their weapons. The thug lizard, not fully grown, was about as big as a man's arm span from one index finger to the other. Still, they were known for their short tempers and an inexhaustible ability to keep fighting creatures twice their size.

"Don't shoot, don't shoot," Cole said as the thug lizard scurried down the tree, closest to Dan/Danny. Its tail was up, it's head hunkered to the forest floor, it's blue tongue uncurling as it eyed Dan/Danny. Before the thug lizard could run away or attack, the latter of which Null doubted, given their party size, Dan/Danny stuck out his weapon and a blue glow, a lightning bolt, emitted with a single sizzling bark and the thug lizard's head became a pile of singed gore. Null began to realize why the emissaries had laughed at his club, which would have needed up to three good strikes to crack the thug lizard's tough skull.

"Can we keep track of our footprint here? Come on . . ." Cole said and with the danger gone, Null couldn't figure out the cause of his desperation. Something bothered him, perhaps something that stuck with him from whichever lands the emissaries of the gods call home.

For a while, the most unexpected thing the party encountered was a brief rainstorm. To Null's confusion, the emissaries, even Cole, began to act like children. They danced around one another, cheering. Cole tucked his gun away, raised his hands to the sky above that so quickly became clogged by grey clouds. "I always dreamed of this," the female said. Dan/Danny cried all through the brief bout of rainfall. The party didn't begin moving again until the rain stopped.

"It doesn't do that where we come from," Dan/Danny said, ashamed by his tears. Cole then reprimanded him for saying too much and Null began to realize that, even if he did ask all his many questions, the gods value their secrets.

Much to Null's relief, the rain did little to overflow the river. The party descended a muddy slope to the entrance of the largest of the caves nearby. Further down the river there were more caves, some that ran deeper than any member of Null's tribe would dare tread, but for gathering crystals, Null knew this spot would do.

"Freshwater, I wonder?" Dan/Danny asked as the party walked along the river's edge, sloshing through ankle-high water. Null actually understood that question.

"Yes," he said, thinking of the salt rivers that were said to lead to lakes so big they ate half of the world.

"Do you and your people fish?"

It took Null a moment to contemplate the meaning of that term before he told Dan/Danny yes, they fished, during certain seasons when the rivers were full. Bigger game, like the elk and tiger woolies offered more meat. He began to deduce, privately, that the gods provided for their emissaries. As fearsome as they seemed, they were also somewhat helpless.

As they wandered over to the waterlogged mouth of the cave, Null spotted something slowly stalking the riverbank. A bottom lurker, a rare crustacean Null had only seen a handful of times before. Growing up, he had been taught that unlike crayfish and many forms of beetle, bottom lurkers were poisonous and could not be eaten no matter how much meat was packed into their claws. Null waved Dan/Danny aside, and crouched, as the lurker approached him. A dim-witted beast, it rose out the water with its long claws clicking Null's way as he raised his arm and brought it down with one glorious smack. With his newly healed arm having gone numb, there was little satisfaction from the kill. The beast's skull burst into yellow gunk as Dan/Danny yelped with surprise.

"That was like some kind of alien!" Dan/Danny began shouting.

"Is there more danger within?" the female gestured toward the blackness of the cave.

Null shook his head. "The bottom lurkers prefer only the edge of deep water. Stick to the shallows and we should be fine," Null said and then nearly fell back into the arms of the river when the female shot light, pure and as bright as the sun, from the end of her rectangular device. Cole and Dan/Danny began to do the same with devices of their own as they ventured into the cave, now made light and clearer than Null had ever before seen it. One of the bottom lurker's broken limbs prodded Null's leg and he nearly jumped, swishing around, eyeing the depths of the river and a second bottom lurker, staying oddly immobile beneath flowing current. Two in one day? Null had never heard of a mating season for bottom lurkers like the one for thug lizards in the middle of the hot season, but it was possible.

Already within the cave behind Null, the emissaries began to yell. More sizzling sounds from their weapons emitted as Null stomped through the water, charging into the eerily glowing cave. Up head, the crystals along the walls pulsated as if with a life and energy of their own. Along the flooded cave floor, bottom lurkers were out of their element, almost completely emerged, clicking and chirping, before the emissaries shot their lightning beams at them.

Dan/Danny was on his back, his helmet filled with blood, the smoldering dead bodies of several bottom lurkers draped over him. The female and Cole were yelling, making quick work of the remaining few bottom lurkers that Null now could see matched the rocks jutting out of the cave floor almost too perfectly, even in the emissary's light. They wandered into the nest before the lurkers had a chance to alert them.

Null turned, partly by chance, partly from a faint twitch of instinct as he discovered a latent bottom lurker attempting to snip through his legs. The beasts were callous, and to the point. Bring the bigger prey down to their level. He bashed it to pieces with ease. He had heard nightmare stories about how they tried to lay their eggs in the bodies of their prey. He had never heard about them emerging from their depths to breed but, the river, running endlessly, was the bringer of new things. New threats, new seasonal wanderers like Null's own clan. What had happened in the cave was no different from any other clash of tribes and cultures.

"He's choking up in there, we had to remove the helmet," the female said as Cole grabbed her by the shoulder.

"He's not going to make it," Cole said and one of the bottom lurker's claws had gone through Dan/Danny's chest and emerged within the see-through confinement of his helmet. The claw now rested against his trembling cheeks as more blood pumped free from his mouth.

"They carry poison," Null said, trying to help. Cole raised his weapon Null's way and the end of it began to glow faint blue, crackling with atmospheric energy. "How could you not warn us?" Cole asked and Null began to feel the shame of his foolishness. He hadn't known, he hadn't had any idea.

"Neither me, nor my people have been here for many seasons," Null said. As the clan continued to grow smaller, they had stuck to the bigger game. Less time for wandering rivers, especially when there were lakes and smaller streams with a better freshwater supply.

The female, the captain, removed Dan/Danny's helmet and pressed a gloved hand to his cheek as he breathed his last. Then she and Cole turned him over, took the tools from his back. "It's going to be hell taking his body back with us," Cole said and Null felt a touch of icy blackness at the translated mention of that word. *Hell.* Where gods fear to tread, Null thought. If the gods didn't walk Null's land themselves, then was this place considered hell? Of perhaps they came from hell, guarded it to protect men like Null.

Unfurling two sparkling silver bags, the female and Cole began to shear the glowing crystals off the wall with a tool similar to their weapons, using the same energy to cut the crystals free from their roots.

"He's a hero, that's how he'll be remembered, colleges will be named after him, all the new children will be called Daniel, it's going to be worth it," Cole kept saying, either trying to reassure the female or himself. The female remained silent, mourning in her own way. While the living emissaries harvested the crystals, Null managed to kill several more bottom lurkers that continued to blend in amongst the rocks.

Once the sparkling bags were full of crystals, the female asked Null if it would be a problem for him to carry both of them, eyeing his arms and the muscles teeming across his chest. Null lifted both bags with ease and Cole groaned in amazement. He had been struggling with one, leaving it in place while he sheared the crystals off the walls and dropped them into the sack. With Null carrying the crystals, Cole and the female positioned themselves by either end of Danny, placing his helmet back on, lifting him up. They nearly ran through the shallows beyond the cave, not spotting a single bottom lurker as they did so.

Satisfied that the emissaries needed Null, given his ability to carry the heavy bags, he marched before them with pride, his club tucked between his arm and one of the bags. He began to wonder how people would tell stories about him, how the day's events would be exaggerated. Dan/Danny/Daniel would be a hero that, from the sounds of it, the gods would remember.

When the charred jungle and the emissary's vessel was in sight, the jungle decided it was still hungry. "Null, a lizard!" Cole yelled from behind Null as he dropped the bags and had his club in his hand all in the same motion. It was understandable, that Cole and the female would not want to drop their friend. As Null turned, he saw no lizard, only the female, holding Dan/Danny/Daniel up by his shoulders, his feet dragging across the dirt. Cole held the weapon Null's way and fired a round into his belly.

Unlike the massive force that came with the emergence of the vessel, Null wasn't thrown back. Instead a hole burned through his stomach where he stood, as he looked down in confusion.

"Cole!" the female, the captain yelled as Cole raised his weapon higher, toward Null's head. Dan/Danny/Daniel fell to the ground as the captain grabbed Cole's arm, jerked it away and a sizzling shot rippled to Null's right.

"He could mean the end of everything! You know the argument. What's he going to tell his people? Think of what'll happen. The new cults and religions that'll rise, slowly. The influence this will have on mankind. He knows the crystals are important now. What if they get mined into extinction earlier because of it?" Cole sneered as Null continued to stare at the hole going through him. Smoke was wafting through it. The hole wasn't that big. Then Null began to feel the pain along his back, and he knew the exit wound was wider, worse. Like the pulverized thug lizard's skull. The emissaries could heal him though, couldn't they? Would they?

"That is one theory of thousands! Our reality will always exist. It's what we're bringing back that matters, this isn't our world, it's a what if, it's a . . ."

"You don't know that!" Cole pulled away from the female, made to aim Null's way and Null should've known. Not that Cole would kill him, but the blood Dan/Danny/Daniel's body was dripping all through the jungle. Thug lizards love blood, and Null spotted one righteous monster, bigger than the emissaries vessel, stalking through the underbrush.

"Captain!" Null shouted before the beast went for Dan/Danny/Daniel's body, consumed by bloodlust. Not as adaptive as a jaguar or a fox. The thug lizard's tail swept the captain and Cole onto their backs. Cole fired, missed and the female was too close to the gory mess that was Dan/Danny/Daniel as one of the beast's talons swiped across the front of her suit. Null took a step forward, reflexively gripping the club, oh his faithful club that he still held onto, pain disregarded. He took another step, and then fell, but as he did so he brought his club forward and bashed the thug lizard's body.

The beast hissed, it's claws scrambling, making a mess of the female's insides as Cole let loose several rapid-fire shots through the beast's flank. The female had her own weapon drawn as she backed away and fired into the thug lizard's head. Its skull was too thick and in desperate need of Null's final swing, which he delivered with one mighty exhale of breath as the club ground the beast's simple instincts into mush.

It was some time later before Null's mind began to come back together, as he lay on his back, having passed out from his wound. The female had sobbed at one point before Cole healed her, Null assumed. Presumably they carried Dan/Danny/Daniel's body back, along with the crystals. There they stood, man and female, god and goddess, over Null. The female was healed, wincing, limping, her flesh back together. But internally she was still damaged, just like Null's numbness in his arm.

"Thank you," the captain said, before turning, limping off, leaving him to Cole.

"I am sorry," Cole said, raised his weapon, but then lowered it. "I know death seems scary, but I want you to know, you are a hero. Like our friend. You may have only known your tribe, but there are many people out there. Many people from where we are from. They are all indebted to you. You will be remembered, even if everyone you know here forgets you. I will do that. I will. I realize now, how you matter. I hope you can understand me."

And in a way, Null did, as his world became filled by a blue glow that got brighter, just for a moment, before he was returned to the mud, and fossils.

Nick Manzolillo is another bearded Manhattanite wizard whose writing has appeared in over thirty publications including Thuglit, Wicked Witches: An Anthology of the New England Horror Writers, Grievous Angel and the Tales to Terrify podcast. He has an MFA in Creative and Professional Writing from Western Connecticut State University, and by day, he works as a content operations specialist for TopBuzz, a news app.

With the diversity that exists within our own solar system and what we are finding exists within our galaxy, what will we find beyond our galaxy? What strange things will exist as we explore our Universe? If other Universes exist what will separate them from ours and what will the similarities be?

Dark Reflections

Tom Olbert

Parallel Universe JRN117.53

Blinding light, followed by darkness, as every crossing between universes. Like dying and being reborn a billion times over in a micro-second. Every nerve in Daniel Kwan's body seared in anguish as he shifted through the intercosmic rift, materializing in normal space.

He cursed silently, the usual nausea and dizziness passing, his brain implant compensating as he found himself in a dark chamber. He drew a deep breath, his eyes slowly adjusting to the gloom. He winced. Stuffy. The smell of musk and sweat and the sound of rustling cloth. He started at the sound of a woman's scream. He threw aside a dark, thick curtain and emerged into a dimly lit bed chamber. The sight that next met his eyes made his blood freeze. A young woman lay dead, obviously by violence. Her blue eyes stared lifeless into his, burning into his soul. Eyes he had known well in another life.

Her killer looked up, his dark eyes flaring in anger. "Who dares . . ." he froze, the bloodied knife slipping from his numbed fingers onto the bed covers. He stared at Daniel with shock, the blood draining from his face, the ugly scar running the length of his jaw a dark purple against his pale flesh. "Who . . ." he gasped out in a strangled whisper.

Daniel's hatred for the man was too intense to bear. Snarling in a bestial rage, he focused his anger and attacked. He drew and activated his sonic blade in one fluid motion, the blade vibrating, a silver blur on the air. He crossed the chamber in two easy strides, driving the blade into the other man's heart even as the murdering devil reached for the alarm button. Daniel chuckled in sweet delight as the pig fell lifeless to the floor at his feet, the expression of horrified disbelief still frozen on his face. Daniel stopped, the smile slipping from his own face as he saw his reflection in the gilded mirror over the bed. The same evil smile he'd seen on the face of the man he'd just killed. The same eyes. The same scar, with all the memories it carried. He trembled in hatred at his reflected image. An enraged roar rising from his lungs, he smashed the mirror into a thousand pieces.

Unable to bear the sight of the murdered young woman's eyes, he threw the bed covers over her. "Alex, forgive me," he whispered, tears in his eyes. If only he'd arrived a second earlier. He looked down. Her blood was now on his own hands. And, on the hands of his other self, now lying dead before him. How many times had he played this scene out, on how many parallel timelines, he asked himself. "How many times must I kill you?" he demanded of his dead other self. "Is it my hell to keep killing you forever?"

"M'lord, are you all right?" a man's voice called out, a fist pounding on the chamber door. Daniel looked up in shock. Pulling himself together, he quickly pulled his scanner from his belt and activated it, running it down the length of his doppelganger's body. He activated the duplicator, the nannite swarm quickly rearranging the constituent molecules of his own clothing into an exact replication of the clothes worn by that version of himself indigenous to this universe. He pressed his thumb on the *cleaner* switch, and the nannites broke his dead other self down into atoms. The man simply faded into nonexistence, as so many other versions of Daniel had done. Like erasing a flawed sketch, he thought grimly.

"Come," he said, keeping his voice as steady as possible as he pressed the button unlocking the door.

The door slid aside as two guardsmen entered, their energy blasters drawn. "Are you quite all right, M'Lord?" one of them asked.

"Yes, of course I am. Must your squeamishness interrupt my pleasure?"

"I . . . forgive me, Your Grace," the man said with a respectful bow, both guards holstering their blasters. "I meant no intrusion. I heard you cry out, and was concerned for your safety." The man glanced over at the dead woman lying under blood-soaked sheets. "Shall I arrange for another selection to be brought to you from the slave pits, M'Lord?"

Daniel had to turn away to hide the look of disgust on his face. "No," he said through clenched teeth, fighting the nausea. "Just . . . remove the body, clean up that mess and leave me alone."

"As M'Lord wishes." The guardsman signaled for other palace guards and servants. Daniel seated himself numbly, his back to the horrid scene as the body and shattered glass were cleared away.

"A matter of state, M'Lord," the voice of another man said.

Daniel looked up with annoyance, a man in a palace clerk's uniform standing there holding a computer pad. "Later," Daniel muttered, rubbing his throbbing head. The clerk pressed a button, the door closing. Daniel stood. "I said . . ." He stilled his voice as the air shimmered and rippled, the holographic illusion of the clerk vanishing. In its place stood Alex Veraan, the same young woman he'd just seen murdered. Or rather, the Hub Universe parallel version of her.

She adjusted the voice masking device at her uniform collar, speaking to him now in her natural voice. "As usual, Agent Kwan, I see you couldn't resist the urge to add a touch of carnage to what should have been a standard terminate and replace." Cold and professional, her lovely blue eyes stern and set, her beautiful face now a hard mask. He remembered the laughing face of the nineteen-year-old girl he thought he'd loved, once, in another reality. The young woman he'd hurt. A lifetime ago, now, it seemed.

He felt both relieved and guilty as she stood before him. Guilty that he'd failed to prevent her death, relieved she wasn't dead at all. Irrational, of course. He sighed. "I'm in place. That's all that matters, isn't it? You didn't have to risk coming here."

She crossed her arms. "I. C. A. Command is a bit leery of letting you into the field without an on-site handler, especially after that last mission. I'm sure I don't have to remind you . . ."

"You don't," he said, not meeting her eyes. He'd seen her so many ways. In love. In pain and betrayal. In anger. In battle, beside him. Dead.

***

Months later . . .

Man's multi-galactic empire spanned half this alternate universe. Star cruisers traversed a cosmic network of artificially generated trans dimensional wormholes, honeycombing a continuum that was rapidly expanding. Expanding far beyond the feeble perceptions of man, its galaxies racing further and further apart, across the accumulating eons, toward the cold darkness of cosmic dissolution.

Twin red suns hung like glowering demonic eyes over the scorched dry ocean beds of Telesta, the base world of humanity's empire in this parallel universe. Incoming starships slipped in silently, their grey bulks dully reflecting the bloody red sheen of the suns, their shadows moving slowly across the dusty gray plains as they descended to the landing pads atop the imperial palace.

Daniel Kwan . . . or, Daniel Alexander Kwan, Overlord of the Telestan Empire, Warlord of Andromeda and the Magellanic Clouds, as he was known in this reality . . . reclined on his throne. He drummed a finger pensively at his lips as he took in the impressive gathering of nobles now filing into his audience chamber at the summit of the palace. The visiting satraps of a half-dozen subject galaxy clusters respectfully bowed before him in their flowing robes as they approached at his bidding. "Welcome, lords," he said as servants knelt before the visiting dignitaries, offering them wine in golden chalices. Scantily clad dancers in swirling silks performed to soft and entrancing music amid the twisting columns, arching ceilings and gilded bay windows looking out on a bloody, red sky where great winged beasts circled over the distant mountains. Bejeweled courtiers whispered to each other in the shadows, observing the most powerful warlords in the Empire.

Alex Veraan, ever the watchful overseer stood close by Daniel's side, now holographically camouflaged as an old man in black robes and a long grey beard, passing herself off as the Overlord's trusted adviser. "Take careful note of Lord Belesarrio," she whispered in Daniel's ear. "Intelligence believes he may be an Extraverse operative."

Daniel looked Belesarrio over. The man looked deceptively innocuous with his thinning grey hair and soft, sagging frame. But, Daniel could see the keen light of shrewdness in the old man's eyes. This was, after all, the warlord who had orchestrated the construction of the intergalactic energy grid that had powered half a universe, enriching his elite class at the expense of the lower tiers of imperial society. And, the one with most reason among all the galaxy lords to despise Daniel for what he had done since stepping into his doppelganger's shoes. "Approach, Lord Belesarrio," he said cordially, beckoning with his bejeweled fingers.

The old man approached the throne and bowed with his usual false respect. "Your servant, M'Lord," he said.

"No need for formality, My Lord," Daniel said with a genial smile. "Not from so distinguished a benefactor of the Empire. Rise, and state your business."

A slight grin tugging at the corner of his mouth, Lord Belesarrio pressed a button on a hand-held holo projection device. The audience chamber around him became a holographic depiction of the Telestan Empire, its reach extending across several multi-galactic clusters. Belesarrio strode through the shimmering silver galactic spirals like some cosmic giant. "Tremendous investments of imperial resources went into the construction of the matter/antimatter conduction spheres," he said, the hologram zooming in at various points, power stations the size of small planets orbiting strategically located suns in one galaxy after another. Now, being dismantled.

Daniel fought to hide a smirk. Matter/antimatter conduction, indeed. Merely a cover for what those power stations really were. Intercosmic rift gates that actually admitted dark energy from another universe, accelerating the expansion of this universe, across billions of years into a dead future. Extraverse technology, obviously. The only question was whether Belesarrio knew that or was merely an unsuspecting pawn of the Extraverse intelligence. Daniel manipulated a hand-held communicator, linking into the A.I. memory core. Taking control of the hologram, he zoomed in on his own construction projects, already spanning solar systems in several galaxies. Outwardly packaged as quark fusion generators, they too were rift gates, but produced by Hub Universe tech and primed to convey neutron star matter from another universe into this one while siphoning out the dark energy, slowing this continuum's expansion and laying the foundations for its eventual unification. "With all due respect to your approach, Lord Belesarrio . . . frankly, the Empire was losing money on it. Additionally, the radiation waves the M/A spheres generated were ecologically destructive to many life-sustaining systems in the outlying galaxies."

"Alien systems," Lord Belesarrio grumbled, his grey eyes flaring angrily.

"Did you wish to interject, Lord Belesarrio?" Daniel demanded, deactivating the hologram.

"Oh, no, Overlord," Belesarrio said with a mock bow. "Your efforts to improve relations with the alien races are widely known." Daniel cast his eyes about the room as a low murmur swept through the courtiers and visiting dignitaries. Daniel glanced at Alex. He knew full well Belesarrio's political power base was built on fear of the alien civilizations, and the military stockpiles Belesarrio justified by milking that fear. So public an insult was obviously intended to make Daniel appear sympathetic to the alien empires. Daniel would not let the challenge go unanswered.

"Far too many of our planets go hungry because of your obscenely bloated military emplacements, Lord Belesarrio," Daniel said, enjoying the angry tension in the other man's face. "Our people suffer almost as much by the cost of energy generated by the M/A spheres. The quark fusion reactor approach is considerably more effective in creating employment, and generating energy affordable to even our poorest territories."

"Causing a devastating loss of profit to the great houses," Lord Belesarrio pointed out. "The sector lords are growing restive."

"Are they?" Daniel said through clenched teeth, not bothering to hide his anger. "Well then . . . perhaps it would behoove me to redistribute some of your impressive military stockpiles among the local militia's I've been raising in the proletarian sectors." He paused a moment, to see the reaction. The soft murmur among the crowd grew into a commotion. He smiled. Like tossing a pebble into a lake and watching the ripples spread. "Yes . . . the people are squarely behind my efforts. They like the increase in employment, the lower cost of energy . . . more of them swarm to the militia recruiting stations every day."

The crowd grew increasingly ugly. "Creeping populism," he heard from somewhere in the crowd. "He sells us out to the rabble," one of the nobles said. "Traitor," several said.

"Who said that?!" The security commander, William Quaast shouted in anger, his hand on his blaster. "Who dares accuse the Overlord of treason? Identify yourselves, cowards!" William's bright green eyes flared from his handsome dark face, his brow now creased with anger. Even in this parallel reality, the passion in the man touched Daniel's heart. How his heart longed for the strong arms and loving embrace of the other William Quaast . . . *his* William, from the Hub Universe. Daniel instinctively glanced at Alex, the coldness of her stare sending a chill through him.

"Calm yourself, Commander Quaast," Daniel said, raising a hand. "I respect the right of my nobles to speak their minds. I welcome their counsel, in fact. That is one reason I called this assembly. Stand at ease." Quaast reluctantly stepped back, his eyes radiating deep concern. Daniel reassured him as best he could with his own expression, without sacrificing propriety. Daniel knew William meant well, but Daniel welcomed this as his opportunity to determine who his allies and who his enemies were. "Now then, Lord Belesarrio . . . Did you have something you wished to add?"

Belesarrio's face grew cold and dark. "No, Your Grace," he said in an icy whisper that seemed to cut through Daniel's flesh. "I believe the time for talk has passed." Daniel's eyes flared, the blood draining from his face as Belesarrio's aged body twisted and warped into an obscenely distorted mockery of its human form. The crowd gasped and drew back in fear as the old man's face twisted in an anguished snarl into an elongated, grotesque maw of fangs, his body turning inside-out, bone and flesh and internal organs warping into a horrific, writhing mass of tentacles and glistening, slimy-moist stingers.

Daniel's battle trained reflexes snapped automatically. He leaped aside as a stream of fluid spewed out, the throne where he'd sat a moment before dissolving as though touched by acid. Nobles and servants screamed as they trampled over each other fleeing the audience chamber, William Quaast and his men firing at the alien abomination with their energy blasters. The blinding white bolts rippled upon contacting the monster, as though it generated a natural energy field of its own. The few scraps and bits of the monster's grey flesh that were torn away by the blasts quickly regenerated, growing into hideously scampering multi-limbed offspring which attacked the guards like rabid dogs, tearing out their throats.

"Run, William!" Daniel shouted without thinking, reflexively reaching for the gravity wave disruptor hidden under his cloak. Alex gripped his arm. "No," she whispered urgently in his ear. "Nothing incongruent to this continuum." As William and his surviving men incinerated the smaller offspring organisms and concentrated their fire on the parent organism, Alex stepped in front of Daniel and pulled the energy blaster from the holster at his hip. Setting the power pack to overload, she tossed the blaster straight into that mass of writhing flesh.

"Down!" she shouted, tackling Daniel and falling protectively on him as the blaster exploded in a blinding flash. The alien monstrosity screeched an unholy wail.

Daniel winced, his vision slowly returning from dull grey as the flash passed. His ears still ringing, he stood, slowly, Alex helping him to his feet.

"Are you all right?" he whispered to her. She nodded. "Casualties, Commander Quaast?"

"Three of my men are dead, Sire," William answered, breathless, his fine features glistening with sweat. "Several more injured." Daniel followed William's gaze along the steaming trail of scorched flooring the monster had left as it fled the audience chamber.

"Organize a search team at once to track that . . . creature down and destroy it."

"Yes, M'Lord, but . . . should I not first summon a transport to take you to safety?"

"No. I shall take direct command of the search." Alex clutched his arm in a strong grip. He shook it off.

William's eyes flared. "Sire, I must advise . . ."

"You have your orders, Commander," Daniel said firmly, silently thanking the Multiverse that William was safe.

William stiffly bowed and turned to go, his gaze lingering with apparent suspicion on the supposedly aged court advisor whose startlingly heroic actions had saved the Overlord's life. Daniel put his arm around Alex, apparently supporting her as she resumed her role as a decrepit counselor. As Daniel got Alex out of sight, he heard the voices of William's men behind him. "What in the seven black hells was that?" one man asked. "I've seen alien life before, but nothing like that."

***

Daniel had sent William and his men to search the lower caverns below the palace while he and Alex used their spatial trackers to determine the true location of the dark matter Extraverse being that had taken over Belesarrio's body. Alone with Daniel in the murky caves, Alex had dropped her holographic disguise and now appeared in her true, comely form. "Need I list every one of your transgressions, Agent Kwan, or merely express my general displeasure?" Her voice trembled with anger.

He sighed. "This is hardly the time . . ."

She roughly grabbed his arm and turned him to face her. "I have to know I can trust you, especially now."

He pulled his arm free. "Meaning?"

"First you nearly blow your cover at the reception, forcing me to jeopardize my cover as well, and now you've sent your precious William to safety and put yourself at risk yet again."

"We stand a better chance of facing that devil together than you would alone, and I sent William away for the very purpose of protecting our cover," Daniel protested.

"You were clearly the target!" she said in an angry whisper. "It's you it wants. The strategically sound course of action would be for you to return to the Hub Universe immediately."

"And, how would my disappearance be explained now? Besides . . . so brazenly revealing itself to the primitives was a desperate attempt by the Extraverse to fan the flames of anti-alien fear on this parallel. And, to undermine my position here. If I run, I appear weak, or sympathetic to alien incursion. If I lead the attack and slay the alien, then I secure my position. And, if I am the target, then what better bait to lure the enemy?"

She rolled her eyes, her teeth clenched. "Why can't you just admit . . ." She glanced at her spatial tracker. "It's close," she whispered, drawing her gravity wave disruptor. Daniel did likewise, noting the strangely elongating pattern of warping space, as though enough dark energy were concentrated in one place, he realized, perhaps to . . . "Down!" she shouted.

The dank air rippled as solid matter and shadow merged, the monstrosity appearing with a bone-curdling shriek as it morphed out of the cavern wall, a writhing nightmare beast of twisting limbs and slavering fangs. Daniel leapt aside and rolled, coming up on one knee and taking aim at the boiling black mass coming towards him. He saw that Alex was already firing from the opposite side of the cave and he coordinated his fire accordingly. Bombarded by twin waves of concentrated gravitational force, the monstrosity shrieked and grotesquely bulged and rippled, its mutating form half solid matter, half shadow. One final hellish wail, and the monster dissolved, like dark mist in sunlight. Dark matter dispersed as the conventional matter it had shaped collapsed into dissolving protoplasm.

Daniel drew a trembling breath as he and Alex cautiously approached what was left of the abomination, their disruptors still at the ready. He breathed a bit easier, lowering his weapon as he looked down at the smoldering, scattered bits of half-melted metallic parts and fused circuitry. The cybernetic implants inside Belesarrio's body that had channeled the living dark matter, he realized. "It must have taken every bit of lingering dark energy still trickling through the few remaining rift gates to have powered this potent a manifestation," he said, wiping sweat from his brow.

"The enemy's last-ditch effort to eliminate you," Alex remarked, relief visible in her voice as she holstered her weapon. "And now, we go home."

"No," he said, holstering his disruptor. She looked up at him, her eyes burning. "If they were willing to sacrifice Belesarrio, then he wasn't their primary asset on this parallel. There must be someone else. Probably right here in the heart of the empire. I have to stay until I find out who."

She strode towards him. "I am ordering you . . ."

"Don't bother, Alex. I.C.A. Command will see it my way, and you know it. We've come too far in this universe only to see all our work torn down by the next puppet Overlord the Extraverse inserts here. We have to eliminate their primary agent. And, I can only do that by making him come to me."

She clenched her fists and writhed. The look that next entered her eyes as her body slowly relaxed was one he knew didn't come easily to her. Pleading. A desperate, silent plea to let her protect him. His gut soured with guilt as he realized he was hurting her yet again. But, he had no choice, he reminded himself.

***

Weeks later . . .

Daniel pulled back sharply on the reins of his skrill mount, the beast's mandibles spreading wide in a sharp squeal as the animal's leathery wings stroked wide under the red suns. Across the dry ocean bed below, the shadows of the Overlord's hunting party fell upon their monstrous quarry. A full-grown sand serpent. Its dorsal spines rose from the sand as it crested and dove. "Launch!" Daniel ordered. His gunners turned their skrills, flanking the serpent and fired their shoulder-launched lancer missiles. The twin explosions forced the great beast to the surface, its full size exposed. At least forty feet in length. Daniel's eyes widened in awe of the beast.

He'd wanted to outlaw this barbaric sport, but the risk to his cover would have been too great, his deceased doppelganger having been so avid a serpent hunter. "Bowmen, strike!" he ordered as his men swooped in on their skrills, their explosive-tipped arrow bolts exploding against the serpent's black, scaly hide. The monster roared, its fearsome forward spines extending as Daniel spurred his mount and attacked, swooping down on the serpent. As his skrill's wings stroked and folded, he dismounted, swinging from his saddle onto the monster's back. He leapt forward, driving the explosive tip of his spear straight down into the creature's central brain node. The fever of the hunt and the risk coursed hot through his blood. That raging blood turned rapidly to ice as he saw the red detonator light on his spear tip flashing. The delayed timer had failed.

The enemy had finally made its move. An attempt to bring about the Overlord's death and make it look like a hunting accident. Daniel slipped his hand behind his cloak and activated his anti-grav belt. He sprang thirty feet straight up just as the explosive charge went off. The heat of the explosion rising like a searing wave below, he seized the harness of the nearest skrill. The animal squealed as its rider, one of Daniel's men drew his blaster and pointed it at Daniel's head. Daniel shouted a curse as he grabbed the man's wrist and twisted it. Using his own weight to pull the man from his saddle, he grabbed the harness again and swung up into the saddle as his would-be killer plunged to his death.

Daniel grabbed the reins and fought to control the wildly panicking skrill. He'd stand a better chance of survival if the skrill's flight remained erratic, he realized, as searing white energy bolts coursed around him in the hot mid-day air. The sky under the bloody suns was now a wild free-for-all, his men swerving about on their mounts, firing at each other. He drew his own blaster and scanned the battle. He couldn't tell the loyalists from the assassins. Until one man spurred his mount straight at Daniel, firing his blaster. Daniel pulled the reins sharply to the right and leaned aside, the energy bolt searing his shoulder. Gritting through the pain, he returned fire, blasting the other man's head off, his skrill flying free.

A shadow fell upon him from the left. He turned and raised his weapon just as another skrill rammed head-on into his, knocking his blaster out of his hand. He looked up and froze with shock. The attacking rider was William Quaast. "William . . ." he choked out in a strangled whisper. "Not you." William snarled viciously, his handsome face creasing in pure hatred as he drew his scimitar. Daniel drew his. They stood in the stirrups of their skrills, the two animals now reverting to instinct and snapping wildly at each other as their riders dueled. William hacked wildly, Daniel parrying his thrusts, steel sparking on steel. It was like some mad nightmare, the mirror image of the man he loved trying to kill him.

Wounding each other, the two skrills spiraled down to the parched ground. William leapt, tackling Daniel and knocking him out of his saddle. Daniel grunted as his back hit the ground. He rolled with the impact, ramming his knee into William's chest as he flipped the other man backwards over him. Rolling and quickly recovering, William sprang up, his sword at the ready. "This is how it should be," William said through clenched teeth, sweat and blood intermingling on his face. "Man to man." He attacked in Telestan duelist tradition, and Daniel responded in kind, defending himself.

"Why, William?" he demanded as they faced each other, their swords touching. Daniel's eyes pleaded, his heart in a vice. "My love . . ."

"Don't call me that!" William shouted, more in pain than rage. "You're not him! You murdered him!" He attacked again savagely, his pain driving him to carelessness. Using a move William's other self had taught him, Daniel slipped around him and brought the edge of his sword to William's throat. William glared up at him, defiantly. "Do it," he demanded.

Daniel breathed heavily, trembling. He couldn't. "William, if . . ."

William moved swiftly, knocking Daniel's sword aside and kicking his legs out from under him as his sword hilt swept up and collided with Daniel's chin. There was a flash of stars. Daniel shook his head, his vision clearing as he found himself flat on his back, William standing over him. In the lurid red sunlight, he caught the sight of a tear sliding down William's cheek. "For Daniel Alexander," William said in an anguished whisper as he raised his sword over his head, poised to plunge it into Daniel's heart.

Daniel didn't even try to move, a part of him welcoming the pain and the peace to come. His eyes flared in shock as the bloodied tip of an arrow bolt emerged from William's chest. The man's eyes flared in shock, then faded to darkness as he dropped his sword and fell, the arrow shaft protruding from his back. Behind him stood one of Daniel's men, lowering his bow gun. The hologram image rippled and faded as Alex Veraan appeared. "William!" Daniel shouted as he pulled himself up and examined the body of the man he loved. William's eyes stared up at nothing, his blood darkening the sand, the skrills screeching hungrily overhead as their shadows circled the field of human corpses. Daniel slumped over William's body, the tears flowing freely. He groaned in anguish, gently closing the dead man's eyes. He looked up, his heart splintering with anger. Alex stood there, her gaze cold, her long dark hair blowing in the hot wind.

***

The Hub Universe.

A stable, unified continuum. Across billions of years, galactic civilizations of ancient, pre-human life forms had evolved beyond corporeal form into immense beings the size of galaxies, their vast intellects telepathically linked via networks of sub-space relays spanning the universe, each galactic entity but a neuron in the larger cosmic brain that was the Hub Universe itself. The Hub Verse was linked across alternate timelines with other such cosmic beings, forming connections sustaining the evolutionary development of an eventual sentient Multiverse.

Many space-faring races, from many parallel timelines co-existed in peace in the Hub Verse, its gateways taking them to many other parallel realities, many other universes.

At the heart of the central system of the I.C.A., the Intercosmic Correction Agency, a hundred worlds were linked as one through a central stellar nexus. Daniel Kwan and Alex Veraan emerged from the quantum gateway, materializing on one of many reception pads at the heart of a vast transparent dome. The usual numbing pain of light and darkness passing, Daniel looked up, his vision focusing. Above the humming silver trams of the interplanetary railways hung the graceful blue curve of the home world and its many moons. Its beauty was lost on him. Unable even to look at Alex, he felt only coldness.

"Daniel!" Daniel turned away, wincing as William Quaast ran eagerly to him through the crowd. Daniel pulled himself together, hiding his grief from the man he'd seen die scarcely half a day before. "Daniel . . ." William said with a broad smile, taking Daniel by the shoulders. "Welcome home, love." They kissed. Daniel had so longed for William's touch, but . . . it was too soon, the blood and the betrayal too fresh. He felt himself stiffen at his lover's touch. "Daniel, what's wrong?" William said with concern, his brow furrowed as he pulled back. "Alex . . . are you two all right? I heard the mission concluded successfully, though there were no details . . ."

"We're fine," Alex said coldly. "But, Daniel's due in de-brief. I'm afraid your re-union will have to wait an hour or so."

"I'll be at home, waiting," William said, softly, kissing Daniel's hand in parting.

The worry Daniel saw in William's eyes was like an arrow through his heart. "What you did back there must have been very satisfying for you," he said in quiet anger, turning back to Alex. "How many times have you fantasized killing him?"

She slapped him hard, across the face. "Go to hell," she hissed through clenched teeth. "And, you're welcome, by the way."

He rubbed his face. "You could have stopped him without killing him."

"He was a threat to the mission, and my decision was strategically sound, as you very well know. You seriously think I acted out of jealousy? Do you have so little respect for me, to think I'm still the teenaged girl you hurt a lifetime ago? I have moved on since then! And yes, despite my better judgement, I do still care about you. And, if you gave a damn about William, you'd admit to yourself you have a death wish." Her lip quivered, the glint of a tear in her eye. "That's why you stayed, against orders, why you put yourself at risk, why you always put yourself at risk. However many times you kill yourself, it will never be enough. And, unless you find some way to stop hating yourself, you are going to end up destroying a man you claim to love."

He stared at her, numb. "Alex . . ."

"Get to debrief," she said, walking away. "Your collective's waiting for you."

***

Daniel floated weightless, immersed in the soft orange light of the link chamber at the heart of the central nexus. His mind reached out through the sub space relays, across the Hub Universe to the other three members of his collective . . . his link to the higher consciousness of the galaxy beings.

"You have long been absent from communion, friend Daniel," one of his link mates, Kol said, its thoughts passing instantaneously from its distant galaxy. "We have missed you." Kol was a being the size of a star. Evolved from a civilization that had broken down the matter of their entire solar system and built it into a spherical shell around their sun, harvesting its energy, their minds eventually merging into one singular consciousness. Kol's perspective was solitary and pure.

Daniel sometimes envied Kol. "My mission took me away."

"Well do I read the scars of that mission, Daniel," another link mate, Trell, said in her almost melodic, soothing voice, her thoughts touching his like a loving balm. Trell was an immense, floating organism, her translucent form miles across, electricity flowing down her long, trailing tendrils as she slowly drifted with her herd through the methane currents of a gaseous giant planet in a remote galaxy. Her kind knew only love and freedom. He had always felt unworthy of her.

"Many shadows haunt you still, Daniel," said Saav, the final member of their collective. A liquid-breathing organic colony organism the size of a continent, swimming through an ocean of thick, cloying protein fluids on a planet in a galaxy far across the Hub Verse. Its knowledge was the accumulation of eons, yet ever fluid, ever changing. Saav seemed to know all, yet was surprised every moment, every event merely another discovery to a mind that never stopped searching. At times, Saav's merciless search for truth was painful.

Daniel screamed in anguish as Saav took him back to that memory of his boyhood, in his native continuum. The day Daniel's life had been torn apart when hostile aliens had attacked the space colony where he'd lived with his family, near Earth Outpost III. He saw the alien fighters blasting the orbiting space wheel to fragments. He felt the explosion of the bulkhead splintering, the metal shards tearing open half his face as he was thrown to the deck. He could still hear the shrieking hiss of atmosphere venting into space as he'd struggled to reach the launch bay, his own blood filling his eyes. He'd jettisoned himself in an escape pod, leaving his parents and his siblings to die.

"Stop it, Saav," Trell said, pulling Daniel back to the present, shielding him with her mind. "You're cruel." Daniel's mind reeled with pain, as though he'd just been thrown naked into a vat of boiling water.

"No," Saav said in its cool, analytical tone. "Daniel must destroy himself if he does not face the source of the darkness that seeks to devour him. That moment in his life is the point at which his timeline splinters, a score of parallel versions of him radiating like a disruptive vibration along the time strings. This Daniel is the key to all the others. Only by accepting that can he ever be whole."

"Saav is right," Kol interjected. "We saved this Daniel from his native continuum and raised him here in the Hub Verse because of his quantum synchronicity with so many versions of himself in key link universes that the Extraverse would destroy. The many must become one, Daniel. As it is with the Multiverse, so it must be with you."

"How?" he asked, lost and adrift, like a piece of flotsam buffeted this way and that by waves on a pitching sea. "How can I?"

"Only by forgiving yourself, Daniel," Trell said, her loving thoughts caressing his mind. "Hate is your enemy, whether turned inward or outward. You must stop hating yourself."

He reached outward, towards the light. But, looking within, saw only a growing darkness.

***

Parallel Universe KXL213.91

A dying universe, all but consumed by darkness.

Intergalactic wars raging on for millennia, whole races ruthlessly exterminated. At the heart of the dark inter-galactic empire that ruled what little was left, planets were split to their cores by destructive technologies, transformed from green, life sustaining worlds to lifeless volcanic furnaces, their metallic ores stripped, destroying the lives of the many to satisfy the greed of the few. Stellar harvesting projects turned suns into black holes, contracting this universe into eventual collapse and final darkness.

At the fringes of this parallel, the Extraverse, the dark matter intelligence that hungered at the fringes of all universes, greedily consumed what life remained, like a ravenous predator licking dry the bones of its slaughtered prey.

Cassias stepped into the dark heart of the interface chamber at the core of the empire, where the dark matter intellect spoke to him, its acolyte. The darkness closed in around him like a choking wave, entering his mind. "Cassias . . . We have suffered a defeat in JRN117.53," the voice of the Presence, the dark matter cosmic intelligence that was the Extraverse said in his thoughts. "Daniel Kwan has set forces in motion there that will eventually reverse the expansion of that continuum. One more link universe that may in a billion years become one more component in the tyranny of a Multiverse intelligence."

Cassius's fist trembled. Hatred boiled in his blood at the mention of the enemy. "Command me, All-Seeing."

"Kwan's continuing mission will next take him to JRN117.54, the connecting universe, the other half of our plan for that all-important link. There, he will hand you the key to the Hub Universe, and you will use it to open the gateway. Preparations have already been made in the 5-4 continuum. Are you prepared to depart?"

"I am, All-Wise. All-Seeing. The darkness purifies. The darkness is peace." Cassias-Marcellus Daniel Kwan contemplated darkly, running a finger along the scar on his face. He looked forward to watching his other self suffer excruciating torment before destroying all he loved. He smiled, coldly, and the darkness smiled back.

***

Parallel Universe JRN117.54
A universe rapidly contracting toward eventual collapse and destruction.

Intercosmic Transmission to I.C.A. Command.
Field Report 17, Agent Daniel Kwan reporting.
Since terminating my alternate self in this universe, I have successfully replaced him as Chancellor General of the New Earth Intergalactic Federation. Having ordered the dismantling of the rift gate energy system my other self had put in place, a system which was accelerating the contraction of this universe, I have implemented the construction of a new rift gate network which has effectively reversed the interaction between this continuum and its mirror counterpart, JRN117.53, the Telestan Empire universe. This continuum is now exporting neutron star matter to 5-3, thereby reversing that continuum's expansion and simultaneously importing dark energy from that universe, reversing its own contraction, the two now balancing each other toward the stabilization of both parallels.

Beta IV, one of the key rift gates in my new network has apparently stopped functioning. As this is too vital and too well monitored a station to be an accidental malfunction, I must conclude it is an attempt by the Extraverse to sabotage our efforts. I am therefore taking command of a Federation space task force to investigate.
End Transmission

"Now entering orbit around Beta IV," the Federation navigator reported, a nervous edge to her voice as the small recon cruiser approached the planet.

Daniel studied the icy gray horizon of the cold, dead little world through the viewport. "Still no response from the surface?" he asked.

"Negative, Chancellor General," the young comm officer reported, his brown eyes betraying fear as he glanced up from his console. "No response on any frequency."

"Tactical report?"

"Long-range scans indicate the base structure is intact, Chancellor General," the tactical officer reported.

"Very well. Bring us in for a landing at the main pad. All hands prepare to disembark. Weapons on kill force. I will lead."

The ship's commander—the William Quaast of this universe—looked up sharply. "Chancellor General, I must officially protest. Your safety is—"

"Your concern is noted, Commander Quaast," Daniel said, glancing into the other man's eyes and probing them desperately for some hidden sign of betrayal. "Nevertheless, my order stands. Make preparations." Was William friend or foe in this parallel? Daniel dreaded the answer, yet felt compelled to find out, one way or another.

***

Daniel looked down into the seething dark purple/black pit of the artificial black hole at the station's heart.

He drew a trembling breath, the quantum energy of the rift gate sending a vibrancy of molecular excitation through the air as he and his crew circled the edge of the pit. Like a million swarming mites crawling over his skin. In the dim light of the subterranean chamber, he could see it was having an unnerving effect on the primitives. And, on him. The gate had stopped functioning, radiation building up at its core, he realized. Obviously, sabotage, and not by indigenous life forms. "Any response from the station crew?" he asked, loosening his uniform collar.

"None, sir," William responded, looking increasingly nervous, clutching his blaster. "It's as if they all just—" He glanced up. "Look out!"

Daniel looked up, the air rippling as holographic blinds dropped, humans in black cybernetic armor appearing from every corner of the dark chamber, floating on anti-gravs as they attacked. Daniel's heart raced as he fired, his blaster bolts deflecting harmlessly, apparently encountering energy shielding clearly not of this parallel reality. The enemy soldiers fired with gravity wave disruptors, cutting his men down in seconds. "Run, Daniel!" William shouted, throwing himself directly in the path of an enemy soldier as the hostile flew straight at Daniel. With cybernetically enhanced strength, the attacker knocked William aside with a back-handed blow, sending him sprawling over the circling guard rail and straight down into the churning black light of the pit.

"Noooo!" Daniel shouted as he drew his own grav disruptor and fired, blowing the enemy trooper apart. A surge of energy blasted through him like a lightning bolt, crashing through his nerves as the disruptor slipped from his numbed hand. As he dropped to his knees, the chamber swirling around him, he saw the enemy troopers standing around him part as a man stepped forward.

"I've waited a long time for this, Daniel," a strangely familiar voice said. As the man stooped towards him, his face was illuminated in the dim light. Daniel's mouth dropped as he recognized his own face. His mirror image snarled as his back-handed blow sent Daniel's brain reeling into darkness and swirling stars.

***

Daniel awoke to find himself spread-eagled against some kind of apparatus.

He struggled, unable to move, his arms and legs pinned by restraints. He looked around. He was in a huge chamber. All around him, lined up row upon row in glass tubes were human beings, apparently growing, like giant fetuses in incubators. *A clone soldier factory*, he realized. Long-since banned in the Hub Universe, but still very much in use on parallels controlled by the Extraverse.

"Don't bother trying to quantum shift," that familiar voice said. He looked around, finding his other self also spread-eagled, locked into a similar apparatus, directly facing his. "Your brain implant is now locked with mine," his doppelganger said. "We're now in perfect sync."

Daniel started as the air seared and boiled white hot, an inter-cosmic rift opening. Squad upon squad of cyborg clone troopers mobilized, marching into the rift. Daniel's heart nearly burst from his chest as he realized what was happening. By entering this universe, he'd shown the enemy the way into the Hub Verse. Using his other self to mimic his own quantum resonance frequency, they could open a rift into the very heart of I.C.A. Command. *No,* he thought as he struggled against his restraints. *William. Alex. No!*

***

The Hub Universe.

Panicking crowds scattered madly as the white-hot shimmer of the rift gate opened, black-armored cyborgs streaming through from the other side. Alex Veraan gasped as the attacking clones morphed into dark-matter warped monstrosities, merging into gigantic hydra-like titans, crushing trams and platforms, hundreds falling to their deaths. She grit her teeth, cursing Daniel's collective for insisting I.C.A. Command let him take this mission alone.

Mounting an anti-grav sled, she attacked, a roar rising from her lungs as she fired her grav disruptor. William Quaast came up close beside her, firing into the writhing mass of claws and fangs ahead.

***

"How does it feel, Daniel," his other self mocked, laughing in sadistic delight, "to know you're responsible for the deaths of the ones you love most? Just as it was before, remember, at Earth Outpost III? You ran, like a coward, leaving everyone to die." His face—Daniel's face—winced in familiar anguish.

"You couldn't bear the pain of the guilt, so you gave up," Daniel shouted. "That was the true cowardice. Giving in to the hate and the darkness. We both did." He remembered his life in his home verse after the death of his family. He remembered joining the space militia squads that attacked alien space transports and butchered them indiscriminately. Hate was all he knew after the attack. Until he met Alex. She was the first person he'd ever loved, before he even knew what love was. He'd learned what it truly was when he'd met William. He'd feared to admit his feelings at first, having been taught they were wrong. When the truth finally emerged, it was Alex who suffered for it, and again he hated himself.

He surrendered to his pain . . . to the truth Saav had showed him as he allowed himself to slip beyond his solitary existence, his brain implant taking his thoughts across the many timelines, the many versions of him, taking the Cassias version of him along. So many driven to darkness by the pain and self-hatred.

"What are you doing?" Cassias demanded.

"Going where you haven't dared." He remembered what Kol had said. He had to become one. He remembered Trell's words. Hate was his enemy. Only by forgiving himself could he be whole. He opened himself, surrendering to William's love. To Alex's. He let the love flow outward, throughout the time strings, the pain and the love becoming one. He felt himself coming back together, the many divergent strings of his life merging across the lines.

"No!" Cassias screamed as his control ebbed. Freed from Cassius's dominance, Daniel quantum shifted, effortlessly freeing himself from his restraints. He felt Cassias melting into him as Daniel's hands touched his anguished face.

"Let it go," he whispered as he and Cassias and all the others merged into one.

***

The Hub Universe

The cosmic rift closed, and the Extraverse mutations, no longer sustained by the flow of dark energy from the other universe, dissolved. William heaved a sigh of relief, lowering his disruptor. Relief quickly gave way to concern. "Daniel," he whispered.

Alex's hand rested on his shoulder. "He's safe," she said. "He's all right now." He turned to her, and she smiled.

***

Parallel Universe JRN117.54

The life support system shut down, the nascent clones dying. The system had been controlled by Daniel's other self, and that splintered version of himself was gone, he realized as he looked at the now-empty apparatus where Cassias had been. Daniel was whole.

He silently willed it, and a rift gate opened to the Hub Universe. He smiled as he walked towards the light of the rift. Towards home, where William waited.

My short fiction has appeared in **Volumes II-VI** *of* **Visions,** *as well as* **The Future is Short, Vol. IV** *and in anthologies such as* **In the Bloodstream, An Improbable Truth: The Paranormal Adventures of Sherlock Holmes,** *and* **Curious Incidents: More Improbable Adventures.** *My dark science fiction novella* **Black Goddess** *is available from Mocha Memoirs Press, and my full-length science fiction novel* **Dissent: Book I of the Nexus** *is available from Phase5 Publishing.*

About the Editor

Carrol Fix writes and edits for Lillicat Publishers. She is the editor of the *Visions Series*, science fiction short story anthologies describing human exploration of space, including *Visions: Leaving Earth, Visions II: Moons of Saturn, Visions III: Inside the Kuiper Belt, Visions IV: Space Between Stars, Visions V: Milky Way, Visions VI: Galaxies* and the current *Visions VII: Universe*. She also is the editor of *The Future Is Short: Science Fiction in a Flash, The Future Is Short, Volume 3: Science Fiction in a Flash,* and *The Future Is Short, Volume 4: Science Fiction in a Flash* and numerous novels and short story collections.

Carrol is a short-story author and novelist whose science fiction work includes *Mishka: Book One of the Quadrate Mind*, winner in the Pikes Peak Writers' 2000 Paul Gillette Memorial Writing Contest, and the Published Fiction Third Place Award in the 2005 Arizona Literary Contest and Book Awards. In addition to her editing, she is writing the second book in the *Quadrate Mind Series*, while working on a young-adult fantasy novel, *Worlds Apart*. Her most recent short stories appear in *Visions: Leaving Earth, The Future Is Short: Science Fiction in a Flash, The Future Is Short, Volume 2: Science Fiction in a Flash, Twisted Tales IX: Wunderkind,* and *Perihelion Science Fiction Online Magazine*.

A former computer consultant who has lived in six different states, Carrol currently resides near San Diego, California, USA, in a household containing three generations of grandmothers, of which she is one. Her brother, W. A. Fix, a frequent contributor to the *Visions Series,* occupies a well-deserved spot on her list of favorite authors.

http://www.lillicatpublishers.com
http://www.mishkabook.com

Visions VI: Galaxies

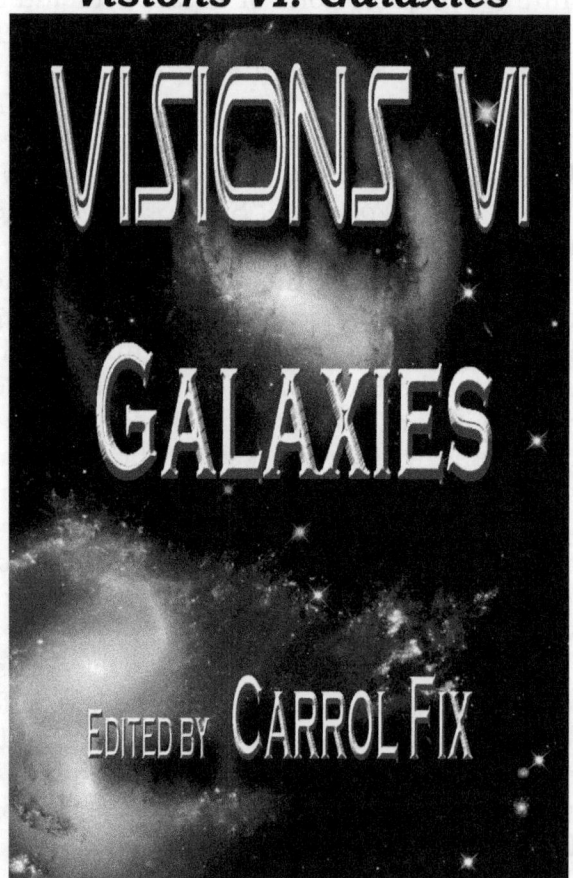

Visions V: Milky Way

VISIONS V

MILKY WAY

EDITED BY CARROL FIX

Visions IV: Space Between Stars

Visions III: Inside the Kuiper Belt

Visions II: Moons of Saturn

Visions: Leaving Earth

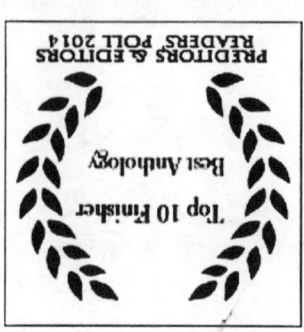